THAT'S WHAT FRENEMIES ARE FOR

THAT'S WHAT FRENEMIES ARE FOR

A NOVEL

SOPHIE LITTLEFIELD
AND
LAUREN GERSHELL

BALLANTINE BOOKS
NEW YORK

Copyright © 2019 by Sophie Littlefield and Lauren Gershell

Published in the United States by Ballantine Books,
an imprint of Random House, a division of
Penguin Random House LLC, New York.

BALLANTINE and the HOUSE colophon are registered
trademarks of Penguin Random House LLC.

Hardback ISBN 9781984817969
Ebook ISBN 9781984817976

Printed in the United States of America on acid-free paper

randomhousebooks.com

2 4 6 8 9 7 5 3 1

First Edition

Book design by Diane Hobbing

For Lauren K., who is made of smarts and heart and grit and glitter
—SL

For my grandmother Ida, who was the best friend I ever had
—LG

THAT'S
WHAT
FRENEMIES
ARE FOR

PROLOGUE

Every woman of a certain age secretly hopes she'll meet someone at a wedding—and not just because it makes a good meet-cute story. Kind of the opposite, actually. Emotions are already running high, and the drumbeat of one's waning fertility is never louder than when the best man gets up and recounts some anecdote about the groom's younger, wilder days, the moral of which is that standing before the crowd is a changed man eager to take on a mortgage and issue progeny, transformed by the love (and persistence) of a worthy woman.

If she can do it, the still-single woman thinks, *so can I.*

But here's a little tip: funerals are where the *real* action is. In fact, I met my husband, James, at the funeral for one of the associate partners at the branding firm where I worked after college. I barely knew the deceased. I'd been pulled in on his project a month before he was T-boned in a rental car headed back to the Peoria airport after a pitch, and since everyone on the team was going to the funeral, I did too.

James was at the funeral because he and the dead man had been in the same fraternity at UPenn. Later, he told me he'd been planning to bolt after half an hour at the reception, until he saw me signing the guest book. I was wearing a basic black Helmut Lang that did wonders for my ass. I don't often wear black—but a funeral isn't the place to stand out.

James brought me a bourbon, neat, and told me I looked like I could use it before introducing himself. A gamble on his part, especially given the diamond ring on my finger, but I admired his boldness. Funeral talk, even among strangers, is more intimate than cocktail-hour chitchat at a wedding reception, fueled by skimpy flutes of champagne from which the bubbles are fast disappearing.

Also, some girls just look best sad. For instance, my smile often looks uneven and insincere. But when my expression is serious, I've been told I look "tragic," and obviously there is nothing more alluring than that.

Every man likes to think he's someone's savior.

Lydia Dickinson's memorial service takes place at the Metropolitan Club, which is practically as old as the city itself, with a soaring marble entrance hall, gilded walls, scarlet carpets, and coffered and frescoed ceilings. It's packed, which isn't surprising given the fact that Lydia served on half the boards in both the city and Greenwich, and her husband's private equity firm has made many of the wealthiest people here even wealthier. Also, their daughter has followed in her mother's socially ambitious footsteps—Gigi McLayne knows everyone worth knowing on the Upper East Side.

I'm among Gigi's many friends who are here to support her. (Actually, in the interest of getting this story off on the right foot, let me clarify: I'm a *former* friend, and no one is really here to provide support. Any real grieving has been dispensed with between Mrs. Dickinson's unexpected death and the reading of the will, and the real reason we're all here is to avoid having our absence noticed and discussed behind our backs.)

I smell Tatum Farris before she murmurs my name. Her perfume is Heure Exquise—I've heard her tell people she's worn it *forever,* but I happen to know that she'd never heard of it before a grateful client brought her a bottle from Paris. I have a fraction of a second to arrange my features in an appropriate expression.

I turn toward her as she reaches for my hand and gives it a squeeze.

"Such a tragic loss," she murmurs sadly.

"Tatum," I say, pulling back my hand. "What a surprise to see you here. I wasn't aware that you knew Mrs. Dickinson."

"Lydia came to my classes," Tatum says defensively. "She was interested in the Kegan Diet and we bonded right away."

I regard her with suppressed fury. "Guess you dodged a bullet, then."

"I haven't the faintest idea what you're talking about."

That is a lie. Though the public story is that Mrs. Dickinson's embolism came out of nowhere, everyone knows the truth. Seized by panic at the approach of her fortieth class reunion, Mrs. Dickinson forged her doctor's signature on the medical forms for a brutal week of fitness and spa cuisine at River Rock Ranch in Arizona, and dropped dead during the first sun salutation. Given her sky-high blood pressure and sedentary lifestyle, it was a miracle she didn't stroke out when Tatum first let her on a bike.

Tatum is wearing an honest-to-God Chanel bouclé. The suit may have been a hand-me-down from one of her clients, or it might have been a gift, but rest assured that the effect is calculated. If one had any doubts, the nearly translucent white silk blouse and five-inch peep-toe Louboutins ought to confirm it. Tatum thrives on that contrast, the razor edge hidden under layers of decorum.

Also, Tatum is wearing a brooch I have never seen before. I squint at it, trying to decide if it's real. Eight diamond-crusted platinum legs extend from a center moonstone to form a gaudy jeweled spider. It looks like a Schlumberger from the sixties, with the hallmark enamel detail.

Following my gaze, she looks at the brooch and laughs. "Like it?"

"A bit . . . macabre for the occasion, don't you think?"

"Oh, I don't know," she says, stroking the smooth surface of the moonstone. "I think it's pretty."

"Sure," I say, giving up the ruse, since it's just the two of us. "Especially with that blouse and those shoes. I'm sure your goth mall fantasy is just the way Gigi wants her mother to be honored."

"I can't believe you said that." Tatum's indignation is almost convincing. "Gigi's one of my *best friends*."

A waiter passes with a tray and she taps him on the shoulder. The poor man nearly collides with a bystander as she leans in and favors him with an exquisite view of her cleavage, even though all she wants is a drink. That's classic Tatum Farris, always bringing the biggest gun to every fight.

"You can drop the act now," I say. I can't help myself, even though the only smart move is to stop talking. "You've got a lot of nerve showing up here considering that you're really just the hired help."

"I've got every bit as much right to be here as you do," she retorts. "I mean, when's the last time you and Gigi even did anything together? Speaking of which, she and Coco and I found the most amazing little sake bar in the Village a couple of weeks ago. It's great because nobody knows about it yet so you can actually have a conversation."

This from a girl whose biggest thrill used to be getting pulled out of a line at a club to serve as chum for big spenders. I hate her for worming her way into my circle of friends; I hate them for being careless enough to let her. Instead of gloating over my downfall, maybe they should stop and consider what I really am—a cautionary tale.

But I can't afford to give in to defeat. It has been several days already since our very public humiliation, and James and I must show the world that we will endure. I had promised myself that I would ignore the sideways glances, the whispering, the snubs, but it seems I'm no longer a don't-give-a-fuck kind of girl. Underneath my formerly confident façade, I've turned out to be as disappointingly insecure as everyone else.

I hurry away from Tatum toward the bar, where I hope I'll find James lubed to compliance and ready to go. He is standing with a man I don't know in front of the enormous fireplace, pale and cowed, recent events having worn him down to the point of unrecognizability.

I take his arm and give the stranger a curt nod. Across the room I see Tatum accepting a glass from a waiter. She turns and smiles at me. She is dazzling.

Even now, I can't quite quell the bitter shock of seeing everything I worked for, my dream, my masterpiece, taken away from me. And what a cruel irony that Tatum escaped unscathed.

But then again, she's a survivor. It's in her blood.

CHAPTER 1

There is a particular species of shrew that injects a dose of anesthetizing venom into its prey so it can feed at leisure while the victim is still alive. Maybe it's a kindness; more likely it's just nature's inclination to keep you still and compliant as disaster strikes. You only realize you're fucked when it's too late.

Think about it: markets crash when investors are feeling fat and happy. Spouses leave when their jilted partners are convinced things are finally on the right track again. And when it's your turn, there's nothing you can do. You're the mouse. That short-tailed shrew bearing down on you with an oily grin? That's that old familiar bastard, fate.

In my case, the early months of the new year passed in not-unpleasant monotony, our household bobbing along in the privileged waters of the Upper East Side. My husband worked hard and made a lot of money. I was a stay-at-home mom of two young children, a pampered wife with a busy social calendar, a sought-after friend with a reputation for the mildly outrageous.

At least, I had been for a time, when everything I touched turned—if not into gold, at least into Instagram posts with hundreds of likes and invitations to every party worth going to and the fawning admiration of those on the fringes of my circle.

Dear reader, allow me to give you a little preview of my story: I had it all, once, but I let it slip away. I'd been a golden girl all my life: rich, spoiled, attractive, confident, with a talent for cultivating envy. But as I reached the mid-point of my thirties, I grew sloppy or lazy or distracted—it's hard to remember exactly why I stopped trying—and I lost my luster. People noticed; they drifted away. When I realized how far my star had fallen, I became desperate to fight my way back. Naïvely, I thought it couldn't get any worse than to be irrelevant.

I lost my way. And then I lost my nerve. And then I made a mistake.

It was a chilly evening in May, and James and I were attending our daughter's lower school play at the exclusive Graylon Academy on the Upper East Side of New York City, where our children would soon be finishing kindergarten and second grade. James had been working around the clock on a new deal, a former nursing home in Chelsea that his firm was turning into luxury condos, and I'd ordered him to take a night off and come to the performance. You don't show up to such an event without your husband unless you wish to answer for it all night. Managing our husbands is one of the skills on which we judge each other.

I had asked our nanny to stay late and watch Henry, our younger child. I'd already dropped Paige off at the school to get ready for the play, in which she had a minor role as a mushroom. The play was a morality tale about inclusivity, as far as I could tell, told through vegetables.

Benilda's contract was for 8:00 A.M. to 5:00 P.M. each weekday plus additional hours "as needed," for which we paid her extra. James had asked me several times why we couldn't cut back on her hours now that both Henry and Paige were in school. James didn't grow up here—he's from Allentown—and he could be insensitive to the fact that certain things simply weren't done. Our compromise was to ask Benilda to take on the housekeeping and laundry, which allowed us to let our twice-a-week housekeeper go.

At work, James had no problem managing a staff of eleven. But Benilda—with her thick black bob cut precisely jaw length, her acid-washed jeans, the rapid-fire conversations she had on the phone in

Tagalog with her daughters—could reduce him to silence with a single "Not so fast, Mr. James."

This, in fact, was what she said as we were leaving, our contribution for the evening's charity collection in my hands, a stack of women's thermal underwear still in the Gap bag. "Not so fast, Mrs. Julia. Take this for school."

She handed me a small box wrapped in shiny, cheap paper I didn't recognize. I'd always encouraged Benilda to help herself to my gift-wrap closet: before the holidays I mailed her packages to her daughters in Sorsogon myself.

"What's this?"

"Paige wanted to buy her own gift for poor kids. We went to CVS. She used her birthday money."

I was torn between pride in my daughter and resentment that Paige had confided this wish to Benilda and not me. Lord knows I'd tried to foster a generous spirit in her, but empathy tends to be in short supply among eight-year-olds.

"What is it?"

"Nail polish kit. Deluxe kind with six colors." Benilda nodded with satisfaction. I had no choice but to take the box from her. "They wrap for free!"

In the Uber, James brought it up. "I thought we didn't let Paige wear nail polish?"

I rolled my eyes. "It's the school that doesn't allow nail polish. Which is all the more reason for her to want it. But it can't go in the collection. There was a very specific list. *Practical* things." Socks, phone cards, notebooks. Clothing in plus sizes. All of it to be donated to our sister school in the Bronx.

"So what are you going to do? Toss it in the trash in the ladies' room?"

James could only ask such a question because he never had to deal with dilemmas like this. To him it was amusing.

But I had an even better solution. I simply left the nail polish in the Uber, a black Escalade so new it smelled like the showroom floor. Maybe the next rider would have a creative idea for it. Or a young niece. No longer my problem, at any rate.

Our driver dropped us off around the corner from the school on Madison Avenue; the street in front of Graylon was as crowded as any weekday pickup. The evening's highlight was the play, but there was also the sister school collection and a silent auction. Graylon Academy never missed an opportunity to squeeze a few bucks from the parents on top of the fifty thousand dollars per child we paid for tuition every year. Missing these events did not go unnoticed. Few parents dared risk it.

"Jesus," James said, surveying the line to check in, snaking out through the open doors from the lobby. I could make out Hollis Graves at the desk, flipping through her spreadsheets, checking people's names off the list.

"Yes, well, welcome to my life." I shouldn't have said it. It was petty and not even accurate. It was true that I served on a lot of school committees and put in a ton of volunteer time, but many of my duties were fairly pleasant, involving lots of wine-drenched "planning" lunches. And I'd learned to avoid the worst tasks—you wouldn't find me sitting at a desk checking off names under the glare of all these parents' impatience.

We stood in line, not speaking. Behind us were Emery Souza and her mother-in-law. I said a perfunctory hello, but things had been cool between me and Emery since she ran against me for treasurer in the PTA election two years ago and won.

When we finally reached the sign-in table, I was ready. "You're such a trouper to do this, especially all by yourself."

Hollis gave me a thin smile. "Poppy was supposed to be helping me, but *apparently* she threw her back out."

"Oh dear," I said, already turning away. "Oh look, James, let's check out the silent auction."

These auctions, as you can probably guess, are tedious. The amount of effort that goes into them hardly justifies the return, or the annoyance of having to lug home whatever prize you accidentally overbid for. Last year, I bid three hundred dollars on a Nambé platter, never imagining I'd win. I offered it to Benilda, who said she didn't have room for it, and it went directly into the Goodwill box.

But you have to bid on something. Several somethings, really, if you want to show you're a team player. And occasionally there are amazing lots, like a weekend at someone's place in Aspen, which was literally next door to Jessica Biel's. It ended up going for over twenty thousand dollars.

We strolled along the raffle table with the other parents, more relaxed now that the onus to make conversation was off. James was not at his finest at school events, where he tended to be testy and restless. I bid a hundred dollars on a manicure at Bliss, and another two hundred on a miniature Graylon Academy uniform for an American Girl doll.

Then I saw a frilled and bow-tied basket with a vaguely familiar red and orange logo on the card. TWO PERSONAL SPINNING SESSIONS AT FLAME! the hand-lettered sign read, and I realized where I'd seen that logo before: a boutique gym had popped up a few months ago in a basement retail space on Eighty-fourth Street off Lexington Avenue that was once occupied by a video rental store. SPINNING * BOXING * HIIT * MINDFULNESS, the sign out front promised, and I'd been intrigued by the clientele I'd seen coming and going whenever I walked by: firefighters from the station down the street, students, artsy types, merchants, waiters, cops. Everyone, it seemed, but people like me and my friends.

That was my catnip. I was an urban bloodhound trawling for treasures that went unnoticed by others, and I was famous for my finds and my willingness to go my own way, eschewing the clothes and restaurants and decorators everyone else flocked to. My style was often copied but never duplicated. I wasn't rebelling against the life I led; I just loved to bring back shiny bits from the teeming world to feather my nest—and, in the process, feed my status as a maverick and tastemaker. Being admired is addictive, and I'd been mainlining that drug since my adolescence as a black-sheep daughter of old-money Boston Brahmin stock.

The raffle basket contained an orange ribbed T-shirt, a coffee mug, an orange-handled jump rope. Its bid sheet read, in a slanting and girlish hand, *Great for newbie's and spinning experts! Tatum will make you LOVE your ride!!! Value $220!*

"Wait, James," I said, bending to add my name to the list. There were already two bids, for $200 and $225. I debated only a moment before writing $300 next to my name.

"Don't we already belong to a gym?" James said.

This is a little game we play, where he pretends to tighten the purse strings and then gives in to pretty much anything I want.

"The spin classes at our gym are terrible. Besides, I've been thinking of trying something new." Not entirely true, but not untrue either—I'm *always* thinking of trying new things.

We moved on, got our glasses of wine, and filed into the auditorium, which smelled exactly like my own days back at the Winsor School in Boston. The program went as these things always do. *Adorable,* Coco Choi sighed when Paige uttered her single line, and I returned the favor when her twins, dressed as a single head of broccoli, stumbled onto the stage.

"Make a break for it," James whispered in my ear when it was over and the aisles began filling. "Let's grab the little monster and get out of here."

"You get her," I said. "I need to check something. I'll meet you out front."

I broke away before he could object, dodging between two tottering grandmothers in pastel cardigans. I hurried to the auction table and checked my bids. I'd been outbid on the manicure and the doll dress—and the Flame sessions, which had reached $350.

I deliberated only a second before writing in $500, underlining it twice.

I told myself it was for a good cause.

CHAPTER 2

I picked up the raffle basket from the school office the next day and promptly forgot about it. I was occupied with the kids' activities as well as my class mom duties. James was so busy with work that he was spending occasional nights at his office, a habit that went back to when we first started dating; he'd get lost in whatever he was doing until the wee hours of the morning and crash on the couch in his office, then shower at the gym in the morning and keep going.

But there would soon be a break in the madness, at least for me. Like many Graylon families, we'd be opening up our summer house in the Hamptons over Memorial Day weekend, and as soon as school was out the kids and I would move there for the summer, James joining us whenever he could. Which, given all the delays and obstacles with Mercer House, was unlikely to be very often.

I put up with James's hours because he made a very good living as a real estate developer, and his work ethic had everything to do with his success. I was superstitious that if I tried to change his habits, his business might dry up and we'd be left penniless. Well: not penniless, obviously, but I had my mother's Yankee sensibilities when it came to money. Though she'd come from a fortune that spanned generations, she never stopped keeping an eye on the coffers, and I was at the age where I was beginning to realize I wasn't so different from her in a depressing variety of ways.

On the Thursday before Memorial Day I met my best friends, Lindsay Parker and Grace Dexter, for lunch. It was one of the last times we'd get together before we all decamped for the summer. I would see lots of Lindsay, whose summer house in Bridgehampton was ten minutes from ours, but Grace was spending the summer at her family's compound on the Virginia coast and wouldn't be back until Labor Day. We'd made reservations at our old standby, La Goulue, and were gossiping and drinking Pinot Grigio when my phone rang.

"So sorry, you guys, it's James," I said, getting up from the table. "I'd better take this."

James almost never called me in the middle of the day. "Hang on," I whispered as I threaded my way toward the exit. But James started ranting before I even made it to the door.

"We have a big fucking problem, Julia. I just talked to Bart."

"Bart Grissom?"

"What other Bart do we know? A goddamn pipe burst."

"*Now?* You've got to be kidding!"

"Pipes don't just burst in the winter, it can happen anytime. There was apparently some galvanized pipe left, which obviously I didn't know, since I paid those crooks a fucking fortune to run copper when we bought the place."

This was a dig at me, because I'd insisted we use local contractors instead of James bringing one of his own crews like he'd wanted. I tried to make him understand that you don't show up in the Hamptons and rock the boat, especially because we'd only bought the house a few years earlier and weren't known around town yet. I didn't so much as sneeze without getting the permit expediter in— not just to push our permits through, because that can usually be helped along with money, but to make sure we weren't pissing anyone off. If it was true that the crew we'd hired had messed up the job, we'd simply have to suffer the consequences.

"Okay," I said cautiously. "Did he call a plumber?"

Bart Grissom was our caretaker, the man who opened up the house in the spring and closed it in the fall and, in between, was supposed to stop by every few days to check on the place. The job of Hamptons caretaker, as far as I could tell, involved calling other people to fix things and looking the other way when the recycling bin was piled with liquor bottles or the family's teenage offspring snuck friends into the pool house.

"This isn't a minor leak, Julia. We've had a couple hundred gallons of water a day pouring through the walls for who knows how long. Bart hadn't been there in weeks—he says one week, but I don't believe it, not this time of year. I've got one of my guys headed out there to check it out, but it sounds like it started in the upstairs hall bathroom and came through the kitchen ceiling. That's potentially floors, fixtures, electric, every goddamn thing."

"Oh no," I whispered. James was right—given that virtually everyone wants their place opened for Memorial Day, Bart had undoubtedly bumped us down the list below his more important clients, the ones whose waterfront homes run to the tens of millions. We'd bought our own 1930s cottage in town for a comparatively modest three million and done an extensive remodel. I thought of the custom-built cabinets, the tiles I'd picked out one by one at a funky little studio in New Jersey.

"Let me put it this way—unless Bart was shitting me, we aren't going to be in the house for months. Probably all summer. And I'll tell you one thing, Julia, this time I'm using *my* guys, and the Preservation Society can suck my dick."

"*Please,* James."

"I'm sorry, Julia, but this had to happen *this* summer, when I'm ass deep in Mercer? Maybe it's a blessing, since I probably wouldn't have been able to get there much anyway."

A blessing? Really? The children and I had planned our entire summer there, ten weeks away from the stench and humidity of the city, and now there was a big gaping hole where those long, languorous afternoons and Sancerre-laced evenings should have been. James was relentlessly focused when it came to his job, and while he wasn't being deliberately thoughtless, it didn't change the outcome. "Well, no sense thinking about that until we know how bad the damage is."

"Yeah. Gotta run. More when I know more."

He hung up before I could say goodbye, and I was left staring at the phone, my heart sinking. The timing of this disaster was terrible. With James distracted by work, he wouldn't be able to give his full attention to the repairs. I knew I'd never convince him to hand the job over to someone local, even though summer was the only time of year contractors were hungry for work in the Hamptons—James was a control freak who liked to have his fingers in every part of a job.

A summer's worth of plans collapsed in my mind. There went Tonawanda Lake Camp for the children, the clambakes, the beach bonfires. There went lazy afternoons spent reading in the hammock, and Friday night patio dinners in town with our friends, and lovely leisurely afternoon sex while the children were at the golf club with Benilda.

Numbly, I made my way back to the table. "What's wrong?" Grace asked immediately.

"Is it that obvious?" I asked, taking a big gulp of my wine, which the waiter had thoughtfully refilled while I was gone. "Well, it looks like the kids and I are going to be marooned in the city all summer."

As I explained about the house, the horror on my friends' faces underscored the gravity of the situation. Being stuck in the city all summer was like being sentenced to solitary confinement; everyone I knew would be out of town. Even the working moms took half days Fridays and headed out of the city the second they could slip away. The kids' friends would be gone, and I'd have to find activities and entertain them on the weekends, and since we'd be out of sight and out of mind, we'd be left out of any plans people made for when summer ended.

"Maybe you could find a rental . . ." Grace suggested, but we all knew that was hopeless. People book their rentals months in advance if they don't own, and besides, it's just an entirely different vibe. "You have to stay with us for the Fourth," Lindsay said. She and Garth always threw a party on the Fourth of July, a barbecue that showcased their beautiful property overlooking the ocean.

"God, thanks. I didn't even think of that."

"And you and the kids should come down to Cape Charles for a week," Grace said. "The kids can go to sailing camp with Nora and Clay and the cousins."

"Oh, you guys," I said, my eyes misting. I'd never take Grace up on that offer—she had four sisters and something like fifty nieces and nephews and their rambling old seaside family compound barely had functioning plumbing, and we both knew I'd never survive the roughing-it charm of the place no matter how many of her signature Splenda bourbon sours I drank. But it was generous of her nonetheless. "I'm going to miss you both so much."

"What are you going to do about the house?" Lindsay asked, as the waiter refilled her glass. They'd ordered a second bottle while I was talking to James.

"James will deal with it, I guess. He'll get his guys on it, probably go out and check on it every week or two, make sure it's on track."

"You're so lucky," Grace said. "Matt wouldn't even know which end of a hammer to use."

"Yeah, but I wish he'd just let me hire a contractor. At least then there'd be a chance someone would do what I tell them for once."

"Come on, Jules, that's not fair—James let you do whatever you wanted with that place!"

It was true—he hadn't said one word about the finishes and furnishings. I worked with a young designer I'd met at a gallery opening, and we'd made plenty of unconventional choices—like the X-rated toile wallpaper in the master bath and the bar made from an old library card catalog cabinet, the sides painted with quotes from Anaïs Nin and Henry Miller—but James never batted an eye. "I know, I know, he's a saint."

"All I'm saying is that not every man would put up with a pink dining room."

"It's not pink, it's cerise," I said. "That grass cloth is hand-dyed!"

"Also—hard hat," Lindsay chimed in, winking. It was an old joke among us, that all the school moms lusted after James after he'd showed up for pickup one day wearing a hard hat. It was absolutely untrue, but he *had* been wearing an ancient pair of Carhartt work pants and a faded T-shirt and looked every bit the construction worker he'd once been. My husband, if you haven't figured it out, is a good-looking man. But more important, he's the extremely rare guy who can fix your sink and also afford to buy your anniversary gift at Cartier.

"It won't be the same without you," Lindsay sighed. "Who am I going to go to the Hampton Classic with?"

"At least you won't have any excuse not to call me," Grace said. "I'll probably murder one of my sisters the first week, but maybe they'll let me FaceTime from jail."

"I'll drink to that," I said, and we raised our glasses.

Somehow, I'd muddle through until September, when the city would come back to life again.

Mom and Dad took pity on me and decided to visit, to take the sting out of missing the official first summer weekend in the Hamptons. Dad was recently retired, having built his family's regional grocery chain into a multinational conglomerate. He and Mom spent the winters at their condo in Captiva, and in the summer, they traveled and visited me and my brother and our families.

"We'll be there by lunchtime on Saturday," Mom said, "so you can have the afternoon all to yourself. And then you and James can go out to dinner."

The idea was for my parents to take the kids to the Central Park Zoo, and then spend the evening in the living room with movies and pizza. Sunday we'd go out for brunch, maybe hit a museum or a show, and have a quiet dinner at home. The kids would be happy and entertained, and my parents would catch a cab to the airport Monday morning and be back in Boston in time to attend a Memorial Day barbecue at some Marblehead estate.

I envied them. What must it be like to live solely for oneself again? My own privileged childhood seemed like it had belonged to someone else entirely. I couldn't remember the last time I'd spent twenty-four hours alone, or made a sandwich without cutting the crusts off.

I'd been thinking I'd use my few hours of freedom to do a little shopping, but as I was checking on the linens in the guest room I noticed the Flame gift basket sitting on the dresser, where I had stashed it weeks ago. I picked up the card and reread the handwritten note, wincing again at the errant apostrophe. I'd barely managed to get to the gym in weeks, and as much as I loved to shop I knew that some exercise would do more for my mood, so I called the number.

"Hello?" She'd evidently used her personal number rather than the club's. Her voice was fresh and youthful.

"Hello, Tatum?" I said, reading from the card. "This is Julia Summers. My kids go to Graylon Academy, and I won the personal training sessions at the auction. I know it's last minute, but I was wondering if there was any chance you could squeeze me in this afternoon?"

"Oh my God, I'm so glad you called! This is just so fantastic. I've been worried no one bid on them."

I smiled at her enthusiasm. "There were quite a few bidders, actually. I was just the most persistent."

"That's great. And today is *perfect*. With the holiday and all, they canceled a bunch of the classes, and the studio's empty after the one o'clock until five-thirty. Would two-thirty work for you?"

"Um . . . I think I could get there by three?" It's an old reflex from my dating days—never take the first time someone offers you; always make them conform to your schedule—and I'm not sure why it surfaced just then.

"Three, then. Do you have spin shoes?"

"No, I haven't had time to shop yet. Does Flame rent them?"

"They're on me," Tatum said, a touch grandly. "See you soon!"

As I hung up, I felt lighter. I had somewhere to go, where someone was going to be happy—or at the very least, *pretend* to be happy—to see me.

I tidied the kids' rooms, mounded the laundry on the washer, and changed into my favorite leggings and a top that camouflaged my midriff bulge, so that I'd be ready to go as soon as I'd greeted my parents and gotten them settled in with the kids. There might even be time to stop for a skim cappuccino, maybe window-shop the sales on my way to Flame.

I didn't want this lovely illusion of freedom to end.

CHAPTER 3

I wasn't a total spinning neophyte. I'd tried it once before at my old gym, choosing a bike as far back as possible, but when the instructor kept yelling at me to pedal faster, I picked up my water bottle and walked out, leaving my towel puddled on the handlebars. I was unimpressed, unmoved, unmotivated, and I returned to my treadmill slogs without feeling like I was missing anything.

But in the last few years I'd gained over twenty pounds and developed a band of pale, flabby flesh around my midsection that made me look like my grandmother in her Speedo swimsuit. The weight had snuck up on me; I'd been blessed in my younger years with a body that had kept its shape without any effort, and I missed the attention it had once brought me. From James, of course, but the truth was that I was motivated most by the judgment of other women. (It's not my fault I grew up on an endless stream of diet articles and airbrushed fashion photography and undressing in the dark for lovers. You younger girls discovered body positivity, and thanks for that—but body shaming is one of the key currencies of my generation.)

When we first moved to the Upper East Side and popped out the kids in short order, I was at the top of my game. I shed the weight effortlessly after giving birth, and I had another advantage in those early mommy-and-me classes and coffees and playgroups—I was younger than most of the other mothers by a decade or more. Many of the women had established careers before stepping aside to have kids, and others had married later. At twenty-six, I was almost radically young to have my first, and as the kids got older and we found ourselves in the school parent scene, it was an advantage I played to the hilt. I never got tired of hearing myself referred to as "the young one," of other women telling me they hated me for my flat stomach and perky breasts and the lack of gray in my hair.

But you don't get to be the shiny new object forever. Every year a new crop of moms arrived, and there were always one or two who stood out: pretty ones, young ones, filthy rich ones. My star faded with the extra weight and a general lack of effort, and now I needed help to get it back. I hoped I could find at Flame the motivation I'd been missing.

After I got my parents settled with the kids, I walked the ten blocks to Flame. There was the familiar sign, the sleek letters in relief against an ombré background of red fading to orange. As I started down the narrow stairs, two women in workout gear emerged from the entrance and I had to reverse course to let them by. They were in their twenties, with good highlights and gorgeous skin and perfect bodies.

I averted my eyes from all that smooth, unblemished flesh.

Inside, I was greeted by the muted, primitive beat of drumming coming from hidden speakers and a pleasant scent of lemongrass. The small, cocoon-like reception area had burnished walls and concrete floors inset with bands of quartz. The receptionist, a woman around my age with delicate pale skin and biceps I'd trade a year of my life for, adjusted her casual chignon and didn't bother to conceal her appraisal of me.

"Are you here for sophrology?"

"Soph . . . what?"

"The sophrology class? Because it's completely full. Did you sign up?"

"I'm sorry, I don't know what you're talking about."

The woman gave me a faint smile. "It's from the Greek. *Sos* for harmony and *phren* for the mind."

"Oh. Uh, actually, I'm here for a personal training appointment. With Tatum?"

"Tatum doesn't do personal training. She's too new." The receptionist tapped a discreet ivory card in a polished wooden stand, which was hand-lettered with the late policy (*If you arrive after the class start time, you will be respectfully asked to reschedule*) and the class fee, a whopping thirty-five dollars.

A pretty blond woman came hurrying down the hall. She had a smattering of freckles and a high ponytail, and bright pink bike shoes with yellow socks peeping from the top. "Julia!" she exclaimed, as though she was delighted to see me.

"Hi," I said, relieved. "You're Tatum?"

"I am! I'm so thrilled you're here!"

"She says she has a personal training session," the receptionist said grudgingly.

"Ken knows about it," Tatum said. "It was a charity auction thing. For a supergood cause."

The receptionist shrugged and went back to her phone.

"Let's get you some shoes. What's your size?" Tatum asked, moving behind the desk and opening a cabinet that held wire bins filled with plain black spin shoes.

"Um, seven?"

The pair that she handed me was shabby and disconcertingly damp.

"Don't worry, it's just sanitizing spray."

Tatum led the way down a corridor. On one side were the doors to the locker rooms; on the other were studios with windows in the doors. The classes only seemed to be about half full, despite what the receptionist had said.

"You're sure this is all right? I don't want you to get in any trouble—"

"No, no, don't worry! It's fine, she probably just didn't know about . . . So anyway, let me show you the locker room."

"Wow, Tatum, this is amazing," I said, as we entered a room that resembled a yogi's secret sex den. The lighting was dim and sensuous, though lighted makeup mirrors lined the wall above the half dozen sinks, each a raised copper bowl that looked like some strapping Italian artisan had hammered it under the Umbrian sun centuries ago. Snow-white towels were stacked in austere lacquered black shelves, the floor was etched French limestone, and more of the hippie-dippie tribal music was being piped in. Personally, I found the décor over the top and more ostentatious than original, but it certainly got the point across—big money was spent here.

I locked up my stuff and followed Tatum's bouncing ponytail down the hall. The largest of the three studios was at the end, a huge space with three rows of bikes facing an elevated podium. The smell in here was part vanilla, part citrus—very posh, nothing like the antiseptic-and-sweat smell of my old gym. Industrial light fixtures and speakers hung from the ceiling; the walls were covered with graffiti that had clearly been done by an artist—no taggers from Crown Heights would ever enter these rooms—with a few key words standing out in the whorls and splatters: *Journey, Strive, Battle, Obsession.*

"Let me just light these," Tatum said, picking up a lighter and going to the front of the room, where thick white candles of different heights were lined up casually on a ledge spanning the length of the studio. "They're supposed to be just for classes, but I love them."

"Is that where the name comes from? Flame?"

"I guess. Ken—he's the owner? He got the idea from some retreat he went on in Bali. It's, like, his signature."

Nowadays, you'll find candles in half a dozen other gyms in town—they're so ubiquitous it's hard to remember that they ever weren't part of boutique gym culture. But Flame was the first.

"So!" Tatum said, taking a laptop from a messenger bag decorated with a Tinker Bell decal. "Let me put some music on, okay? What do you like?"

I shrugged. It's a loaded question, isn't it? A generation ago you could draw conclusions from a person's bookshelf, but no one has books anymore, so we look for clues in people's playlists. "Oh, you know . . . a little of everything."

"I'll play something I like to warm up to," Tatum said. She opened her laptop on a podium carved from gleaming dark wood and plugged it into a hidden jack, and the room was suddenly filled with rather lugubrious rap with unintelligible lyrics, other than the occasional *ride my dick* and so forth.

"What is that?"

"It's a playlist that one of the other teachers uses a lot. Her riders love it."

I tried to imagine who would love exercising to this music: no one I knew. And though I'd just met her, I didn't think it suited Tatum at all—like blasting death metal into a kindergarten classroom. Tatum beamed upbeat, positive energy; she wore bright colors and a perpetual smile, and her voice was girlish, the vowels flat and midwestern. She was all cheerleader, but the nice kind, the one who helps pick up the contents of the nerdy kid's backpack after the jocks throw it on the floor.

She draped a clean towel over the handlebars of the center bike in the front row and patted the seat as though it was a beloved pet. "The first thing we're going to do is set your seat to hip bone height—like this."

She grabbed the narrow front of the black saddle and lowered it smoothly, then crooked her arm in the space between the seat and the handlebars. "See? Elbow to fingertip, it's almost an exact match. Neat, huh?"

She pushed the pedal, and the gray spokes spun and flashed, whirring smartly. *I'm hot cuz I'm fly*, the singer insisted. *U ain't cuz u not.*

"Okay, climb on up."

"I had trouble with clipping into the pedals the last time I tried this," I confessed. "I finally got it to work, but I couldn't tell you how."

"There's kind of a trick to it—let me show you. Go ahead and slide the ball of your foot forward, then push down toward the floor when you get to the bottom. Tell you what," Tatum added after I'd been struggling for a few moments, "go ahead and take those shoes off for a sec."

I dismounted and took them off, and Tatum slipped them on and jumped gracefully onto my bike and the shoes clicked into place.

She got off and motioned for me to take her place, and after I'd climbed up on the bike and slid my feet into the shoes, she bent and strapped them. There was something in the moment—her kneeling, me elevated above her—that made me feel both uncomfortable and perversely energized.

"Great! Now I'm going to stand next to you and guide you on your form before we get started." Tatum placed her hands over mine and moved them gently along the handlebars. "You'll want to find your comfort spot . . . not too far back, you're going to want to lean a bit. Don't grip too hard—you want to work your abs and butt."

I glanced at her butt—perfectly toned and firm—as I slid my hands down the slightly padded gray handlebars, giving the pedals an experimental spin.

"Good . . . soften your elbows, relax your shoulders . . . there's nothing stiff, nothing too, you know, trying too hard."

Pop that pussy like a zit, I thought I heard the singer belt out.

"I'm sorry," I said, "but did he just say—"

"Don't listen to the words, just focus on the rhythm," Tatum scolded.

I tried to do as directed, exhaling and willing my body to relax. It was hard, though, as my pose felt so unnatural, the bike so unfamiliar. I wished I'd taken a few more spin classes before having a private session, but then again, it wasn't my responsibility to impress her.

"Now that you're clipped in, let's have you stand up and come out of the saddle. You want to push down with your thighs, right? Like you're climbing up steps? But it's better if you think about lifting your knees *up* instead. Like you're doing knee lifts . . . and move your butt as far back as you can—do you feel that in your core? Good!"

The music had segued into something frenetic and electronic. Tatum reached down to the big round control knob between my knees. She had to raise her voice to make herself heard over the music. "This is your resistance. To the right is harder, left is easier. In the class, they'll tell you when to increase it, okay?"

"Okay." I was still breathing pretty easily, but Tatum gave the knob another twist to the right and it became harder.

"If you need to brake at any time, just push the resistance knob."

I rode for a few minutes, my breathing growing more ragged, while Tatum swayed and snapped her fingers in time to the music, the encouraging smile never leaving her face.

"So now I'm going to take it all off and have you go faster, so you can feel your body adapting to the motion." She twisted again and I felt the wheel lighten. "Your hips are going to want to move with your feet, and you might find that you're moving to the music, kind of following the beat, right? One, two, one, two . . . yes, like that—that's what I'm looking for."

She increased and decreased the resistance as the music changed, making minor adjustments to my hips, hands, and shoulders with her hands, and complimented me for the slightest shows of competency. I felt encouraged, excited, eager to please, even as I grew winded and exhausted.

"You're doing great, Julia—you'll be ready to learn choreography in no time."

I snuck a glance at my watch; we'd been at it for half an hour already. I didn't think I could last much longer. Other than my prior attempt at spinning and a torturous session on a two-person bike on my honeymoon, during which I almost murdered James, I hadn't ridden a bike since childhood. I hated the way my stomach folded on itself, the bulge doubling; when I stole a look in the mirror along the side of the room, I saw that my face was beet red.

But Tatum was undeterred. "Nice form!" she said. "And you've got good arms. Do you work out with weights?"

"Sometimes," I said, not wanting to admit that my exercise was often limited to gossipy strolls around the reservoir with my friends after school drop-off.

"Hang on," she said, jogging toward the back of the room. "Just keep doing what you're doing."

In moments—too soon, since I used her absence as an excuse to slack off—she was back with hand weights.

"These are only one pound each," she said, handing me the

smaller set. "I just want you to try them and see what you think—we can squeeze in some weight training while you pedal."

I started pedaling slowly while gripping the weights, and Tatum had me increase my resistance until my legs were barely moving. She picked up five-pound weights and began doing an arm series with the weights in time with the music, her motions fluid and graceful, calling out encouragement. I followed along as best I could—biceps curls, triceps, and other moves that soon had my muscles screaming.

After what seemed like forever, Tatum took the weights out of my hands. She changed the music again, and *Imma go hard like a motherfuckin' boner* segued abruptly into Taylor Swift's "Teardrops on My Guitar."

"I love to cool down and stretch to this song," Tatum sighed, sitting down to put on her own spin shoes, which she'd stashed behind the podium. Of course she loved it; it was the song they would have played when they crowned her corn princess and drove her down Main Street in a convertible with the mayor. "I'll ride this one with you!"

She climbed up on the podium and mounted the instructor bike. "God, this feels *great,*" she said, and while I sweated and gasped and prayed for it to end, she threw her head back and pedaled to the beat, her ponytail flying behind her. "Ease your resistance to the left a few turns. Come out of the saddle and go ahead and close your eyes. Find your rhythm. That's good . . . pay attention to your breathing. Gorgeous.

"Can you feel it, Julia?" she asked, closing her eyes as she finally slowed, moving her arms languidly. "Can you feel yourself absorbing all that amazing energy, taking it inside you, body and spirit . . . getting stronger?"

"Yeah," I gasped, and the funny thing was that—especially now that she'd turned off that god-awful music—I *did*. I was sure I'd be sore tomorrow, but I was proud of myself for keeping up, for doing everything she said.

Tatum slowed her speed until we were coasting through the final bars of the song. She leaned over to tap on her laptop and lowered the volume, switching to a nineties ballad that had probably been recorded when she was a child, a song that reminded me of my first kiss behind the snack shack at our swim club. She dismounted the bike and podium and knelt down next to me as I coasted to a stop.

"I'll get this," she said, removing my feet from the pedals, the loud snap of the metal jarring me out of my come-down trance. "Next time we'll practice some more. Clipping in and unclipping are the hardest parts of spinning—it takes some people months to get it."

As I dismounted, she handed me a clean towel from a bin by the podium. "You did so well today, Julia."

I knew she was lying, but I was grateful. "Thank you. I'm in awful shape, though. I thought I was going to have a heart attack trying to keep up. Maybe we could take it down a notch next time?"

"Absolutely. Whatever you need! And we've still got another session together, right?"

"Right." I remembered something. "I've got the card from the auction in my bag—do you need it? To show your manager or anything?"

For a moment she looked confused, and then she laughed. "Oh, don't worry about that. It's not, like, official or anything."

"If you don't mind me asking, Tatum, what's your connection to Graylon, anyway? Do you know one of the moms?"

She blinked, and then her cheeks turned a pretty shade of pink. "No, actually. Ken wanted everyone to help spread the word to recruit new members and I just, you know, it seemed like such a good cause. The charity, the sister school, and all. So when do you want to schedule your next session?"

We retrieved our things from the locker room and compared calendars, settling on noon the following Tuesday. After I'd changed back into my own shoes and retrieved my things from my locker, Tatum walked me out to the lobby, where the receptionist barely deigned to acknowledge me other than to cast an assessing glance at the sweat patches on my clothes. I tossed my rental shoes into a woven sea-grass bin and asked for a schedule, only to be told that class reservations were handled through the app and that I'd find a complete schedule there.

"You need to sign up exactly twenty-four hours in advance or you'll end up on the waiting list," the receptionist added.

"Oh, come on, Paz," Tatum protested. "That almost never happens. I mean, look around! There's hardly anyone here!"

Paz? Seriously? She pursed her lips and raised her chin, fingering a delicate silver necklace with what looked like a chunk of petrified wood suspended from it.

"I'll keep that in mind," I said in my deadly-sweet fuck-you voice.

"I just thought you should know," Paz said. "I would *hate* to have to turn you away."

Tatum was starting to hop from foot to foot with agitation. "Don't worry," she muttered, "there's almost never a wait list for spin unless Brooke is teaching."

"There was a class discount for newcomers last month," Paz went on as though Tatum hadn't spoken. "What a shame that you missed it."

"It's no problem." I angled my bag so she couldn't miss the logo, so she'd know that I didn't need her damn discount.

I said goodbye to Tatum and headed out the door, still fuming over the encounter. It was just so unnecessary. Plenty of people would be impressed by Paz's zenner-than-thou routine, her jaw-dropping body; she didn't need to be such a bitch.

I'd walked three blocks before I realized that Tatum had never answered my question, and I still didn't know how her basket had found its way to Graylon.

CHAPTER 4

I stopped by the liquor store for a few bottles of rosé and as I waited on line, I thought about my session with Tatum, the combination of sensory stimuli in the studio, from the pounding beat of the music to the vanilla-and-citrus-scented candles to the gears whirring between my legs. I knew I would feel the workout the next day, but it wasn't exactly revolutionary. Still, there was a kernel of something— the contrast between Tatum's sunny countenance and her almost primitive energy when she got on the bike, perhaps.

Given how empty Flame was, I doubted it was breaking even. It hadn't found its audience. The lobby and locker room practically dripped with condescension, and the owner had obviously spent aggressively—I had a pretty good idea what the tumbled quartz mosaic and the Dornbracht faucets cost—but it still struck me as nothing short of brazen to charge thirty-five dollars per class.

The shadow of an idea wouldn't quite come into focus in my mind.

During the three years between my graduation from Dartmouth and getting pregnant with Paige, I had worked in brand management at Feral Hare, a boutique branding agency that you've probably never heard of that was known in the industry for taking a tired tableware manufacturer to industry dominance. It was a sought-after job and I was good at it.

You can't work in branding for any length of time without developing a sort of experience blindness. I can't buy mascara or test-drive a car without reverse-engineering everything from marketing copy to visual branding to demographic cues. From the moment I entered Flame, I'd been subconsciously evaluating its strategy. I thought it was smart to offer several different forms of exercise rather than focusing on just one like other boutique studios. The décor was exquisite, even if it wasn't my taste: the muted colors and contrast in textures and lighting created a sense of awe—you wanted to whisper, right up until you wanted to shout.

And then there was Tatum—she was adorable, but there was more to her than her lip-glossed, pep-rally charm. I had a strong feeling that she was working her own game, with the auction basket that the receptionist had never heard of and the obvious antipathy between them, and I was intrigued enough to want to find out what she was up to.

Just call me Encyclopedia Brown. School was almost out for summer, I had a mystery to solve, and maybe Flame could be my new clubhouse. If it lived up to my first impressions, I'd make it my own, tackling a few problems in one bold stroke: I'd get back in shape and start paying attention to my appearance again, and when everyone returned at the end of the summer, I'd let my friends in on my secret find, restoring my reputation as a trendsetter and influencer. In short, Flame would give me back the envy of others.

It would take work, and not just the sweat-and-grunt variety. I'd have to develop Tatum with care, refining her assets and helping her smooth over her rough edges, while letting her believe my sole goal was to mentor her. By the time I brought in a raft of women with free time and gobs of disposable income burning holes in their YSL purses, I'd have cemented Tatum's loyalty, which would only underscore my insider status at Flame. My plans might seem self-serving and manipulative, but Tatum would benefit too. I would *make* her and Flame succeed—already I was getting a rush from the idea.

When I walked in the door with the wine a few minutes after five, Mom suggested that we open it and have a glass—"Just us girls"— while Dad played Candy Land with the kids in the living room. We repaired to the little nook off the master bedroom that I had furnished with peacock blue chaises and cushions made from vintage batik fabric rescued from an upstate artists' colony. It was the only space in the apartment that was truly all mine, and I had envisioned relaxing there in the evenings with a cup of tea and a biography (in my domestic fantasies, I'm always reading biographies), but I mostly used it to hide out during Benilda's frequent cleaning frenzies.

I'd chosen a French rosé as my mother had an aversion to American wines, and filled a bowl with roasted pistachios. We tucked our feet under our legs like girls at a sleepover. Mom had already made a few comments since she arrived about how run-down I looked, how I had lost my glow, but now she got right to it: "What's wrong, honey? Is James having an affair?"

I burst into tears.

I wasn't concerned that James was having an affair—unlike many of my friends, I had a sturdy, loving marriage. But my mother was making a painful calculus, gauging how far I'd let myself go to determine if I'd sabotaged my marriage. I was suddenly acutely aware of my missed appointments with my dermatologist and colorist, the shapeless clothes I'd taken to wearing rather than shop for a new wardrobe for a body I was ashamed of. I often went without makeup, and sometimes I skipped a shower, and it was a good thing James had been too exhausted to feel frisky because I was growing a veritable hedge down there.

"Oh dear," Mom said, and handed me my glass and a cocktail napkin, which in our undemonstrative family amounts to a display of unbridled love and concern. "Has he admitted it?"

"No, Mom, it isn't James. I mean, he's not having an affair, I'm positive. It's just—" I gestured vaguely around the bedroom. "I don't know. The kids are in way too many activities, and it's a nightmare trying to keep up. And then this stupid deal James is trying to get off the ground, all the issues that have come up—I swear he's only home to sleep and sometimes not even then. I mean he *wants* to be home, he just . . . can't."

"If you're sure," Mom said delicately. "The important thing is that you take care of yourself. You know, you have to put your mask on first before you help the children, isn't that what they say? What about Benilda, isn't she picking up the slack?"

I used the napkin to dab at my eyes. "Sure, I guess, but she leaves early to go see family in Queens a couple times a week, and she doesn't like to stay late in the evenings, even though we always pay for an Uber home."

"That's ridiculous!" my mother said. "She's lucky you give her carfare. Our housekeepers never expected to be driven around when you were growing up."

"It's different now, Mom. A decent nanny can pretty much write her own ticket. I mean, it's one thing if you want some twenty-year-old from Iowa—"

"—or one of those Bulgarian girls," Mom said darkly. She had developed a deep distrust of Eastern European nannies after Dad's CFO got the family nanny pregnant.

"But Benilda's got great experience, she knows how to drive, and she keeps the apartment spotless. She does laundry every day, and she'll make whatever I ask for dinner."

"Well," Mom said, draining her glass. She'd brought the bottle with her, and now she topped us both off. "Maybe you should start looking for someone for nights and weekends."

I laughed. "James would love that. Do you know he asked me if Benilda could start taking the kids on the *subway* when he saw the Uber charges last month?"

Mom rolled her eyes. "Tell him he's welcome to take them to their lessons himself for a while if he's so worried."

"Mom . . ."

"I know, I know. We love James, you know that. It's just . . . hard, to see you like this."

She gave my knee a pat, and for a few moments we were silent, sipping our wine, lost in our own thoughts.

I knew my parents didn't "love" James, but that was all right. James made lots of money and mostly let me run our household without interference, and my parents had made their peace with him despite the inauspicious start of our relationship, the fact that I drunkenly made out with him in the coatroom at a funeral while I was engaged to another man.

"I'd better order the pizza," I said, my voice husky. "James will be home any minute, and I want to get the kids fed so you don't have to deal with it."

"All right, honey," Mom said, collecting the bottle and her glass. "But you know I'm always here for you, don't you?"

I hid a smile on my way out of the room, because when my mother said she was there for me, she meant our brisk Sunday phone calls and their quarterly visits to the city, not the late-night tête-à-têtes and giddy shopping sprees I'd once longed for. Still, Mom loved me, and she adored my children. In her way, she gave me all she had to give.

In the living room, Dad was lying on the floor with Henry balanced on his knees pretending to be a jet. Paige was on her stomach next to them, turning the pages of the book Mom had brought her. I experienced a rush of love and comfort that made me believe that better days were ahead.

CHAPTER 5

The rest of my parents' visit was uneventful. After they left on Monday, the skies turned gray and I took guilty pleasure in knowing that a rainstorm was heading for the Hamptons, ruining all those barbecues we weren't attending.

Tuesday morning I stood in my walk-in closet, trying to decide what to wear. It was less than two weeks until the end of school, and I was determined to be relentlessly upbeat and polished, so the last impression people had of me for the summer would be a good one. By the time Benilda arrived, I was running late.

"Can you get the kids fed and dressed?" I called. "I'm going to take them this morning."

I could have asked Benilda to drop off the kids every day if I wanted, but people notice—unless you work, it's considered poor form to send the nanny too often. And besides, the best way to make sure you're not being talked about is to be the one doing the talking. Anyone who believes we all show up solely out of maternal concern is being naïve: we're there to catch up on the gossip, to evaluate and judge each other, to jockey for position. It used to be exciting—back when something as simple as a vintage coat I'd found downtown won me admiration and envy—but lately it had become tedious. So much effort just to stay in the game.

"Yes, Mrs. Julia," Benilda called back. I heard the low, soothing murmur of her voice as she made the kids finish up their breakfast and take their plates to the sink and wash their hands. I felt both gratitude and guilt around Benilda, who never lost her patience with the kids and insisted on good behavior. Imagining the daughters she'd left behind in the Philippines, deprived of their mother while she raised someone else's children, always made me feel slightly ill.

I spent extra time applying my makeup and blow-dried and flat-ironed my hair. The day was pleasant, so I settled on a forgiving jade wrap dress that I'd bought in Paris and a pair of delicate birdcage earrings. I'd have plenty of time to come back and change before I headed to Flame for my second session with Tatum.

I timed our arrival at drop-off for a few minutes before the principal emerged from the huge carved oak doors to usher the children up the steps and inside. Henry dawdled as usual, while Paige chattered away about her friends and teachers and what was for lunch. At eight years old, she was starting to show the first signs of mean-girl behavior, and I was resigned to the fact that she had inherited from me a fondness for the spotlight.

"Hello, Lily," she said haughtily as we walked up to Emery Souza and her daughter. "I hope you don't still feel bad about making our team lose the reading challenge. Everybody's probably forgotten about how it was your fault we didn't get ice cream."

Poor Lily Souza flushed and stammered a response, but Paige had already moved on, headed for Clara Otedola, who was showing off her new smart watch—not one of those colorful kids' models but an actual Apple watch. Great—now Paige would want one. And I was stuck with smoothing Emery's ruffled feathers.

But Celeste Zapata beat me to it. "That damn reading challenge," she muttered, shooing her daughter Esme off toward the steps, out of earshot. "How are they supposed to find time to read extra books? Esme's got Latin twice a week, on top of gymnastics and soccer."

"It's ridiculous," Penelope Epstein said, pushing her stroller up next to us and setting the brake. Isabel, her third, was only eighteen months and Penelope was pregnant again—one of those women who claims to love everything about motherhood while experiencing most of it from a distance as her live-in nanny kept things afloat with the help of a second one, who lived out. "Chauncy *loves* to read—he'd spend all his time with his nose in a book, if I let him—but we're committed to maintaining a practice of family dialogue every night. You know, unstructured time to simply be together."

I suppressed an eye roll—word was that she and Adam were on the brink of divorce.

"Are those Jakobine's?" Milly Prasad asked, peering at my earrings. "They're gorgeous! Is she working on a new line?"

I stood a little taller and smiled modestly. "She is, actually, but it's still in the design phase."

"Oh, I hope she does more with topaz," Milly said, sticking out her wrist, from which hung a bronze bangle studded with golden stones. "Have you seen any of it yet?"

"Sorry, you know I can't talk about it," I said, feigning regret. "I barely got it out of her myself."

The doors opened, and Zarine Parekh, the principal, came walking out with Mrs. Edmonds from the office behind her, and the children began streaming up the stairs. "Bye, Mom," Henry said without a backward glance as he barreled away.

For a moment we all watched our children, which gave me a chance to bask in the glow of the talk of Jakobine. I'd discovered her a few years ago, when I was browsing the Dumbo Flea Market. She was sitting at one of the vendor tables, wearing enormous sunglasses with opaque black lenses that would have made her look like a human fly if it weren't for her white-blond bob. She was reading a dog-eared book that, when I looked closer, turned out to be a Dutch-English dictionary, and laid out in front of her on a white dish towel was a collection of striking jewelry: delicate rings and pendants worked in jet-black fretwork, studded with pavé brown and black stones.

It turned out she was from the Netherlands and had come to the United States to work as an au pair, but her real love was designing jewelry. Her name was Jakobine, and she wanted her own store someday, but for now she worked in inexpensive materials—rhodium-plated silver and brass, flawed gemstones that other jewelers wouldn't touch—and sold her work all over the city. Her English wasn't great, and neither were her teeth, but she was working on the former and saving for the latter.

I took her number and bought half a dozen pieces and started wearing them everywhere, and a month later, when I invited a handful of friends for a private viewing in my apartment, Jakobine sold everything she brought at the 50 percent markup I'd insisted she add. I convinced a friend to get her husband to fix Jakobine's teeth in exchange for a custom piece, and people spread the word until Jakobine had more business than she could keep up with. Eight months after we met, she moved to Brooklyn and opened her own tiny gallery, hired a few assistants, and began selling her designs from her new website. Last fall she had pieces featured in *Bazaar* and *Vogue,* and several celebrities were seen wearing her "Dagger" rings. And most important, she never forgot that I gave her her start.

The last of the children filed inside and Zarine gave us all a brisk nod before the doors closed, leaving us to finish our conversations and make our plans and pair up for coffee or rush off for appointments or head to the gym. Half the moms—and the one dad—were dressed in workout clothes.

"You know," Milly said, as though she'd just thought of it, "Maybe *I* should host Jakobine's next launch party. I must have twenty of her pieces by now—and since we've bumped out the solarium, we could do a drinks thing there."

Nice try, I thought, but there was no way I was giving up the launch party, not when people hinted for invitations for weeks. I hadn't had a big win on the board since Jakobine, and I wasn't about to loosen my grip on her until I did. "That is *so* thoughtful," I said, "but she's already planning to have me do it and—"

"Julia!"

I winced and forced a polite smile as a woman in a baseball cap and baggy leggings came racewalking toward me, arms outstretched.

"Hi, Janet," I said, accepting her hug. "We were just talking about the end of the school year."

"Finally!" Janet said. "I can't wait to have Willa all to ourselves. We're teaching her to drive this summer, can you believe it?"

"Surely not in the city?" Celeste said, staring at Janet's shapeless yellow T-shirt, which was printed with KINGSBRIDGE HEIGHTS COMMUNITY CENTER CLEANUP DAY 2011.

"Oh no." Janet laughed. "We're driving across the country, all three of us. Terry just has to finish grading finals, and we've rented one of those pop-up campers. We're going to stop and visit his parents in Ohio, and the idea is that by then Willa can help drive the rest of the way to Washington."

"Aren't you brave," Emery said. "It's like World War Three in the backseat when we go anywhere."

"Well, it's probably easier with an only," Janet said, starting to march in place. "Listen, I need to keep my heart rate up—Terry wrote a program to track our heart rates and body fat and we take our numbers on Wednesdays."

She went striding up Madison Avenue, hips swinging and fists pumping as she dodged hydrants and pedestrians, oblivious to the looks she was getting.

"That's insane," Emery said when she was out of earshot. "They could afford to *buy* a plane to get them across country. And instead they're *camping*? What, like in KOA Campgrounds?"

"Did you see how gray she's getting?" Celeste asked. "I bet she's never even had highlights."

"And that T-shirt!" Penelope looked to me. I knew they were expecting a zinger from me, but I felt a little queasy.

"Yellow isn't her color," I said uncomfortably. "Hey, I need to talk to Lindsay—"

But before I could extricate myself, Lindsay came over to join us. "Just who I wanted to see," she said, handing me a lumpy envelope. "The keys are in there. I'm sure nothing's going to happen while we're away, but since you'll be in town all summer—"

I snatched the envelope and stuffed it into my purse, but I hadn't been quick enough.

"You're staying in town?" Emery asked in surprise.

I wasn't going to be able to keep it secret forever. People had already noticed that we weren't in the Hamptons over Memorial Day—I got a bunch of texts asking where we were—but I had been hoping to keep it quiet until everyone was gone, so I wouldn't have to keep reliving the disaster and trying to put a positive spin on it.

"Oh, we're just having some work done on the Hamptons house," I said. "But we'll be out for the Fourth."

"What kind of work?" Milly asked, her eyes narrowed. Oh, how she wanted a piece of me.

"You'll be the first to see it when it's finished," I gushed, taking Lindsay's arm and steering her away.

"Sorry, sorry," she said once we were out of earshot. "You know she's going to be driving by the site all summer to see what they're doing."

"She just offered to give Jakobine a party," I confided.

"She didn't!"

"I heard she and Jay didn't get invited to Elizabeth Kim's fortieth birthday party. She's getting a little desperate."

"Yeah, they invited four couples to their place in Park City over spring break and every one of them declined," Lindsay said. "And then there's Janet, who simply does not have one fuck to give. Was she really wearing crew socks with capri leggings?"

I felt that same vague nausea again. "I don't know, you kind of have to admire her," I tried. "Not caring what anyone else thinks."

"Of course you'd say that," Lindsay scoffed. "But there's a difference between being a free spirit"—she gestured at my bag, a chrome yellow version of the Mansur Gavriel bucket bag that everyone else owned in black—"and being a freak. You know she only gets away with it because—"

"—she's richer than God," I finished. "Yes, I know. But still . . ."

Lindsay rolled her eyes. "You're sweet to defend her. Call me later?"

We set off in our separate directions. I was grateful for the walk, for time to ponder the last twenty minutes: Paige's meanness to Lily, Milly's grasping for Jakobine, the fact that the news of our summer disaster was out.

And the Eriksons: Terry, a classic absentminded professor and physics genius; Willa, an ungainly tenth grader who'd finaled in the state spelling bee . . . and Janet.

Janet and I had a history. When I'd moved to New York after graduation, Mom called her college friend Cecelia Van Cordt, Janet's oldest sister, and asked if she'd make an introduction, since I knew few people in the city other than my roommates and a handful of Dartmouth classmates. Janet and Terry had taken me out to dinner, and I'd spent an evening listening to stories from their Peace Corps days. We didn't keep in touch, but after Paige had been accepted to Graylon, I found out that Janet had written a letter on her behalf.

I had actually enjoyed my evening with the Eriksons, but I thought of Janet as my mother's generation, though she was only ten years older than I was. When Paige started at Graylon, I carefully distanced myself, making excuses every time Janet suggested coffee, until she finally stopped. I'm ashamed to admit it, but I knew from the start that she'd be a social liability. The Eriksons were invited everywhere, but only because they donated insane amounts of money to the school and dozens of other causes and charities; behind her back Janet was the object of endless ridicule.

I felt bad for the way I'd treated her, but now wasn't the time for me to be taking chances. I sometimes thought of my life like a stock ticker, the graph line trending up or down with my social status. Throw a winter solstice party that ended up all over Instagram—the line ticked up. Lose the PTA election, and it slipped back down.

Conspicuous absence from the Hamptons scene all summer . . . it remained to be seen how far my stock would fall.

CHAPTER 6

James called me a few hours later as I was walking to Flame.

"Well, I'm here," he said, not bothering with hello. "Scene of the fucking crime."

It took me a moment to realize he meant our Hamptons house. "I thought you weren't going out there until the middle of the week."

"Yeah, well, things got moved around a little. Got to say, Bart wasn't exaggerating. Hole in the ceiling three feet wide. Floors are toast."

My heart sank. The floors—ten-inch-wide planks reclaimed from an old North Carolina textile mill, polished to a gleam during our renovation—could not be replaced, not with anything I'd love as much.

"Bart got a couple fans in here, but they aren't doing shit. I've got Servpro coming, I'm gonna have them run 'em the rest of the week, around the clock. Got a dumpster coming too—Dante's going to start demo tomorrow."

"Did you talk to the neighbors?"

"Seriously, Julia? If they've got a problem with a dumpster in front of the house—that I'm paying a goddamn premium for, it's criminal how they rip you off out here—they can walk over and tell me. But they might want to save their breath for when the excavation starts. It's going to be a hell of a mess."

"Excavation? Of what?"

"Well, that's what I'm calling to tell you. I went down in the crawl space and I don't know how Bart managed to miss this, which tells me he wasn't doing shit that was in his contract, but there's been water coming in a hell of a lot longer than just this week. My guess is, when they open up the walls they're going to find more leaks in the galvanized pipe. So now the mortar's shot and the foundation's rotated and it's all going to have to be fixed before we can touch the inside."

"I don't understand anything you just said." I was trying to keep calm, but James wasn't helping. "Are you telling me that they have to dig up under the house?"

"The house was built in 1910," James said, slowly and deliberately, like he was talking to the kids. "The cripple wall was built for shit then, and it sure as hell hasn't gotten any better over time. I knew when we bought the place we were going to have to shore it up eventually, but I never saw this coming."

I didn't know what a cripple wall was and I didn't think now was the time to ask. "So they have to replace it?" I asked, then braced myself for another incomprehensible torrent.

Instead, there was silence, though I could hear him breathing.

". . . James?"

"It isn't just . . . Look, I'll explain it later. I've got the insurance guy meeting me here in a half hour, and I want to take some pictures." He'd actually toned it down a little, which somehow made it worse. "All you need to know? We won't be back in there for a year if we're lucky, but on the bright side, you get to decorate it all over again. Gotta go, Jules."

I put my phone back in my purse slowly. *You get to decorate it all over again.* Was that really what James thought of me? That the highlight of my existence was making trips to showrooms and poring over sample books?

I'd always put a lot of time and effort into our homes. I sought out undiscovered and outsider artists, combined vintage pieces with contemporary ones, and created rooms that sparked conversations but were comfortable and durable enough for a family with young kids. I'd even thought that if circumstances were different I might design homes for other people, maybe even go back to school for a master's.

James's casual dismissal stung. He was supportive, in his way—he never complained about what I spent, and complimented the results, but I had a feeling he neither noticed nor cared about the details. I once took a pair of fleece-stuffed dolphins my parents sent the kids from the San Diego aquarium and tacked them up over the mantel as though they were kissing mid-leap, and asked him what he thought. His "looks nice" was no more or less enthusiastic than when I'd hung a Rouault lithograph I'd bought at an estate sale in the foyer.

I went home to change and return some emails and got to Flame ten minutes early. Paz was at the desk, dressed in a shapeless brown linen shift and jute sandals that looked like some Cub Scout had made them at camp, her hair twisted and secured with a leather barrette. She was talking to another woman in workout clothes, a lithe creature with full-sleeve tattoos and inky black hair and pale gray eyes rimmed in makeup that looked like she'd slept in it. When she saw me, she gave me a nod of faint acknowledgment.

Tatum came flying around the corner, gathering her damaged, bleached hair up into a bun, a hair elastic between her teeth. Her top was shiny and covered in an abstract, swirling print in shades of purple and yellow. Her capris, unfortunately, matched.

"Sorry, sorry!" she said, taking the elastic out of her mouth and securing her bun. "Have you been waiting?"

"No, I just got here."

"Paz says you're doing a private," the tattooed woman said. "You mind if I grab a bike and get a workout in? I'll be quiet—I'm stuck here until my two o'clock."

Tatum's grin slipped a bit. "Sure! Of course! That'll be great! This is Brooke," she said to me. "The one with the really great music?"

I put it together: *I'm hot cuz I'm fly* . . . the septum and lip piercings, the tattoo that stopped just short of her neck. The chipped black nail polish and the Flame tank top that she'd taken scissors to so the hem ended in a shredded fringe over her leggings. More tattoos on her ankles and calves.

"Of course," I said. "Nice to meet you. I'm Julia."

"I saw you learned how to use the app," Paz said, as if I'd exceeded her wildest expectations.

"It was easy." I made a show of checking my watch, the Cartier Tank James gave me for our first anniversary.

"Well, let's get your shoes and get started," Tatum said.

I felt for her—she was clearly the new kid on the block, subject to the mean girl initiation that takes place in some form, I'm convinced, in every gathering of women from the glittering heights of Manhattan to the factory line in Arkansas. I followed her down to the spin room, walking awkwardly in the spin shoes, Brooke jogging ahead. By the time we entered, Brooke had already mounted a bike in the back corner and was warming up with her eyes closed, swaying languidly.

"Listen," I said to Tatum. "How about this time we just work out to your favorite music? Like that cooldown—that was nice."

"I don't really have favorites," she said doubtfully. "I mean songs, yeah, but not like a playlist or anything. I've just been borrowing my music from other teachers."

"Okay, how about we use mine then?" I suggested. I just couldn't stand another rap-blasting session, especially not with Brooke in the room; I didn't trust her. I figured she was here to intimidate Tatum. Already she'd increased her speed to an alarming pace, her ebony hair falling over her face as she bore down. Under all that ink, her muscles flexed and rippled. I bet the firefighters loved her.

"Sure!" Tatum said, looking relieved. I grabbed her laptop and logged in to my Spotify account; the first few bars of "Don't Know Why" by Norah Jones filled the room.

"Oh my God!" Tatum squealed. "I love this song—it's from my favorite movie ever!"

"Really? Which one?"

"*Maid in Manhattan.*"

"The one with J.Lo? I don't think I ever saw it but—"

"Yes, that's the one! It came out in 2002, when I was ten years old. J.Lo plays this maid who accidentally gets mistaken for a fancy socialite, and Ralph Fiennes is this superrich guy who falls in love with her but he doesn't know she's actually a maid. And it's set right here in New York!"

What I had been going to say before she cut me off was that I was familiar with the film from a class in women's studies at Dartmouth. Her assessment of the movie was a bit different from the one our professor had put forth, in which viewers are forced to view J.Lo's character through a white, male, classist lens while the white couture outfit she wears in a key scene signals an effort to maintain the purity of white identity, at the same time suggesting that social mobility for women of color can only be achieved through sexual congress with powerful men. Triple-strike feminist-racist fail, but Tatum's Cinderellaish version was sort of touching.

"Maybe you'll meet an amazing guy here at Flame," I said. "You never know!"

Tatum shrugged. "I don't know, I'm not really looking. Besides, all I really want is to help people be the best that they can be."

"Well, you're welcome to make *me* be the best I can be," I said, pinching my stomach flab. "Starting with getting rid of this."

"That's easy! Come on, let's get you on the bike!"

This time, I felt a bit more confident. I found that I enjoyed the sensation of rising off the seat, extending my legs as far as they could go, feeling the power in my body, the beat vibrating through the soles of my feet. Brooke only stayed for about twenty minutes before wandering out; Tatum rode on the instructor bike in front of me for most of my session, calling encouragement, singing, cuing me to sit down or adjust my resistance.

"You did great," Tatum chirped when we finished the cooldown and had unclipped and come off the bikes. "And your music is amazing."

"Thanks," I said. "I just hope all my evil fat cells are getting the message."

"Spin will help with weight loss, and the weight work will really tone you," Tatum promised. "Besides, I can tell that you're motivated. People don't realize how much they can change about themselves if they try. You just have to be determined."

"And disciplined."

Tatum nodded. "So true. A lot of people are so weak it's pathetic. They say they want to change, and you show them exactly how to do it, but then they don't do the work. People like that deserve to stay the way they are."

I was surprised by the harshness of her words, so at odds with her usual gumball optimism. "Listen, you want to get coffee? My nanny's picking the kids up from school."

"Gosh, yes!"

We changed our shoes and freshened up in the locker room before setting off to find coffee. I only half-listened to Tatum's chatter as we walked, imagining the barely disguised envy of my friends when they returned at the end of the summer, the conversations I'd already been practicing in the shower.

You're so kind! It's true, I did lose weight, but mostly I've just shifted the way I think about the mind-body connection. It's amazing, the clarity that comes from honoring that balance—it's like training my body has almost become a spiritual practice.

Tatum? Oh yes, she's amazing. As soon as we started working together, I could tell that teaching was more than just a job for her—it's her calling.

We were devastated about the Hamptons house at first, but it's been a blessing in disguise. Having to replace virtually everything made me really focus on what James and I value most, and we're working with local artisans and an amazing sustainability consultant . . .

When we arrived at the coffee shop, I bought us each a macaron to go with our cappuccinos, and we found a table in the corner by the window.

"So tell me about you," I said.

Tatum shrugged. "Not a whole lot to tell. I'm from Missouri, a little town called Versailles. I was in theater in high school and on the dance team and I sang in the choir, and when I was a senior one of my teachers asked me if I'd ever thought of majoring in theater in college, but I decided to skip college and come here for the real thing instead." She glanced at me shyly. "Ridiculous, right? I was such an idiot—I thought I'd saved up enough to get a place but I ended up only being able to sublet a room in a walk-up in Alphabet City—

you don't even want to know. I got a job at a restaurant supply store and waited tables at a diner around the corner on weekends. And then I moved in with this old lady on the Upper West Side who needed help in exchange for room and board, and I lived with her until she went into a nursing home. And the whole time I was taking acting classes and going on auditions and, you know, that whole grind. I'm back in Alphabet City now."

"Did you ever get to Broadway?"

"Oh . . . yes, but it was just a chorus part, and the show closed halfway through its run. I mean, don't get me wrong, it was my dream, and I'll always be supergrateful I had that experience, but I had to accept that it wasn't going to happen."

"How did you end up at Flame?"

"Through Brooke, actually. I met her through a friend a few months ago, and she told me I should apply to Flame. A spin teacher had just quit, and they needed someone to cover her classes fast, otherwise I don't think Ken would ever have hired me."

"Just like that? Had you done spin before?"

"Oh yeah, I had a friend who used to sneak me into her gym, and I'd taken a bunch of classes. I *love* spin, and I think it showed when I auditioned for Flame. What about you?"

"Me? I think you've seen the grand sum of my fitness experience—not much, unfortunately."

"No, I meant, how did you end up here?"

"Here . . . the Upper East Side? Well, I grew up in Boston, and after college I got a job in the city. I lived with a couple of friends in Murray Hill, and then I met my husband and we got engaged three months later." I left out the part where I was already engaged—I always edited that out of the version I told people. "James is a real estate developer . . . he works a *lot*. You already know about my kids—Henry's six and just about to finish kindergarten, Paige's eight—and that's about it, really."

"You make it sound so easy," Tatum said, which gave me pause. *Easy* was a funny word for it.

"I've been blessed," I said and changed the subject. "Do you like working at Flame?"

"Yes, except I can't get enough classes," Tatum said. "I don't have any seniority so I mostly fill in and cover for people, I don't get regular time slots. I mean, I love it, obviously, but Ken says we can't add more classes until we get more members, and none of the other teachers are willing to give up any of their slots."

"Well." I dabbed at my mouth with my napkin and pushed my plate away. "I may be able to help you with that."

I told her about the work I used to do, how I was trained to build brands for companies. "Building a personal brand isn't much different," I said. "You just have to be strategic—and disciplined."

"Brooke has a brand," Tatum said. "People *love* her."

"That's because Brooke distinguishes herself, from what I can see. I mean, she's not my cup of tea, but she doesn't have to be. That's one of the key tenets of branding: you don't have to reach every consumer, and in fact you shouldn't even try. The first step is to identify your customer, and after that, everything you do, every decision you make, should be focused on her. Who would you say is the core Flame member? The person who feels at home the minute they walk in?"

"I'm not sure we have one. I mean, we've got twenty-somethings, people in their first jobs. When Flame first opened—before the remodel—it was cheaper than Equinox, but we lost a lot of members when the prices went up. We've got guys from the firehouse who mostly box—Ken gives them a discount. Medical people from Sinai. A few older people. And just a lot of random members."

"See, now that's a problem," I said. "There's no way to target a group you haven't defined. Let me ask it another way: who do you think would be the *ideal* member? Someone who can pay a premium, fill day classes and not just nights and weekends, who would bring their friends and grow the membership?" I already knew the answer, of course, but I wanted to see if Tatum got it.

"Well, women like *you*," she said. "Neighborhood moms who don't work, who have time on their hands."

I smiled. "I have a theory to run by you, Tatum. I think you already knew that. In fact, I think it was your idea to donate that basket to the Graylon Academy benefit, because you saw the value in recruiting the moms." This wasn't much of a leap; a casual call to the school's Development Office had confirmed that a "cute blond girl" had stopped by and said she'd heard about the benefit and wanted to contribute.

Uncertainty and surprise flashed across Tatum's expression. "That's—I mean—"

"Don't worry, there's nothing to be embarrassed about," I reassured her. "I think you did the smart thing. You had a need—to get more classes—and the determination to make it happen. Did you make sure your boss took notice of your efforts?"

She smiled uncertainly. "Um . . . he *did* ask us all at a staff meeting to spread the word to find new members, but I think I was the only one who really tried."

"So you came up with the basket, the personal training sessions. Did your boss know you were going to do that?"

"No," Tatum admitted. "But I told him about it after. I thought if we could get more rich moms, maybe they'd tell their friends." She hesitated. "The honest truth is, he was going to let me go. I mean he actually did let me go, he said he just didn't think I was working out, because I wasn't filling classes when I was subbing, but I asked him to give me one month to show him I could do better."

"Why's it so important to you, Tatum? You could probably get a job at any gym in town."

"Yes, but not up *here*." She looked around the café with an almost innocent sense of wonder. "I live in a studio on Avenue A. When I come out the front door every day, I see homeless people, trash, filth. There's a Chinese restaurant on the corner that smells like something died inside it. A little grocery store where you can't even get a decent head of lettuce. I guess to some people, that's the city, you know? But for me . . . when I was taking care of the old lady, I used to walk across the park to the Metropolitan Museum. Remember I was telling you how much I love *Maid in Manhattan*? There's a scene where J.Lo goes to this party at the Met, and everyone's dressed in these beautiful gowns and there's music and champagne and she gets to dance with Ralph Fiennes. And it's like—it's like—"

Words, it seemed, had failed her, but I thought I knew what she meant. Even I could still come around the corner after walking around the reservoir and catch a glimpse of the sun on the marble of the grand old buildings along Fifth Avenue and experience a little shiver of awe.

"But it isn't just the museums, or the architecture or whatever," Tatum went on. "It's the way people *are* up here. The stores, the restaurants, people still care about, oh, I don't know, details. And quality. And having things that last. It's . . . elegant."

This was hardly an original sentiment, but it made me feel warm toward her, this girl in her cheap clothes with her fake-leather bag and her midwestern twang, carried along by this very ordinary dream, with no idea how she revealed herself with that too-eager grin.

She was raw potential, misguided in her style and awkward in her enthusiasm. To be a fitness instructor was a touchingly modest goal, but I saw how it encompassed so much more for Tatum—it was her ticket to a neighborhood that represented everything she dreamed of.

I, with my privileged upbringing in Boston, had never questioned whether the city would open her arms to me. But Tatum had come from nothing; she'd had to fight for everything she got. Now I had a chance to do something good for her while I pursued my own goals, to help her fit in on the Upper East Side, maybe even eventually make it her home.

"I know exactly what you mean," I said. "Now let me share a few thoughts—I think you can be even more successful here than you've imagined."

That night I was in bed reading when James came in carrying his laptop and got into bed next to me.

"O-*ho*," I said. "Really?"

"Yup. It's your lucky night. Now be quiet so I can send these last two emails."

James used to bring his laptop to bed all the time, until I made a rule—he had to go down on me for the same amount of time he spent on his computer. I excused myself to comb my hair and dab on a little perfume and exchange the ancient Dartmouth tank top I'd worn to bed for a silk negligee, and when I returned, he'd closed the laptop and was waiting for me.

"Turn off the lamp," I said as I crawled across the bed to his side. "I'm under construction. You have to wait for the finished product."

"What the hell does that mean?" James asked, guiding me on top of him so I could feel his erection under the sheet. After all this time, I knew his contours, his moves, and we fit like a favorite old pair of jeans. It might not be fireworks every night, but it was good, and often better than good.

"It means I have to lose twenty pounds," I said. "But this new gym is going to whip me into shape—watch out."

"How boring," James said. Easy for him to say, when he still had a construction worker's build—broad shoulders, flat stomach, muscles for days. "Turn around, cowgirl."

The next twenty minutes made me forget all about the fact that the light was on. Afterward, he finally turned it off and I curled up in his strong arms, which was the second-best part of sex with my husband. He was even good for a little pillow talk before falling asleep.

"What new gym?" he asked, yawning. That's one of James's talents—he can pick up a conversation wherever he left off after an interruption, whether it's the kids or a work call or causing his wife to thrash around and make undignified noises.

So I told him a little about Flame and mentioned I'd found a teacher I liked.

"At least you'll have something to do this summer." He was quiet for a moment. "I really am sorry about the damn Hamptons house, Jules. And all the work you put into it."

"I know," I said. "And it's not your fault. It's nobody's fault, and we'll get through it."

"About that . . ." He stroked my back. "It may be good we're here all summer. At least for work. There's some things going on with Mercer—"

"Oh, no," I groaned. *Things going on* was usually code for shit hitting fans, a prelude to James announcing he was missing dinner or the kids' events or some benefit he didn't want to go to anyway. Already, the Mercer project had been plagued with problems. There had been some bad press and protests when they shut the nursing home down and moved the few remaining residents, though all of that had happened before James ever bought it. Construction had been supposed to start in April, but it had been delayed by some sort of zoning problem. "Is it the city council thing?"

"Yeah, sort of." James didn't mind that I didn't follow the details of his job; I think he preferred it, because it took forever to explain all the complex rules and realities of redevelopment in the city. "Fucking Cora's fucking with me again."

Cora Rivera was the city councilwoman in the district where Mercer House was located, and where James had had a few other projects over the years. She'd come to our Christmas open house, along with a few of James's other acquaintances from work, and cornered one of my friends who used to practice sports medicine to ask for advice about her knee issues. What Cora lacked in social skills she more than made up for with a barracuda-like instinct for controversy, or so you would think if you heard her on TV, blaming everyone from the mayor to her fellow council members to developers to transit authorities for everything that went wrong in her district. The only people who weren't targets of her wrath were voters, and she wasn't above treading ethically murky waters to keep her seat. When James had done a townhouse conversion in her district a few years back, the myriad code violations and multiple inspections didn't get settled until he made a substantial donation to her reelection fund.

"Is it bad?" I asked.

"Eh, you know. Nothing I can't handle. Man stuff—don't you worry your pretty little head over it."

I snuggled in closer, lulled by the steady beat of his heart against my cheek. Ordinarily I'd give him hell for a crack like that, but here, in the refuge of our bedroom with his arms wrapped around me, his words made me feel safe and cared for as I drifted off to untroubled sleep.

CHAPTER 7

By the time the last few days of school arrived, I was ready for everyone to be gone. Word of our misfortune had gotten around, and every time I ran into one of the other moms, I had to endure the oh-poor-you thing all over again. You'd think I was grieving the loss of a parent rather than a few months at our vacation home.

On the second-to-last day of school I decided I'd drop the kids off but have Benilda pick them up so I wouldn't have to endure more of the excited chatter, the invitations to clambakes and cocktail parties I couldn't attend. Instead, I got on the Flame app and signed up for a spin class Tatum was teaching at 3:00 P.M.

As class parent for Paige's grade, I had a huge bag full of end-of-year gifts to deliver, so I called an Uber. Our theme was Lazy Summer, and people had donated books, beach towels, flip-flops, and bottles upon bottles of wine. Paige and Henry carried boxes of cookies Benilda had made for their teachers.

As we arrived at the school, I saw Emery struggling with an enormous potted fern. Paige's little mean-girl episode last week hadn't helped the tension between us. Since Emery was about to be out of my life for the summer, I decided I might as well make amends, and as Paige and Henry ran to join their friends, I dragged my bag over to her.

"Let me help you with that," I said, "and then maybe you can help me carry this—it weighs a ton."

Together, we carried the fern and the bag of gifts up the stairs and into the school office.

"Thanks for the help," Emery said, as we walked back outside.

"By the way, I'm so sorry to hear about the Hamptons. But there's something to be said for simplifying too. I swear, some summers I think we really ought to sell our place—I spend more time yelling at the kids not to track sand in than I do relaxing."

That seemed a bit extreme, considering I'd heard they'd leveraged everything to buy it, even though it was on the North Fork. "It's just one summer," I said, laughing. "We've got all winter to get the repairs done—I think we'll survive."

"Oh—you're not selling?"

"What?" I blinked. "Who told you that?"

"I don't actually remember. I heard that—I guess I misunderstood."

But she didn't seem at all flustered . . . in fact she seemed a bit smug.

"Wait a minute. People are saying we're selling the Hamptons house? Because that's not true. There was a leak—there's water damage, that's all."

"Right. It's just . . ."

I regretted my spontaneous show of goodwill as I stifled the urge to reach down her throat and yank out the truth. "Just what?"

"Like I said, I probably misunderstood, but I heard that it was underinsured, and the repairs . . ." She shrugged. And now I got it.

Emery was implying that we couldn't afford to keep the place. Which in this crowd was as bad as suggesting that I had joined a satanic cult or molested the captain of the varsity tennis team: being broke was an unforgivable sin.

Grace had arrived for the tail end of the conversation. "Can you believe this?" I asked her. "There's a rumor going around that James and I are losing our house."

"That's the problem with Hamptons real estate," Grace joked. "You lose your shirt every time, am I right?"

"Listen, Emery, you really must come for dinner next summer. Since we have to make all those repairs, James and I decided we might as well put in an outdoor kitchen." That would be news to James, but I'd deal with him later. "The North Fork isn't too far from Southampton, is it? I confess I've never been."

I smiled at her placidly, proud of my two-pronged rejoinder.

"Got time for a coffee?" Grace asked me, turning her shoulder slightly toward Emery in a show of loyalty.

"Why not?" I asked, linking arms with her. "But let's make it a quick one—I've got to FaceTime with my architect in an hour. She wants me to check out this cabinetmaker in Vermont who doesn't use the Internet—he refuses to post pictures of his work online because he says you can't appreciate the spirit of the wood. You have to drive three hundred miles to his workshop—or pay someone two hundred and fifty dollars an hour to do it."

We both laughed as Emery stood there looking like she hoped a delivery van would come out of nowhere and mow me down.

"So nice to see you, Emery," Grace said.

"Have a wonderful summer if I don't see you," I added.

Grace waited until we were out of earshot to say, "I suppose there's not really a cabinetmaker in Vermont?"

"I'm sure there are dozens," I said innocently. "Maybe even hundreds. They're thick on the ground up there, from what I hear. Listen, let's check out the new stuff in the windows at Lululemon—if I'm going to be stuck here all summer, I might as well be comfortable."

"So no coffee and no Vermont carpenter. You're a very bad girl, Mrs. Summers."

I laughed hollowly along with her. "Good girls never get anywhere worth going," I replied.

Grace and I hit a few stores, and it was past lunchtime when I got home. I changed into my new gym clothes and made a salad for lunch, using fat-free dressing and skipping my usual blue cheese and croutons. Then I stepped on the scale. Usually I only weighed myself first thing in the morning before I'd had so much as a sip of water, but I figured I might as well face the ugly truth as I launched my summer transformation. Still, the number took my breath away: I weighed almost thirty pounds more than I had on my wedding day.

I gave myself a little extra time to get to Flame so as not to draw attention to myself in my first real class. I'd used the app to select a bike near the back of the room, and I was arranging my towel on the handlebars as I'd seen Tatum do when she bounced into the studio. She squealed when she saw me and ran over to give me a hug—it was like being hugged by a giant monarch butterfly; she was wearing orange leggings and a striped orange and yellow and black tank top, and she gave off a cloud of cheap floral perfume.

"I'm so thrilled you came!" she said. "Listen, can you give me the sign-in to your Spotify so I can use one of your playlists? I'm nervous—this is the most people I've ever taught."

"Sure, and I'll send them all to you so you'll have them," I said, following her up to the podium, where I picked a playlist I'd made to listen to when I walked the reservoir. Semisonic's "Closing Time" filled the room.

"Want a little advice?" I asked, looking out at a dozen or so riders getting their bikes set up.

"God, yes."

"See that girl over there? I overheard her telling her friend that she loves Erika's classes because she knows everyone by name. Erika makes her feel important, or at least recognized."

"But I don't know any of these people!"

"You can still make them feel singled out. Special. Just—like her, see?" I nodded toward a heavy woman in her twenties who had chosen a bike near me in the back of the room. "She's probably trying to get into shape, and if you comment on her effort, I bet she'd appreciate it. Or that guy—he's probably a little self-conscious about being one of the only men here, right? So make a joke of it, let him know you're glad he's in the class."

Tatum nodded, looking around the room. "I can do that."

"And then try to learn their names. Seriously, you'd be amazed how much that means to people." It was a trick I'd used when we were looking at preschools—after every presentation and interview I'd written a thank-you note to each person we'd met.

"You can see who's registered, right? In the app?" I went on. "Before class, write down every single name and whatever you know about them. And then use your notes during class to call them out, compliment them, whatever. Talk to people after class and add whatever you learn to your notes. And this is important—every time you see someone you recognize, even if it's just in the lobby, say hello and casually mention when you're teaching and how much you'd love to see them in class so they get in the habit of looking for your name on the schedule. When people are paying this much for a spin class, they want to feel like the teacher knows them, that you *care* about them."

"Okay." Her eyes were wide and serious. "Thank you, Julia, truly."

"You've got this," I said, giving her arm a squeeze before I headed back to my bike.

Tatum took a deep breath and adjusted her headset microphone. "Welcome, everyone! My name is Tatum, and it's so great to be here with every one of you. For the next forty-five minutes we're going to take care of our bodies and our spirits. This is *your* time, and I want you to celebrate your strength and your essence! Leave the stress of your lives at the door, okay?" She looked around the studio, making eye contact. "I haven't met all of you yet, but I can't wait to get to know you. Come on up after class if you've got any questions or just want to introduce yourself."

Well, well. Not bad at all. I felt a little thrill of satisfaction to see Tatum following my advice.

She turned the music back up and started with an easy warm-up. She ran the class as she'd run my personal sessions, her voice bright and encouraging, lavishing praise on us as we followed her lead, combining upper-body moves that she'd given cutesy names to— *dippy dip, bear hug*—with intervals of varying speed and resistance. Halfway through the class she got off the bike and wandered among us, complimenting riders and correcting their position or adjusting their resistance with a wink or a flirty smile.

"Your form is perfection," she gushed over the heavy girl.

"Keep this up and you'll be taking my job," she teased a woman in her sixties who skipped some of the more challenging moves.

"Ladies, who thinks this handsome man should ride in the front row next time so you can all enjoy the view?" she called out next to a middle-aged man with a paunch and a bald spot, to much laughter.

As the class ended and people swarmed the podium, I watched how Tatum interacted with them. She was a natural—full of praise and encouragement, touching people's hands or arms as she spoke. She was warm to the women and flirtatious with the men, but in a sweet, squeaky-clean, girl-next-door way.

I waited until everyone else was gone before I joined her. "You did a fantastic job, Tatum."

"You really think so?"

"Absolutely. Listen, I was thinking—I liked how you came off the bike and actually *talked* to people during the class. People ate it up."

"I'm trying to do what you said! I'm going to make notes." She was a Disney princess in spandex, her girlish enthusiasm making her eyes sparkle and flushing her cheeks.

"That's great. I was thinking, though, maybe you should have someone ride the instructor bike when you're down on the floor. Just so everyone can see what they're supposed to be doing, because when you weren't up there, people seemed kind of lost. I'll be glad to do it if you want—I know I'm new to this, but we could go over it in advance so I'd be prepared."

"That's an *awesome* idea! You'd really do that?"

"Sure," I said generously, though the truth was I wanted that podium bike for my own purposes. With the other riders' eyes on me, they'd come to see me as special, an insider. If I worked my ass off, there would be no doubt in the fall that I belonged there. "Listen, want to get coffee again? Or a drink? I mean, if you have time."

"Heck yeah!" (Yes, Tatum said *heck*. Back then, she never swore.) "We've earned it, right?"

I laughed. "Sure, let me just tell my nanny."

I dashed off a text to Benilda letting her know I might be a bit later than I'd said, adding heart-eyes emojis and gratitude hands to sweeten the deal. In seconds she texted back **OK**.

We went to a place that Tatum chose, a sterile, generically upscale little lounge in the Eighties on Second Avenue. We sat at the bar and

Tatum released her hair from its elastic and let it cascade around her shoulders. I ordered a California Malbec in a pointless rebellion against my mother, and Tatum asked the bartender if he knew how to make a Sweet Seacrest Blue, which turned out to be a Tiffany-blue cocktail based on a sticky-sweet fruity liqueur, a girl's drink if there ever was one. She offered me a sip and I laughed, feeling an almost maternal fondness for her.

"Tell me something," I prompted, after the bartender had asked Tatum if she liked her drink. He wasn't the only one riveted by Tatum: a group of guys in suits at the end of the bar were favoring her with yearning, drunken looks. "How have you been managing to make ends meet, since they don't give you many classes at Flame?"

"Well, I'm still waitressing," she said. "At the Alibi Room at the Marmont—do you know it?"

The Marmont Hotel was a few blocks from Penn Station and catered to a business clientele, but it was a far cry from the Carlyle or the Mark, and the bar attracted a younger, rowdier crowd. "I do," I said tactfully. "I imagine the tips are good, but it must be hard work."

"It's okay. I used to be full-time, but now it's mostly weekends. I've been there long enough I can mostly get the shifts I want. But I'd way rather be teaching at Flame."

"Then let's make that happen. Keep it up like you did today, and word of mouth will do the rest. Once your classes start filling up, you can push for a raise."

"God, I hope so. I'm a little tired of eating ramen for dinner."

"What's your long-term goal? If you don't mind me asking."

"To be a part of this world," Tatum said immediately. "I want to be able to walk into a place like this and feel like I belong, to order anything on the menu without having to figure out if I've got enough in the bank to cover it. I want to stop buying my clothes second-hand, maybe find an apartment where the heat works and I don't have to listen to people fighting all the time."

It was a touchingly modest goal, but not easy in this city. "How long have you been keeping this up, working all these jobs?"

"I came here eight years ago, when I was eighteen. At first, I took anything I could get. I told you about my first few jobs, but I also cleaned apartments and worked retail. I bought food in Chinatown every few days and lived on the leftovers, and the only time I ever really ate a full meal was on dates. Eventually I got the job taking care of the old lady, and then when she went into a nursing home, I got the job at the Alibi Room and the place I'm living now."

"Boyfriends . . . ?"

"No, unfortunately." Tatum shrugged. "I don't know what it is about guys in the city—they always end up not telling you some big huge thing. Like, that they're married, or living with their ex, or reporting to prison to serve a two-year sentence the next week."

"No—seriously?"

Tatum laughed. "That only happened once. And it makes a good story. I'm mostly off dating right now—I'm really trying to get my life together. With the babysitting and Flame, I'm hoping I can quit my waitress job eventually, which would be *awesome,* and I really want to move, so I need to save up for that."

My ears pricked up. "Babysitting?"

"Yes, it's great—all cash, you know? I work for someone I met at Flame a few months ago, a single dad who gets his kid one week and one weekend a month. Like he still has to work, right? He pays me twenty bucks an hour and half the time the kid's asleep—he's only four."

This was getting better and better. I did the calculations in my head: I paid Benilda thirty dollars an hour for overtime, and it came with the added cost of enduring her aggrieved attitude. "Tatum, I'd love to hire you sometimes. If you can fit it in."

"Seriously? Oh gosh, that would be fantastic."

"We're always looking for someone to help when our nanny isn't available. Maybe you could come over and meet the kids? Next week, when they're out of school?"

"I'd *love* to. I bet they're adorable." She paused before adding, "But, Julia . . . why are you being so nice? Why are you helping me?"

I chose my words carefully. "I had a mentor, when I first went to work at Feral Hare," I said, though I'd had no such thing—all of us new recruits were thrown in cubicles jammed into a former conference room and pitted against each other to see who rose to the top. "She really helped me during my first year—I don't know what I'd have done without her. Now maybe I can do the same thing for you."

"So I'm like your project?"

"Maybe." I smiled. "But in a nice way. I just want to see things come together for you."

"You're amazing, Julia!" She took my hands in hers, the pale, milky skin of her wrists exposed and vulnerable. "I accept your offer. Make me over. Make me something new."

I signaled for the check, though Tatum protested, sweetly. When we got outside, she gave me a little hug and made a dash for the subway, threading her way through traffic. I watched her go, her blond head bobbing like the flash of a lure on a lake.

CHAPTER 8

James and I spent a quiet Friday night in front of the TV, each of us lost in our own thoughts. School had been dismissed at noon for summer break, and Lindsay left for the Hamptons right after. Grace and her family were driving to Virginia the next day. Already the city felt forlorn and empty.

If I was honest with myself, I was uneasy about the three of us being apart all summer. Three-way friendships are prone to tension, because it always seems like two of you are closer at any given time and the third gets left out, but we'd weathered the dynamic for years. Lindsay was from a powerful family, sure of herself and sometimes dismissive; I was the spoiled daughter of old Boston money and known for my sense of style; and Grace, the daughter of one of the first African American principals with the Metropolitan Opera, was beautiful and reserved and could come off as shy to people who didn't know her.

For a long time, Lindsay and I were the ringleaders and Grace was our sidekick, content to play second fiddle, but recently that had begun to change. Grace's husband had founded a media company whose success propelled him to the outskirts of the celebrity arts community, and Grace discovered that she liked it there. Suddenly she was dropping names and going to parties hosted by people Lindsay and I didn't know. Meanwhile the wife of the managing partner at Lindsay's husband's law firm took a shine to Lindsay and started grooming her to take over the gala she'd chaired for years, one of the most coveted invitations in town with a guest list dripping with money and social ambition.

Only I was struggling to live up to my promise. James worked long hours and I balanced running the household and raising the kids, and there never seemed to be enough time left over for myself. Or maybe I just lacked discipline, because I made time for my friends and committees and wine in front of the television most nights. Whatever the reason, I'd grown duller, fatter, and less interesting— at least that's how I'd come to feel when I was with Grace and Lindsay, and I couldn't help noticing that the two of them seemed to be getting together without me more than usual. And now that I was spending my summer in exile, my vague discomfort threatened to blossom into full-blown insecurity.

But I still had a spark of my old determination, a hunger to regain the attention and admiration I'd once commanded. With the long, empty summer looming, I resolved not to take defeat lying down. While James tapped morosely at his laptop, muttering about some new issue with the engineering reports, I sipped mineral water and set up the weight loss app I'd downloaded. When the leftover pasta started calling my name, I went to bed before it could lure me to the fridge. And as I drifted off to sleep, I thought about what I'd buy myself as a reward for losing the first five pounds.

In the morning James's mood seemed to have recovered, and he announced he was taking the kids for breakfast and then to buy new baseball gloves that would end up moldering in the closet like the last ones he'd bought. I never said no to these weekend impulses; I knew that James modeled these excursions on his own childhood. I could picture taciturn Ed Summers taking his boys to the local diner for milkshakes after they finished their chores, and I loved James for trying to re-create the memory.

And just as important, I'd scored a morning to myself. I grabbed my phone and pulled up the Flame app, but Brooke's spin class was already full and Tatum wasn't teaching until Monday. I hesitated only for a moment before signing up for a HIIT class, even though

I'd never tried it before. Time to get serious about whipping myself into shape, now that summer had officially started.

I was still sore from Tatum's class two days before and I had a feeling I wouldn't make it all the way through forty-five minutes of HIIT—I'd seen the sweat pouring off people as they struggled through sets of plank jacks and mountain climbers—but nothing great was ever accomplished without pain. And besides, nothing could be as bad as staying home on the couch and scrolling through Instagram photos of my friends sipping cocktails at sunset, their children building sand castles on pristine beaches.

Over the next week, we settled into a new routine. Benilda kept the kids busy, taking them to Victorian Gardens and the zoo and an aquarium in Queens, while I scrambled to line up activities for them. I called a friend who knew the director at Camp Hillard and got the kids enrolled. They'd start the following week, and a bus would pick them up a few blocks from our building at 7:45 A.M. every weekday for the forty-five-minute drive to Westchester.

I canceled the housekeeper we used in the Hamptons and called the pool and landscape guys to cut back on the schedule—the lawn would still need to be mowed and the hedges trimmed, but there was no reason to fill the pool or tend to the flower beds this year. I placed a huge FreshDirect order full of fresh produce and healthy snacks and ingredients for low-calorie recipes I'd found on my app—and a few bottles of champagne, which had almost 40 percent fewer calories than my favorite Viognier. I texted with Lindsay to get the Hamptons gossip and forwarded celebrity scandals to Grace and forced myself back onto Instagram to remind people I was still around.

I went to Flame nearly every single day, taking spin when I could, HIIT when I couldn't (though after that first class I was so sore I could barely get out of bed). Paz now greeted me grudgingly by name, and I made a point of introducing myself to the rest of the staff and chatting with the teachers after each class. There was Zion, a beautifully sculpted man in his mid-thirties with dreadlocks past his shoulders and a habit of singing along to the music; Ido, who'd done a stint in the Israeli army and was a favorite among the older women with his beautiful accent and soulful brown eyes; and Erika, whose fine hair was shorn to an inch and dyed sea glass green and who'd been a professional volleyball player until she was sidelined by an injury. And of course Brooke, whose style was about what I'd expected: as her playlist segued from metal to rap to electronic tracks that made me feel like someone was drilling into my skull, she snarled and yelled and threw her hair around while she pedaled. She pushed us to the point where I wasn't the only one who looked like she was going to pass out, and then reproached us for slacking.

Tatum taught only evening classes that week, so I didn't see her at Flame, but on Friday night she came to watch the kids for the first time so James and I could go out to dinner with some people on the city council's land use committee.

These evenings might have been fun, since James always took business associates to great restaurants and ordered bottle after bottle of good wine, but he had never been comfortable with small talk, and I knew almost nothing about public siting and planning and zoning. Also, James didn't drink much while he was doing business, and I always paced myself so I could make sure everyone else was enjoying themselves. The conversation usually went over my head until everyone but James and I were drunk, but I knew these were important relationships to cultivate.

Tatum arrived at a few minutes before seven, while James was in the shower, and spent the next five minutes exclaiming over the décor I'd worked so hard on, nearly speechless when she saw the walk-in closet our architect had created from a dim little former bedroom. I gave her a tour of the kids' rooms, laid out their pajamas, and showed her around the kitchen and told her to help herself to whatever she liked.

"Bedtime's nine on the weekends," I said. "But if they fall asleep in front of the TV, just leave them and I'll put them to bed when I get home. I mean obviously it would be great if they didn't spend the *entire* night in front of the television."

"I'm sure we'll be just fine—won't we, Paige?"

My daughter had been following us around, clearly smitten with Tatum, who had complimented her artwork and admired her American Girl collection and promised that they'd do something special later, just the two of them, after her brother went to bed. For his part, Henry was digging through his toy chest looking for his light-up swords, which the rest of us had long ago tired of playing with him.

"We shouldn't be too late," I said. "It's a work thing for James."

James emerged from our room in the sport coat and Hermès tie I'd given him for his birthday, his hair still wet from the shower. "You must be Tatum," he said, shaking her hand.

"It's so nice to meet you! I've heard so much about you."

"Don't believe it all." He grinned, giving her a dose of his aw-shucks charm.

"Text me if you need anything, Tatum, anything at all."

"I will," she promised. "We're going to have so much fun, right, guys?"

Tatum was true to her word. When James and I finally got home, well after eleven, having practically poured one of the committee members and his wife into a cab, the evidence of the fun they'd had lay all around: Paige was curled up on the couch asleep in her Tiana costume from last Halloween, her hair French-braided and her nails painted green, and the living room floor was littered with Magna-Tiles. The counters were smeared with ketchup and the sink was full of dishes, but Tatum swore the kids had been angels.

After that first time, I felt comfortable leaving the kids with Tatum in the evenings and on weekends when she wasn't waitressing or teaching. I paid her in cash, stacks of bills fresh from the ATM, and she always jammed them into the outside pocket of her backpack without counting them.

Paige loved Tatum, who talked to her more like a girlfriend than a child. We compromised on the nail polish—I told Paige she could only wear it until school started again—and when I saw traces of makeup on her face I didn't complain.

Between Benilda and Tatum, I was getting to Flame nearly every day, sometimes two classes back to back when I could fit them in. I was already seeing results—I lost five pounds in the first two weeks, and the HIIT classes no longer made me painfully sore, though I still couldn't keep up with the punishing pace. I took spin with Tatum whenever I could, but because Brooke had a lock on the prime 9:30 A.M. slot, I was in her class just as often. I still didn't think much of her attitude or music, but I had a certain fascination with her raw energy and blatant sensuality, the unabashed way she watched herself in the mirrors along the sides of the room, as though she was performing only for herself.

In fact, I got an idea from one such class. We were all struggling to match her furious pace as Tyga sang *ba-back that ass* when Brooke jumped off her bike and flashed the lights off and on while she yelled what passed for encouragement. ("You call that your best?" "When are you going to stop whining and start trying?" "Do you want to make people just notice you or do you want them to *fucking hate themselves when they see you*?") When the lights were off, everything else seemed to come into exquisite focus—the sound of the wheels whirring, the grunts and breathing of the riders, the scent of the candles.

The next time I took a class with Tatum, as we were chatting at the podium—I'd ridden the instructor bike a few times now while she walked among the riders—I suggested she try turning the lights off for the whole class.

"I don't know," she said. "We already turn them off for the cooldown, and I get nervous when I can't see people's faces."

"If you keep them off the whole time, everyone's eyes will get used to it. Let's try it—if you don't like it, you don't have to do it again."

It was a huge success. I'd made a playlist just for Tatum, timing the progression from warm-up to higher intensity to the cooldown, choosing music that my friends and I loved—songs from when we were in college interspersed with newer ones. As the candles flickered and "Blue Monday" played in the dark, someone started singing along in the back, and then we were all singing *Tell me, how do I feel? Tell me now, how should I feel?* dissolving in laughter.

Can I tell you something? I *loved* being up there on the bike, high above the others. Once I had the technical part down, I really got into having everyone's eyes on me. I didn't show off, I stuck to Tatum's script, but afterward when people came up and made small talk, I realized that they not only admired me, they *envied* me.

What I live for—I could mainline that shit every day of the week.

In a matter of weeks, as the weight came off and I started feeling better about myself, I began to regain my desire to stand out. I replaced all my old workout clothes with things I found in boutiques and online. I bought a beautiful mustard-colored cashmere wrap and custom-painted spin shoes and instead of a gym bag, I carried a big tote I found on Etsy that was made from cotton mud cloth appliquéd with a genuine beaded Hmong tribal collar. I reveled in the compliments I received at the gym, but I was already dressing for the audience I'd have in the fall, when I planned to fill those classes with women I knew. Especially my rivals—like Coco and especially Milly, who'd tried to horn in on Jakobine. *See that, bitches, it's my firm ass up here in front while the rest of you sweat and grunt.*

Working out had become my obsession, and I began supplementing my visits to Flame with long walks with the kids and toning exercises I found on the Internet when I was at home in the evenings. James went out to the summer house to check on it, but little could be done until the insurance company finished their investigation and paid out. He had his guys remove the ruined flooring and insulation and temporarily shore up the foundation, but he wasn't willing to move ahead until he received the check.

James was working so much that his gym bag now always held a change of clothes in case he ended up sleeping in his office. I knew James loved being able to wake up, shower at his gym, pick up coffee and a bagel from a sidewalk cart, and arrive at the same time the crew did.

He didn't talk about work much, and I didn't ask—it was enough for me to know that it was in the shitstorm phase, and the less said the better. It happened on every big project: bids came in high and contractors disappeared and inspections revealed unexpected issues and investors pulled out and council members demanded all kinds of unrealistic accommodations. To his credit, James rarely took his frustrations out on me—he turned them inward, going silent and brooding, and stayed away. It was always worth it in the end, when the issues were finally resolved and the project completed—then he lavished the rest of us with attention and gifts and, just between you and me, a lot of *appreciation* in the bedroom.

As June came to an end, I had to admit that being marooned in the city hadn't been as bad as I'd feared. Benilda had been asking for extra time off—she had a cousin in Queens who'd been sick, and she was in some sort of family caregiving rotation—but Tatum was happy to pick up extra hours. In fact, I'd asked her to come along to Lindsay's over the Fourth of July to watch the kids, since Benilda couldn't make it and Tatum needed the money.

In another interesting turn of events, Tatum had a friendship with Brooke, and the two of them convinced me to go out for drinks a few times. I hadn't seen my friends for weeks and I was desperate for female companionship, but I always left after a single glass of wine. The minute I got up, the happy-hour businessmen started approaching like alligators up the banks of a swamp. Maybe it was my wedding ring, maybe it was the curious fact that two girls in a bar are easier to approach than three, but I had a feeling that the real fun started after I left.

Brooke tolerated my presence but made little effort to include me in their conversation, which was fine with me because I was filing away every morsel of Flame gossip: who was sleeping with who, who taught while high, who had an eating disorder, who used steroids. The drug use among the instructors didn't really shock me, especially because I suspected that the female Flame teachers favored drugs over alcohol because of the calories. I'd smoked my share of weed and done a bit of coke in college, and prescription drugs were rampant on the Upper East Side. Everyone I knew had a script for Xanax or Klonopin; any number of doctors were making a very good living taking care of all our anxiety issues.

Talk often turned to how to get more new members, more "butts on the bikes," more classes.

"It's fine for you," Tatum said to Brooke, one night over drinks. "You don't need the money."

"Oh, do you have a second job?" I could picture Brooke tending bar in the Village or making lattes in Brooklyn.

Tatum giggled. "Julia, she's Brooke *Timms*. You know, Timms Pharmaceutical?"

How had I not known this? Marty Timms routinely made the *Forbes* list, and Glad Timms was a well-known socialite and philanthropist. I'd been introduced to her once at the New Yorkers for Children gala, and while she was perfectly gracious I felt completely out of my league. Around her neck was an emerald the size of a quarter, and she was seated for dinner next to Carly Fiorina, who was delivering the keynote.

It was hard to square that woman with the girl in front of me, who was wearing a distressed denim vest and a tiny skirt and heavy black boots.

"I believe I've met your mother," I said.

"That's unfortunate—she's a piece of work." Brooke smirked at me over the rim of her cocktail glass.

"But at least they pay your rent," Tatum said. "I mean, they can adopt me anytime."

Tatum was tipsy. It didn't take a whole lot to get her drunk. I decided to change the subject.

"I've never asked you about *your* family, Tatum. Are they still in Missouri?"

Instantly, Tatum's expression changed—or rather, it seemed to collapse. In a second she was smiling again, but it was strained. "My parents are dead," she said. "And I'm an only child."

"I'm so sorry."

"It's okay. They died in a car accident when I was a senior in high school. I was almost out of the house anyway."

Brooke covered Tatum's hand with her own, and they exchanged a look. So they'd talked about this already; they had grown closer than I'd realized. Maybe, underneath her off-putting exterior, Brooke had a heart. And Tatum could certainly use a friend. From what I could tell, she didn't have many.

I signaled the bartender. "Please bring another round for these ladies, and then I'll take the check," I said. I usually picked up the tab when I left, but the extra round was my way of apologizing.

"I'm so sorry I have to go, but Benilda will be furious if I don't get back."

"Got to keep the help happy," Brooke said, and I couldn't tell if she was making a joke.

"Thank you so much for the drinks," Tatum added, jumping off her barstool to hug me. "One of these days you have to go *out* out with us! We'd have so much fun!"

As I headed home to an evening of baths and bedtime arguments and waiting up for James in front of the television, I wondered, *Why not?*

CHAPTER 9

On the first day of July, James called me while I was on line at
Dean & DeLuca. We were leaving for Bridgehampton on Wednesday, and I was picking up snacks for the drive and something for
dinner.

"You'd better be calling to say you're on your way home," I said
in a mock threatening tone.

"Julia . . ."

I sighed, loud enough for him to hear. "I'm standing here with
forty dollars' worth of artichoke dip and salumi in my basket and I
swear to God if you're not coming home tonight I'm going to send
it home with Tatum." It wasn't much of a threat, but tweaking
James about money was always a direct hit.

"Look, it isn't exactly a picnic over here. Want to know what I
had for lunch? A street cart pretzel and Oreos from the vending
machine. You know they still have Fifth Avenue blocked off to one
lane between Fifty-sixth and Fifty-fifth? I didn't, which is why I have
to stay late tonight. By the time I got to my appointment this afternoon, the guy was gone, and now he's pissed and I had to reschedule
for Wednesday morning and I've got to submit the docs all over
again."

"But, James—I wanted to get on the road early! We're already
cutting the trip short—"

"Look, it was meet him then or wait an entire week. You guys go
on out, I'll take the Jitney later. I'm sorry about this, Jules."

Poor James—he was apologizing to me so often these days I

barely registered it. I knew he couldn't afford the time away; we'd compromised by agreeing to come home Friday, which I didn't really mind. I'd just as soon miss the whole cleanup effort the next day, not to mention the holiday weekend throngs at the beaches.

"No, *I'm* sorry, I didn't mean to snap at you. I'm just frustrated because this line is like thirty people long. And—and I was hoping we could . . . I mean, we aren't going to have any privacy at Lindsay's." I was surrounded by strangers, so I couldn't exactly tell him what I had been hoping to do to him that night. Suffice it to say that the better I felt about my body, the more I wanted to put it to good use.

"You think I wouldn't rather be home in bed with you? Look, Jules, this is all going to wrap up in the next month or two. Fall at the latest. And then, I swear, things are going to settle down."

"Okay," I said. "So you're going to stay over at the office again?"

"I'll try to get home, but that's all I can promise for now. I'll check in later, okay?"

"All right." I stared at the mauve-shaded perm of the elderly woman in front of me. "Love you."

"You too," James said and clicked off.

When I got home with my two heavy shopping bags, the apartment was quiet. Benilda had had to leave early, so I'd asked Tatum to come at three to take over when the kids got home from camp, and for a frantic moment I wondered if she'd forgotten.

I found her in Paige's room, reclining against the pillows and looking at her phone while Paige knelt at the end of the bed digging in the box of bandages from the linen closet. Tatum must not have heard me come in because when she saw me, she immediately stuffed her phone in her pocket with a guilty look on her face.

"Mommy!" Paige cried. "I'm giving Tatum a pedicure!"

"Not with nail polish," Tatum said hastily. "We're just pretending."

Paige had wrapped gauze between Tatum's toes, and when I looked closer I could see that she'd applied tiny stickers to each of Tatum's toenails. I had to admit that it was a pretty clever way to keep Paige occupied. "Fantastic," I said. "Maybe you can work in a nail salon when you grow up."

"Don't say that, Mommy," Paige said, pouting. "I don't want to be poor."

"What—where did you ever get that idea?"

"Tatum says the nail polish ladies are all poor. And the ladies who do Daddy's dry cleaning. And the ones who work at the Food Emporium."

"Paige!" Tatum scolded. "That's not what I said! I was just trying to explain to her why I live downtown. I told her that a lot of the people who work in this neighborhood live in other places because it's too expensive if you have an ordinary job. I'm sorry, I didn't think—"

"Forget it," I laughed. "Out of the mouths of babes, and all that. You'll see when you have kids of your own—they never listen when you need them to, and then you find out they were paying attention when you wish they hadn't been. Where's Henry?"

"Napping," Paige said. "He was superbad so he had to go to his room."

"He was fine, he just got a little wound up so I had him lie down for a bit," Tatum corrected. "He fell asleep right away, so I think he must have needed the rest."

"He knocked your phone on the floor!" Paige said indignantly.

"I'm so sorry," I said. "They must have gotten overtired at camp."

"It's no big deal, really. Oh—that reminds me, Benilda said to tell you she found their swim goggles, she put them on the washing machine."

"Oh, thank God," I said. "She really is a miracle worker. Listen, do you want to stay for dinner? James has to work and I've got all this food."

"Are you sure?"

"Absolutely. Don't make me drink alone!"

So, drink we did. I set out the prosciutto and artichoke dip and a wedge of Reblochon and sliced the baguette I'd picked up, and let Paige nibble at it too so I didn't have to make her dinner. We made it through the wine I'd bought to share with James, and then another bottle, the first one I pulled out of the wine fridge. A Pinot, I think. Henry slept until seven o'clock and woke up groggy, and I made him a peanut butter sandwich and let him and Paige watch TV in my room so that Tatum and I could talk in the living room. At nine, well into the second bottle, I remembered I had never put them to bed, and I found them asleep.

"So cute!" Tatum had followed me down the hall, wineglass in hand. I pried Henry out of the tangled covers, waking Paige up in the process, and she stumbled to her room while I carried Henry to his. No baths, no toothbrushing, and now I had crumbs in my bed—but it was worth it; life had been lonely since school ended. I got a package of Oreos from the kitchen and didn't even bother to put them on a plate. As I plopped back down on the sectional, "Gives You Hell" by the All-American Rejects came on over the living room speakers, and I grabbed my phone and turned it up.

"You'll have to remember this one for when my friends start coming to your classes," I advised. "It's like an ode to wifely rage."

Tatum looked at me, her gaze unfocused. "What do you have to rage over? You have everything."

I was drunk, but not so drunk that I wasn't struck by the baldness of her words. Tatum wanted what I had, I realized, with a tiny frisson of . . . not discomfort, exactly, but a sort of dissonance. It happened sometimes with Tatum—she'd say or do something to remind me of how far she'd come from her old life, and how hungry she was for more.

She reached for the bottle and topped off our glasses. "You really think you can get your friends to come to Flame? I mean, like, a lot of them?"

"I *know* I can. When Lindsay sees how much weight I've lost already . . ." I looked down at my arms, which were beginning to develop some nice definition, and pushed the Oreos away. Now wasn't the time to slack off, not when I'd managed to resist the cheese and have just a few slices of prosciutto. I was down nine pounds in three weeks, and I wanted to lose at least another ten by September.

"Although, they're not going to like Paz," I said, my mind drunkenly stumbling from topic to topic. "She's got way too much attitude."

"Not anymore," Tatum said slyly, pulling her phone from the pocket of her jeans. "At least, not with me. Check it out, I'm sending you something."

It took her a few tries, but when my phone pinged a new message from her, I clicked on the link and found myself looking at a blurry video of Paz—naked from the waist down, her shoes and pants on the floor with her legs wrapped around the waist of a gray-haired man whose own trousers bagged at his ankles. The quality was terrible and it was only a few seconds long, but you could hear the man grunting and Paz moaning as he pounded into her against the wall.

"Wow," I said.

"Do you recognize where they are?"

I looked closer. "Is that the hallway? At Flame?"

"Yup! The hall security camera's broken, and it was after closing so she thought they were safe, but I left my jacket in the spin studio with my keys in the pocket. She didn't hear me because I came through the service entrance. Anyway, that's Phil Heising, who's running for comptroller in the next election. He comes here to box. And to *bang*." More giggling at her little joke. "Can you imagine if this got out?"

"Wouldn't do much for his campaign, I guess."

"I mean for *Paz*. Just the other day a delivery guy dropped off this huge box from Veda—he bought her eight-hundred-dollar leather pants!"

I had to admit, I was impressed. "What are you going to do with the video?"

"You mean, what did I already do?" Tatum gloated. "I made Paz give me admin access to the app. Now I can see everyone's class lists, not just mine, and I can make changes too. Like, I can make sure you always get in even if there's a wait list. Or move people to a better bike, stuff that only the desk staff are supposed to be able to do."

"That could be handy, especially if my friends start coming

here—trust me, they'd be very appreciative of that kind of favor. And they're discreet."

"Leather-pants appreciative? Or just, like, Starbucks-gift-card?"

I laughed. "Well, let's just say they'd take good care of you at the holidays."

"Then I'll take good care of *them*. God, I'm so bad," she moaned, sloshing more wine into our glasses. "All this wine? On top of the baguette and cheese, that's like three thousand calories. I'm not going to be able to eat all weekend."

"Oh, please, you're tiny."

But she pulled up her sweatshirt and grabbed at her stomach, squeezing it between both hands. "I'm disgusting," she said, and there was something in her tone that alarmed me, along with how quickly her mood changed.

"You're *not*," I said, patting her ankle. "You're beautiful, and smart and fun."

She shook her head. "And I *hate* all my clothes. They're old and—have you ever noticed that hardly anyone up here wears patterns? Or bright colors?"

Of course I had, but I didn't bother pointing out that anyone who could afford Flame's class fees probably didn't buy their gym clothes at Walmart. "People here tend to be more reserved in the way they dress," I said diplomatically. "I could help you pick out a few new things, if you want."

She nodded and dabbed at her eyes. I was drunk enough to have missed the cues, but sober enough to worry we were headed for one of those crying jags that nights like these sometimes morphed into. I sat up straighter, ready to get up and make coffee, toast, whatever she needed. "Or I could give you a few things I've outgrown," I amended. "I know money's tight for you—"

"It's not even that, it's just . . ." she said, her voice wobbling. "I have a lot on my mind right now. The thing is, my apartment . . . my landlord . . . he, uh." She stared down at her hands. "He broke into my place the other day. I got home and things were all out of place. Like my underwear was in the wrong drawer, all wadded up. And some of my clothes were on the floor of my closet. And my computer—well, I'm not sure about that, actually, but I don't think I left it open."

"That's horrible! Why do you think it was him?"

"He wanted me to, like, have sex with him. When I was late with rent. I mean I know it was my fault I was late, it was a few months ago and he came up and I let him in, I shouldn't have but I wanted a chance to explain. I was going to have the money the next night, from tips—I was only short like eighty dollars—and I was in the middle of all of that when he shoved me up against the counter and kissed me. I pushed him off me and he got all mad and said if I was ever late again, he'd just take what he had coming. Like, a threat, you know? I stuck the money under his door the next day—he lives on the first floor—and I've paid early since then."

"Tatum," I said, truly alarmed. "Have you reported him?"

She was already shaking her head. "I can't. I can't afford anything else. Not right now, anyway. First and last months' rent—and the security deposit, it's so much money. And now that I'm only wait-ressing on weekends . . . I don't know, maybe I should just go back to waitressing full-time."

If Tatum did that, there went my protégée, and probably my babysitter too. Sure, I could still bring my friends to Flame, I could still take credit for discovering the place, but who else was going to put me up on the bike in front of the room?

"Okay, look," I said, sobering up fast. "You have *got* to take what I'm telling you seriously. You have an opportunity at Flame, a chance to build a following and make some real money. We'll figure the apartment situation out, but the last thing you should do right now is quit. Did you know the top instructors at City Barre make over three hundred dollars a class?"

"They only pay me fifty," Tatum snuffled. "Brooke gets one fifty."

"But once you build a following you'll be able to demand more. And you can make extra money doing private sessions if Ken will keep letting you use the studio. You could charge a hundred, one fifty—maybe even two hundred per session, once you're established. Trust me, my friends can afford it. Look, I really *believe* in you.

You've just got to have a little faith in me, and you have to do everything I tell you. Can you do that?"

Tatum nodded hopefully. "I can."

"Stay here tonight and we can talk about it more tomorrow. We'll come up with a plan." Then, like my mother, like her mother before her, I threw money on the problem for good measure. "And first chance we get, I'm taking you shopping."

CHAPTER 10

When Benilda arrived in the morning, Tatum and I were sitting at the kitchen table drinking coffee. Maybe it was my imagination, but Benilda seemed irritable, declining to have a cup of coffee with us before disappearing down the hall to get the kids ready for camp. I figured she was probably annoyed at having to clean up after Tatum, who'd left the guest bed unmade and damp towels on the bathroom floor.

But we had work to do. I'd woken up thinking about last night's conversation, determined to help Tatum fit in better. I'd gone through my old things only to realize that nearly all of them would be too big for her, and set aside the few pieces I thought would fit. But Tatum's most glaring shortcomings had more to do with her grooming than with the way she dressed. Everyone has a few unflattering pieces in their closet, but a bad haircut or overplucked brows are harder to overlook.

As Tatum made toaster waffles, I gathered all the fashion magazines I had lying around and piled them on the kitchen table, then went to my salon's website and made an appointment for her with the only available stylist for a keratin treatment, cut, color, and a mani-pedi.

"So listen," I said as she set two plates of waffles drowning in syrup on the table. I was touched by the effort, even though neither of us was likely to eat more than a few bites. "I'd like to treat you to a makeover. I've been thinking of what you said about—well, how people dress up here, but it's more than just the clothes. It'll be so much easier to stand out at Flame if you know you're projecting a look that really represents who *you* are, the moment you walk in."

"Do you mean like Brooke's tattoos? Or Erika's green hair?"

"Sort of, but real style—the kind I think suits you—isn't about gimmicks so much as it is about identifying a few key features and really playing them up. In your case, I think it's all about freshness— your perfect skin and big blue eyes and your smile. You don't want to fight those—instead, I think you should play to your strengths, but up the ante a little with a good haircut and a few changes to your regimen."

I could feel my excitement growing as I talked about the make-over I wanted to give her. It reminded me of watching *The Swan* with my college roommates, riveted by the shocking transforma-tions of frumpy women into sexpots. All of us knew better—it was clearly established on college campuses by then that our appear-ances should not be dictated by the hetero male gaze—but we'd watched too many Miss America pageants with our mothers and spent too many sleepovers dancing to the "Oops! . . . I Did It Again" video. The hunger for that particular poison, I'm afraid, will never leave us.

"I'd *love* that." Tatum sniffled, her eyes shiny. "I've been cutting my own hair to save money."

Well, that explained some things. "I made you an appointment at my salon. It's not for a couple of hours, but I want to pick up a few things for you on the way," I said. "Now don't say no—you've been so helpful, I don't know how I would have gotten through the last month without you, so this is my treat. And I thought I could loan you a few things to wear on the trip, from before I gained weight. Especially since you'll be coming to the party."

"I will?"

"Sure, we'll just put the kids in front of the TV—the guesthouse is right there, we can check on them. And you'll be meeting Lindsay, who—she's totally going to come to your classes, you'll see, and she knows *everybody*, so this is our chance to start talking up Flame."

"That all sounds amazing, Julia."

I was so relieved that she didn't hate the idea that I plowed ahead.

"I've got a really cute beach cover-up, and a dress for the party that would look great on you, and some other stuff. We can go through it after the salon if you want."

"You're being so nice! I mean, this is already a vacation for me."

I reached across the table and squeezed her hand. "Let me do this. Do you remember what we talked about last night?"

Tatum smiled ruefully. "I wasn't *that* drunk."

"I just want you to remember that you said you'd trust me. Do everything I say, make these changes in your clothes and appearance, and before long you're going to have all the classes you want—and lots of fans to spread the word. If you build an effective brand from the start, you can go anywhere. You see those girls on Instagram—the ones from City Barre and Nova? Companies *pay* them to post with their products and clothes, and it's real money. Some of them even get TV work. If they can do it, I know you can too."

Tatum's eyes were bright; I could see the wheels turning. "I don't even know how to thank you, Julia."

"Don't thank me, just take this seriously. That's all I ask."

She nodded. "I will. I promise. So . . . I have to cut my hair?"

"Nothing extreme. Listen, Tatum, as gorgeous as you are, there are a few things that could take you to the next level. Not unattainable—we want women to be inspired by you, not intimidated—but a little more polished."

"I know my hair's kind of damaged—"

"It can be fixed, you'll see." Her hair, to be blunt, was a mess—overprocessed, the ends jagged and split, the color obviously a home job. Men wouldn't notice, because put a long blond wig on a woman and it triggers the same animal response as five-hundred-dollar Oscar Blandi highlights—but my friends would. "Don't worry, they won't take too much off the length. And then we'll have them even up the color and give you a keratin treatment. Trust me, you'll be amazed."

"Whatever you think."

"And another thing. If you can't squeeze in a professional manicure, it's best to just go with bare nails."

Tatum looked at her nails; in addition to the chipped polish, they were all different lengths, some vampire-long, others torn and ragged.

"Ask for Rose Chemise—it's a great pale pink. This place seriously does the greatest gel jobs, they last forever, especially with a light color like that."

"Wow. I'm excited—it's been ages since I had a real manicure." Tatum's smile lit up her face, and I was flush with a feeling of lovely benevolence. How nice to have someone in my life who was actually grateful for something I did for them.

We stopped at Lululemon, where I picked out three pairs of plain black leggings and four tank tops (three white, one gray—no more bubblegum shades) and a beautiful, soft gray fleece wrap cardigan that set off Tatum's pale, creamy skin. In total the clothes set me back almost nine hundred dollars, a figure I concealed from her as I signed the credit card receipt.

She thanked me all the way to the salon. I stayed for the consultation, discussing her hair with the stylist as Tatum sat mute in a black silk robe clutching her glass of champagne, my own stylist, Nina, coming over to weigh in. When we'd agreed on a plan, Nina said Tatum would be there for at least five hours, and I headed home with her bags of clothes.

When I got home, I found Benilda standing at the living room window, staring out at the muggy haze blanketing the city. The apartment was neat as a pin, the kitchen gleaming and fresh vacuum tracks on the carpet, but she looked exhausted, dark circles under her eyes and a grayish cast to her skin.

"I wanted to tell you when we are alone," she said. "My cousin has cancer."

And then she began to cry. It was the first time I'd ever seen her cry, and I was alarmed. I tried to remember what she'd said about her cousin—I couldn't even remember if it was a man or a woman. "Come sit down," I said, and she allowed me to take her arm and guide her to a kitchen chair.

I poured her a glass of water and sat down across from her. "Do you want to talk about it?"

She had stopped crying by then. She was wearing the shiny royal-blue blouse that Paige had picked out for her last Christmas, and the gold cross that she never took off, its minuscule diamond twinkling under the kitchen lights.

She stared at the glass of water without drinking. "Cancer of pancreas. Very bad. She should have gone to doctor sooner."

"Oh, no," I said. I knew a death sentence when I heard one. "Is she . . . is there someone taking care of her?"

Benilda shrugged. "Her husband is back in Philippines. He's no good. Her son, he's in Texas, he has wife and three kids."

I didn't like where this was going. "But other family that lives near her . . . friends?"

"I will help," Benilda said firmly. "She is very sick."

I tried a different tack. "What about home health aides? Is she on public assistance? Does she have insurance?"

I personally had helped Benilda fill out the New York Obamacare application and paid her extra for the premiums, and was astonished at the quality of care she received for a tiny fraction of what James and I paid for health insurance. If Benilda were to get sick, she'd get Cadillac treatment right here in the city.

"Mrs. Julia, these questions, I don't know. Right now I just need to make sure she gets to the doctor. She has so many appointments!"

"Okay," I said, buying time while I struggled to stay calm. This had to happen in the summer? *This* summer, when we were stuck here in the city with only one six-week summer camp session to occupy the children, and James working around the clock? "I'm sure we can adjust your hours. And we'll look into other solutions, like maybe we can set her up with an Uber account—"

Benilda reached across the table and put her hand on my arm. She pressed hard, making it clear that the gesture was meant to silence rather than reassure me. "Thelma can't take Uber, she doesn't speak enough English. And besides, she's *sick*. I have to take her."

Shit, shit, shit. I thought of Tatum, wondered how I'd convince her to pick up the slack if she succeeded in getting more classes. I imagined having to deal with the kids every afternoon, cranky from their full day at camp and long bus ride. And it wouldn't even do any good to have Benilda make up time in the evenings, since there was nowhere for me to go and no one to see. "I understand" was all I could say—but Benilda wasn't finished.

"You can fire me if you want to."

"What? Benilda, don't be ridiculous."

She was shaking her head, as stubborn as I'd ever seen her. "I can get job in Queens. Be closer to Thelma."

"No, no, don't say that." I'd known two people who had pancreatic cancer; one had died two months after making her diagnosis public, the other had held on for four. We could last four months if we had to—that would take us into early November. The timing was horrible, since those would be the worst months for James and I'd be dealing with the back-to-school chaos, but we'd just have to make do. I couldn't lose Benilda—the idea of conducting a search for a new nanny now was unthinkable. "We'll figure this out, Benilda."

"But I can't work all day every day—"

"We'll figure it out," I repeated. I considered suggesting that she might ask her cousin to schedule her appointments to coincide with camp, but immediately felt guilty—the poor woman was *dying*, after all.

"Why don't you make a list of her appointments tonight, and tomorrow we'll sit down and figure out the schedule."

But Benilda was already shaking her head. "Sometimes she goes for doctor and then she has to get test. Blood test, lab test, all kind of test. And sometimes she feels sick after visit or we have to get her medicine. And the pharmacy has such long lines."

I counted to ten, trying to rein in my panic. "I understand that you can't give me *exact* times, and that we need to be flexible, but I'm sure we can work this out, Benilda."

She didn't bother to respond to that, lifting her chin and staring sorrowfully out the window. "I can ask my friend to help you."

"No, don't do that. I'll see if Tatum can help out."

Tatum and Benilda had encountered each other in passing plenty of times. Neither had much to say about the other. But at the mention of her name, Benilda dropped her slightly wounded air and stared me right in the eye. "Better I will ask my friend," she said.

I should have taken her up on the offer.

CHAPTER 11

I spent the rest of the day scrambling to get ready for our visit to the Parkers' house in Bridgehampton. I picked up a hostess gift for Lindsay and several bottles of wine that I hoped would meet Garth's standards, and then I started packing. The party invitation specified "festive patriotic," and I'd bought a pair of cropped white sailor pants with gold buttons on the pockets. I added a silk halter top in a wild red paisley that I'd bought on a trip to Italy, along with navy sandals with a four-inch heel.

Tatum had texted me photos from the salon. The stylist had managed to get all the brassiness out of her hair, and it now lay in shiny ash-blond waves with subtle lowlights. Her brows looked a hundred times better, and she even sent me a photo of her nails, which were painted the pale shell pink that was my staple shade, trimmed short enough to suggest she played tennis or sailed in her free time. All that remained was to figure out her wardrobe.

I laid out the clothes I'd chosen for her on my bed: a Tory Burch beach cover-up and the simple navy Alexander Wang cocktail dress I'd worn to my parents' anniversary party a few years ago to make my mother happy, as well as a few other classic pieces. When she came home, I poured us each a glass of wine—a small one—and Tatum tried on clothes. Each time she changed into a new outfit and checked out her reflection in my full-length mirror, slowly turning to see every angle, it was like she was meeting herself for the first time.

I folded everything and put it in the bags with the Lulu purchases and walked her to the door.

"This means so much to me, you don't even know," Tatum said, holding the bags to her chest. "I'm going to work so hard, you'll see."

I basked in the glow of her appreciation all afternoon, sending Benilda home early and letting Henry help me make a salad and set the table while Paige worked on a friendship bracelet she'd started at camp. James came home at a little before five, looking like he hadn't slept much the last two nights at the office. He went straight to our bedroom to shower, and when he didn't come out after I called him to dinner, I discovered him asleep on top of the bedspread, a damp towel still wrapped around his waist.

"Where's Daddy?" Paige asked as I ladled out the corn chowder I'd picked up at Citarella. The sun had given her a sprinkling of freckles across her nose.

"Resting," I said. "But tomorrow Daddy will meet us at the Parkers' house, and then we get him all to ourselves."

"Yay!" Henry cheered.

"I'm going to show him my dream catcher!" Paige said.

They chattered about all the things they wanted to do with their father on vacation as they ate their soup and grilled cheese sandwiches and I picked at a salad. My new pants were a little snug, and I wasn't about to ruin my diet now, when all I could think about was how thin I would look in photos.

James was already gone when I woke the next morning. By the time I had the kids dressed and fed, Tatum arrived with a suitcase so battered and ugly that I insisted she repack in one of mine.

Holiday Hamptons traffic was one of life's humbling realities: you couldn't beg, threaten, or steal your way out of the backup on the Long Island Expressway. For two thousand dollars, a family of four could book seats on a helicopter or seaplane, and there were times I thought it would be worth it. Though if this was an ordinary summer, I would have moved out of the city by now and wouldn't return until Labor Day, so it was usually James who was stuck doing the trip.

But any sympathy I had for him evaporated when he called to argue about the list I'd left for him on the dresser. I would have packed for him myself, but the last time I'd done that, he'd complained all weekend that he didn't have anything "comfortable" to wear.

"Come on, Jules, it's a barbecue. I'll look stupid in a jacket. And I hate that goddamn pink shirt, you know that."

"It's just one night. You'll live. And I already compromised on everything else." It was true—Garth would be in Nantucket Reds and Lacoste polo shirts most of the weekend, and I was letting James bring cargo shorts and T-shirts, though I drew the line at his old sneakers.

"I'm not wearing that shirt. It's going down the trash chute."

I sighed. "Just bring the rest, okay? Please, James, this is our one event with our friends this summer."

"I see my friends every day," he said. "And they don't give a shit what I wear."

I knew he was just trying to get a rise out of me. He was friendly with everyone from his accountant to the guys who sold tamales out of their trunks on job sites, but they weren't really his friends. He liked some of the Graylon dads well enough, but his true friends were the guys he'd grown up with back in Allentown.

I let it go. "And you shaved today, right?"

"Watch it, woman," he growled. "There's a Yankees game on tonight and I'm perfectly happy to stay right here on the couch."

"I love you too," I said and hung up. "God forbid that man should make an effort. If I let him, he'd show up in cutoff jeans and a Led Zeppelin T-shirt."

"Maybe he just feels awkward around your friends, especially if he doesn't know them very well," Tatum suggested.

I laughed. "Tatum—we've known them for years." Though James complained that Garth Parker was boring, because he didn't watch sports and his only hobby was wine.

"Well, I'm certainly looking forward to meeting them!" Tatum said, her voice bright with what I took to be anxiety. She kept tugging on the hem of the Ulla Johnson shift that I'd loaned her for the drive.

I'd explained the situation to Lindsay on the phone—that I'd met Tatum at my new gym, that I'd gotten to know her better when she started babysitting for us, that she was an amazing young woman who was struggling to survive in the city while working several jobs. I didn't elaborate on her past—better to keep that vague if we were going to unleash her on this crowd. Unfortunate details would come out if anyone dug too far into her story, asking her where she went to college, for instance, but at some point Tatum was going to have to show a little initiative of her own and find a way to work it.

I believed we were aligned in our aspirations, given Tatum's nervous anticipation and her stream of questions about our hosts, the guests, what people talked about and wore and drove. In a gesture that amused me, she'd tied a scarf to her bag as I had done the prior week—I didn't have the heart to tell her that I'd done it only because the tag itched and I didn't want to lose it.

I admit: her emulation was intoxicating.

Lindsay and I had met at a Dartmouth alumni event shortly after James and I started dating—her husband, Garth, had gone there for undergrad—and become fast friends. Lindsay was the third generation of women in her family to attend Wellesley, and the second to get a law degree from Columbia; her grandmother had been an adviser to both Bush presidencies, and her mother had cofounded a global women's health research NGO. She was also brash and arch with a penchant for sidelines snark.

Despite her lofty pedigree, Lindsay was unapologetic about her decision to give up her career to stay home with her kids—but she could be competitive about some things. There'd been tension between us when James and I moved to our current apartment, which was significantly larger than hers and Garth's. She never failed to remind me that Audrey, who was a year younger than Paige, had tested as gifted. And there had been an awkward episode at a New Year's Eve party when she accused me of flirting with Garth and stopped speaking to me for a month, even though it was Garth, not me, who drank so much that he was kissing other people's spouses when the ball dropped.

So I was nervous about introducing her to Tatum, fearful that she'd pick apart Tatum's naïve enthusiasm, that she'd see through the haircut and borrowed clothes. But Lindsay seemed to take to Tatum the minute they were introduced, and installed her in the guest room in the main house. The rest of us were given the guesthouse by the pool, a cozy little space with bunk beds for the kids and a tiny kitchenette and a washer and dryer for towels.

Once I got the kids settled, I asked James to watch them while I helped Lindsay with dinner, but first I knocked on Tatum's door. She opened it an inch and then, seeing it was me, let me into the guest room dressed in her underwear with a curling iron in her hand.

"What should I wear for dinner?" she asked. Everything she'd packed was on the bed, and it looked like she'd been trying it on. "Is it like supercasual or—"

"Relax," I said, taking the curling iron from her hand. "Your hair already looks perfect—you don't want to look like you tried too hard, not for something like this. And tonight's just the five of us, so maybe . . ."

I looked through everything she'd brought, settling on navy piqué ankle pants and a simple linen tank. "Try these," I said, "and definitely the copper flats."

She took the clothes from me and disappeared into the bathroom. A moment later she came out, shy as a virgin bride, and turned in a circle with her arms out to the sides. Her hair fell in a smooth sheet against her bare shoulders; the tank was just transparent enough to hint at her beautiful body underneath. The old Tatum, with her gummy lip gloss and vinyl purses, was gone, and in her place was this elegant creature that I'd helped create.

"It's not too . . . plain?" she asked.

"Not at all. But you know what it needs . . ." I took off my earrings, the Mikimoto pearl studs James had given me for my thirtieth birthday.

"Are you sure?" Tatum asked, her eyes wide.

"They're perfect with that outfit. Now put them on, and we'll go see if Lindsay needs any help."

By the time James finally arrived and we got the kids fed and Garth had the barbecue lit, we'd made it through the first bottle of wine, and Tatum had finally relaxed. I caught Lindsay staring at the pearls in Tatum's ears, but she complimented her on my sandals and asked her where she had her hair done and kept her glass filled. Tatum took the kids back to the guesthouse to get them ready for bed, and I helped Lindsay set out platters of salad and summer corn while the guys grilled chicken. When Tatum returned, the hurricane candles were lit and the moonlight shimmered on the water.

As often happens during these summer holidays, everyone stayed up too late and drank too much that first night. Even through my gin-and-tonic haze I judged that Tatum had acquitted herself well, making her midwestern childhood sound wholesome and wry and asking Lindsay thoughtful questions about TomorrowMakers, the foundation whose gala she had inherited from Garth's boss's wife.

"So do you help choose the kids?" she asked. TomorrowMakers paired underprivileged high school students in the city with sea-soned professionals in the law and public policy, providing mentor-ship and support and financial aid.

"God, no." Lindsay laughed. "The only time the committee ever deals with them is when they send us one to speak at the gala. And as you might imagine, the ones who make it that far are a bit more polished than most of the others."

"But didn't you say a hundred percent of them go to college?" I detected a hint of envy in Tatum's voice, and I wondered if she was thinking about how different her life would have been if she'd had access to such a program. "They must be smart, at least."

"What I said was that a hundred percent *enroll* in college," Lindsay corrected her. "What we don't put in the literature is that a lot of them can't hack it—we lose almost thirty percent in the first year."

"You mean they just drop out? What happens to them?"

"Well, they don't have to pay back the financial aid. But the foundation doesn't keep data on them after that—we believe in focusing our resources on the ones with the drive to make the most of the opportunities we've given them." The words rolled so smoothly off Lindsay's tongue, I knew she was going to be perfect in her new role. Any genetic predisposition to beneficence that she'd inherited from her forebears was eclipsed by her fierce pragmatism, a critical tool for coaxing big checks from wealthy donors.

"I can't believe they just quit!" Tatum said indignantly. "After all you do for them?"

"The world's a tough place." Lindsay shrugged. "You cut your losses and move on."

"Well, I still think it's awesome that you give so much time to a cause like that."

"You're not kidding," Lindsay said. "Running that gala's going to be my full-time job. Julia's too, once I appoint her assistant chair."

I sat up a little straighter. I'd been hoping, of course—but Lindsay had never come out and said it before. "So we're really doing it?" I said, aiming for a casual tone.

Lindsay gave me a sly smile over the rim of her glass. She knew exactly what she was offering by appointing me—visibility, publicity, cachet, a springboard to a chair position of my own—and I knew she would make me work for it. "Of course we are. I couldn't do it without you."

"You guys are going to have so much fun!" Tatum sighed.

We were all drinking our share. Garth kept going to the cellar and bringing up bottle after bottle of Beaujolais Nouveau. He and Lindsay had been in France for the release the prior November, and he had an attentive audience in Tatum, who wasn't familiar with the custom. He regaled her with stories of the Lyon warehouses being unlocked at midnight, the barrels being rolled down the street. Lindsay rolled her eyes and pronounced the wine *imbuvable,* then tipsily rose from the table.

"Come with me," she said, taking my hand. She picked up the bottle of Sancerre she'd been drinking and I grabbed our glasses and we headed down the stairs to the ocean, where we kicked off our shoes and walked barefoot across the sand and sat down on the splintery edge of a log that had washed up on the beach. Lindsay dug a pack of cigarettes and a lighter from the pocket of her pants.

"You're so bad," I said with a laugh. "I thought you quit for good!"

"This doesn't count," she said, puffing delicately, the tip glowing in the dark. "It's a holiday. Almost."

She handed me the cigarette, and I took a deep drag. I used to smoke, like everyone I knew in college—at parties, late nights studying, on the balcony of the first apartment that I shared with James. Since the children were born I was afraid to keep cigarettes in the house.

"So . . . thank you," I said. "For asking me to help with the gala."

"Well, it was either you or Grace, but she doesn't have time, not with the Players and entertaining Matt's clients." The Players Club was a century-old private club founded in support of the arts, and since she and Matt were invited to join, six months ago, Grace had really thrown herself into it. "Besides, you may not be thanking me a year from now. We'll have to get cranking as soon as they announce the committee in October."

"I can't wait," I said, though I was going to have to nail down our evening child care arrangement by then, since assistant chairs had to attend all the subcommittee meetings.

"So what's Tatum's story?" Lindsay said, as we passed the cigarette back and forth between us.

"I told you. She came here to act, it didn't work out—tale as old as time."

"Nope."

"What do you mean, nope?"

"The only place that girl's acted is in the manager's office at Macy's, trying to explain why she was walking out the door with merchandise in her purse."

"Lindsay! You're just jealous."

She raised one eyebrow and looked at me coolly as I realized my mistake. "If you're referring to her flirtation with my husband, you don't need to worry. Garth's tastes are a little more urbane."

"I know she doesn't have a lot of polish," I said hastily, anxious to move the conversation back to safer ground, "but she's smart and she works hard. I thought maybe she'd enjoy meeting your niece and her friends." Lindsay's niece was twenty-four, and I'd hoped Tatum would get to know her and her friends, maybe meet a young investment banker or one of those tech startup types who biked to work and paid cash for their first apartments.

"Your little Eliza Doolittle transformation might fool most people," Lindsay said crisply, "but you need to introduce her to a proper tailor—"

"It was last minute," I protested, annoyed. "She needed something to wear—she can't help it that she's two inches taller than me and two sizes smaller."

"—and maybe get her some elocution lessons."

"You're such a snob."

Lindsay laughed. "Don't be so touchy. I like your little pet, I do. I just wouldn't leave her alone in the apartment with the good silver. And I hope you remember to get your earrings back."

"Don't be mean," I said. "She's got it tough." I told her about Tatum's landlord, about how she was working so hard to try to make ends meet.

"I mean, thank God she's babysitting for us. I should probably give her a huge raise, especially since Benilda just told me her cousin's dying of cancer and she has to take all kinds of time off to go up to Queens and help."

"Oh no," Lindsay said, exhaling a thin stream of smoke. "That's horrible. I mean, it's sad about her cousin, but—you don't think she's going to quit, do you?"

"God, I hope not. I'll never find anyone over the summer."

"Well, the solution to your problem is obvious—move Tatum into your guest room. That way she can help out when she's not working her other jobs, and Benilda can take some time off, and— how long does this cousin have?" She stubbed her cigarette out in the sand. "Not to be indelicate."

"I don't know. Weeks? Months, tops."

"So it might even work out perfectly—it'll give Tatum time to find a new place and save for the deposit and first month's rent and all that. And you won't lose your mind trying to keep everything together. And you can keep going to that gym. Though if you lose any more weight, I'll never speak to you again."

I grinned in the dark. "You're a genius. Want to head up before our husbands drink you out of house and home?"

"Sure," Lindsay said, getting up and dusting the sand off her pants. "But I'm not too worried—I think we can afford a six-pack or two."

Leave it to Lindsay to take a dig at James for drinking beer. In the weeks since I'd seen her last, I'd forgotten that her friendship came with a price—you never knew when she was going to put you in your place.

CHAPTER 12

The party the next night proceeded as these things do. Guests arrived as the sun was setting, golden beams glancing off mirrored sunglasses and diamonds, the women's high heels sinking into the lawns. Glassy-eyed caterers circulated trays of appetizers, ducking behind the shrubs to get high as the bartenders raced to keep up. Lindsay had done a retro picnic thing, with tiny cheeseburger sliders and shot glasses filled with ceviche, and a pig roasting on a portable spit on the back deck.

A couple hours in, Lindsay rescued me from a pair of thousand-year-old matrons, true old-school stalwarts in the same bright Bally flats and Lily Pulitzer skirts they'd been wearing since their school days, and dragged me to the bar to replenish our wine.

"Your husband saved the day," she said, as we watched the men gathered around the pig on the lower deck, in a cloud of billowing smoke. "The propane ran out and the caterers couldn't change the tank—something about the valve being stuck. James found some pliers in the garage and sprayed it with olive oil, of all things—*et voilà*."

"He's certainly handy," I agreed lightly, trying to ignore the familiar edge to her praise, the veiled suggestion that James was little more than a laborer. "If only he could dress himself."

James was telling a story, waving his cigar around for emphasis, to a group of men that included Garth Parker with his ever-present Beaujolais and his navy blazer with monogrammed gold buttons. My husband could always hold this audience in thrall with tales of the building trade, and I knew that played on Lindsay's insecurities.

"Everything going okay with the Mercer deal?" Lindsay asked, sipping her wine.

"I guess. I mean, there's been the usual hassle with permitting and the city and all that."

"You're sure?"

"Why? What?"

"It's nothing—just something Garth said this morning. I guess the guys were talking last night, when we were down on the beach. Garth said James was pretty animated."

"James is always pretty animated," I said, but an unpleasant feeling was taking root in my gut.

"You're right. Like I said, it's probably nothing."

I didn't miss the frisson of satisfaction that flashed across her face, but I couldn't help myself. "Just tell me, Linds."

"It's just . . . maybe Garth got it wrong, he was pretty wasted. But he said James had a visit from a federal antitrust agent."

"*What?*"

"I mean, it could have been anything. I wouldn't read too much into it."

"What would they want with him? It's all local, the regulations and codes and all that."

"Well, there's bid rigging, price-fixing, subcontracting issues— any kind of fraud, really." I always forget that Lindsay had been an attorney herself once—she met Garth at the firm where she'd been a summer associate. "But he's got good legal, right?"

"Yes, of course," I said. Stewart Marlowe was a humorless man of few words unless you got him started on real estate or tax law. "At least, he's ungodly expensive and he has a nice office."

Lindsay nodded. "Anyway, enough about that, I shouldn't have even brought it up. Let's head down—I think they're about to carve the beast."

Tatum disappeared before dessert was served.

I only noticed because she'd been so excited about the sundae station, the glass jars filled with nonpareils and gummy worms and flaked coconut. Two college girls in pink and white striped aprons stood ready to scoop, as the guests—many of them inebriated—lined up. I went looking for Tatum, thinking I'd say good night and then collect James and head back to the guesthouse. Lindsay's comments were nagging at the back of my mind, and—though surely none of it amounted to more than the inevitable hassles associated with nine-figure development projects—I was worried about James's loose lips.

I checked the multilevel deck, the entire main floor of the house, the front drive, where a knot of people were smoking. I scanned the beach and asked a couple of the caterers if they'd seen her, and when I couldn't think of anywhere else to look, I checked the bathrooms. Just as I was about to give up, I found her.

The caterers had left the side door of the kitchen open to vent the heat from the oven, and I could see out into a little patio surrounded by a lilac hedge. It was shielded from view of the driveway and backyard by the hedge, and I would never have thought to look there if the door hadn't been open.

Tatum was tucked into the corner of a wicker love seat, talking to a man in a flag-print shirt and huaraches. From the back I could see only a ring of gray on his otherwise bald head. The compact size of the love seat meant that they were sitting awkwardly close, Tatum balancing a paper plate holding an untouched ear of grilled sweet corn on her knee, and as I watched, the man laid his arm across the back of the love seat, his fingertips inches from her bare shoulder. Surprise, surprise, he was wearing a wedding band. I, like every other woman over the age of thirteen, knew that move, the oh-shucks-how-did-my-arm-get-there technique that adolescent boys use to advance to second base. But Tatum seemed oblivious, leaning forward to laugh at something the man said so that the wrap front of the dress I'd loaned her gaped open, revealing the lacy edge of her bra.

"Tatum!" I exclaimed, my voice overly bright as I headed through the door, closing it behind me to prevent anyone else from catching this little tête-à-tête. I plopped into a matching wicker armchair and pulled it close so my knees were almost touching theirs. "They're serving dessert, and I remembered you wanted some."

Tatum's smile slipped. "Oh, hi. We're just taking a little break— it's so loud around the pool."

The last I'd seen her, she'd been talking to some of the younger guests, girls with tan lines and good jewelry and men green enough to still relish their Wall Street jobs. Somehow she'd gotten separated from the pack. I gave her companion a frosty look, and then I recognized him.

"Augie," I said in surprise. "Julia Summers—we met when James did that project in Brooklyn Heights."

"Julia!" Augie didn't look happy to see me, edging away from Tatum on the love seat. "Is James here?"

"Uh-huh, I think he's on his third round of ribs. Tatum, Augie and James worked together on an apartment building a few years back."

"James did all the work," Augie said, recovering some of his swagger. "I just wrote checks."

"It was a syndicated deal," I said, not really in the mood to explain it to Tatum—Augie was one of half a dozen investors on the project, one of the largest James had ever done. "Actually, you and James met at this same party, didn't you?"

Augie nodded vigorously. "I've got Garth to thank for that. Speaking of which—I think I'll hunt that bastard down, give you girls a chance to catch up. Nice meeting you, Tatum."

"Please say hello to Nan for me," I called after him.

"I didn't know he was in real estate," Tatum said. "He told me he was an importer."

"He is," I said coldly. Was she really naïve enough to be impressed by his gaudy Rolex, his golf tan? Or worse—did she think she had a *chance* with him? "Listen, Tatum, when I said you should try to get to know people, I did not mean a married lech old enough to be your father. Do you really want people's first impression of you to be that you're a gold digger?"

Her mouth dropped open, her eyes wounded. "We were just talking! It was loud, and he wanted to get another drink, so—"

"Tatum, don't be stupid! I'm sure you get hit on all the time, but this isn't just some drunk guy trying to grab your ass—the Crafts know *everyone*. Nan's probably friends with Brooke's mom, for God's sake. And trust me, you do *not* want to make an enemy of her."

"I didn't mean anything." Tatum looked close to tears. "You know her?"

"James and I had dinner with them when Augie first got interested in the deal. She's not someone to mess with." Nan was a well-maintained blonde in her mid-fifties who held a course record at Shinnecock. I'd recently heard she'd made her assistant chairwoman cry when the caterers brought the wrong color tablecloths to the Sloan Kettering luncheon. On the plus side, Augie wasn't known for philandering, as far as I knew. "Did people see you leave the party with him?"

"Of course not!" She clenched her hands, and the paper plate fell to the ground, the corn rolling into the ivy. "I mean, we were just *walking* together, getting a drink. And, like, I could have just been coming in to go to the bathroom. Does it seriously matter?"

Disaster scenarios raced through my mind. "Did he ask for your number? Touch you?"

"No—"

"Because I want you to avoid him from now on. Go back to those people you were talking to before. In fact, try to get one of those guys to ask for your phone number. And act excited about it."

Tatum fell silent, staring ahead at nothing. A moment passed before she said, "Okay. Okay, I understand."

"I mean it wouldn't be the worst thing. Those guys have good jobs, Tatum. They're very well paid."

I hoped that I didn't need to spell it out for her. Seeing her distress, I relented. "You're right, it's probably no big deal. I'm sorry if I overreacted. It's just—look, Nan Craft is exactly who you want to get in your classes, Tatum, and women like her. They've got time and they've got money and influence. And you can get them to *adore* you, but not by flirting with their husbands."

"Okay—"

"You're the girl next door, remember? You're—you're Betty, not Veronica."

"I don't know who they are."

I let out a breath in frustration. "You're *sweet*. You're the girl who doesn't get dirty jokes, but will stop to help an old lady who drops her keys. You've got this hot body but all you care about is getting your riders to be as healthy as they can be, to feel good when they leave. You can't even tell when a man is coming on to you or a woman is being passive-aggressive, because you assume the best of everyone."

"I understand what you're saying, I just don't get—I mean, people here are so sophisticated. They're not like where I'm from. Like, when Brooke—"

I wanted to shake her. "Brooke has her thing," I said. "You have yours. There are a lot of people out there who don't actually enjoy being yelled at."

I didn't want to lean too hard into the idea that her appeal came from her naïveté; I didn't want to insult her. Sure, there were women who'd take one look at her and try to mow her down. But here's the thing: despite Tatum's obvious ambition, her charm was genuine. She was the kind of girl you wanted to be friends with—a surrogate sister, an eager sidekick, a babysitter who let a little girl put stickers on her toes.

Not a girl who let men put their hands on her thighs while their wives were holding court a few yards away.

Tatum gave me a weak smile. "I'm sorry I embarrassed you. I'll—I'll do better."

"All right. Good. And just to be on the safe side, I'll mention to Lindsay that Augie followed you into the house because he was drunk." We stood up and I let her lead the way back into the house.

I could have told her it was no big deal, not to worry about it, everything was fine—but it wasn't. Seeing my friends gathered here tonight had reminded me how much was at stake. How much I was counting on her. She couldn't fuck this up.

CHAPTER 13

Before we left the next morning, I took Lindsay aside to tell her what happened with Augie Craft, implying that Tatum had merely been trying to be polite and hadn't known how to fend him off.

Tatum was silent on the trip back to the city, wedged between the kids in the backseat, while James talked on his phone and drove the way he usually did. I'd long ago given up trying to convince James that he was endangering us all, that a speeding ticket wasn't worth it, that he was setting a bad example for the kids.

In his mind, he was modeling appropriate behavior for Henry. In James's view, driving aggression was a skill that all males needed to learn, just as he'd wanted Paige to take dance lessons and wear a dress for our annual Christmas card. Yes, these were stale values, but the truth was that his old-school attitudes were part of his appeal. A man like James might not watch a TED talk with you or read *The Atlantic*—but if the building caught fire he'd get everyone out, on his back if he had to, which was more than I could say for many of my friends' husbands, who probably couldn't even change a lightbulb. James had threatened men who catcalled me, slammed his fist on the counter of the mechanic who'd overcharged me for a brake job, and he never did tell me exactly what he'd said to the co-worker who'd taken credit for one of my campaigns at a company party, but afterward, the guy apologized and kept his distance.

This was how I knew I'd married the right man. My mother still hadn't forgiven me for breaking my engagement—Ryan Walker was the whole package: his grandfather had been a popular Delaware senator; his father ran a successful hedge fund; and his parents gave generously to all the right causes and owned homes in Arizona and Cap Ferrat in addition to their Main Line estate. The family diamond Ryan had set for me in a ring he designed himself was insured for over a hundred thousand dollars, and his trust fund would have bought not just a starter home but an entire city block.

But Ryan barely managed to graduate from Skidmore, and he frequently used the wrong word in conversations and got irritable if I corrected him. His passions were online gaming and the films of Wes Anderson, and I suspected that his father had called in favors to land Ryan's job at a regional bank. I'd fallen for him because of his generally sunny disposition and what I mistook for confidence, but it turned out that he'd simply never been told no before. When I broke off the engagement the day after meeting James, the strongest emotion I felt was relief.

In contrast with the man in the driver's seat next to me, drumming on the steering wheel to Nazareth and copping a feel while Tatum dozed, there was no comparison.

Once we'd made it through Southampton and Tatum woke up, James made his version of polite conversation. "So, Jules told me about your asshole landlord."

"James," I said automatically. We kept up the pretense that swearing wasn't allowed in our family, though I was almost as bad as he was.

"Sorry. Anyway, you want me to go over there and beat the shit out of him?"

"James!"

"Just kidding. Hey, listen, I agree with Jules. Come stay with us for a bit—I know she'd appreciate the help with the kids, and that'll give you a little time to find a new place."

I'd relayed what Tatum had told me, the first morning when we were still in bed in the guesthouse. James had been sympathetic and agreeable to my idea, but I was surprised he was bringing it up now, in front of the kids.

"That's so incredibly generous," Tatum said. "But I couldn't impose like that."

"You'd be helping us out," James said. "Jules has her hands full this summer and I'm sure she'd love the company too."

Then I got it—he was trying to line up a babysitter for *me*. I'd been pretty vocal with my complaints about being stuck in the city, and James saw Tatum as a chance to off-load his obligation to keep me entertained.

"It's true," I said, turning to check on the kids. Paige was playing some game on her iPad and Henry was gazing out the window and clutching his stuffed bear, a beloved and threadbare Gund my mother had given him when he was a baby. "We'd love to have you. It's not safe for you to stay where you are. And listen, don't pay another cent in rent. If your landlord tries to come after you, James can have his lawyer make a call."

"Yep," James agreed. "Stewart Marlowe, human wrecking ball. We'll have him break a few fingers, just to get the point across."

"Oh, you guys . . ." Tatum said. Her eyes were shiny.

"Can Benilda live with us instead?" Henry asked.

"Henry!" I chastised him. "Benilda already has a home. And a family that needs her. If Tatum stays with us, she can play with you more."

"Okay."

"I'm sorry," I said to Tatum. "He's just tired. So it's settled—go home and pack your stuff and you can move in anytime this weekend. Benilda won't be back until Monday, but we can figure out the schedule for the week then."

I'd texted Benilda several times over the last few days to try to find out how it was going with her cousin—and received only one cryptic text back. **Thank You Mrs. Julia every Prayer is answered in GODS Time.** Was Thelma (it *was* Thelma, wasn't it?) doing better? Worse? Experiencing a miraculous cure? At death's door?

"I have to throw up," Henry announced.

"You do not!" Paige yelled. "Oh my God, you are *killing* my ears!"

Henry leaned across Tatum and tried to slap Paige's hand, but she yanked it out of the way.

"You are *so* annoying," she announced triumphantly.

She was developing a propensity for the last word.

I didn't hear from Tatum over the weekend, but I was occupied with unpacking and getting the kids back on a schedule.

Monday morning, Tatum texted to say she'd be over in time to shower before her 5:00 P.M. class. At a little before four she arrived with our building's porter in tow, carrying a huge duffel bag.

I showed her the guest room, the towels I'd put in the guest bathroom. "Do you need to go back for the rest of your stuff? Or do you have somewhere to store it?"

"This is it." Tatum shrugged, giving the duffel a little kick. "My old place came furnished."

Benilda was banging pots around in the kitchen. I knew she'd heard Tatum arrive, but she hadn't come out to greet her. Benilda had been moody and silent since her return from Queens, clucking to herself while she worked. I had concluded that Thelma wasn't going to linger.

"Listen, Julia," Tatum continued, the expression on her face hopeful, tentative. "I was wondering . . . I want to take you out to dinner. Like a thank-you? For letting me stay here and taking me with you for the Fourth and—and everything?"

"Sure," I said, touched. Obviously she'd done some thinking since the Hamptons; maybe the episode with Augie Craft had been a blessing in disguise, and my warning had sunk in. I hadn't been looking for thanks, but it was nice to be acknowledged. "I'd love to."

I hadn't had a real night out since everyone left town, and Benilda certainly owed me some hours. I'd bought some new things since losing weight—a fitted boatneck top that looked like something Gina Lollobrigida would have worn in Capri, and the first size 6 jeans I'd worn in years. If the clothes didn't quite make me feel twenty-five again, they at least didn't scream *mommy*. My new out-fit and I deserved a night on the damn town.

"Yay! I'm so excited! Do you mind if I invite Brooke too?"

Tatum and Brooke had recently become almost inseparable. I'd see them getting dressed together in the locker room or bent over their laptops, going through their playlists, one shiny blond head and one tousled and darker.

"Of course—it'll be fun," I said, though I would have much pre-ferred a Brooke-free evening.

"Great! I'll figure out some dates with her and let you know."

Tatum left to teach and I ran to the drugstore, and when I got back, Benilda immediately started gathering her things, casting a pointed glare at the tote bag Tatum had left on the floor of the foyer.

"Benilda, wait," I said. "Did you talk to Thelma today? How is she doing?"

Benilda sighed and set her purse back down on the counter. "Is no good, no good," she said. "Her belly? Is filling up. And her eyes are the yellow." She patted her stomach the way a pregnant woman does, running her hands gently over its contours.

"Her . . . belly? You mean with, um, gas?"

"No, no. Is . . . water?"

"Oh, fluids?" This was often how we communicated, Benilda try-ing out words that I countered with a host of alternatives until I landed on the one she wanted.

"Yes, *fluids*. The cancer, it is in her liver now."

"Oh, no. I'm so sorry." Though did it really matter, at this point? I'd heard the pain could be terrible in the final weeks—that patients were doped up on morphine most of the time. I was pretty sure I'd choose that route myself if it came to it. "Were you able to . . . um, spend some quality time with her last week?"

"Oh, yes. Friends are coming, her son and his family are trying to get here, but is so expensive. All the way from Texas."

Benilda looked at me hopefully—but maybe that was my imagination. Truth be told, Benilda's expression rarely changed, her emotional spectrum ranging from slightly sour to sorely affronted when speaking to me and James. But now I wondered if she expected me to offer to help with her cousin's travel. If she wanted, Benilda could dip into her own savings, of which I suspected there were plenty, as she spent almost nothing and occasionally talked about the house she and her husband planned to build in the hills above Taytay when she retired.

"Well, I'm glad you were able to spend the holiday with her," I said firmly.

Benilda looked pointedly at Tatum's bag again. "Will *she* be staying here?"

"Yes, for a while." I found it annoying that Benilda refused to say her name. "I'm sure she'll keep out of your way."

"I hope so," Benilda said curtly. "Good night, Mrs. Julia."

The friction between them was something I'd probably have to deal with eventually, though I resented being caught in the middle—was it so much to ask for everyone in my house to make an effort to get along?

CHAPTER 14

It ended up taking a couple weeks before we managed to find a night that worked for all three of us. The plan was for Tatum and Brooke to get ready at Flame after Brooke's 5:30 P.M. class on Friday, and then they'd meet me at the restaurant at 8:00 P.M.

Late Friday afternoon I locked my bedroom door while Benilda fed the kids dinner. She'd been silent and brooding all day, snapping at the children to put their wet swimsuits in the hamper after she picked them up from the bus. Lately she had been coming in later and later, ignoring Henry's wailing when he couldn't find his teddy bear. But she didn't want to talk about it; she'd just shake her head when I asked after Thelma. I'd been juggling the kids and the household tasks myself in the mornings, but Benilda more than made up for it when she arrived—ferocious bouts of cleaning seemed to provide her an outlet for her stress.

I took my time in the shower, shaving all the way up my thighs, and spent an hour on my hair and makeup. We'd arranged to meet at a little tapas place tucked away in a pocket of the West Village. Incredible aromas wafted out when I opened the silvered glass door. Inside, beautifully dressed people waited to be seated. Other than a gorgeous zinc bar, the space looked like it had been furnished with castoffs from a defunct convent: unadorned plain long wooden tables, a mishmash of lath and stick and brace-back and bow-back chairs, all treated to a coat of black lacquer. Mercury glass sconces, exposed brick, and the original scarred oak floors.

I was so over that vibe, but the place was packed and the hostess was turning away people without reservations. I spotted Tatum and Brooke in the corner next to the bar at an intimate little four-top.

Brooke was wearing a steel-gray silk bustier that showed off her breasts. In the soft light, her tattoos looked almost like Dürer sketches. Her hair fell in loose waves around her shoulders, and her lips were painted blood red. By contrast, Tatum channeled eighties Madonna: lots of black eyeliner, hair teased and sprayed to massive volume, a black mesh top that revealed her bra, and over that, a shiny ivory leather moto jacket. I wasn't sure where she got the inspiration for her look, but there was something familiar about that jacket, and for a second I wondered if she'd borrowed it without asking—but despite my shopping habit and walk-in closet filled to bursting, I was pretty sure I'd never owned anything like it.

A bottle of champagne rested in an ice bucket next to the table— Feuillatte, nice but not terribly expensive. Melting ice and empty shells were all that was left of a platter of oysters. I was only a few minutes late; obviously they had arrived early and started without me.

"Julia!" Tatum shrieked, jumping up and jostling the table. She sat back down with a plop, giggling. Brooke slid out of her chair and laid her hands lightly on my shoulders, her kiss landing almost on my ear.

"You guys clean up fast," I said, "seeing as you were on bikes uptown just over an hour ago."

"Oh, I found someone to sub for me," Brooke said. "Since it's my birthday."

"It is? You didn't have to invite me—"

"I *wanted* you here," Brooke said, touching my arm. In a few moments she'd shown me more attention than in the entire time I'd known her. "I wanted to thank you. Tatum says you're going to bring all your friends to Flame."

I searched her expression for signs of sarcasm as she slid back into her chair but found none. Her gratitude seemed genuine. Who knew—with her rent covered by her parents, $150 a class might cover the rest, though her black bag was Valentino and the diamond studs in her cartilage looked real. I wondered how she had fallen so far from the family tree, and what her parents thought of her career choice.

"I'm famished," I said. "Did you already order?"

"Just the oysters," Tatum said. "Should we get more?"

We did, and some small plates—razor-thin carpaccio with juniper berries, crostini with salted cod—but the three of us only picked at the dishes. Those calories don't burn themselves.

I figured I'd end up with the bill, but I didn't care. It was such a pleasure to be in a restaurant with a linen napkin in my lap, the buzz of interesting conversations around me. By the time we finished eating, well into a second bottle of Pinot Grigio, it was almost ten-thirty. James had texted me a little after nine that he was home, and I felt wistful that my night out was coming to an end.

But they surprised me.

"I'll get this," Brooke said, snatching the bill off the waitress's pewter tray.

"But it's your birthday!" Tatum exclaimed.

"At least let me contribute," I said, reaching for my bag.

"Nope. You guys can get rounds at the club. But I meant what I said—I wanted to show you that we appreciate everything you're doing, Julia."

"Well—it's my pleasure, and thank you, Brooke."

"I've never been to Constellation," Tatum said, getting unsteadily to her feet. "I can't wait!"

Constellation was the sort of club that had sprouted recently around that part of town, lushly appointed with ironic lounge décor just made for Instagram posts, bottles of house-made tinctures lined up behind the bar, little pots of chalk in the bathrooms to encourage people to write on the walls. Matt Dexter's media company had hosted an event there shortly after it opened, and while he entertained clients, Grace and I took selfies in the brocade chaises and sampled artisanal bourbon and flirted with the DJ.

I feared I'd be the oldest person in the club, but the alternative was to head home, to climb into bed and read a few paragraphs before nodding off.

"Oh, I love that place," I said. "They make this amazing yellow cocktail, with tequila and turmeric and fresh herbs."

The two of them exchanged glances and I feared I'd gone too far, but then Tatum gave me an impulsive little hug. "Of course you've been there! Oh God, you're the best, Julia."

I could feel people watching us as we wound our way through the cramped gauntlet of tables, and I decided to believe that some of that admiration was meant for me. Your mother probably told you how to project confidence that you don't feel: stand up straight, keep your shoulders back, smile and look people in the eye. She may have added that everyone else is just as unsure of themselves as you are.

This isn't true, of course. Some people *do* walk around like they own the place, either because they actually do or because they believe they truly are better than you. That's the real trick: keep reminding yourself of everyone else's flaws. I gave a table of drunk investment bankers a withering gaze as I passed them.

Adventure ahead, and I was suited up and ready.

CHAPTER 15

Brooke knew people. At the front of the line of hopefuls outside the club was a bearded young man in thick-framed glasses—velvet ropes and muscled bouncers being hopelessly out of date—who waved us over when he saw us.

"How've you been?" he asked after they kissed. "Benny's into Chartreuse right now and he's barrel-aged a couple of new cocktails—you've got to try them."

"Definitely," Brooke said smoothly. "These are my friends, Tatum and Julia."

"Hey, how are you?" he said, barely glancing at us.

Inside, nothing was as I remembered. That's not true—the same furniture was arranged in the same self-conscious rumpus-room groupings; the same enormous screens overhead twitched and pulsed with the same blurry images in time to the same music, a bass-heavy, fey instrumental that seemed to feature sitars and steel drums and nineties pop riffs. But instead of a bunch of media executives in creative casual standing around talking work, we navigated a teeming school of the young and gorgeous. A good many of them looking narcotically detached, their pretty eyes unfocused.

While Brooke went to the bar to get drinks, Tatum dug in her bag and pulled out a little round container. She shook out two pieces of chocolate and handed me one. "It's just weed," she said. "Don't worry, one won't get you too high."

I only hesitated for a moment. I wasn't exactly a stranger to edibles, thanks to James's brother who lived in California and sent occasional gifts of cookies and tinctures and topical creams in packages with no return address. Usually James and I hoarded them until a night when the kids were away with their grandparents, and then we got high and had raunchy sex.

I had popped the chocolate in my mouth when Brooke returned with three martini glasses filled with a cloudy pale orange concoction. Tatum grabbed my hand and pulled me onto the dance floor, leaving our untouched cocktails on a ledge. She danced like she spun, her arms lifted, her head thrown back, swaying and laughing. I closed my eyes and gave in to my lovely glistening buzz and let the music guide me. Someone collided with me and apologized, and I smiled, full of goodwill as the weed did its work. We took a break and drank our cocktails and danced some more, until Tatum drifted away from me.

We needed more drinks, but by the time I fought my way to the bar and bought a round, Tatum and Brooke were nowhere to be seen. I was annoyed until I heard Tatum yelling my name overhead: the two of them were seated on a platform on gold kidney-shaped couches with a well-dressed man in his fifties. I made my way unsteadily up the curved staircase, sloshing the drinks, and sat next to Tatum across a tiny cocktail table from Brooke and the man, setting the glasses down amid a litter of empties and crumpled napkins.

"This is Richie," Brooke said. "I've known him forever."

"Richard," he corrected, offering me one of those horrible handshakes where the guy grabs only your fingertips and squeezes. "We met a couple months ago."

Brooke reached across the coffee table and tucked something in my hand, closing my fingers over it. It was an Altoids tin, the little oblong kind that holds the tiny ones. I opened the lid and saw three small pills, mint green and stamped with the image of a dove. Brooke plucked two of the pills from the tin and popped one in her mouth, then fed the other to Tatum, slipping it past her lips.

"It's just Molly," Tatum said against my ear, so close that her lips brushed my skin. "Have you tried it?"

I'd tried Ecstasy in college, just once, because my roommate said it gave you irreversible brain damage. The main thing I remembered about that night was somehow ending up in the kitchen of a fraternity house kissing a man I'd never seen before who was too old to be a student. Two girls had come in looking for snacks and dragged me out.

But I also remember the glinting cheer, the feeling that everything was as it should be, that everything was possible. I suddenly craved that—I told myself I deserved it. And if Brooke and Tatum could handle it on an empty stomach, then surely I could too.

"Don't be afraid," Brooke said, watching me. "You'll love it. You'll see. And you're with us—nothing bad will happen."

Richard was watching me too, looking amused, and the music was thrumming up through the floor into my body. I wanted him to flirt with me too; I wanted to trade in the currency that Brooke spilled like sand from her fists. I held the pill between my finger and thumb, considering.

"Come on, Julia," Tatum pleaded.

"Forget it," Brooke said, tossing her hair over her shoulder. "She's too scared." She turned her back on me and clambered onto Richard's lap, straddling him, and began a languorous bump and grind in time to the pulsing beat. A new song came on, and Tatum shrieked and jumped up, distractible as a butterfly, and danced out into the crowd.

My perilous moment had passed. I'd resisted Brooke and I told myself that it was a victory—someone had to be the tedious adult in the room. I dropped the pill back in the tin and slipped it into my purse, and stood up too quickly, instantly dizzy.

"I'm going to get some water," I announced. Richard had both his hands on Brooke's ass, and neither of them looked up.

At the bar I wedged myself into a narrow space between people and took stock. I was definitely drunk—I'd put away most of the second bottle of wine at the restaurant by myself, not to mention the two cocktails. Thank God I'd come to my senses; I was in no condition to put one more thing in my body until I'd sobered up. As I tried to catch the bartender's attention, I realized I'd left my purse under the coffee table. Someone leaned into me and drawled, in a gust of garlic and beer, "Damn, you're amazing."

My admirer was wearing a T-shirt with a vintage Olympia beer logo and a modest, hopeful thatch of facial hair; he couldn't have been more than nineteen. Okay, twenty-one, since not even the best fake ID would get him in this place.

"Dance with me."

"I need to find my friends."

"You don't need them," He hooked his fingers into my waistband and tugged me into the mass of gyrating, undulating bodies, and I spotted Tatum. She'd taken off the leather jacket and her mesh top slipped fetchingly off her shoulders as she danced with a man with skin the color of walnuts and hair as long as mine. They were doing a contained samba amid the crush of strangers, their hips touching, Tatum's hand on his shoulder. I remembered she'd once been a dancer.

I maneuvered so my new friend was between me and Tatum. I didn't want her to see me. I watched her roll her shoulders and let a strand of her hair get stuck between her lips and thrust out her breasts. People watched her, clearing space around them to make way for one final, whirling spin that ended in—what else?—a nearly acrobatic dip, Tatum exposing the long, pale expanse of her throat, her blond hair dusting the floor.

This was a different Tatum than the one I knew, her peppy cheer giving way to unbridled provocation, as though she was channeling Brooke on steroids. As the music changed, there were catcalls and a smattering of applause—and I went in search of a better vantage point, not even bothering to say goodbye to my frat-boy friend. My purse was right where I'd left it, but the sofas had been overtaken by a bunch of millennials, girls with crop tops and wrists heavy with bracelets, boys in tortoiseshell glasses and European-cut blazers. I snatched up my purse and headed for the ladies' room; I really had to pee, and a splash of cold water on my face would help sober me up.

The line was a dozen deep. I'd been waiting for what felt like an hour when Brooke appeared, grabbing my hand. "I've been looking for you! Come on, this line is ridiculous."

She led me past the bar and through a pair of swinging doors marked STAFF ONLY into a harshly lit, steamy room lined with dishwashers and kegs and racks of glasses.

"Brooke—"

"No, come on, there's a bathroom back here."

She led the way through the room and down a hall, at the end of which was a dull metal door covered with a crude drawing of a cock and years' worth of graffiti. "It's us," Brooke said, knocking, and Tatum opened the door, smoking a cigarette; a girl I didn't recognize was sprawled on a vinyl bench in the corner. Brooke gave me a little shove and locked the door behind us.

"I saw you!" Tatum said gaily, her eyes unfocused as she sat down on the toilet. Her makeup had smudged and strands of her hair were plastered to her cheek. "Who was that guy you were dancing with?"

"Can I just—"

There was no privacy, but I was desperate so I grabbed her hand and pulled her up and basically pushed her into Brooke's arms, then pulled down my pants and sat on the toilet to pee. The relief was almost pleasurable. As I washed my hands, Brooke eased Tatum back down onto the lid.

I leaned against the tiled wall and checked my watch, but it wasn't there, and I couldn't remember if I'd even worn it tonight. I looked in the mirror: my mascara pooled under my eyes, my lipstick was worn off except at the edges. My eyes were red and my hair was a mess. There was dirt on my blouse. I looked like a crime victim.

"I think we should call it a night." I turned on the taps again and splashed my face, getting water all over the floor and mirror.

"You have nice tits, Julia," Brooke said. "Have you had work done?"

"I really don't feel well," I said. The girl on the bench shuddered and made a gasping sound. "Hey, is she okay?"

"Her? Who cares?" Brooke took Tatum's cigarette and used it to light one of her own; she handed it to me after taking a single puff. "Look at those thighs."

I looked: they were dimpled with fat, the lace edge of her panties visible where her skirt had ridden up. "Seriously, you guys, I don't think she's okay."

Tatum stood up unsteadily and started humming, performing the ghost of the dance she'd done for the crowd, watching herself in the mirror. She spun once, twice, closer and closer to Brooke, and then she took Brooke's hand so her long, pale, tattooed arm wrapped around Tatum's body on the final spin. Brooke pulled Tatum into her arms and kissed her neck.

"Poor little girl, you've torn your party dress," she murmured, her hands on Tatum's hips as she kissed her way to her earlobe, Tatum making little mewling sounds. I didn't get it until I saw the tip of Brooke's tongue trace the edge of Tatum's ear. Her hands snaked up Tatum's rib cage until they were underneath her breasts, her thumbs caressing them, while Tatum's head lolled against her.

Brooke grinned wolfishly and winked at me. "You like her too."

"Yes, I like Tatum," I said stiffly. "But none of us are in any condition to—"

What? What were we in no condition to do? Keep drinking? Smoke directly under the NO SMOKING sign screwed into the tile? Molest our friends? I knew what I needed: a taxi, fresh air, a chance to sober up before I had to walk past my doorman. And I was getting ready to say so when Tatum sighed and twisted in Brooke's arms, wrapped her arms around her neck, and kissed her full on the mouth.

A real kiss, a hungry kiss—I'm sure you can imagine. Brooke leaned against the wall, her hands sliding down to Tatum's ass, grinding against her. I couldn't look away—I watched, transfixed, until the girl on the bench started making noises behind me.

I turned around to see her choking. Vomit covered her chin and neck, the stench hitting me a second later. As she gasped for breath, her back arched and she slid to the floor, her skull hitting the tile and her eyes rolling up. There was blood on her mouth and a cut on her shin.

"Call 911!" I yelped, kneeling beside her.

Brooke steadied herself on the sink while Tatum knelt down next to me. "Jesus—what's the matter with her?"

"I don't know, but we shouldn't touch her. Can't you please call?" I had my own phone out by then and I was trying to dial, but my hands were shaking. "Brooke, go get someone, get help!"

But neither of them moved. Brooke seemed immobilized by shock and the drugs, but Tatum started backing away, saying, "We can't be here."

"What do you mean?"

"We can't be here when the paramedics and cops get here, they'll get the wrong idea—we need to *go*. We'll call from outside, she'll be fine, I swear. Come on!"

She tried to take the phone out of my hand, but I held on to it; she grabbed for my wrist, but I pulled it away.

"Tatum, stop!" Brooke said, finally snapping out of it. "What the fuck are you doing?"

Tatum stood up and grabbed Brooke's face and forced Brooke to look at her. Suddenly, she seemed perfectly sober. "Think about it. If something—they're going to want to know what we were doing in here. They're going to want to talk to us, do you get it? Think of your *parents*."

Someone started pounding on the door. "What the fuck, open up!"

"This is serious!" I said, finally managing to make the call. "Let them in!"

But Tatum took one more swipe at my phone, and this time she managed to grab it. She ended the call and set it on top of the paper towel dispenser, out of my reach. "The club will take care of it," she said. "They'll call for help. Come *on*, Julia."

She grabbed Brooke's arm and twisted the lock, and the door banged open. Tatum pushed past the man standing in the doorway, dragging Brooke with her, saying "My friend's going to be sick, let us through, she's sick." I heard the sound of the fire door opening and closing at the end of the hall.

"I was trying to call 911," I said to the guy, who was wearing a long, stained apron and a hairnet and rubber shoes. "There's a girl in here who needs help."

He took one look and yelled over his shoulder, pulling his phone from his pocket. "Elliott! Lara! Get in here *now*!" he yelled, already dialing.

A bartender in a short black skirt pushed into the room. "Oh my God," she said. The girl hadn't moved; blood was trickling slowly down her neck and dripping on the floor.

"She threw up," I said. "And then she sort of fell."

"How much has she had to drink?" the woman asked me. Behind her, the guy was talking to the emergency dispatcher, giving the address, tripping over his words.

"I don't even know her," I gasped. "I just—"

"What were you guys even *doing* in here?"

"What did she take?" the man asked. "They want to know what she took."

"I don't *know* her—"

"Then get out of the way," the bartender said. "Wait in the hall-way."

I backed out of the room, grabbing my phone off the paper towel dispenser on the way.

The girl was okay. Wasn't she? The blood, she'd probably just bitten herself.

She hadn't seen me.

I shrank against the wall, out of view of the open door. What did it matter if she saw me? I'd been trying to help. I didn't even know her. I thought she was okay. I wouldn't have just left her there if I'd known . . . I'd *peed* inches from her face.

I hadn't done anything wrong, other than get really fucked up with two women who were even more fucked up than me and—but Tatum had sobered up so fast, taken in the situation and hustled Brooke out of there. Only now was I going down the same path in my mind: how it was going to look, how the cops would ask for my name—would there be cops? There probably would—how I'd have to tell James. Word would get out, because it always does, no matter how careful you are, and everyone would know I'd gotten wasted at Constellation. My blouse was filthy, my makeup wrecked. If there were photos . . . but there couldn't be photos.

More people were filling the hall. I peered around the door, and the man was on the floor now too, saying, "They're on their way," over and over again while the bartender held the girl's waxy, pale hand.

I didn't dare go out the fire door the way Brooke and Tatum had, not with an audience. I ducked my head and headed back down the hall, through the swinging doors, into the club. The music still blared, the dancers still writhed, the TV screens still pulsed as I fought through the packed club and out the door, past the guy with the glasses, the line of people down to the corner, clutching my purse to my chest. A cab pulled over, and I grabbed the door handle before it had even come to a stop. I got in, gave the driver my address, and huddled low in my seat.

And then I started to cry.

CHAPTER 16

I was all done with my little crying jag by the time the cab pulled up to my building. I walked stiffly into the lobby the way you do when you're trying not to appear drunk.

"Good evening, Mrs. Summers," Chetan said, though it was no longer evening.

The apartment was quiet. James had left the lights on. There was an empty pretzel bag on the sofa; Paige's markers were all over the floor. I turned off the lights, and on the way to our room I changed my mind and headed for the guest room instead, unable to face James.

I'd forgotten that it was now Tatum's room. I surveyed her belongings strewn around the room, more than I ever would have guessed would fit in her duffel and backpack. I picked up piles of clothes she'd discarded on the bed and tossed them on the floor and set her laptop on the nightstand and accidentally stepped on what turned out to be a dinner plate with a sheen of grease, my foot skidding on its slick surface. I stripped down to my underwear and folded my clothes and laid them on the dresser. I was getting under the covers when I noticed a familiar bit of scarlet peeping out from a pile of dirty laundry on the closet floor.

It wasn't actually scarlet, but a distinct shade of brick red that the salesgirl at Loro Piana had called "antique cinnabar." I knew this because my mother was so enraptured by the color that she bought herself the same cashmere dressing gown she bought me right after Henry was born. I'd barely ever worn it—even Mom was too young for such a matronly item, in my opinion—but it hung at the end of the rod in the section of my closet devoted to unwanted things too expensive to give away.

I got out of bed and dug down in the mound of clothes, and sure enough it was my gown, wadded and wrinkled. I pressed it to my nose and inhaled Tatum's department store perfume.

What was my dressing gown doing here? Well, that was obvious— Tatum had gotten it from my closet. There had to be an innocent explanation—she didn't own a robe, she didn't want to parade around in just a towel after her shower. Likely she would have asked if I'd been home, or she'd meant to tell me and forgotten. After all, how was she to know that it cost nine hundred dollars?

At least I'd found it before Benilda accidentally put it in the washing machine. It was so soft in my hands that I slipped it on, but then I took it off again before I got back in bed and turned out the lamp. I felt too dirty to wear it.

When I woke, light was coming through the shades and I was alone in the bed. Tatum either had never made it home or was passed out elsewhere in the apartment.

I listened for James and the kids—but the apartment was silent.

I replayed the night before, events coming back to me with sobering clarity. I—we—had left an unconscious girl bleeding and choking on her own vomit in the bathroom of a nightclub. I didn't know if she was all right, if she was even alive, if it would have made a difference if we'd called sooner. We were cowards, no better than hit-and-run drivers.

But I'd tried, hadn't I? I'd been calling—trying to call—for help. My first thought was for the girl, and I hadn't hesitated, hadn't thought about myself. It was Tatum who grabbed my phone from my hands, who dragged Brooke with her out the door. At least I'd stayed.

But I couldn't trust my memory of the details. The image of Tatum and Brooke kissing, Brooke's hands on Tatum's ass, Tatum's hands in Brooke's hair . . . that I remembered clearly. I don't know how long I would have watched, if the girl hadn't made those terrible sounds—and after that it was all confused. I remembered the cold, rubbery feel of the girl's legs, the red blood against her grayish skin, my knees on the hard tile.

But it wasn't *my* memory that I needed to worry about—would the bartender remember me? The dishwasher? And was it a crime to leave the scene of a—whatever had happened? If she really was fine, it probably wouldn't matter, but . . .

I grabbed my purse from the floor and took out my phone. It was nearly out of power, but I searched "Constellation" for the last twenty-four hours and found nothing other than a few Instagram photos. I tried "overdose," "accident," "hospital," but nothing surfaced.

The girl must be okay, or something would have turned up. I was blowing it all out of proportion. Right now she was probably lying on her couch watching Netflix and nursing a hangover. She might have a wicked bump on the head, but otherwise, good as new. No harm done.

Though James . . . James wouldn't see it that way.

He'd been an Eagle Scout; he'd done ROTC in high school. He had old-fashioned ideas about right and wrong, and nothing made him yell at the television more than news stories about bystanders letting terrible things happen while they did nothing. This impulse was one of the things I loved him for. Once, when we were driving in a snowstorm to see his parents before we had kids, he stopped and changed a tire for a car full of elderly women; I'd made him pull over at the next exit and we had sex in the backseat.

If he knew I'd left that girl lying there . . .

I couldn't stand thinking about it. I grabbed my robe and purse and last night's clothes and carried it all to my own bed, which James had left unmade. I threw on one of James's flannel shirts and a pair of leggings and headed for the kitchen. A note was propped up against the coffeemaker: *Took the kids to Sarabeth's.*

I couldn't believe I'd slept through their departure, but I'd only been asleep for—I checked the clock on the stove: six hours.

I waited for the coffee to brew, checking Tatum's and Brooke's

Instagram accounts, but there was nothing. I thought about calling Tatum, but the memory of her wresting away my phone stopped me. I went back to the guest room and stood in the doorway, staring at her mess, trying to understand how she could have just *left* that poor girl like that. There was a pile of magazines peeking out from under the bed, and I knelt to look through them: *Town & Country, Westport, Greenwich,* and a copy of *Vogue* dog-eared to an article about antiaging technology. None of it made much sense—as far as I knew she didn't even know anyone in Connecticut. I was putting the magazines back under the bed when the facing page in the copy of *Vogue* caught my eye.

The ad was for Bottega Veneta, the luxury Italian leather purveyor, and it featured a gaunt model reclining on an emerald green velvet chaise, wearing silk palazzo pants and an ivory leather moto jacket.

Tatum's jacket.

I stared at the photograph—had Tatum's jacket had that slightly asymmetrical burnished gold zipper, that stitching detail along the side pockets, the pale pink silk lining? A jacket like that easily cost five thousand dollars.

I returned the magazines to where I'd found them and arranged the bedcovers as I remembered, shoved messily to one side. Then I did a thorough search of the room, not even sure what I was looking for.

I poked through the clothes on the floor, the contents of the dresser, the closet. Among the unexpected items I discovered were oversize mirrored sunglasses and a diamond-studded charm in the shape of the letter *T,* a folded pair of ripped white jeans with the tags still attached, a boar-bristle hairbrush in a tiny black Barneys bag—and Henry's teddy bear shoved into the drawer of the nightstand.

I stared into Gruffy's beady plastic eyes, trying to make sense of what I'd discovered. I almost put him back in the drawer, but I couldn't do that to Henry, who had been devastated when he discovered Gruffy was missing. I'd give him his bear back—and then I'd figure out what the hell Tatum was up to.

I took a long, hot shower and carefully removed every trace of the makeup I'd worn the night before, then dressed in clean jeans and an old sleeveless cotton shirt. I grabbed the Tylenol and poured myself a tall glass of water and had barely sat down when I heard keys in the door and flinched. But it was just James and the kids.

"Hey, mamacita," James said, handing me a paper cup with the name *Angelina* written on the side in marker. Angelina had been James's nickname for me when we first started dating—he used to sing Dylan's "Farewell, Angelina" whenever I left his apartment. I gave him a weak smile.

"Mommy! Daddy made them put extra whipped cream!" Henry yelled, hopping toward me across the kitchen. The hopping was a new thing.

"Walking feet, walking feet!" I reminded him automatically. Mrs. Simon, the crotchety downstairs neighbor, called to complain whenever the kids got out of hand. "Into the bathroom, you two—wash your faces and hands."

"You're kind of a buzzkill, aren't you," James said, bending to kiss the top of my head. "Yikes. How much did you drink last night? I can still smell it on you."

I covered my mouth and pushed him away. "You don't need to tell me. I'm never drinking again."

"Where's Tatum?" he asked, going to the fridge for a Diet Coke.

He'd been polite to her since she moved in, but he stayed out of her way. I knew he didn't like having guests, even if he'd been the one to invite her. It had been the right thing to do and he'd done it, a thought that made me queasy.

I wondered what he'd have said if he'd seen her bolting out the back door of the club.

"She spent the night with a friend," I said lightly.

"Hey, what's up with Benilda?" Now he was rummaging through the pantry, trying to find his Doritos. I threw them out every time I found them, and then he'd just buy more at a bodega on Lexington Avenue and hide them behind the cans of soup and jars of tomato sauce. "How's her aunt doing?"

"Cousin," I corrected. "I mean, terrible, obviously. Sounds like it's nearing the end. And Benilda won't talk about it."

"Well, shit, Julia, can you blame her? I mean, Jesus, something like that happens to me, just shoot me, okay?"

Paige came running into the kitchen, Gruffy in her hand, Henry hot on her heels. "Look what I found! Is there a reward?"

"Gimme him!" Henry wailed, as Paige held Gruffy out of his reach. "He's mine!"

I snatched the bear out of Paige's hands and handed him to Henry, who clutched him to his chest and went running down the hall. Seconds later his bedroom door slammed.

"Paige," I scolded. "*I* found him, and you have no right to tease your brother that way. He wouldn't do that to you."

"He would *too!*"

"James . . ." I pleaded. "Can you deal with this?"

"Honey," he said patiently, "I kept them out of your hair all morning. I've got to head downtown. Didn't you say Benilda was coming today? She can help when she gets here."

"I guess," I sighed. Something occurred to me. "Hey—I thought you had to meet someone this morning."

Something flickered in his expression, and then was gone. "Meeting canceled. This guy, Christ, I ought to send him a bill, he's rescheduled so many times. I'll probably have to stay late tonight though, okay?"

"On a Saturday? Really?"

"Yes, *really*, if you want to keep the lights on and pay the cable bill."

There was an edge to his voice that I didn't like. I almost asked him why he was snapping at me, but I didn't feel like starting anything. He hadn't asked me about my night out; I wouldn't ask him what the hell was going on with him.

Maybe my mother was right—maybe James *was* having an affair.

"Whatever," I said and picked up the paper cup he'd brought me. Still hot. A man who cheated on his wife wouldn't walk two extra blocks to get her a latte, would he?

But then again, you wouldn't think a woman who cherished her family would be in a nightclub bathroom drunk and high at three in the morning as a stranger lay bleeding and unconscious and the cops came around the corner with lights and sirens on.

By the time Tatum rolled in, late that afternoon, I was exhausted. I'd cleaned up the lunch dishes, and then I let Paige watch a movie in my bed so Henry could watch *PAW Patrol* in the living room. Benilda was supposed to work a half day to make up for time she'd taken off during the week to go to Queens, but she'd sent a text around noon: **Sorry, not coming today Thelma too sick I will make up hours.**

Tatum rang the bell, even though she had her own key. When I opened the door, she was standing there looking even worse than I felt. There were purple circles under her eyes, and her hair hung limp around her face.

She was carrying an enormous bouquet of peonies, which I'd once told her were my favorite. They weren't in season and must have set her back quite a bit. She held them out to me without a word, still standing on the other side of the threshold.

"Tatum—"

"I'm so sorry about last night." The words came out in a rush. "I never should have had so much to drink, and the pills—the Molly— that was so stupid. I can't even remember how I got home. God, I'm so sorry we left you to deal with that girl."

I stared at her, thinking of Lindsay's words—*I just wouldn't leave her alone in the apartment with the good silver.* I remembered how she'd fought me for my phone, how she hadn't seemed at all confused in that moment.

As if reading my thoughts, she added, "I vaguely remember trying to call 911 . . . All I can say is I'm just so sorry."

"But you weren't calling 911," I said. "*I* was."

"But you couldn't dial the numbers," Tatum said. "I remember that. I remember thinking I could make the call faster, that we had to get someone to come help that poor girl."

She was right about that at least; I couldn't seem to get my fingers to work right. Was it possible that she really *was* trying to help, and that I'd confused her panic with something else? "But why did you leave? You and Brooke—you left me there."

"Julia," Tatum said, looking wounded, "I was trying to get you *out*. Don't you get it, I was trying to protect you. I know you and James don't need the extra scrutiny right now."

"What the hell is that supposed to mean?"

"Just—because of the investigation."

"*What* investigation?" I felt like screaming.

Now it was her turn to look confused. "I'm sorry, maybe I didn't—"

"Tell me," I demanded, taking the flowers from her and tossing them on the hall table, petals falling to the floor. "What investigation are you talking about?"

"I—I just heard them talking. Him and Garth, the first night in Bridgehampton. James was telling him about some federal agent looking into his project—it sounded like he was asking Garth for advice."

I clenched my fists to stop myself from strangling her. "I already *know* about that."

"You know about the investigation? The fraud thing?"

"Garth is an *intellectual property* lawyer, Tatum," I said in a withering tone. "There's no way James would ever ask him for legal advice. That would be like—like me asking you what I should wear."

It was a cruel thing to say, but I was pissed. I didn't care what she said, Tatum's excuse for leaving the club didn't hold water, and now she was trying to turn the tables on me.

I wasn't stupid—the business of construction in New York City was full of unscrupulous people, and sometimes James cut a corner or two. But if Tatum was trying to intimidate me, it wouldn't work: my husband would never do anything serious enough to warrant an investigation.

Still, the truth didn't matter if word got out that James was in trouble. A rumor like that metastasizes as it spreads, and it can happen to anyone. It's worst for the people with the most money and power, because so many people want to see them taken down; envy is dry tinder that needs very little to combust.

Tatum's expression was cool, and I regretted insulting her. I didn't know exactly how it had happened, but she'd gained the upper hand.

"Okay, look," I said in a softer tone. "This sort of thing happens all the time, Tatum. The inspections are complicated—there's like dozens of pages on every form, and it's really easy to miss details, and things fall through the cracks." I was making shit up for all I was worth. "And a firm the size of James's, it's impossible to cross every *t* and dot every *i*—it's like health inspections. You can take the best restaurant in the city, they're just as likely to get shut down as a greasy diner in Hell's Kitchen. The difference is that the best places know how to fix it, they throw money at the problem and push through the paperwork and it gets taken care of. That's how it is sometimes with these conversion projects. And with the historic nature of the building, there's that much more that can go wrong."

I was good at this, always able to talk myself into or out of anything. And the more I talked, the more credible it sounded, until I almost believed it myself. "So I'm sure it's nothing. Thanks for telling me, but you don't have to worry about it."

"Okay," Tatum said skeptically. "The important thing is I just wanted you to understand that I was trying to help you guys. Look, we would never have left that girl if she was really in trouble. But her eyes were open and that guy was calling 911—there wasn't anything more we could have done."

I stared at her, trying to figure out if she was telling the truth. I was almost positive the girl's eyes had still been closed. But it had been so chaotic. Maybe Tatum was right . . . maybe I would only have gotten in the way. There was hardly any room in that bathroom, and the paramedics would have cleared everyone out anyway.

I'd been planning to tell Tatum what I'd seen in the guest room: my robe on the floor, Gruffy in the drawer, the picture of the jacket, but things had changed. Tatum's concern about James didn't feel real—it felt like a warning.

We were still going to have that conversation, just not now, not with Tatum convinced she had something on me.

For now, I knew how to get ahead of the rumor about James. I'd casually mention the investigation to someone like Celeste Zapata or Poppy Blackhurst, women who couldn't keep anything to themselves if their lives depended on it, and I'd laugh and say something about how James's new office manager actually panicked but that it was nothing, so funny to think of James involved with something like that—Boy Scout James, the guy who sat in the dunk tank at the school carnival. Even if people didn't entirely believe it, the story would go around and people would see the investigation for what it was—an unavoidable cost of success.

"So thanks for the flowers," I said. "I'm pretty tired, so can we—"

The front door opened again. James was always bringing work home; he'd probably forgotten some papers or something.

But it wasn't James. Benilda came walking into the kitchen like a zombie, her eyes huge and red. She looked around as though she didn't know where she was or how she got there. Her gaze landed on me and her face crumpled.

"Thelma died."

CHAPTER 17

Later, I'd think about the fact that Benilda came straight from the subway to the apartment, that I was the person she turned to in her grief. After she found her cousin unresponsive in bed, after she called the paramedics and the undertaker and all of her cousin's family, after she worked out the most pressing details with Thelma's son and his wife and looked after their children so they could have some time alone with their grief, Benilda had gotten on the express train back to Manhattan like any other workday.

I wish I could do it over again. Benilda had never been emotional, she didn't care for expressions of affection from anyone but the children, and so I was brisk with her. Of course I asked how we could help and told her to take as much time as she needed, but I didn't hug her or take her hand or even offer her a tissue, not that she cried—she just sat in the kitchen chair letting her coffee get cold, barely responding when I asked her questions, and then she stood abruptly and picked up her purse.

"I will call you," she said, and I repeated that she should take her time. I followed her to the door and held it for her and watched her walk down the hall. At the elevator, she stared straight ahead, clutching the handles of her purse as though someone was trying to take it from her.

Tatum had taken the children to Paige's room and kept them busy while I dealt with Benilda. Since I assumed Benilda would be gone for at least a week, I had incentive to keep things civil with Tatum.

I went to Paige's room, where Tatum was on her knees, zipping up the dress that Paige had worn for Easter, a yellow organdy Bonpoint with a smocked bodice and a wide sash. On the floor, three other dresses lay in a heap. Henry was playing with his toy cars.

"Oh, hi," Tatum said brightly, as though we hadn't argued. "We were just trying things on."

"Tatum's going to teach me the princess walk!" Paige said excitedly.

"How fun," I said.

"Is everything all right?" Tatum asked.

"Yes. Benilda just left." It occurred to me that I would still have to explain to the children what had happened. All we'd told them was that Benilda's cousin was sick. "Umm . . . listen, kids, I need to talk to Tatum for a bit, okay?"

"But she was going to show me the princess walk!"

"She can do that in a few minutes," I said firmly.

The two of us went to the kitchen. "So," I said, "just to wrap up. Let's put last night behind us."

Tatum nodded. "Absolutely. I know I could have handled things better."

"And I'm sure I don't need to say it, but this has to stay between us. I mean . . . I assume Brooke understands that?"

"God, yes. And speaking of Brooke—look, I should have told you, before. About us."

"Your personal life is none of my business," I said stiffly.

"No, no, it's just—well, it's kind of new. I mean, we've been hanging out for a while, but it's only recently that we . . ." She trailed off.

"Tatum," I said. "I don't care who you date."

"Stop saying that," Tatum pleaded. "You're my *friend*. You're *important* to me. That's why I feel bad about not saying anything. It's just, we never really talked about, um . . . I wasn't sure how you'd feel about it. About me being bi, I mean."

"I'm *totally* fine with that," I said, affronted that she'd even wonder. "I have tons of gay friends. Seriously, James and I have no judgment."

"I've mostly been with men. Actually, before Brooke, I was only ever with a girl one other time."

"Huh." Despite everything that had happened, I couldn't help wondering what Brooke was like. All that savage energy—the raw, almost violent edge to the way she behaved when she taught—I wondered if she was like that in bed. I thought of those tattoos on her arms, her back; I imagined them flexing and rippling as she writhed in a tangle of sheets.

I'd made out with girls myself in college. I think I knew even when I was doing it that it had little to do with desire; it was just another ineffectual stab at my parents, another pointless rebellion. But last night was nothing like my experimentation; there was a shocking hunger in their kiss, in the way they seemed to forget I was there as Brooke ground against Tatum. I hadn't been able to look away.

Was it possible that Tatum was actually in *love* with Brooke? Brooke was dark energy, venomous and raging; Tatum was . . . I once would have said innocent. Vulnerable, even. Now, I wasn't so sure.

"So, is this serious?"

"Julia!" Tatum said, blushing. "I just told you we barely began dating."

"But you like her."

"I do. I really do." She seemed to relax in her chair, sipping at her coffee. "It's funny—I was the one who kissed her first. I didn't even know I was going to do it. We'd gone out for tea after her class one day and ended up talking for like two hours. And then we walked to the subway, and the downtown trains were delayed, and we talked some more, and then finally her train was coming and I— I just kissed her. On the lips, like this." She tapped her fingers to her lips, a gentle brush. "But then she grabbed me and kissed back, like, *really* kissed me, and then she got on the train and I was standing there like, what just happened? But then a minute later I got a text from her. And it was only a question mark. And I texted back— I mean, I still can't believe I did this. It's so not me. But I texted back 'yes' in all caps and then she texted 'stay where you are.' She got off at the next stop and ran all the way back."

"That's pretty romantic," I said—though I was imagining the pulsing heat of that kiss. "How long ago was that?"

"Only a couple of weeks. That's why—I mean, I *would* have told you, eventually. I guess also I kind of wanted to see if it's, you know, real. If it's turning into something, I mean."

I remember how they'd looked that day at Flame, bent over the laptop. They were about the same size, though Brooke was lean, with pronounced hip bones and rock-hard biceps and calves, while Tatum had a softness to her, a roundedness that no amount of working out would erase. When you saw them together, the contrast somehow made them both even more striking—a girl-on-girl fantasy.

"Are you trying to keep it a secret at work?"

"Sort of," Tatum said. "At least for now. I mean, there's no policy about people dating or anything, but the last thing we want is everyone talking about it. God," she added. "Listen to me! For all I know, this will be over next week."

"But you don't want it to be."

"I—I'm not sure. But I really like her. She's not like anyone else."

"Well, then, I'll keep my fingers crossed that it works out."

"Thank you, Julia. But I'm still sorry for the way we . . . you know, right in front of you. Honestly, it was the Molly." She seemed to remember something. "Hey, were *you* okay? I mean, with the Molly and everything?"

For some reason, I didn't want to admit that I hadn't taken the little pill Brooke gave me, didn't want to add to the prudish feeling I had when we were all together. "Sure. I probably could have done without that last round of drinks, but yeah."

"I know. I couldn't even get out of bed until noon—I was afraid I'd hurl."

"Speaking of which," I said, "I need to eat something. And the kids are going to need dinner."

"I'll help!"

I'd actually been trying to end the conversation, to hint that it would be best if we gave each other some space, but Tatum was back to her old self. She rooted through the refrigerator and announced she was going to make quesadillas, and while she grated cheese and scooped salsa into a bowl, I poured myself a glass of wine.

I had another with dinner, and then I told the kids to pick a movie.

"I want *Beauty and the Beast*!" Paige said. That was no surprise— Belle wore a yellow dress like the one she'd been trying on.

"Oh my God, I *love* Disney!" Tatum beamed. "I dressed up as Snow White for Halloween three years in a row."

Of course she did. Of all the princesses, leave it to Tatum to pick the fairest of them all.

Benilda came back after a week, glum and uncommunicative. I was a little put out that she hadn't let me know the funeral arrangements, even if it saved me a trip to Queens. At the very least I would have sent flowers. Though she was back to her regular schedule, Benilda was spending her free time with Thelma's son and his family, who had apparently decided to take over Thelma's lease, and was frequently late, or asked to leave early.

I'd been able to tack on an extra session at the camp, and the kids came home tired and happy most days, their hair bleached by the sun and their rooms overflowing with nature souvenirs and craft projects.

Nothing else went missing around the house, and my uneasiness receded. I went through Tatum's things from time to time when she was out, and didn't find anything suspicious. She even bought me little gifts—a Flame tank top, a candle—and asked for help refining her style. The skimpy H&M miniskirts and polyester tops gave way to classic pieces that she picked up at consignment shops. For teaching, she still wore the Lululemon clothes I'd bought her, but she started wearing Flame gear in her Instagram photos, tank tops and sweatshirts and tote bags and baseball caps.

As Tatum's look had evolved over the summer, so had her social media. Her former aversion to technology had given way to a veritable obsession. She got all of her riders to follow her on Instagram and asked them to comment and repost, and her likes and follower numbers shot up, quickly surpassing those of all the other teachers. She posted on Facebook and Twitter and learned to edit and enhance her photos and create graphics so that the look and feel of her posts were consistent across platforms, something I would have encouraged her to do if she'd still been asking me for advice. She still took notes after every class she taught and memorized the names of every newcomer and hung around even when she wasn't teaching so that she could rub elbows with gym members she hadn't already won over. She cultivated an intimacy with everyone that I almost couldn't distinguish from the real thing, and even without the benefit of a single one of my friends, her classes began filling up.

As her photo-editing skills grew, she started posting carefully curated shots taken all over the city. A photo of her in a white cotton sundress drinking wine on the Great Lawn with the city skyline behind her got over a thousand likes. Another of her and Brooke doing handstands in front of Flame got even more.

I'd been posting a lot myself, my best shots from Flame and my reservoir runs. I never mentioned my weight loss directly, but I made sure it was obvious, and the comments and likes piled up. Lindsay wasn't much of an Instagram user, but Grace liked nearly all of my posts, and I did the same for hers, though her artful photos of her and her sisters and attractive people I didn't know left me feeling increasingly disconnected from her. Despite trying to call every week or so, we'd only managed to speak a handful of times since the beginning of summer, and she was always having to cut our conversations short to handle some family drama or crisis with the kids and their cousins. Lindsay, too, would let days and even weeks go by without calling or texting. I was starting to wonder if it was worth it—despite all my efforts to stay in touch, we seemed to be drifting further and further apart.

I increased my efforts to keep up with my other friends, commenting on their posts and scheduling lunch or drinks when they were in town, but often plans got canceled at the last minute. I texted so much that my thumbs hurt, but the effusive, exclamation-point-ridden stream of chatter was no substitute for real conversation.

I channeled my loneliness and insecurity into my workouts. Since Ken had noticed Tatum's popularity and given her a regular schedule, and with Benilda back, I was able to spin every day. I always rode the instructor bike now; I talked to Tatum after class about what had worked and what hadn't. We talked more at Flame than we did at home. My weight loss had reached twenty-three pounds—I'd gone right past my goal, and my calves and thighs and arms and butt were toned and muscular, my stomach nearly flat. I looked better than I had in years.

On a Thursday afternoon in late August, I ran into Janet Erikson at the supermarket.

"You're back from your cross-country trip!" I said. "How was it?"

After one of her aggressive hugs, she started telling me how wonderful it had been. National Parks, quirky roadside diners, fishing in Montana, camping in the desert, blah blah blah. I made the appropriate noises, thinking that maybe James should have married someone like Janet instead of me.

"Listen, you should come to dinner tomorrow night," she said, when she was done telling me about their travels. "We're having people over for a potluck."

Damn, she was persistent. I might be desperate for company, but not if it meant hanging out with her weird hippie friends. "Thanks, but Friday's family night. James hardly ever gets home in time for dinner during the week."

"Absolutely," Janet said. "Family time is so important."

Then her mouth twisted and she put her hand on my shoulder. "Hey, I've been meaning to say something to you. But . . . I didn't know how to bring it up, so maybe running into you was—oh, listen to me beating around the bush."

Great, I thought. *Here it comes.*

"I just wanted you to know that Terry and I don't believe James would ever force elderly people out of their homes. I know this stuff gets misreported all the time, everyone's always looking for a story and, well . . . we firmly support smart urban redevelopment and mixed-income housing, and of course that doesn't happen without disruption. So I hope you won't let all the talk get you down, is all I'm trying to say."

I felt the blood drain from my face. Where the hell had this come from? "I'm not sure I even know what you're talking about," I said, my jaw aching from smiling.

"Oh, sweetie, it's *me* you're talking to," Janet said. She grabbed my hand and squeezed it. "I don't give a shit about gossip, but some of those vultures . . ."

I swallowed. "Do you mind me asking . . ."

Her expression was pained. "Well, that's what I thought was so . . . I mean, isn't Lindsay Parker one of your closest friends?"

The look in my eyes must have signaled my shock. "I was visiting my cousin last weekend in East Hampton and I ran into Lindsay when we were out to dinner," Janet went on. "She'd been drinking, and . . . anyway, I just thought she should be talking *to* you, not *about* you. That's what we always tell Willa—we don't want her affected by this toxic frenemy culture."

"No, no, I'm glad you told me." Now that I knew, I couldn't back away fast enough. As clueless as Janet was most of the time, she seemed to have a weird sixth sense when it came to me. "Lindsay overheard Garth and James talking, she probably just didn't understand. I mean, Mercer used to be a nursing home, but it was vacant when James bought it. So anything that happened before that—and you're right, James *cares* about people. He really does."

To my mortification, I had started to cry. This time when Janet hugged me, she was gentle, rubbing my back and making *tsk*ing sounds.

"You know, ever since I first met you I knew you were special," she said. "You've got a big heart. Hang on to that—as long as you stay true to yourself, nothing else matters."

I extricated myself from Janet and finished my shopping, but I couldn't stop thinking about the conversation. The initial shock of Lindsay's betrayal had given way to anxiety over the practical implications. Drunk or not, she was spreading rumors, which meant the story wasn't going away. I'd never brought the investigation up with

James—I'd meant to, but as the days passed and things seemed to calm down with Mercer, it was easier just to assume that everything was fine. And maybe it was, but I still needed to find out exactly what was going on before everyone came back to town in a couple weeks—because if they sensed any weakness in my denial of the rumors, they would pounce.

I had to be strategic, though. Putting James on the defensive would only lead to a fight, so I decided to try one of my most reliable old tricks. It amazed me that James fell for it every time, but when I delivered the medicine with a spoonful of sugar, I could often get him to do what I wanted while thinking it was his idea all along.

Dressing for James wasn't exactly rocket science: I chose a silky top that made my boobs look enormous and the tight jeans I'd bought to replace the ones that were now way too big. By the time he got home I was June freaking Cleaver, meeting him at the door with a kiss while a chicken roasted in the oven.

The kids had picked up on the special effort I was making and had been waiting excitedly for James to get home. "Daddy!" they yelled, tackling him.

"You're my favorite ever," Henry said, wrapping his arms around James's legs.

"Can I go to the Cardi B concert with Charlotte?" Paige asked, tugging his arm. Meanwhile I posed in the kitchen like a fifties pinup, brandishing the beer I'd poured for him.

"I've got something special for you," I purred.

It was easy, right up to the point I finished cleaning the kitchen and found James in bed with his laptop.

"Just answering a couple emails," he said, winking, "and then I'll be happy to pay the fine."

I felt a little guilty for hoodwinking him with wifely foreplay. I took the laptop from him and set it on the bedside table.

"James," I said, sitting cross-legged on the bed so I could look at him while we talked. "I want to talk to you about something. I've been hearing things."

"Oh?"

"When we were staying with the Parkers, Lindsay told me she

overheard you and Garth talking about the feds investigating you. Tatum heard it too. And now apparently Lindsay's telling people you forced people out of the nursing home with nowhere to go?" I had to work hard to keep my tone calm. "It's made it all the way to Janet Erikson, which, I shouldn't have to tell you, means *everyone* knows."

"Jules." The change in James was instant. He straightened up and took my hands, suddenly serious. "Anything she overheard—that was months ago."

"And maybe I should have talked to you then. I just, you were under so much stress, but lately you've seemed better, and I thought—I hoped, maybe that meant whatever was going on was taken care of. Seriously, all I'm looking for is for you to tell me that. Look me in the eye and tell me that there's nothing to worry about with Mercer House, and I won't bother you about it anymore."

But he didn't. Instead, he let go of my hands and blew out a frustrated breath. "In the first place, I don't know where you're getting this—"

"I just told you," I interrupted. "Lindsay, Tatum, Janet—but it all goes back to what you apparently told Garth. I mean, you didn't even tell *me*!"

Uh-oh, the look in his eyes telegraphed. "It's not a big deal. Seriously. Yes, someone from the feds came to talk to me, okay, but I've worked with them before, don't you remember those protests in Dumbo? Or that industrial conversion thing that had the city council shitting their pants?"

"Okay, well, then why didn't you tell me about it? If it was no big deal. I mean, are you being sued or something?"

"No!" James's chuckle sounded about as genuine as one of Paige's apologies. "Look. The feds thing was a dead end, and Lindsay— probably what happened is she heard me complaining about the community organizer wackos. Yeah, they're upset, but their complaint is against the original operator, who by the way has filed for bankruptcy and, I mean I didn't have anything to do with that. The deal was clean, Stewart was on it every step of the way. I'm sorry you have to put up with the bullshit, but people are going to run

their mouths no matter what you do. You just have to learn to ignore them, honey."

Easy for him to say. James had a black belt in ignoring what other
people thought, but he wouldn't last a week in my shoes. "I can't
just ignore them! These are my *friends,* James, the people I see every
day. Your children's friends' *parents.* I don't have a job like you, I
can't just shut the door to my office and tell everyone else to go to
hell!"

"Well, maybe that's the problem," James shot back. "If you *did*
have a job, or even a goddamn hobby, maybe you wouldn't go
around acting like any of this shit matters."

"You're saying what I do doesn't matter?" I knew I should stop,
but I couldn't. "I'm sorry if you think our children's happiness
doesn't matter. Or the volunteer work I do. Or the opinions of the
people I care about. Yeah, maybe I should get an eighty-hour-a-
week job too—we'll just tell the whole world to fuck off, and Benilda can home-school the kids."

"What happened to you?" James said, suddenly deadly calm,
looking at me like he'd never seen me before. "No, seriously, J.
What the hell happened to what you always said you wanted?"

I squeezed my eyes shut, willing him to stop. I knew where he was
headed, and it was going to hurt.

"When we met, you didn't care at all about this stuff. You said
you never wanted to turn into your mother. You said you wanted to
live in an old farmhouse in Vermont, remember that? That our kids
would grow up knowing how to fish and garden and we'd raise lla-
mas and I'd play guitar and you'd write all my songs?"

"That was . . ." So long ago. Before everything changed. And I
had never been serious, obviously. It wasn't fair for him to even
bring it up.

"I've put up with this for nine years, Jules. I've put on the monkey
suit and kissed ass at fundraisers for things I don't even believe in.
I've watched those teachers try to beat every last bit of independence
out of our kids. I never said a word when you spent more on a fucking purse than my mom spends on herself in a year. I thought it was
all worth it because it made you happy. Except you don't seem very

happy to me, not anymore, and now I'm wondering what the hell we're doing to each other."

"James, I—"

"Maybe you should think about what you really want," he said, getting out of bed and picking his jeans up off the floor where he'd dropped them. "Because I don't work as hard as I do to come home to a wife who doesn't believe in me."

Neither of us said anything as he got dressed and grabbed his wallet from the dresser. I waited to cry until he'd closed the bedroom door behind him.

CHAPTER 18

School was starting in less than two weeks. Tatum had posted a photo of me on the instructor bike holding five-pound weights, my biceps sheened with sweat, and after I reposted it and two dozen women from Graylon commented, including Coco Choi, who wrote **you look like a #GODDESS** 💪 I had an inspiration: I'd host a fundraiser at Flame for Tremont Academy, Graylon's sister school in the Bronx, to coincide with the annual school supply drive. Not only would all my friends come, but with the blessing of the PTA board, so would everyone else. We'd charge $250 per person and hold it after drop-off the second week of school and do gift bags and a raffle, and I knew Ken would be willing to donate the studio time in exchange for the publicity.

I'd have Tatum teach the class, but I'd script it, with lots of references to all those needy kids at Tremont, and I'd ride on the instructor bike and afterward we would serve iced coffee and pressed juice and scones made from ancient grains. I'd wear my new color-block Michi leggings and I'd knot the tank top high enough to reveal my toned midriff. I was almost delirious with anticipation.

I approached Tatum with the idea before talking to Ken. "You don't think Brooke will mind, do you? I mean, you've got as many classes as she does now, and—"

"Brooke doesn't care," Tatum said. "She's not really competitive that way. And even if they cut her schedule, it's not like she needs the money. Her parents pay for her apartment. And they still give her an allowance."

Lots of my friends from high school had stayed on their parents' dole until they got married—but that largesse came with certain expectations: make sure that your behavior reflects well on the family, show up when invited to dinner, date appropriate men, comport yourself with dignity—none of which Brooke bothered to do. If I'd so much as gotten a belly ring in my twenties, I'm sure that my "just because" checks from my mother would have dried up. Given that the Timmses led an especially public life, one would think that Brooke's behavior was a concern, if not an outright embarrassment.

"They're not expecting her to"—I searched for the right words— "work toward some larger goal?"

"She's been thinking of law school. She's going to take the LSAT."

Not the answer I expected—but maybe I'd underestimated her.

I scheduled the fundraiser for Monday morning of the second week of school and got the PTA to email an announcement. Within a few hours, the entire fundraiser had sold out and we'd raised over twelve thousand dollars for Tremont, with promises of more from the raffle and day-of donations.

Lindsay came home from the Hamptons the Wednesday before school started, and I invited her over for a drink on Thursday. I was still irritated that she'd been spreading the rumor about James, but I was also so relieved to have things back to normal that I vowed to put it behind me. James put the kids to bed while Lindsay and I drank the Pouilly-Fuissé that Garth had sent with her, and we talked about the new uniform standards and a rumor going around that one of the school counselors's partners had left him for his personal trainer and, of course, Lindsay's concerns that Audrey wasn't being challenged enough academically. Nothing seemed to have changed after all, to my great relief; I decided my isolation had made me paranoid.

I didn't bring up what Janet had told me, because in retrospect I decided I was making too much of it. Not that people weren't talking about James, but my guess was that Janet had overheard only part of the conversation, and that it was someone else who'd floated the stuff about the tenants after hearing about the investigation. Besides, I wasn't naïve enough to think any of us could be counted on to keep secrets. After all, I had let it slip to a few people when Lindsay had CoolSculpting on her stomach last year.

When Lindsay looked at her watch and said she needed to get going, I asked if there was anything I should be doing for TomorrowMakers, mostly to make sure she hadn't forgotten our conversation about me being assistant chair.

"No, there's not a lot we can do until after this year's gala is over. Oh, by the way, the development director wanted me to thank you for your donation—she's giving you the table next to mine, up front."

That was the least she could do, considering I'd included a twenty-thousand-dollar check with my table reservation for the gala, which was still almost two months away.

"We should talk about who we want at our tables," I said. Divvying up our friends posed the challenge of navigating various feuds and alliances, but it also provided an opportunity to bestow favors, especially since TomorrowMakers had become such a popular event on the gala circuit. A seat at the front of the room was a perk I could trade on later.

"Sure—maybe once we get through the first week of school? I'm swamped with all the kids' forms and supply lists and I still need to take them for their physicals and Pritchard's speech therapist just took a job in Cleveland so I've got to find a new one."

"It never ends, does it?" I said as I walked her to the door. She gave me a quick hug, and I returned to the living room to finish off the last of the wine.

I had called Grace too, but she said she was too busy unpacking and getting everyone settled to meet up before school started. I was almost relieved; something was bothering me and I hadn't figured out how to bring it up with her yet.

Despite my misgivings about her family's rustic seaside compound, I'd been so starved for company that I'd decided to take the kids down to Cape Charles for a week after all—but the invitation never materialized despite some not-very-subtle hinting on my part.

And then in late August I saw on Instagram that Shayla Otedola was visiting with her kids. Grace posted photos of the two of them at the ice cream stand and on the boat and with the kids at the beach and out for dinner in their sundresses and strappy sandals. I hadn't even known they were friends—but Shayla was a former model and her husband's brother had a minor role in a Netflix series that had led to a bigger part in an upcoming movie. Over the summer Shayla had posted pictures of her and Dayo and his brother on set and out to dinner with Chris Pine and B. J. Novak and their girlfriends.

My eyelid twitched when I saw that. I couldn't help feeling like Grace had dumped me for Shayla. I was both irritated and jealous, and though I wasn't proud of it, I was counting on my new and improved appearance and the Flame fundraiser to remind Grace of the value of our friendship.

The three of us made plans to get coffee after drop-off the first day, and I wore a halter-top romper that I'd bought specifically to debut my new body. Planting myself firmly in the middle of the group of moms and kids waiting for the Graylon doors to open, I greeted everyone I hadn't seen since June and basked in their thinly disguised envy. Penelope Epstein told me she hoped I'd be crushed to death under a barbell, and Emery Souza pointedly said nothing at all about my appearance and instead asked in a loud voice, "Where were you all summer again?"

Once Grace and Lindsay and I walked to our favorite coffee shop and were seated at a table with our skim lattes, Lindsay brought up the fundraiser.

"Gigi's telling people that PTA officers should have gotten priority," she said. "It sold out before she could sign up. You might want to talk to her—you know how she gets."

"I held back a couple of bikes for exactly that reason," I said. "I'll call her."

"And you're sure Tatum can handle it?" Lindsay asked. "I mean, has she ever even done anything like this before? Does she understand who she's dealing with?"

"She's an amazing teacher," I said, a little defensively. "She's really good in the studio. Wait until you see her."

"I still can't believe you're letting her stay with you," Grace said.

"It's only until she moves into her new place. I mean, come on—her landlord practically *raped* her."

"So she says," Lindsay said ominously. I wanted to punch her. "You should have seen her, Gracie—trying to talk to all my mother's friends in this dress Julia loaned her that barely covered her lady bits."

"Yeah, but that photo of her yesterday, the one with some girl who looks like a heroin addict—it got two thousand likes," Grace said. "She's got followers all over the world."

"Tatum's gotten really good at Instagram," I said, pleased that Grace had noticed. "She uses all these apps to edit her posts and adds quotes she gets from Pinterest—people love those. There was one she put on Facebook that got shared almost nine hundred times. Not exactly viral, but—"

"But close enough," Grace said shrewdly. "So I guess she's your new Jakobine."

"I have to hand it to you, Julia," Lindsay said. "When you first brought her to my house, I figured she would have stolen your identity and gone back to Missouri by now."

"Let's hope she can pull it off next week," Grace said, "or they'll eat her alive—and you along with her."

I forced a smile and said, "The only thing that matters is that it's for a good cause."

CHAPTER 19

When I arrived at Flame the morning of the fundraiser, Tatum was already there, wearing the tank top I'd designed for the event over Cushnie et Ochs leggings with intricate detailing along the sides. There was no way she found those leggings in a consignment store—Bergdorf's was completely sold out. Tatum had come a long way in the few short months since I'd dressed her for the Hamptons; she'd been studying the magazines I'd given her like a law school grad preparing for the bar exam. It was almost shocking, how quickly she'd gone from pliant acolyte to this newly confident version of herself—unless you knew her like I did, unless you'd seen the hunger in her eyes when she talked about the Upper East Side, and the raw determination on her face when she thought no one was watching.

I took my seat at the table Ken had set up in the hall outside the spin studio. A second table held the silent auction items, the usual stuff plus a Flame gift basket with logo gear and private training sessions and a custom playlist to be created by Tatum, though we both knew I'd be the one doing it. Paz was already there, squaring up the stack of donation forms, replacing caps on the pens. Paz, despite her peace-to-the-people vibe, was apparently a control freak.

"It's so nice of you to help out," I said, taking my clipboard from my bag, "but it's really not necessary. I need to talk to everyone as they arrive anyway to check them off the list."

"I can check them off," Paz said. "And you can just—" She waved her hand vaguely.

I wasn't getting rid of her, which was interesting, because why would she be here if there wasn't something in it for her? Tatum had once told me that Paz wanted to teach—maybe she was trying to raise her profile. Everyone had an angle, and with the new bonus structure Ken had instituted, it was possible to make real money if you could fill your classes.

I kept the clipboard to myself, and as people began to arrive, I greeted them warmly and said things like "Paz, can you give Greta a donation form so we can move the line along?" just to make her twitch. Many of the moms from the lower grades were there, and I made sure to introduce myself to the few I didn't know. I directed women to the changing room and lockers, to the cart laden with refreshments, to the bike assignment chart I'd made. (I'd had some fun with that, though I told people it was random. I'm sure no one believed me.)

Lindsay and Grace were among the last to arrive. They were holding paper coffee cups, and I felt an unpleasant chill, knowing they'd gone to Starbucks together.

The music started inside the studio, and I twisted in my chair to see Tatum bound up onto the podium, gleefully clapping her hands. "Look at all of you beautiful women!" she exclaimed, the mike carrying her voice to every corner of the room, encouraging and cheerful and welcoming. "We're here to do some good in the world, am I right?—and we're going to take that gorgeous generosity and save just a little of it for ourselves, because we need to turn some kindness inward if we're going to be strong for all of those who depend on us."

There was a smattering of applause, murmurs of appreciation. Two women I recognized from school, mothers of high school students, arrived apologizing for being late, and after I checked them off I decided that the few names left were probably no-shows. I stripped off my sweatshirt and entered the studio, only to see Vix Ballmer standing next to Tatum on the podium.

"I'm sure many of you already know Vix," Tatum was saying. "She came to my class for the first time last week, and she's a natural. I'd like you all to give her a hand for being brave enough to help out!"

Cheers went up, along with a few whistles and hoots. Everyone knew Vix; her daughters were the fourth generation in her family to attend Graylon, and her in-laws had donated the money for the Ballmer Science Pavilion in the nineties. She was a good sport, waving and blowing a kiss.

"I'm not here for my own workout today," Tatum said when the cheers died down. "My job is to make the next forty-five minutes the most rewarding part of your day. And to help me do that, Vix is going to ride my bike for me so I can be on the floor coaching you."

And then Vix mounted the bike—*my* bike—while my clever little acolyte looked on. Tatum had changed the plan without telling me, giving away the prize I'd worked so hard to earn. As Vix pushed her feet into the pedals, Tatum gazed serenely around the room, making eye contact with everyone.

Except for me.

"This is such a great cause! Tell you what, Vix, I'm going to throw in a personal training session with me, to thank you for helping out today. And for the rest of you, if you enjoy your workout today and want to take it to the next level, I'm happy to talk to you about setting up your own private spin sessions!"

More cheers, as I realized my mistake. Tatum hadn't chosen Vix Ballmer randomly. She'd never planned to have me ride up front at the fundraiser. She'd done her research, and I had to hand it to her, she'd picked the best-connected woman in the room. Vix's family had quietly reigned at the top of Manhattan society for almost a century, her husband was rumored to be considering a mayoral run, and her teenage daughters had started their own foundation to raise money for refugee children.

Tatum turned up the music, and the warm-up song came on, and it was Earth, Wind & Fire's "Dancing in September" . . . crafty girl, I couldn't have done better myself. She led everyone in an easy jog as the wheels hummed and the ladies moved happily to the beat.

"Our hearts were ringing," Tatum sang along with her eyes closed, her arms stretched high over her head, her ponytail cascading down her back.

"In the key that our souls were singing!" The women surrounding me picked up the song, singing for the pleasure of it, for the joy of it, as I made my way unnoticed and unremarked to an empty bike near the back.

Afterward, I fielded questions about Tatum's class times and private sessions while people bid on the auction items and wrote donation checks and helped themselves to juice and scones. Paz was nowhere to be seen, and I quickly ran out of Flame brochures, and instead of basking in my triumph I might as well have been a towel girl who'd gotten called in to help. By the time the crowd thinned, Grace and Lindsay were gone, as was everyone else except for a handful of women still talking to Tatum.

I almost went back inside the studio and joined them, but I could see how it would go, Tatum ignoring me while everyone politely made room for me in the circle without taking their eyes off her, waiting their turn to tell her she was amazing, they never knew spin could be so much fun, she had such an encouraging way about her, and how could they get on her waiting list for private lessons?

I stuffed the stack of checks into my bag and pulled on my Flame sweatshirt. I took a last glance at the used cups and plates, the chart with the bike in front highlighted in yellow because it was supposed to have been *mine*—and then I left.

CHAPTER 20

As the texts rolled in that afternoon, I felt better. Everyone agreed the event was a huge success, and the PTA president sent me an email thanking me and copying Zarine Parekh and the entire board. Grace came running up to me at pickup to say she'd had the best time and she'd already signed up at Flame and asked if I could go with her to one of Tatum's classes.

"I don't know what Lindsay was talking about," she said. "She's amazing. Gorgeous too, and did you see those leggings?"

"Yeah, you really pulled it off," Lindsay said, walking into the conversation with her phone at her ear. "No, no, I wasn't talking to you. See you tonight, okay? Gotta go."

She stuffed the phone into her bag. "Garth seriously couldn't figure out how to make his colonoscopy appointment online and I had to talk him through it. I'm amazed they let him have a computer. Anyway, Julia, I have to hand it to you—she's a whole different person in the studio, and spinning isn't as boring as I expected it to be. I've got myself halfway talked into joining."

"You *have* to!" Grace said. "I mean, look at Julia—three months working with Tatum and she's got a body like a Cowboys cheerleader. And think how fun it would be to take classes together!"

Relief flooded through me. I'd overreacted—I should have given my friends the benefit of the doubt. Of course they were on my side; of course they wanted me to succeed. It seemed ridiculous now, the insecurity I'd allowed to grow unchecked, the jealousy and second-guessing. It was worse than being in eighth grade all over again.

There had been days—as far back as our move uptown, but more frequently in recent years—when I wondered if it had all been a huge mistake. It was never James's dream to live up here or move in these circles. My children could have thrived anywhere. It was only I who needed the rush that came from being surrounded by wealth and society, who sought affirmation from women who were often too self-involved to give it.

But when things were working—when the *Town & Country* photographer took our photo at a charity event or a wealthy heiress asked me for an introduction to Jakobine—the high was like nothing else, a balm for every hurt I'd ever endured, confirmation of my value as a human being. I'd gotten hooked on it; I couldn't go without it. The lines between friendship and social commerce blurred until I couldn't tell the difference—all I knew was that I needed more and more just to get through the day.

I had a sudden brainstorm, an idea that would both reward my friends for their support and ensure that it continued. I would prove to them how much they meant to me, and remind them of what I could offer in return.

"Hey, Lindsay, your birthday's coming up," I said.

"Not again," she groaned. "Can't we skip it this year?"

"Absolutely not!" Grace said. "It's a tradition. Besides, I can't miss the four months of the year that you're a whole year older than me."

"It doesn't work that way," Lindsay said, rolling her eyes. "And besides, we'll both always be five years older than Julia."

"Or six, in your case," Grace teased.

"You guys can stop bickering, because I'm going to handle the whole thing this year," I said. "It's going to be a surprise. Your birthday's on a Sunday, so how about we do the Friday before?"

"Are you serious?" Lindsay asked in surprise. "I mean, it's not even a significant number. Forty-one seems like a good one to skip."

"I, uh . . . just wanted to do something nice since I barely got to see you all summer," I improvised. It hadn't occurred to me that she might not welcome the attention.

"Well, why not?" Lindsay said. "It's not like Garth is going to plan anything."

"I'll put it on my calendar," Grace said. "It'll be fun. Let me know if you want help."

By the time I got home with the kids, I'd convinced myself that everything was going to be fine, that I could take back control of my project and count on my friends' support. All I had to do was manage Tatum better, and remind her where she fit into my plan—and that just as I had built her up, I could tear her down. Sure, she was feeling full of herself after the fundraiser—but there were lots of ways to tarnish the reputation she was just beginning to build, vulnerabilities that she wasn't even aware of. And as soon as she came home, I was going to lay them all out in a way she was sure to understand.

And then I would ask—no, *tell* her that I needed a favor: a private session just for me and Grace and Lindsay. It would be my birthday gift to Lindsay, but it was intended for Grace too, a reminder that I was still the glue that held us all together.

Grace might have her exclusive new club, Lindsay had the gala, but I was the one who'd discovered Flame and Tatum and made them what they were. Without me, they would be one more failing little health club and a cocktail waitress who moonlighted as a personal trainer.

But Tatum didn't come home that day—she didn't even text. The next morning, she wandered in still wearing the tank top from the fundraiser, her face scrubbed clean and her hair up in a messy bun, and went straight to her room, closing the door behind her. I waited until she came into the kitchen to get a Diet Coke twenty minutes later.

"Did you have a fun night?" I asked pointedly.

"Yeah, I guess. It was pretty chill."

"Look, can you sit down a minute? I actually don't give a shit what you did last night, but I want to talk to you about yesterday."

"Sure. I wanted to talk about it too—I thought it went great, didn't you? Everyone seemed to have fun, and I got a lot of people asking about privates. And all my classes for the rest of the week have wait lists!"

"Yes, you really hit it out of the park," I said sarcastically. "Except I thought we had agreed that you were going to run it like a regular class. The way you've been doing it all summer. Or should I say, the way *we've* been doing it all summer."

"I was just trying to help," Tatum said innocently. "It was such a great cause, and I thought—I mean, you're always talking about engaging people one on one. And they're all so nice!"

She was going to make me say it. "Actually, Vix Ballmer isn't really all that nice. She's just very rich."

"You're mad that I didn't have you ride up front," Tatum said, adopting a patient tone. "I get it, but you're up there all the time. People have said things about it to me. I didn't want to hurt your feelings, but some of the other regulars wonder why they don't ever get to ride up in front, you know? And I thought we were supposed to be trying to get these women to contribute more, so—I mean, I handed those pledge envelopes out to every single person who came up to talk to me. Check the donations, I think you'll be surprised how much came in."

"You and I both know that no one gives a fuck about the donations," I snapped. "Especially you. All you were doing was promoting yourself."

Tatum tilted her head, her expression serene. "But isn't that what you've been telling me to do from the start? You always said you wanted me to succeed, that you wanted to help me."

"Yes, but there was a specific way—a *plan*—" But that wasn't the way to do this, not by reminding her I'd been using her. "I took you to the Hamptons. I bought you *clothes*, I—"

"And I'm really grateful, I've told you that," Tatum interrupted. "I learned a lot from you. But I have ideas too, Julia. At some point I have to do this on my own, I can't just let you prop me up forever."

"Well, you've made that pretty clear," I said, losing patience. "Maybe *Vix* can be your next mentor."

Tatum's face crumpled. "Don't be like that," she pleaded, her calm façade disintegrating. "I never meant to hurt your feelings. I only picked her because I recognized her from other classes. I thought it would help."

I couldn't argue that point, or fault her for her preparation. I'd given her a copy of the fundraiser bike chart, complete with notes—and the Graylon moms had loved that she called them out by name, that she knew things about them.

But I had one last card to play.

"Just one more thing." I reached into my pocket for the plastic bag and handed it to Tatum. "Benilda found this in the laundry. It isn't mine."

I watched her open the bag and take out the necklace, the pavé diamonds glinting in the light.

"That's a six-thousand-dollar necklace." I'd looked it up on the Barneys website.

"It's a friend's. I borrowed it," Tatum said, dropping it back into the plastic bag. "Tell Benilda . . . no, let me talk to her, I'll thank her myself. It must have gotten snagged on my sweater."

"Which friend?"

Her eyes narrowed. "You don't believe me?"

"I'm not sure why I should. Convince me. And while you're at it, maybe you can tell me which friend loaned you the Prada dress. Or those Gucci sneakers or that Hermès belt."

Her face went through a series of expressions. It was a strange thing to watch, but I'd seen it before—it was like she was trying them on until she found the right one. It happened so fast that I'd chalked it up as a sort of tic in the past.

When she spoke, her voice was tremulous. "You went through my room? Wow. Okay, look, Julia, I'll tell you whose stuff it is, only . . . if you could keep it between us? Because the thing is . . ."

I rolled my eyes. "What?"

"Most of that stuff is Brooke's mom's. Brooke borrowed it all ages ago and she and her mom aren't really speaking right now and so she hasn't had a chance to give it back but—I mean Brooke totally knows I wore that necklace, that's not the problem, I just wouldn't want—" She buried her face in her hands. "God, it's such a mess."

Surprise, surprise, Brooke and her parents had a difficult relationship. "What part is a mess?"

"It's just that they want her to, like, already *be* in law school. And she *did* take the LSAT last year, but she wasn't happy with her score and she wanted to take a prep class before she took it again, but they didn't offer the one she wanted until fall and—and her sister is like this certified genius and supersuccessful and that doesn't help. Anyway her dad asked her to lunch and I guess . . . I wasn't there but—and it's not like her folks didn't know she was gay, but . . ."

"Is there a point to this story?"

Tatum looked wounded. "They've cut her off. And the thing is she could get a cheaper apartment, I guess, but that takes *time*. It's not like you can instantly be like, yeah, I have to break my lease because my parents are mad at me, you know? And they're upset because she didn't tell them she'd been drawing down her trust, and now they've blocked that too, something with their lawyers and—and—"

"Poor Brooke. To have her own parents question her character—especially after all the generosity she's shown you."

"Julia!" I'd finally jolted her out of her little act. "Just say it—you think I took that necklace without her knowing."

"Or shoplifted it," I said blandly. "There's always that possibility."

She stared at me a moment, and I could see her trying to figure out how to play it. "It's kind of ironic, you being so suspicious of me," she muttered. "Especially since—look, I didn't want to say anything, after everything she's been through."

"Who?"

Tatum twisted the hem of her sweatshirt anxiously. "Maybe I should have brought this up with you a lot sooner, but I didn't want to get Benilda into trouble. I hate to say it, but I think she's stealing from you."

"Oh, *really*."

"I think it started a couple of months ago. I caught her . . . well,

I don't want to go through the whole thing, because maybe I'm wrong, you know? And I *like* her, I've always liked her and maybe there's an explanation, but—"

"Just tell me what you think you saw."

Tatum drew a deep breath. "Okay, look. Do you have a gold Patek Philippe?"

"Yes . . ." My mother had given me the watch a few years back when Dad bought her a new one. I rarely wore it; I didn't care for the mesh band, which seemed gaudy and dated.

"Well, I saw Benilda take it. You can go check if you want to see for yourself that it's gone."

"I think I will," I said icily. I went to my room, thoughts swirling in my head, and opened my jewelry drawer. I checked the compartment where I kept the pieces I rarely wore, and then I checked everywhere else.

"This doesn't prove it was Benilda," I snapped when I came back. "When exactly did you say you saw her take it?"

"About a month ago, I guess. I'd only gone into your room because I wanted to return your rain jacket. Remember, that one time there was that huge storm and I borrowed it to get to Flame? Anyway, I didn't even know Benilda was here, but when I came in she had your jewelry drawer open and the watch in her hand and she kind of jammed it into her pocket. And then I forgot about it until she was here the other day and I don't think she knew I was home and when I passed by your room I could see her in the closet, and she had your drawers open again. I hate to say it but maybe you should check and see if anything else is missing."

I couldn't imagine Benilda—who dressed in neat, pressed elastic-waist jeans and polyester blouses, who wore her reading glasses on a chain around her neck and smelled like Jean Naté—having any interest in my gold watch. "How would you even know what kind of watch it was, especially if you only saw it from the doorway?"

She didn't even miss a beat. "Come on, it's totally distinctive. That band? If it wasn't a Patek Philippe it would've had to have been a knockoff and I know you wouldn't ever buy a knockoff."

Was that a dig at me? I'd made her get rid of a fake Gucci tote she bought on Canal Street that wouldn't have fooled a high school girl in Tenafly. At the time, she'd been embarrassed. But now, after her summer of reinvention, she seemed so sure of herself.

"I hate having to tell you this," Tatum said sadly. "Maybe Benilda got into a jam and didn't know what to do and thought she could sell it. I know what it's like to feel like there's no way out. I mean, that's how I ended up in that situation with my landlord, it was—"

"Just *stop,* Tatum. Why didn't you say something at the time, if you were so worried?"

"Because I didn't want to get her in trouble. And also I thought, with all the funeral expenses, with everything she's had to do for her family . . . I was torn, you know?"

"I have a very hard time believing Benilda would ever do something like this." Benilda had about as much guile as a potted plant. When she'd asked me for a fifty-dollar-a-week raise, she'd actually offered to show me her CVS receipts to prove her new blood pressure medicine was twice as expensive as her old one.

"Why would I lie, Julia?" Tatum said, her lip quivering as though she was about to cry—as her eyes remained as dry as a bone. "I care about you. And I care about her. She needs *help,* I'm not saying you should fire her—"

"Are you sure?" I interrupted. "Because it's not like the two of you have ever gotten along. And besides, what about the necklace she found in the laundry? Why wouldn't she have just kept it, if she's a thief?"

"Because—"

"Here's something you may not know. That night of Brooke's birthday—when you didn't come home—I slept in your room. I found my cashmere dressing gown in your stuff. And Gruffy. I mean, that bear isn't worth anything to anyone—except for Henry."

"What? I don't even know what you're talking about. I mean yes, I borrowed a bathrobe one time, I had no idea it was cashmere— I didn't even know anyone made bathrobes out of cashmere—I guess I forgot to return it, which is absolutely my bad, and I'm really sorry. And as for Gruffy, haven't you seen how Paige hides Henry's things sometimes, like she'll hide his Dinotrux in the cabinets just to mess with him?"

She had a point. I'd seen Paige hide his favorite toys and then act like he'd lost them himself. She was my budding little gaslighter, but it wasn't so different from the way my brother and I had treated each other growing up.

I'd been so sure, but now I wasn't. Paige could easily have been the one to hide Gruffy in the drawer. And maybe Tatum really didn't realize that my cashmere robe wasn't just some cheap polyester one from Bloomingdale's.

As far as the watch went . . . I had shut Benilda down every time she mentioned money and her cousin. I thought she'd been angling for help bringing her family to town, but what if Benilda had been helping pay for all of it—the doctors, the medications, the funeral? What if she'd taken the watch out of desperation?

But even as I wavered, I couldn't shake the feeling that Tatum wasn't telling the truth—at least not the whole truth.

"What about the rest of it? I saw all the stuff in your room that still had the price tags on. Those Illesteva sunglasses? And that Helen Ficalora charm, those things are like six hundred dollars! Though maybe you can afford it now, since you're living with us for free."

Tatum looked at me as if I'd slapped her. And yes, I'd meant to hurt her with that crack.

"Fine. If you must know," she finally said, with an air of wounded dignity, "they were gifts. I have a friend. Brooke knows about it."

"A friend—do you mean like a sugar daddy?"

She shook her head impatiently. "A *friend*. It started as just conversation—I met him at a party. His wife is awful to him. She belittles him every chance she gets, even though he's one of the most generous people I've ever met."

I should have seen this coming—should have known that a big enough fish would make her bite.

"Just curious—how did you manage to get from 'just conversa-tion' to his wallet?"

"You're the one making this ugly." She sniffed. "I know you

won't believe me, but I invited him to one of my classes because I thought it would do him good to let off some steam, and he liked it so much he started spinning a few days a week. I never expected it to become anything."

"And now you're having an affair. With a married man. And you want me to believe that Brooke doesn't care?"

"She's not thrilled about it, which is why I've turned him down every time he offered to help me get my own place. And also, I didn't want you to find out because believe it or not, I care a lot about what you think of me."

"You have a funny way of treating the people you say you care about."

For a moment we just glared at each other.

Tatum got up from the table. "I have to say, I don't feel especially welcome here anymore. Don't worry, I'll move out today. You can search my things first, if you want. So you can make sure I didn't *steal* from you."

"Wait—hang on just a minute!" I said, pushing my chair back so that it screeched on the polished floor. I'd had the upper hand coming into this discussion, I was *justified*. But somehow Tatum had managed to make it seem like *I* was the petty one. "I never accused you of stealing. You were the one who accused Benilda! All I've ever done is try to help you."

"Well, you don't have to anymore. Thank you for the hospitality, but I think it's best if I don't impose any longer."

"So you're going to go beg your married lover to save you?" I was so angry my hands were shaking. "Don't you think he's going to wonder why your only real friend kicked you out? You think he'll be so eager to get you that little First Avenue walk-up studio then?"

Tatum gave me a withering smile. "I spent the morning in bed in a suite at the Mandarin Oriental with a view of the park," she said. "So I don't think I'll be settling for a studio."

CHAPTER 21

I fumed in the kitchen while Tatum packed. She had the doorman send the porter up, and he took the heavy duffel and two garbage bags in which she'd stuffed the rest of her things, while she carried her purse and a Louis Vuitton weekender I'd never seen before.

"Thank you again for all of your kindness," she said sarcastically.

I didn't even answer. I'm not sure what I'd expected—a tearful admission maybe, a cry for help, an apology? Even the porter seemed to take her side. He avoided looking at me while he followed Tatum, then glared at me when the bags got stuck in the door and I didn't jump up to help.

When the door closed behind them, the enormity of what was happening began to sink in. My project, my plans, my comeback—all of them in jeopardy now. I didn't believe that Brooke didn't care—I wondered if Brooke even knew.

The more I thought about it, the more likely it seemed that she didn't: as long as Tatum lived with us, she could see her married man whenever she had an eye on some new bauble, and spend the rest of her free time with Brooke. I doubted Tatum would ever move in with Brooke because her parent-funded one-bedroom would be a major step down, and because she'd have to tell her boyfriend, who probably wouldn't be pleased. Also, letting him put her up in an apartment would give him access to her whenever he felt like it, according to the unspoken rules of this sort of arrangement.

Viewed through this lens, staying with us was the best of all worlds. Tatum got to live at a fashionable address where the doormen knew her name and put her in a taxi whenever she wanted one, her relationship with her hot girlfriend never devolved to whose turn it was to change the kitty litter, and she had to fuck some old geezer only when he made it worth her while.

Now that was over, and Tatum had put her Plan B in motion without even stopping to catch her breath. She'd obviously had the married man's apartment on the back burner, had maybe even promised to move in, but hadn't been able to resist holding on to her freedom for as long as possible. Now she just had to find a way to spin her next move that would satisfy both Brooke and Daddy Warbucks.

I'd seen her in action enough to know she'd come up with something—but I had a head start on her. There was nothing stopping me from telling Brooke the unvarnished truth while Tatum was still in transit.

This was a bit too complicated to do over text, so I took a chance and called Brooke. As I expected, she picked up—I'd counted on her seeing the area code and assuming it was someone wanting to schedule a private session.

"Hi, Brooke, this is Julia Summers."

"Julia," she said after a beat. "What's up?"

"Oh, not much . . . other than the fact that your girlfriend is moving out of my home as we speak, into an apartment paid for by a man she's been seeing behind your back."

There was a short silence, and then Brooke burst into laughter. "She hasn't been seeing him *behind my back,* Julia. God, you're too funny. I've met him—he's one of her riders. I told her it was fine."

So Tatum had been telling the truth. Some of my righteous indignation evaporated. "Why would you do that?"

"Because she wanted a pair of suede jeans that cost almost three thousand dollars, that she happens to look totally fucking amazing in. And it's not like *I* could buy them for her, not after my parents cut me off."

My mind was reeling. "You're telling me you don't care at all? Even though they're . . . ?"

"Listen, Julia, you should see what he was willing to do for a threesome. Let's just say nobody at Bulgari batted an eye when he bought us both the same bracelet and had us wear them out of the store."

Brooke seemed to be enjoying my shock. The terrible thought that perhaps Tatum was there with her—hand over her mouth, shaking with laughter—flashed briefly through my mind.

I dug deep for a shred of dignity. "Well, I guess I should congratulate you on your open-mindedness. Tell her if she comes across anything she borrowed and forgot to return, let me know."

"Look, don't make this into some big drama, Julia," Brooke said. "There's no reason for me to be jealous. It's not, like, torture for her to be with him or anything, but she doesn't have *feelings* for him. Everyone gets what they want—if more people were honest about this shit, the world would be a less fucked-up place, you know?"

Maybe she had a point, but it didn't make me feel any better. "Whatever," I said petulantly, as though I was in middle school. "I need to go."

"Thanks for letting me know," Brooke said. "Look, sorry if I was a dick about it. You just sounded so, like, outraged. I mean, aren't you kind of glad to get rid of her?"

"I'm confused," I said. "I thought you were on her side."

"I am. I fucking *love* her. But every time she comes over, it's like a tornado came through my place. I told her we're never living together until we can afford a maid twice a week."

"Okay," I said. "Well, good luck."

I hung up before she could respond, went to the sink and poured a glass of water. The leaves of the African violet in a little pot on the windowsill were turning brown. Soon it would be dead—a victim of my neglect and indifference.

I was exhausted from the emotional roller coaster of the last week, feelings of hope and excitement and pride alternating with disappointment and despair, sometimes in the same day. Maybe I was just getting what I deserved for running what was basically a long con, for being willing to play with someone else's life the way I'd manipulated Tatum—even if she'd turned out to be as devious as me in the end.

Or maybe we'd been playing each other all along.

I took out my phone and sent James a text, because I needed someone to like me, to reassure me that I wasn't a terrible person.

Tatum moved out. Let's celebrate

I added the winking and blowing-a-kiss emojis before sending it, but when he didn't respond, my mood slipped even further, doubts pressing in on me from all sides. I felt alone and scared and disgusted with myself. I needed a workout—if only I could spin until I was on fire, to burn away all my fears and insecurities by pushing myself harder and harder until I lost myself in the hum of the wheel and the limits of my endurance, the music reaching deep inside of me and taking me to another place.

But for once, Flame was the last place I wanted to be.

I didn't sleep much that night. I *was* relieved that Tatum was no longer under my roof, but it would have been so much better if I could have claimed to have encouraged the move, to have helped her get settled in her new place. Now, with her own apartment and a generous beau and more personal training clients than she could handle, she didn't need me for anything at all.

At least half the women I'd brought to Flame seemed interested in joining, but without Tatum's cooperation, it wouldn't do me a bit of good. Not to mention the fact that now I had to come up with something else for Lindsay's birthday. I'd promised something special— I had to deliver.

I didn't feel like facing everyone at drop-off, but I didn't dare skip a day the second week. When we got to the school, people were still talking about the fundraiser. They loved Tatum, they loved the music and the workout, they had already downloaded the Flame app, we should totally take a class together. Maybe I could ask Tatum if she'd like to donate a private session for their upcoming fundraiser? Did I happen to have her contact info? Did she help me lose all that weight?

Missing from these conversations was any recognition that Tatum was *my* discovery, *my* project. They gushed about her; they'd followed her on Instagram; they were going to try the Kegan Diet— a combination of keto and vegan—which she swore by. And wasn't she *inspiring*? They'd heard she'd escaped a terrible childhood, that she'd made it through with sheer grit and hard work, that she especially loved helping newbies and those struggling with lifelong weight issues and the differently abled and, oh my God, she might as well have shit diamonds the way they went on about her.

I smiled until my face hurt and agreed with everything they said and the whole time I was looking for Grace and Lindsay, but they'd both sent their nannies that morning and I had a horrible feeling that they were getting coffee without me. Pure paranoia, but I couldn't put it out of my mind. I was so distracted that Paige had to ask me twice for her field trip form, and Henry disappeared with his friends while I wasn't looking.

The doors opened and the children began filing in and I was ready to leave when I saw Annabel Marcus heading toward me. Her son, Mitchell, was one of Henry's favorite classmates, and I'd been meaning to invite him over for a playdate.

But she didn't look happy. "Julia! I'm glad I caught you. Listen, something happened with the boys at school yesterday and I wanted to ask you what you knew about it."

I smiled sympathetically. From what I'd heard, Mitchell was a handful—a bit of a daredevil and apparently not very good at following instructions. Henry was always talking about how Mitchell lost privileges for refusing to take turns on the monkey bars or talking during circle time.

"They're so active at this age," I said generously.

"Yes. Well." Annabel's expression became even more sour. "Even so, I think it would be good to talk to them. When they're coming home with bruises . . ."

"Don't you think—" I stopped, finally picking up on what she was saying. "Wait, you're saying that *Henry* hurt Mitchell?"

"I'm sure he didn't intend to," Annabel said, insincerely.

"I'm sure he didn't. Henry's an active child, but he's certainly not aggressive."

"Well, even so, I think we should try to get ahead of this. I didn't want to bring it up with Miss Chirichella before I talked to you."

I resisted the urge to roll my eyes. Annabel was one of those uptight moms of an only child; on the first day of kindergarten she'd sent an email to the other parents describing Mitchell's allergies and proposing banning a long list of foods from the classroom.

"Annabel, I know it's concerning when your child is hurt, believe me. But kids get into scrapes all the time at this age. Especially active boys like ours. Why don't we monitor the situation, see if it happens again?"

Annabel pursed her lips. "I hardly think that waiting until one of them is *injured* is the answer. Julia, I just want to try to work together toward a solution. I'm not saying that Henry's a bad kid—"

"Thank you for the heads-up, Annabel," I cut in, even though I wanted to smack that accusatory smirk right off her face. "James and I will talk to him tonight."

"I appreciate that." She adjusted her Chanel sunglasses. "I heard the fundraiser went well, by the way. Congratulations. Such an important cause, what with public school support for the arts all but disappearing."

"Thank you." This was the obligatory civil exit line that follows every confrontation in this crowd, no matter how small. "I agree completely."

"And I'm so sorry about your place in the Hamptons. George and I drove by it several times this summer. So you've decided to sell it?"

"What? No, we're not selling. Where did you hear that?"

"Oh! I only thought—because of the dumpster out front—we just didn't notice any construction going on, and so we assumed—but I'm so glad you were able to hold on to it. There are so few reasonable properties left in that area."

I stared at Annabel in disbelief. She'd just implied that we couldn't afford to fix the place, and doubled down by calling it "reasonable"— code for small and shabby. Truth be told, she and I had never been especially friendly; she had about as much style as a fire hydrant and bulging eyes and unusually thick ankles, and I'd always assumed she was jealous of me. But this was on another scale entirely.

"Oh no," I said with a fake little laugh. "James just wants to supervise the renovation himself, and he's got a huge work project right now that's taking all of his attention. But he'll be able to devote more time to the house over the winter so we can be back in next summer."

"Oh, that's good to hear. It must have been awful to be stuck in town all summer. At least you got to spend time at the gym—it even looks like you might have lost a bit of weight."

Seriously, bitch? I'd lost twenty-six pounds and dropped three sizes, and if I did happen to lose my composure and punch her in the face, I was pretty sure I'd take her out. Instead, I looked over her shoulder, waved, and held up a finger in a hold-that-thought gesture. "Thanks! Hey, I need to talk to Celeste about something. I appreciate you sharing your concerns, and like I said, we'll talk to Henry."

"And then maybe we can circle back and—"

"Yes, perfect," I said, already on the move.

James, predictably, did not take the news of Annabel's complaint well when I told him that evening.

"She gave you shit about a *bruise*? Maybe she ought to send her kid to school in bubble wrap if she's so concerned. Jesus, Jules, that place is going to turn Henry into a little freak if we're not careful."

"I shouldn't have even told you."

"You know what the problem is? Henry spends too much time around women. Maybe it's a good thing Tatum moved out."

I hadn't told him about the argument that spurred her exit, but I knew he'd been increasingly annoyed with her. He'd nearly blown a gasket when Tatum let Henry color his nails with markers, and when he found Paige's Liv and Maddie sticker book in Henry's room, he told her we were trying to get the kids to respect each other's boundaries and not to let them take things from the other's room, then lured Henry to watch a Jets game on his lap with a bag of Doritos. I'd been trying for ages to get him to stop encouraging Henry to roughhouse, but at the moment, I wasn't going to argue.

"If you're so concerned about him spending more time with guys, how about taking him to the park when you get home Friday and playing catch with that new glove you bought him last Spring?"

"Oh, sorry, can't. I meant to tell you earlier, I invited Larry De Stasi and his wife over for dinner Friday night. Sorry about the late notice, but we can just do something casual."

Larry headed the zoning committee of the city council; I'd met him a couple of times, but couldn't place his face. "James, that's two days away. Even if it's casual, I still have to shop and cook and clean—"

"So have Benilda help you—isn't that why we have her? Look, I wouldn't ask if it wasn't important—I need to pin him down on the variance. Cora had basically told me it was a done deal, but I guess she didn't run it by the committee first."

"Are she and Josie coming too?"

"No, I want to have this conversation without her, since she basically hung me out to dry on this one. Maybe Larry and I can discuss the real world instead of Cora's mythical fucking peaceable kingdom and get this done."

"Okay." I was used to James's diatribes about city politics, which he believed revolved around screwing developers. If this dinner could move the project along, I was willing to suck it up. "So like rib eyes and maybe a Malbec?"

"Steak's good, and Larry's a beer guy. Pick up a twelve-pack, if you're out. And don't lose your shit if we smoke a cigar after dinner, okay?"

I heaved a sigh. "Sure. I'll just chitchat with the wife—we can share recipes and I'll ask her if she knows any solutions for pesky feminine odor."

"Ha ha, very funny. Just remember, this guy has the power to make my life extremely fucking difficult."

"Oh, I'm glad you told me. I'll try not to get drunk and insult him." I couldn't seem to contain my peevishness. "Seriously, James, I *do* know how to host a dinner party."

"Okay, yeah. Sorry. I'm just—look, I'm just a little on edge. The thing is . . . well, Larry's pretty conservative. You know, old school."

"Old school? What's that supposed to mean?"

"Look, don't take this the wrong way, but could you wear something, uh, plain? And maybe put away the tit sculptures and let me handle the music?"

"Really, James?" The "tit sculptures" were a pair of eighteenth-century carved wooden fertility totems that were the focal point of the dining room. "Those things cost more than my first car, but sure, I'll just shove them in the hall closet. Maybe I can ask your mom to loan me an outfit too."

"Jesus, I knew you'd take it wrong." I could hear real frustration in his voice. "I mean, forget all the times you've made me put on a monkey suit for your friends. All I'm doing is trying to save this deal, but hey, if it *offends* you to act like a normal person for one damn night—"

"*Normal?*"

"You know what I mean," he said, without a trace of warmth. "But if you want to turn this into another fight, I guess I can't stop you. I get it—you're used to everyone fawning all over you. But we all have to grow up sometime. I'm not asking you to put on an apron and buy a minivan, for Christ's sake. But do whatever the fuck you want, I guess. You always do."

And then he left the room.

CHAPTER 22

James felt bad about arguing again. I could tell because he came home on time for dinner the next night and joked around with the kids, peeking at me now and then to see if I was falling for it.

I was still upset over the things he'd said, but I had resolved to help him win the De Stasis over. I'd even googled Larry so I could make intelligent conversation about his accomplishments on the city council, and ordered scalloped potatoes and a chocolate cheesecake from Butterfield Market.

I decided to go the extra mile and put on a knockout evening, to be charming and gracious and send the De Stasis home thinking we were their new best friends. But the morning of the dinner, as I was standing on line for my latte, I got a call from the school.

"Hello, Mrs. Summers, this is Zarine Parekh. How are you today?"

Zarine Parekh, the very cultured, very intimidating principal of Graylon Academy, had not one but two assistants—so getting a call from Zarine herself was ominous.

"I'm well, thank you," I said, stepping out onto the sidewalk for privacy. "And you?"

"I'm quite well, thank you for asking. Mrs. Summers, I'll come straight to the point. There was a worrisome incident recently involving Henry and another boy in his class. Two other boys, actually."

I felt a surge of annoyance that Annabel had gone ahead and made her complaint. "If you're talking about what happened with Mitchell Marcus, I've already talked to Annabel, and my husband

and I have discussed it with Henry. I think it was just a case of the boys playing a little too rough."

"Mmm. It seems that there is some disagreement about what actually happened. At this point I'm not so concerned about the details, but as it is the beginning of the school year, we want to address any unhelpful habits now before they have a chance to become more problematic."

"Well, I can understand that, but—"

"The other parents have asked for a meeting to discuss the incident. It might be useful to brainstorm some strategies that all the families can implement at home. Can you and Mr. Summers meet here next Wednesday at four o'clock?"

"Is that really necessary? Given that this sort of thing happens every day in every classroom in the country?"

There was a pause—long enough for me to regret my words. I could picture Zarine with her sculptural bob, her vintage cat-eye glasses, her inscrutable expression. "I understand that this incident may seem trivial. But research shows that conflict resolution skills learned at this age can affect a person's relationship effectiveness later. Dr. Snyder will be sitting in—I'm sure you'll find his expertise invaluable."

Lamar Snyder was the staff psychologist at Graylon. This thing was turning into a circus. "Fine. I'm sure my husband will do his best to rearrange his schedule, though I can't make any promises."

"Oh dear. We really would like to have both parents present."

"I'll do my best," I said, chafing at her tone.

"Excellent," Zarine said and hung up.

I was about to get back on line when I remembered that Benilda had asked to leave early next Wednesday to help her cousin's son choose a headstone. I texted Grace; we'd often watched each other's kids in a pinch.

Is there any way you could pick my kids up next Wednesday afternoon and keep them until 6:00?

A moment later, she called. "Hey, got your text—Benilda can't stay?"

I heard music in the background—that soulful indigenous music that I only ever encountered at one place. I was surprised Grace was at Flame—she was passionate about her yoga studio, so much so that she had made it clear she was doing me a favor to come to the fundraiser.

"She's leaving early that day," I said, "and I've got a meeting at the school." I'd almost lied and said I had a dentist appointment, but it was too risky; Annabel Marcus was probably telling everyone Zarine Parekh was convening her kangaroo court to settle our dispute over Henry's behavior.

"What about Tatum? Is something going on with you and her? Because I just took her class, and she acted weird when I mentioned you."

"Everything's fine with us," I lied. "She's moving into her new apartment, so she's probably just distracted."

"She found a place? That's great," Grace said. "The only thing about next Wednesday is that Nora already invited Clara Otedola over."

"Oh," I said, stung. Since school started, I'd suggested twice that we get the girls together, and Grace had made excuses both times. I thought of those Instagram photos of Nora and Clara in their little white tennis skirts at the Dexters' club. "Well, maybe they could all play together?"

"I guess. It's just, the girls were going to work on a school project."

"I could probably pick up the kids by five—the meeting's at four. Would that leave the girls enough time to do the project later? I wouldn't ask, but . . ." I almost said, *but this is important,* which would only lead to questions about the nature of the meeting. ". . . but Paige has been asking to see Nora for ages."

"It's no problem," Grace said, though her tone implied it was. "I'm sure it will be fine."

"I really appreciate it."

"Sure. And hey, while I've got you on the phone—book club's at my house next month, remember?"

"I wouldn't miss it."

"So I had the best idea. What if you ask Tatum to come, and then

I can pick *The Kegan Diet*? She says she lost four pounds the first week. Maybe she can do a testimonial, you know, in a lighthearted way, nothing too serious."

Too bad Tatum and I weren't speaking. "I don't know. We've always stuck to fiction."

"But this'll be fun! I feel like people would love to do something a little different, especially after Poppy made us read *House of Leaves*—you know hardly anyone even finished it. We can even do a challenge—like have people write down their weight goals and I'll collect them in an envelope and then we'll pass them out the next month and see how everyone did. You should love that, Julia, you can rub it in everyone's faces how much weight you've lost."

"Sounds fun," I said, startled by the hostility in that last comment. "I guess I could ask her."

I was fuming when I hung up. Sure, Grace had agreed to watch the kids, but in exchange she'd extracted the prize of getting to be the first to host Tatum. I could just picture Grace prompting Tatum to talk about herself, the diet, Flame . . . and inserting herself into the story. Tatum would let it happen, too, once she realized the book group was like a pond stocked with fish, every one of them a prize catch. If she could worm her way into that circle of women, she'd have it made: her dream of belonging on the Upper East Side seemed closer to becoming reality than ever.

My carefully laid plans were falling to pieces. Tatum had landed on her feet without my help, and if I didn't think of something fast, no one would even remember that I was the one who'd plucked her from her wretched little life and given her a chance.

By the time Benilda returned from picking the kids up at school, I had the steaks seasoned and the salad ingredients washed and sliced.

"Benilda, can you please set the table for four and feed the kids in the kitchen before you leave? We're having guests and I still need to shower and get ready."

"Okay, Mrs. Julia," she said wearily.

"Who's coming for dinner?" Paige asked, dumping her backpack on the kitchen table.

"One of Daddy's work friends."

"Can I go to Lily's house?"

"Can I watch TV?"

"No, and ask Benilda."

I escaped to my room and locked the door. Suddenly, I was exhausted; I wanted nothing more than to lie facedown on my bed and stay there.

Despite my spending the afternoon frantically preparing for the dinner party, my thoughts had kept circling back to Grace and the way she'd manipulated our conversation. I did the same thing, but only to women who didn't matter, women who'd gotten on my bad side, women I wished to put in their place while preserving plausible deniability. I'd never do it to my best friends. I don't care if you're in middle school or the nursing home, you understand the rules of female loyalty—and what it means to discard them: it's an act of aggression, a severing of the bond.

But how had I wounded Grace so grievously that she'd treat me this way? What had happened over the summer to put so much distance between us?

Except . . . if I was really honest with myself, I had to admit that the problem had begun almost a year ago, around the time Grace and Matt had joined the Players Club. Its membership included famous actors as well as major benefactors and members of society, and it made sense that Matt would make the most of the networking opportunities, but Grace was the one who gushed about club events and name-dropped all the time.

I was no stranger to private clubs; my parents had belonged to the Algonquin Club forever. But James would never join any organization that required him to put on a tie just to order a hamburger. And it wasn't something I'd ever missed—at least, not until Grace wouldn't shut up about it. I caught myself wondering how I could convince James to at least consider Soho House or the Houghton Club, where I had friends who would sponsor us, before remembering that my marriage was already under strain.

Which brought me back to the evening at hand. I glanced at the clock and stood up in a panic: I'd have to haul ass if I didn't want to greet my guests dripping wet from the shower.

I lit the candles and iced down the beer, arranged the artichoke dip and crackers on a tray, and put on James's favorite bluegrass. I'd barely had time to dress and do my hair and makeup, but I was feeling pleased with myself when James walked in the door with the De Stasis—until his gaze landed on the fertility sculptures. I'd simply forgotten to put them away, but from James's scowl I knew he thought it had been deliberate.

Larry and Jenny monopolized the dinner conversation with such fascinating topics as their newfound interest in genealogy and their upcoming trip to Borneo. I escaped briefly to put the kids to bed, but when I got back they were still sharing the boring details of their ancestry, and James refused to look at me.

After dinner, the men retired to the living room, having finished the beer and moved on to scotch. Jenny De Stasi and I didn't share recipes, but I did have to endure a recitation of their struggles with their children's orthodontia, which had led to them filing a lawsuit against the entire practice. I had trouble maintaining a posture of total absorption while she droned on, but I did manage to finish most of a bottle of Malbec by myself.

When our guests finally left, I retrieved the bowl James and Larry had used as an ashtray with its two charred brown butts, a wad of chewing gum stuck to one of them. James leaned against the kitchen island, drinking a Mountain Dew and staring at the sculptures.

I walked over and pointedly turned the sculptures around so they were ass-out. "Better?" I asked sarcastically.

"All I asked," James said in a deadly quiet voice, "was that you just *try*. For one goddamn night."

"I did try!" I pointed to my black pants, my high-necked sweater. "I'm wearing pearls, for God's sake! I made a special trip to Butterfield for that cheesecake! I listened to Jenny De Stasi go on and on about how she was one-thirty-second Inuit as if she wanted a fuck-ing prize!"

James looked so exhausted all of a sudden that it shut me up. "All *you* talked about was all the weight you lost at that gym. Did you ever stop to think that's not what people like the De Stasis want to hear about?"

I hadn't, actually, and James was right, I'd made a sloppy mistake: Jenny was at least a size 16, and Larry's gut hung so far over his pants you couldn't see his belt buckle.

"Well, I'm sorry. Fine, I'll call her and ask her to coffee or something. But that's not the same as—"

James made a sound between a laugh and a snort. "Don't even bother. Larry won't budge. Says it's out of his hands, which is a total bald-faced lie."

"You're not blaming that on *me*—"

"No, of course not," James said sarcastically. "Don't bother waiting up—I'm going to head down and take another look at the numbers, see if I can figure out just how far up the ass this is going to fuck me if we can't get the variance."

"You're going to the office *now*? James, it's late, you've been drinking—"

But he stalked out of the room before I could finish the sentence, only to return a few minutes later in jeans and a plaid shirt I thought I'd sent to charity. I had started the cleaning cycle to get the burnt scalloped potato crud off the bottom of the oven and turned on the exhaust fan full blast because of the smoke, so maybe he said good-bye and I just didn't hear it.

CHAPTER 23

I was back at Flame for Tatum's 9:30 A.M. on Monday.

Surely, you're not surprised?

True, I'd nearly let our argument get the best of me, and allowed valuable time to pass while I absorbed the blow and calculated my losses. But with a few days to recover and refocus, I was feeling less regret and more resolve; fewer second thoughts and a steely determination to defend what I'd worked so hard to build.

My dad had a favorite Muhammad Ali saying he'd repeat in the mirror whenever he was getting ready to renegotiate a contract: *If you even dream of beating me you'd better wake up and apologize.* I was my father's daughter, and anyone who thought they could take advantage of my unfortunate miscalculation was dangerously underestimating my capacity for course correction.

The responsibility for my failure rested squarely on my shoulders. I should have worked harder to maintain my friendships over the summer instead of betting everything on my transformation and the launch of my new project. I could have done more with social media, building anticipation and securing my association with Flame so Tatum couldn't take it away so easily. I had naïvely believed that I was pulling the strings while Tatum was secretly scheming and working her own game. Now I would have to work my ass off to regain the ground I'd lost, starting with Tatum. She and I didn't have to like or even trust each other for me to get what I was owed. I just needed to figure out how to convince her she didn't have a choice.

And the first step was to retake my rightful place at Flame before

I lost any more ground. I had signed up the minute registration opened to make sure I got a bike in the middle of the front row, where Tatum couldn't possibly ignore me. But when I got to Flame, a few minutes before the start of class, Paz told me that the class was full.

"But it wasn't full when I signed up! I had bike four. I can show you on my phone—"

"It's right here," Paz said, turning the little screen toward me. Sure enough, all the bikes were assigned, and I was third on a waiting list of fourteen. "This class has gotten crazy since the kids went back to school."

I suddenly remembered the night back in July when Tatum had drunkenly admitted to blackmailing Paz for admin access to the app—and yet I was still shocked that she would dare to kick me off the list. But I had one kind of influence that she didn't.

"Listen, Paz, I've been coming here since back when you couldn't have filled Tatum's class if you threw in a happy ending," I said, rummaging in my bag. I took a couple twenties from my wallet and slapped them on the counter in front of her. "I know this mistake wasn't your fault, but I also know you guys hold back a bike in case somebody important shows up at the last minute. So let's you and me pretend, just for today, that *I'm* important."

Paz gave me a slightly reptilian smile and slid the cash off the counter. "I probably shouldn't tell you this, but Tatum's been saying things about you . . . things you probably wouldn't want out there."

I sensed that Paz was the kind of equal-opportunity shit stirrer who was in it for her own amusement, so I turned back conspiratorially. "Yeah, I know. Ever since she accidentally left her herpes medication on the bathroom counter she's been afraid I'll tell everyone."

I thought it was a pretty good line, but when I opened the door to the studio my smug satisfaction evaporated. Lindsay was in the front row on bike 4—*my* bike—next to Coco Choi. Annabel Marcus was there, that sneaky hypocritical bitch, along with Emery Souza and half a dozen other Graylon moms. There was one free bike in the room, and it was next to the last person I ever expected to see at Flame: Janet Erikson, dressed in elastic-bottom sweats that looked like they'd belonged to Terry in the nineties and a too-large T-shirt featuring Rosie the Riveter and the words A WOMAN'S PLACE IS IN THE RESISTANCE. Janet had sent a check for a thousand dollars for the Flame fundraiser, and I really needed to thank her, or I might have been more upset; the last row felt like too obvious an exile.

Tatum was in the middle of a conversation with Grace. I watched her notice me; if she was surprised, she didn't show it. She said something and Grace turned around and they both waved and went back to talking. At 9:29 A.M., Tatum patted the teacher bike—the one I'd ridden all summer long—and Grace jumped up on the podium.

You have got to be fucking kidding me.

I may have mouthed the words, because as I approached the empty bike and dropped my stuff on the floor, Janet said, "Julia! Rough morning?"

I pulled myself together and smiled. "Yeah, you know, trying to get back into the school routine."

"Oh, I know. I hate it when Willa goes back—the house just feels so empty after having her home."

She leaned off her bike and wrapped me in a hug before I could escape. She smelled like fresh laundry and cinnamon.

"By the way, thank you so much for your donation to the benefit!" I said, disentangling myself. "I was so sorry you couldn't make it. When did you start coming here?"

"This is my first time. Everybody's been talking about it, so I thought I'd check it out. I had to ask someone to help me clip into the pedals—God only knows how I'll get out. I'm sorry I had to miss the benefit, by the way, Terry and I were at a bris. I have to say, I don't know if this is going to be my thing—I mean, it's like a disco in here."

As if to prove her point, Tatum lowered the lights, except for the laser display she'd started using. It beamed tiny stars up near the ceiling that pulsed and changed colors to the beat of the music. The candles were lit and a hush fell and then the first bars of "Seasons of Love" from *Rent* filled the room, and I knew what would follow was the playlist I'd made for Tatum the week before she moved out, with exactly this moment in mind: all these women here seeking something new, something that would make them feel alive and inspired while also being just familiar enough that they felt catered to.

"Good *morn*ing, loves!" Tatum said as she adjusted her headset microphone. Her voice filled the room, smooth and cheerful and practically breathless with excitement, and she moved her arms in an arc as though she was trying to hug all of us at once. *I'm here for you,* her manner telegraphed. *This is all for you.*

"I'm so excited to have my friend and personal training client Grace Dexter up here helping out today. We haven't been working together long, but she has absolutely *humbled* me with her dedication and talent and just her gorgeous spirit."

Grace smiled modestly; I seethed. Grace hadn't said a word about signing up for private sessions—and she'd never mentioned going to class together after that first time. But as the warm-up music came on and she started pedaling, she looked pretty damn pleased with herself.

I had no trouble keeping up; at this point I could do this in my sleep and barely break a sweat. I watched Tatum, noting the subtle changes she'd made to her routine in the week since the fundraiser. Her expressions reflected an emotional range from delight to all-out rapture, complimenting one woman and taking another's hands, alternating between inspiration and encouragement and pep squad fervor. She looked right at me as she asked Coco Choi if the allergy treatment had helped her French bulldog, and I'm pretty sure she winked at me when she playfully felt up Milly Prasad's biceps and said, "Guess all that time on the court at the Meadow Club this summer paid off!"

My only solace came from seeing Grace struggle. Despite Tatum's constant stream of praise ("Perfect form, Grace. Everyone, see how far back she is on the bike!"), she was breathing hard and off the beat when we came up from the saddles. She tried to keep her game face, but she kept having to wipe sweat from her forehead, and her makeup pooled under her eyes.

It might have been my imagination, but it seemed to me that Grace avoided looking at me, even during the cooldown, when Tatum told everyone to "look around you and take in the beautiful energy of everyone here, be lifted by their good intentions and bless them in return." Lindsay saw me as she looked around the room and gave me a sheepish smile, making me wonder if she'd known about Grace's little coup. Hell, for all I knew, Lindsay would be riding up there next. I had to hand it to Tatum—she knew how to hit me where it hurt.

I'd paid so little attention to Janet that I was startled when she leaned over and stage-whispered, "If we have to count on Annabel's good intentions, it might be time to head for the lifeboats." Despite myself, I snorted with laughter.

"Everything okay back there, ladies?" Tatum called sweetly, as the rest of the class performed chakravakasana stretches over their handlebars.

"Just fine," Janet replied, refusing to be cowed. When class was finally over, she touched my arm. "Would you want to walk after drop-off one day next week? Frankly, I'd rather be outside getting some fresh air than losing my hearing in here."

"Sure, that would be great sometime," I said vaguely, then left her struggling to unclip and headed to the front of the room, where Grace and Tatum were chatting.

"You looked great up there, Grace," I said.

"Thanks!" She beamed. "Tatum is everything you said she was. I can't believe how much I learned in two sessions."

Two sessions? In the week and a half since school started? I'd heard after the benefit that Tatum's private sessions were booked out through October, but she'd found a way to squeeze Grace in.

I remembered the first time Tatum and I had coffee, when she told me she wanted everything I had. At the time, I'd mistaken the expression on her face for admiration. But she'd taken what she wanted from me like a thresher in a wheat field, leaving the plants alive but worthless.

My instinct was to strike back twice as hard, to drive Tatum back down to the squalid depths she'd clawed her way out of, but I couldn't afford thoughts of revenge. I still needed Tatum to get what I wanted, even if I had to eat some crow.

"That's great. Hey, Tatum, do you have a few minutes to talk?"

She and Grace exchanged a look. "Actually, we were going to get coffee."

"You should come too," Grace said, without a trace of sincerity.

What I needed to say to Tatum wasn't exactly group conversation. "You know what, I'll catch you guys next time. I need to run some errands."

"We'll talk soon," Tatum promised cheerfully, pulling on the Lulu wrap I'd bought her while Grace picked up their water bottles.

Watching them walk out together felt like bleeding from a cut that wouldn't close.

CHAPTER 24

That night I got to work. I called half a dozen friends to set up coffee and drinks dates, emailed the chairs of all the committees I was on to ask if there was anything they needed help with, and planned my outfits for the rest of the week to show off my body while the weather was still warm enough to do so. I spent an hour on Instagram liking and commenting on other people's photos and posted one of my own, a moody shot of myself looking out the window at twilight, my pale yoga cardigan slipping off my shoulders to show the definition in my back and upper arms. I'd made Paige retake the photo over and over until I was satisfied, promising her pancakes for dinner, and by the time the dishes were done my post had gotten almost a hundred likes.

When I got into bed, I stared at my phone for a long time before texting Lindsay. Maybe seeing Grace up on the instructor bike had left her feeling a little frozen out too—and even if it hadn't, I had nothing to lose.

Are you going to 9:30 spin tomorrow? Coffee after?

She texted her emoji-studded regrets back almost immediately. **Would love to but have to get new passport photo. SOON though!!!**

I checked Tatum's Instagram, steeling myself for some BFF-lovefest shot of her and Grace, but she hadn't posted in two days. Good—maybe she wasn't as sure of her next move as she pretended, now that she'd made herself a free agent.

I wasn't about to squander the advantage. The next morning, I brought a prop to class with me, walking into the spin studio moments before class started and heading straight for the podium, where I draped my towel over the handlebars of the instructor bike. Tatum looked up from a conversation with Coco Choi about what brand of spin shoes she should buy and frowned.

"Julia, I'm sorry, but—"

"Is this yours?" I asked, dangling an aquamarine-and-lapis bracelet from Jakobine in front of her.

"No . . ."

"Oh, I just thought—since you borrowed all that jewelry from Brooke's mom, maybe you'd left it at my place by accident."

Out of the corner of my eye, I saw Coco snap to attention. I knew rumors were going around among the staff about Brooke and Tatum—a secret like that doesn't stay secret for long in a place like Flame—and the gossip would soon reach Tatum's newest fans, if it hadn't already.

"I've never seen it before," she said, a faint edge to her voice.

"Okay, no problem," I said, tucking the bracelet back in the stretchy little pocket of my capris. "Oh, and by the way, I'm still looking for those jeggings you thought you left in the guest room, but honestly, I think Benilda might have thrown them out. Let me just replace them, I can pick up a pair at Target."

That earned me a murderous glare from Tatum and a raised eyebrow from Coco, who had probably never crossed the threshold of a Target in her life.

"I don't know what you're talking about," Tatum mumbled. "Look, can we talk later? I need to start."

"Sure!" I said brightly, moving past Coco to take my place on the instructor bike. I saw Tatum mouth the word "sorry" at Coco, but she was already turning away, shaking her head. As the opening bars of the warm-up song played, Coco was forced to take the bike I'd signed up for, in the third row next to a guy who liked to ask women for help adjusting his handlebars just so he could watch them bend over.

As the warm-up segued into the next song and Tatum walked among the riders, I silently complimented myself and picked up my pace. As song after song played and Tatum took us through her routine, I gave it my all, pedaling harder than anyone in the room while keeping a smile on my face to reflect the pure joy of the ride. I pumped my fists in the air and threw back my head the way Tatum did, even letting out a whoop after some of her more mawkish platitudes just to get the point across that we were united in our positivity and good intentions, she and I.

Near the end, when Tatum came up on the podium to cue the cooldown, I held up my hand for a high five, and she had no choice but to give it to me. But instead of slapping her hand, I grasped it and held it up in a victory salute and yelled "Isn't she *amazing?*" and didn't let go until everyone in the room was cheering.

Afterward, Tatum came and found me in the locker room. I was telling Milly Prasad where I'd bought my fitness top, a sky-blue cross-back bra with strategically placed mesh inserts. "It was a bit of a splurge, but the fit is amazing and you have to feel good about yourself to get the most from your workout. *You* taught me that, Tatum," I added, gazing at her adoringly.

She forced a smile that disappeared the moment Milly left. "What the hell was that back there, Julia? I promised *Coco* that bike."

"You did? Oh gosh, sorry!" I said insincerely. "Although—I hate to say it, but I don't know if her form's there yet. And Grace was really struggling yesterday. Tell you what, I'll just keep riding on the teacher's bike until they've had more practice. Don't worry, I don't mind at all."

Tatum compressed her lips and squeezed her eyes shut for a second, and I noticed the fine lines around her mouth and eyes that would someday become wrinkles. It was a preview of how she would look when she was old, when her hair lost its luster and the little pocket of fat under her chin had become a wattle and her round curves had settled into bulges that no amount of exercise could tighten. Time would not be kind to her—but I didn't intend to wait that long for the last laugh.

She took a deep breath and opened her eyes. "Look. I'm grateful for your help over the summer, Julia, but you need to let this go. It's nobody's fault we grew apart—it just happens. Besides, you've learned everything I can teach you, and now I want to focus on my other riders, the ones who need my help the most."

I'd been giving versions of this friendship breakup speech since I was in elementary school, and I laughed. "Sorry—that just reminded me of the look on Coco's face when I mentioned your Target jeggings."

"I never owned *jeggings*," Tatum spat, though I would have bet money she'd worn them at some point in her life, probably with pastel fake Uggs and a sweatshirt embroidered with snowmen or hearts or some other cheesy bullshit.

"It doesn't matter. I put that image in Coco's head, and now it's not going anywhere. The point is that you haven't *arrived*, Tatum, you've barely got their attention. If you can't keep it, the shine'll wear off you so fast it'll make your head spin. You're not ready to do this on your own—you're confusing your little bunch of groupies for staying power."

"You're jealous," she said. "Face it—you're done. You thought everyone would be so impressed with you for losing a few pounds, but no one cares."

I refused to be cowed. "That just proves my point. I was *born* into this world and I still have to fight to stay here. I'm sure you're amused to see my friends giving me the cold shoulder, but you still don't understand how this world works. I'm not going anywhere— I just made a mistake, that's all. And unlike you, I've got money and influence and I know the proper way to set a table."

"What was your mistake?"

"Why, so you can tell all your new *friends*?"

"No. So I can make sure I don't make the same one." Her steady gaze held a warning. "Say what you like about me, Julia, but I do pay attention."

Paige waited until Wednesday morning to tell me that she was supposed to bring photos and mementos for the construction of a "My Family Is . . ." collage they were working on. I was livid, but I needed to do triage if I didn't want to get labeled as a mom who couldn't be bothered.

I called the office and said Paige had a doctor's appointment and would be in late. Then I texted Milly Prasad to say something had come up and I needed to reschedule our lunch date. As soon as Benilda left with Henry, I set up my laptop and photo printer on the kitchen table.

The project description Paige had produced from the bottom of her backpack said students should use family photographs to illustrate brief descriptions of special times spent together, and gave an example from the prior year that included "Helping at my cousin's Special Olympics, apple picking, learning about Kwanzaa at the Natural History Museum, playing Nerf Laser Ops Pro." Like any kid ever came up with that list—some parent had thrown in the Nerf thing to prove that when they weren't saving the world or exploring other cultures, their perfect family knew how to have fun.

I set Paige up with her lap desk in my bedroom to work on the written part of the assignment so I could choose photos without her input. When Benilda returned from drop-off, I tasked her with printing out the photos I chose from the thousands on my computer until we had a tidy stack for Paige to take to school. We'd been at it for nearly an hour when Benilda went to CVS to get glue sticks, and I was looking for a big envelope when Paige wandered out of my bedroom with her hair mussed and a stricken expression. Her face was red and blotchy, perspiration sheening her forehead, and she walked like a zombie, stumbling and bumping into the wall.

"Mom," she moaned, "I don't, I'm sick. Everything is dizzy."

She pitched forward the last few feet, and I barely caught her. I was shocked by the heat of her skin.

"No, don't!" she shrieked, trying to twist out of my grip. I held on to her and felt her neck, her racing pulse.

"When did you start feeling like this?" I asked, trying to control my panic. Benilda had taken her a snack—could it be food poisoning? "Was it before you ate your snack or after?"

"I don't know."

"What did you eat? Did you eat what Benilda brought you?"

In response, she only moaned. I went to the bedroom to see for myself, half-dragging her with me.

From the state of things, Paige had been bored out of her mind. The bedcovers were a mess, twisted and pulled from the mattress. The plate of Triscuits and dried mango sat mostly untouched on the bedside table, but the drawer was open, the contents littering the bed—a tube of hand cream, a couple of bookmarks from a museum visit, my spare reading glasses, matches, and a candle I occasionally lit when James and I were feeling romantic.

And the little Altoids tin that I had forgotten I'd stashed there, open and empty. I searched frantically through the covers, looking for the little green Molly tab. Not finding it, I grabbed Paige's face and forced her to look at the tin in my hand. "*Paige*. Did you eat the pill that was in here?"

She looked at me in confusion. "The candy?"

"Was there a picture on it? What color was it?"

"Green," she said, a tremor passing through her body. "It had a bird. It tasted so *bad*."

"Oh my God, Paige—"

Why had I kept it? Of all the places I could have stashed it, how could I have been so stupid? "Paige," I repeated, trying to keep my voice calm. "Get back in bed and stay right here. I need to make a phone call to find out how to help you."

I knew I needed Poison Control, but I had no idea how to call them—I dug my phone out of my pocket and tried to google, but I was so upset I kept hitting the wrong keys. "God *damn* it!"

Paige had started to get into the bed, but suddenly she slipped to the floor—or fell, I couldn't tell—and began convulsing, eyes rolled back, limbs thrashing.

"Oh God, oh God!" I stabbed the phone, dialing 911. I knelt next to her and watched helplessly.

"911, what is your emergency?"

"My daughter! She took Molly—she's only eight. I mean MDMA. Ecstasy!"

"Okay, tell me exactly what happened."

"She took—it was in my bedside table. There was only one pill there, I'm sure of it, she thought it was candy. Please, she's having a seizure!"

"Did you move any dangerous objects out of the way?"

"There aren't—"

"Do not attempt to hold her down, all right?"

"Wait—wait, I think it's stopping."

"Is she breathing, ma'am?"

I knelt close over Paige's face; I could feel her breath against my cheek. Her eyes were slightly open, but all I could see were the whites.

"Yes!"

"All right, ma'am, I'm sending the paramedics to you. I'm going to stay on the line with you until they get there. If she starts seizing again, tell me right away. Don't move her and don't put anything in her mouth."

As I listened to the dispatcher, I touched my daughter's hair, terrified I'd hurt her, cause another seizure, betray her all over again. In moments, Paige blinked a few times and looked up at me in confusion. I stroked her forehead and kissed her cheeks, weak with relief.

There was a pounding on the door, and I ran for it. The paramedics came through, clanging metal equipment. Two police officers followed behind them.

A short, stocky paramedic with a goatee got down on his knees next to Paige. He and his partner worked on her as I watched in helpless terror.

"What happened?" Benilda had trailed in after the cops with a CVS bag in her hand.

I didn't answer; I didn't have time for her. I needed to focus on watching them work on my daughter. The man with the goatee was asking Paige questions—what was her name, what grade she was in, what was her favorite color. Paige was weak and listless and her answers garbled, but she was responding. She was *alive*.

A female cop with her hair pinned up in a bun put her hand on my arm. "You're Mom?" she said, her voice completely devoid of warmth. "Can you show me where she was when she took the pill?"

"Is she going to be okay? Please—just tell me—is she okay?"

"You need to calm down, ma'am. They're preparing her for transport now."

"Her signs are good," one of the paramedics said. "The hyperthermia and tachycardia are typical in a child of this age ingesting amphetamines. You said she convulsed?"

"Yes—she was shaking, twitching, kind of violently—on the floor, I didn't move her—"

"How long did it last?"

"I—I'm not sure, maybe . . . a few minutes?" I really didn't know. "Her skin turned blue—is that normal?"

"She probably stopped breathing."

"Oh God—"

"Normal in a seizure."

"But you said the signs are good—do you mean she'll be fine? A full recovery?"

"Ma'am, right now we just need to let them get her to the hospital," the female cop repeated. "Can you show me where it happened?"

I led her down the hall to the bedroom, the other cop following. They took in the rumpled bedcovers, my things strewn about. I pointed to the Altoids tin lying open on the bed.

"There was just one—one pill. It isn't mine. Someone gave it to me and I didn't take it, I don't know why I didn't just throw it out—oh, God—"

"Can you describe the pill?"

"Green," I said. "Mint green. A weird shape—like a diamond with rounded points, and there was a dove on it. Stamped, a stamped design, there wasn't any writing."

"Okay." The cops exchanged a look. "Why did you leave the pill in your drawer?"

"I don't know. I should have thrown it out but I—I really don't know."

"You know it's illegal to possess MDMA and leaving it where a child could access it, that's child endangerment."

"I know, I know—"

"Ma'am, let's go in the living room, okay?" the male cop said.

I followed him, still talking. "It wasn't mine, I don't *do* drugs."

He didn't respond. He'd pulled out a clipboard and was writing something. The paramedics had moved Paige onto a stretcher, her head lolling, her eyes drifting closed. They ignored me as I circled around them, trying to get closer.

"Wait! Where are you taking her?"

"We're going to want to talk to your husband," the officer said. "What's his phone number?"

I rattled it off as the paramedics raised the stretcher. "Wait—I need to go with them. Please!"

"That's fine. I just need to get your signature on this." The cop handed me the clipboard; it looked like a speeding ticket.

"What is this?"

"Summons to appear for possession of an illegal substance."

"I—do I have to sign this now? Can I talk to our lawyer?"

"Either sign it now or I'm taking you in for endangering the welfare of a child. I either arrest you, or you sign and then you can go with them."

I was signing before he even finished speaking. I didn't care what happened to me as long as I could be with Paige now. I pushed so hard with the pen that it tore the paper, and then I thrust the clipboard back at him.

"Listen," he said, his tone a bit kinder. "These things, she's probably going to be just fine, okay?"

I didn't even respond. I jumped up and ran to the paramedics, who were maneuvering Paige out the door. I suddenly remembered Benilda, standing in the kitchen looking frightened. "My nanny, can someone please just let her know what's going on?"

"Okay, Officer Montaperto can take care of that. Will your nanny be able to watch any other children while you're gone?"

"She's supposed to leave at five but—" I stopped, remembering that Benilda was leaving early, that Grace had agreed to pick up the kids today. "Never mind, my friend is picking up my son."

Thinking of Grace brought an image of her and Tatum laughing together at spin class to my mind, and I felt a rush of fury. If it hadn't been for Tatum—and Brooke—this never would have happened.

"Listen, I need to tell you who gave me the pill. I never wanted it, I swear. I never planned to take it. She literally forced it into my hand. I'll take a drug test, anything you want."

"Ma'am, you don't—"

"Her name is Brooke Timms."

CHAPTER 25

I called James while I followed the paramedics downstairs, but when he didn't pick up, I left a jumbled message saying Paige had accidentally taken MDMA and was on the way to Lenox Hill Hospital and to meet me there and that I was sorry, so sorry.

The paramedics let me ride in the ambulance, and I talked to Paige the whole way even though she never opened her eyes. I watched her chest rise and fall and I prayed, oh, how I prayed, I who had announced on my first trip home from college that I was an atheist.

Once we arrived at the emergency room, they whisked her away and directed me to the waiting room. I don't know how long it was until they called me back—ten minutes, two hours, an eternity. When I saw Paige, so small in the hospital bed in one of the curtained-off enclosures, I nearly broke down again.

The nurses let me stand next to the bed as they moved around me, taking her vital signs and adjusting her IV. Her fever had come down, and her pulse was only slightly elevated.

When they left, saying the doctor would come soon, I pulled a chair close to the bed and checked my phone. I'd received several texts and three missed calls since I last looked at it.

The first was from Grace saying that when she got to Graylon, Benilda was already there picking Henry up, that Benilda had canceled her plans with her cousin's son to stay with him. I wrote back thanking her and saying that Paige had had a reaction to some medication and that I was at the hospital with her, hoping that would satisfy her; now wasn't the time to worry about people finding out.

The next text was from Benilda, saying the same thing. **I am here with Henry I will stay until you come home.** I texted back to thank her and let her know that Paige was stable.

Then there were three texts from Tatum, the first at 5:20 P.M. **OMG Grace says Paige is in the hospital?????? Call me and tell me what is going on!** The second was brief—**CALL ME!** And the third was just a long row of exclamation points.

I stared at them for a moment, surprised by Tatum's concern. Tatum and Paige *had* been close, in their way—Paige loved the attention, the makeup and dress-up and pretend fashion modeling. The fact that Tatum had reached out almost made me feel guilty about giving the cops Brooke's name. Except that Paige wouldn't be lying in a hospital now if it weren't for the two of them.

The fury came surging back as I texted:

Paige found the molly from that night we went out and she ate it and got really sick. I had to give the cops Brooke's name when they asked where I got it

The little dots appeared almost immediately and seconds later Tatum texted:

I thought you took it why did you even keep it??? Why didn't you give a fake name????!!!!

So much for her concern.

Got to go, was all I wrote.

James arrived, shoving aside the curtain so that it went sailing on its curving rod. I put my finger to my lips before he could say anything, pointing to our sleeping daughter, and he pulled me up and crushed me against his chest.

"Is she okay?" he whispered. "Please, please tell me she's okay—"

"She was awake and talking and the nurse says she'll be fine," I whispered back. He cupped my face in his hands, so gently that I could hardly bear to meet his eyes. "I'm so sorry. It's all my fault."

He took my hand and pulled me into the open area so we could speak normally. "What the hell happened, Jules?"

Now that he was here—now that I wasn't the only one with her—my fragile defenses crumpled and the guilt came rushing in. I started to cry. "Brooke gave me Molly that night we went out. Just one pill. I didn't take it—I should have just thrown it away."

"God, why didn't you?"

"I—I don't know. I truly don't." But in the back of my mind, I thought I might . . . the little pill was a souvenir from my wild night out, a reminder that I hadn't completely left behind a more exciting version of myself. Not so different from the bar coasters I'd kept from a friend's bachelorette weekend in Jamaica. And maybe I wanted to keep the possibility, that someday I might swallow that tab and feel what Brooke and Tatum felt. "I'm sorry I didn't tell you. I was embarrassed. That whole night . . . I should never have gone."

"I don't want you going out with them ever again." Classic James—blunt in the face of a threat, circling the wagons, scorching the earth. If there had been something to hit, he would have hit it. His resolve felt like safety, and I sagged against his chest with relief that he wasn't angry.

"I promise I won't. I swear."

"Thank God she's out of the house."

"James . . . it wasn't her, it was Brooke."

He didn't say anything for a moment, rubbing my back. "I get that. But look—the company she keeps, it isn't a good example for the kids. They don't need to be around that."

"She's gone," I said. "It doesn't matter anymore."

While we were waiting for Paige to be released, James called Stewart Marlowe, who asked to speak to me.

"As you know, I am a real estate attorney," he began, "and you may wish to consult a criminal attorney, because—"

"I get it, Stewart, but can you just skip the disclaimer crap and tell me what we're dealing with?"

I heard his aggrieved sigh. "Did the police give you a summons? Do you have it with you?"

"Yes, but I think I left it at home—honestly, I don't even remember."

"Have James send me a copy. But you probably don't have much to worry about as long as you show up and pay the fine. In all likelihood the police officer won't even bother to come to court."

"But—but aren't we going to have to post bail or something?"

"Given the fact that you've never done anything like this before, that James is an upstanding member of the business community, I doubt they'll waste their time on you."

"You mean . . ." An ugly little puff of hope appeared. "It's not going to be in the news? Not even the crime report?"

"No. Though you'll want to be very careful in the future, because a second offense—"

"Thanks for the tip," I interrupted, hanging up.

I handed James back his phone. "Your asshole lawyer thinks I'm a dope fiend."

James shoved the phone in his pocket and grabbed my hand. "Forget about him. Let's go see our girl."

The doctor finally came bustling in, apologizing for the long wait. She was a cheery sort, my mother's age but round with frizzy gray hair and bright blue glasses. She spent some time going over what we could expect—that Paige would be out of it and irritable for a day or two, and that we should let her rest as much as possible.

"So we can take her home now?" James asked.

"There's some paperwork, and the nurse will need to take out her IV," she said, "but after that, you're good to go."

"Oh my God, this has been . . ." I swallowed hard. "Thank you. Thank you so much for taking care of her."

"I'm glad to see everything work out for you. Some of these situations . . ." The look she gave me, the almost imperceptible shake of the head, made it clear how close I'd come to losing everything that mattered.

It was after midnight when we left the hospital. I texted Benilda from the Uber to let her know we were on our way, and then I texted Grace that Paige was fine and we were bringing her home, and promised to call her tomorrow.

"Maybe we should take a few days off and go to my parents'," James said. "Mom can spoil her and she'll get plenty of rest. And it's not like Henry would miss anything important at school."

Henry. I grabbed my phone again, remembering the three missed messages. At the time, I'd barely registered that they were from Graylon. I played the first message from the school, my heart sinking. "Hello, Mrs. Summers, this is Rhonda Edmonds calling from Graylon Academy. Ms. Parekh was expecting you at four o'clock. Could you call and let us know if you are on your way?"

"Fuck," I whispered.

"What was that about?"

I deleted all three messages without listening to the other two. I didn't need to hear them to know how much shit I was in. "Just a meeting I missed. I'll deal with it. How could you take time off to go to your parents' when you've barely been home all week?"

James didn't say anything for a moment. "I don't know, Jules. Sometimes I wonder if it's worth it. I mean, fuck it, you know? Something like this happens and I kind of wish I was still hanging drywall for Micky McInerney and living in a garage."

James always said stuff like that when the job stress got bad, and sometimes a trip home to Allentown could snap him out of his funk. But right now I didn't think I could bear to spend three nights with Lorraine and Ed in their outdated split-level that smelled like Glade plug-ins and cat litter.

"I don't think traveling is a good idea, James. Paige will recover more quickly without distractions."

"Yeah, you're probably right."

But I made a mental note not to complain the next time we made the trip. If James could forgive me for nearly killing our daughter, I could put up with my in-laws for a weekend.

When we got home, James carried Paige up in the elevator. Benilda was sitting in the kitchen with her back ramrod straight. James barely acknowledged her. "I'm going to tuck her in," he said gruffly and headed down the hall with Paige in his arms.

"You are sure she is fine?" Benilda asked.

"Yes. Thank God." I was exhausted, but I owed Benilda an explanation. I went to the refrigerator and reached for the bottle of Sancerre and then thought better of it and grabbed a bottle of Pellegrino.

"Benilda, I want to thank you for, um, everything you did today. For canceling your plans and staying so late with Henry. I just want to explain what happened." I gave her an abbreviated version of what the doctor had said, that there shouldn't be any lingering side effects other than fatigue, and no long-term consequences. I glossed over how Paige had gotten the pill in the first place, and I definitely didn't say what kind of "medication" it was.

"So, is all big accident, right?" Her voice was strange, hollow and sharp.

Something in her tone made me wary. "Well, yes, but the responsibility falls—I made a mistake having that, er, medicine where a child could find it."

"Paige and Henry, they are good kids."

"Yes," I agreed, wondering what she was getting at. "Yes, they are."

"I treat them like my own."

"And we appreciate that—so much, Benilda, you know that. I always tell everyone, you're the heart of this family." That wasn't *exactly* what I said, but it made my point—we knew we couldn't manage without her.

Benilda made a little sound like air puffing out of a balloon. "I am quitting. I will work next two weeks, but I have a new job in Queens, I can stay with Thelma son family."

"Benilda!" I gasped. "Please don't—I know this was an awful day, and I should have handled it differently—everything—"

"Is not about today," Benilda said, shaking her head, and there it was, her eternal stubbornness; I knew from experience that anything I said to try to change her mind would only make her dig in deeper. "I am more convenient to Queens. You want me to ask friends if they want new job?"

"Benilda . . ." I couldn't lose her. "Mr. Summers and I have been meaning to talk to you about what we pay you. I think we should give you a bonus—everything you've been through, and you still made us a priority, and we want to recognize that—and—"

But she was shaking her head. "New family pays me same as you," she said. "But it isn't about money." She stood, with the dignity of a queen debarking a ship. "I will be here regular time tomorrow and I will talk to my friends. Good night, Mrs. Julia."

I stood also, trying to think of something else to say, some way to pull her back, but she was already gone.

I stared at the front door after it closed, trying to process the fact that Benilda had just left me. Us. James didn't come back. I knew I should go tell him, but the shock of Benilda's departure kept me rooted to the spot.

After a moment I went to the sink and poured the rest of the Pellegrino out and put the bottle in the recycling bin. Then I poured myself a glass of wine, all the way to the brim.

CHAPTER 26

Despite drinking half a bottle of wine before collapsing on Paige's floor next to her bed, under her extra blanket, I was up well before the alarm went off. I showered, dressed, and made coffee.

James shuffled out of the bedroom a little after six. I set his cup of coffee on the table and sat down across from him. "Thank you for being so understanding yesterday," I began. "What I did—I wouldn't blame you for being furious with me."

"It's okay. Look—leaving it in the nightstand was pretty stupid. But it could have happened to anyone. Remember that time Tim had those blunts in his Dopp kit? And Paige brought them out in the living room when we were watching a movie and we were afraid she'd eaten one?"

I shuddered at the memory. "Listen, I know that the most important thing is that she's okay. But we have to think about what this means for . . ." I tried to figure out how to say it; I was afraid Tatum might be angry enough at me for giving the cops Brooke's name that she'd tell people I kept drugs lying around the house. "If people find out."

"What, you're worried about what people will *think*?" A muscle in James's jaw jumped. "Fucking Christ's sake. Do we *look* like the kind of people who leave that shit lying around? Besides, it wasn't even yours! Anyone who wants to judge you isn't worth your time."

It was so simple for James—in his world, the subtleties of the social hierarchy did not exist. People were your friends—or they weren't. There were good guys, guys you only kept around to get the job done, and pieces of shit who could go fuck themselves. His repertoire only included live-and-let-live and full-scale assault, with very little in between.

"Okay, I guess maybe you're right." There really wasn't any point in trying to explain it to him.

I spent the morning doting on Paige and going through the closets and under the sinks, throwing out every old prescription, moving every bottle of toxic chemicals and cleaners to the high shelf of the linen closet. Grace had sent me a brief message saying she was glad Paige was all right, but when I texted her to call me when she had a minute, I didn't hear back. Benilda kept her distance, doing laundry and straightening the kids' rooms. It was awkward—I felt like we had nothing left to say to each other.

Late in the morning, after I'd taken a second bag of household cleaners to the trash chute, Tatum texted me.

Hope your happy Julia?????????????????

I told Brooke you told the cops it was her drugs she's so upset do you have any idea how much trouble she could be in?!?!?!?

I texted back in a blind rage—was I really supposed to feel sorry for Brooke after what she'd done to my family?

Paige could have DIED. It looked like CANDY. Forgive me for caring about my own child!!

Her response came just as fast. **I saw Grace at class she says Paige is totally fine**

That stung—Grace had time to go to spin and chat after class but couldn't bother to call me back?

Yes but that doesn't change the fact this wouldn't have happened if it wasn't for Brooke and before you decide to tell everyone why Paige was in the hospital remember I can always call the cops back and tell them I was confused and the molly was yours not hers

This was a bluff, because Stewart had told James that the cops wouldn't care who gave me the pill, that they wouldn't even have bothered to put Brooke's name in their report.

After a long pause, Tatum finally responded.

We need to talk

Fred's noon Saturday

I spent the rest of the day cleaning up my mess while Paige dozed in a nest of blankets in front of the television, and Benilda dusted the baseboards on her hands and knees. I called Zarine Parekh and, reaching one of her assistants, explained that Paige had been hospitalized due to a reaction to medication, and that while she was expected to make a full recovery, James and I had spent several hours fearing for her life and had completely forgotten the meeting. I didn't even finish my story before the assistant was falling all over herself reassuring me that she understood completely. Zarine herself called me back within ten minutes, and told me that the entire staff was holding Paige in their thoughts. Then she added in a somewhat embarrassed tone that while the other parents had insisted on holding the meeting without me and James, upon review she didn't think the boys' behavior merited more than monitoring after all, and that I didn't need to reschedule.

A bouquet of sweetheart roses arrived for Paige while I was making dinner. The card read, WISHING YOU A SPEEDY RECOVERY, FROM ALL YOUR FRIENDS AT GRAYLON ACADEMY. James said he wished he'd been the first person to send his daughter flowers and put the roses on Paige's desk, where she could see them from her bed. Already she was much better, complaining she was bored.

Grace and Lindsay weren't at drop-off on Friday morning, and Hollis Graves told me that a bunch of women were spending the day on a house tour in Brooklyn benefiting the Brownsville Community Foundation and featuring the work of half a dozen up-and-coming interior designers.

"I would have gone," she added, "but I had a commitment I just couldn't get out of."

So I wasn't the only one who hadn't been invited.

I was trying to politely extricate myself when I noticed a group of women clustered around Gigi McLayne. Gigi's eyes were swollen from crying, and Elizabeth Kim was holding her arm as if to keep her standing while Poppy squeezed her hand.

"What's up with Gigi?" I asked Hollis.

"You didn't hear? Her mom passed yesterday. She had a stroke, I guess it came completely out of the blue."

"Oh my God, that's terrible," I said.

"I *know*. It happened in a yoga class at River Rock Ranch. They won't be able to fly the body back until Monday."

I'd met Gigi's mom at a few events—she was another member of the old guard, a woman who'd spent her entire life on the Upper East Side, leaving only long enough to attend Radcliffe and come back with a fiancé from Harvard. My heart went out to Gigi; I had a feeling our mothers would have had a lot in common.

"I think Poppy's setting up a Meal Train," Hollis said. "And she's looking for someone to take the dogs for the next few days, until after the memorial. Preferably a quiet home with no children."

Gigi had two poorly trained Yorkshire terriers that she sometimes brought to drop-off, where they chased pigeons and got their leashes tangled and barked nonstop.

"Can't they just board them?"

"I guess they're worried about traumatizing them more than they already are. Dogs can sense grief, you know—there's scientific proof. Poppy said Daisy started chewing her paws the moment Gigi got the phone call."

"Uh-huh. Wow, too bad Henry's so active, or I'd offer to take them."

"You're so generous, Julia," Hollis said, touching my arm. "It's times like this when you find out who you can really count on, you know?"

"Oh, do I ever," I said grimly, as we watched Gigi's little group begin their solemn procession to Toast of the Town for cappuccinos.

I told James I had plans to see a show at the Guggenheim with a friend on Saturday, and he told me to have fun and that he would take good care of Paige while I was gone. I arrived at the restaurant on the ninth floor of Barneys precisely at noon and saw Tatum before she saw me. She was already seated at a prime table by the window, a glass of wine in front of her.

She'd dressed for the occasion. She was wearing the ivory leather bomber over a white silk tank, jeans, and a pair of camel suede boots. Her only jewelry was a pair of four-stone diamond studs that looked a lot like the Tiffany Victoria line.

"That looks refreshing," I said, indicating the bottle of Moulin Touchais Chenin Blanc sweating in a bed of ice next to the table.

"I assumed you'd have a glass or two," Tatum said coolly.

It was an excellent choice, which made me wonder with a wave of something like jealousy who'd been coaching her. A waiter rushed to bring me a menu and pour me a glass.

"The salads are very good here." There was something about her tone, a brittleness that only increased my wariness.

"You've been here before?"

Tatum narrowed her eyes. "Yes, twice, in fact."

I didn't believe her—left to her own devices, Tatum's taste ran to places that only tourists went. But I ordered my usual lobster salad, and after the server left, I folded my hands and waited.

"Well, I guess you should be proud of yourself," Tatum said. "Brooke and I broke up, thanks to you."

"*Me!* How exactly am I responsible for your love life?"

"You threw her under the bus. I tried to defend you, God knows why. That didn't go over well."

"If she broke up with you, that wasn't the only reason," I said, but with those two, who knew? "I'm not going to apologize for protecting my child."

"First of all, I didn't say that *she* broke up with *me*, only that we broke up. You always do that—you're constantly trying to pin blame on people, do you even realize that?" She was angrier than I'd ever seen her. "And I don't need an *apology*. I'm here to tell you that you're not calling the cops. And you're definitely not giving them my name."

"Oh?"

"I get that you think what happened to Paige is Brooke's fault. Even though nobody made you come to the club that night—and you could have thrown that pill out anytime. But the point is you're not thinking about the bigger picture."

"Which is . . . ?"

"You know something, Julia, ever since I met you, you've treated me like I crawled out of a gutter somewhere and you're doing me this huge favor by letting me babysit your kids and inviting me to some boring weekend in the Hamptons and then telling me who I can and can't talk to, like I'm some—some little kid who can't even go to the bathroom by herself. Oh, and by the way, thanks so much for loaning me your old stuff that you were going to get rid of. None of it even fit. Were you *trying* to make me look ridiculous?"

"I was trying to *help* you," I retorted. "That first time we had coffee, all you could talk about was how badly you wanted my life."

"Get over it, Julia." I'd never heard this tone before. Gone was any trace of her bubbly charm, her fresh-faced enthusiasm. Sitting here in Fred's with a wineglass in her hand, she looked like any other smug rich girl with a trust fund and an attitude. "The only reason you ever had coffee with me was because *you* wanted to use *me*. You thought if you could take credit for my success at Flame, somehow it would make you more popular, but here's a news flash, Julia—no one cares! In a few months, none of your friends will even remember that the fundraiser was your idea. And the other teachers think you're a freak, the way you're always hanging around the studio, shoving people out of the way just so you can ride on that stupid podium bike." She set down her glass and leaned slightly closer so that I could see the points of her pearly little canine teeth. *"No. One. Cares."*

"You still don't get it." I held the stem of my own glass so tightly I thought it might break. "Do you really think I care what the other teachers think? Or *Paz*? They don't matter—I'm surprised you haven't learned that by now. Maybe you're not as smart as I thought you were. Listen, you're not fooling everyone. Lindsay told me I should hide the good silver when you're around."

Tatum raised one perfectly tweezed eyebrow. "Lindsay just called me to get on my personal training waiting list. I told her I'd do my best to squeeze her in sooner, as a favor to a *friend*."

That one took the wind out of me. To cover, I took a sip of my wine. The waiter came and set our salads in front of us, and Tatum dismissed him with a nod.

"We could go around and around like this all day," Tatum said. "But the bottom line is, out of gratitude for the kindness you showed me, you can still be one of my VIP riders. Just like Grace and Coco and the others. You can have your turn riding up and I'll tag you in my posts. As far as anyone knows, we'll still be friends."

"And in exchange?"

"I'd think that would be obvious. You'll treat me like the friend I supposedly am. Invite me to the right events, introduce me to the right people—and don't ever patronize me again."

I was surprised she knew the word. "And I guess you want me to forget all about our big night out, especially the part where you left that girl passed out in the bathroom."

"Obviously. And stay away from Brooke. Don't talk to her, don't talk *about* her."

That one caught me off guard. Could it be that Tatum truly had feelings for Brooke? "Breakup's been hard on you, is that it?"

"I'm in a new relationship now—I don't need the drama."

"I see." I didn't believe her . . . but knowing her weakness might come in handy at some point. "Listen—since we've cleared things up between us, I need a favor."

"Oh?" Her expression didn't change, that hint of calculation always there in her eyes.

"Lindsay's birthday is coming up. I want to do something different this year, and since apparently she and Grace are completely obsessed with you, I was thinking you could do a private session for the three of us next Friday night." I was counting on Tatum's narcissism to prevent her from recognizing how desperate I was to hold on to my friends. "I'll pay you, of course, and I'll talk to Ken about renting the studio. Nothing over the top, just a few decorations, an easy session with her favorite music—I'll send you a playlist—and cake and champagne after, then we'd go out for drinks or a late dinner. You can join us, if you want."

"Sure," Tatum said. "Lindsay and Grace are both so sweet, I'd love to help."

"Excellent."

"The only problem is that Ken doesn't rent studio space for parties, only for charity events and fundraisers. Don't worry, though, I can give you the code for the service entrance door—we can get in that way after hours and stay as long as you want. And they still haven't fixed the security camera in the hall, so no one will ever know."

"Are you sure?" I would have much preferred to play this straight. "I don't want to risk it if there's any chance of getting in trouble."

"No chance at all," Tatum said confidently. "Trust me."

CHAPTER 27

When I got home, I called Grace.

"Julia!" she said in a rush. "Sorry, I meant to call, but things have been crazy around here. Did you hear about Gigi's mom?"

"I did," I said. "So tragic. How was the house tour?"

"Good," she said, after a beat. "How is Paige feeling?"

I suspected that if I hadn't called Grace I wouldn't have heard from her all weekend, but I let it go. "Much better, thanks. We're just taking it easy this weekend, but she'll be back at school Monday."

"What on earth did she take, anyway?"

Luckily I was prepared for this, having done some online research and come up with a cover story. All Paige knew was that a pill had made her sick; she barely even remembered going to the hospital. I felt terrible about lying to her—but I would feel even worse if people started whispering behind her back. "It turns out that she has a penicillin allergy, of all things."

"You're kidding! How did she go so long without being diagnosed?"

"You know Paige—she's hardly ever sick, she never got ear infections the way Henry does. I told the doctor she'd never had a reaction before, but then I remembered that both times she's taken amoxicillin, she complained about being dizzy and itching. But she can be so dramatic, I just assumed it was from the strep."

"But why was it so much worse this time? I mean what even happened?"

"It was terrifying," I said; at least I didn't have to lie about that.

"Her tongue and throat swelled up so much that she was having trouble breathing, and I got hysterical and that scared her and made everything worse, and I ended up calling 911."

"Oh my God, Julia!"

"I *know*. She went to the hospital in an ambulance, with me sitting there sobbing the whole way next to her." I faked a sheepish laugh. "I definitely overreacted, but you see your child struggling to breathe, and . . . anyway they gave her an antihistamine and she was better in a few hours. And luckily there are other antibiotics that she can take."

"You have got to call the school and get that in her records," Grace said.

I hadn't thought of that. "I'm already on it," I lied, wondering how I could avoid reporting it to the school nurse. In theory all the kids' medical information was confidential, but like everything else, it tended to leak out. I knew which kids had EpiPens, who took ADHD medication, whose nut allergies were genuinely serious. "But they say she'll probably grow out of it anyway, as long as we avoid penicillin for a few years. It shouldn't ever happen again."

"Well," Grace said, her voice turning brisk. "I'm just so, so glad everything's okay! And listen, we should definitely try again to get the girls together once things settle down."

"There was one other thing," I said hastily, before she could make an excuse to get off the phone. "I wanted to nail down the details for Lindsay's birthday."

"Oh, that's right—your little surprise," she said, without much enthusiasm. "Look, you know I'd love to help, but the next couple of weeks are ridiculous."

"Don't worry, I've got it all covered," I said. "All you need to do is show up."

I told her the same thing I'd said to Tatum—just a fun, easy private session in the spin studio after Flame closed, a little cake and champagne, and then we'd go out for dinner. "I'm making a custom playlist, it'll be *so* fun."

"I guess," Grace said doubtfully, "although are we really going to want to get all sweaty before we go out?"

"No, it's not going to be like that, it's not supposed to be a regular class. I mean, it's mostly just about the music and—and Tatum—"

I was floundering; it hadn't occurred to me that Grace wouldn't be thrilled. But then again, she was one of Tatum's star riders now—she could see Tatum anytime she wanted. I felt a flash of resentment, even bitterness—here I was, practically begging my supposed best friend to come to a party I was going to considerable trouble and expense to throw. *Not worth it,* a little voice nagged at me, but I silenced it by thinking of how much they'd all love it, once they realized what I'd done.

"That could be cool," Grace conceded. "We could get some good pictures."

"Definitely!" I said, though I'd have to break it to them at some point that we couldn't post any pictures because we weren't actually supposed to be there. "I was thinking Tatum could pick you guys up while I'm setting up. You could all have a drink at your place first."

"I'd have to see what Matt's up to, but yeah, that could work."

Okay, so she wasn't exactly doing flips over the idea, but at least she'd said yes. And I was so sure Lindsay would love it.

"So maybe nine o'clock? If Tatum comes by your place around eight-fifteen, that would give you time to have a drink, and I can put up a few decorations."

"What—like crepe paper on the handlebars? I think I've still got some goody bags from Clara's party." Grace laughed. "Maybe we can play Red Rover."

I pretended to laugh along, wondering why I'd ever thought this was a good idea. But I was committed, so all I could do now was try to make sure it was a night to remember.

Now that Tatum and I had worked things out, I resolved to make it to one of her classes every day that week, alternating between her morning and afternoon sessions to make sure everyone saw me. I wore my favorite workout clothes and used primer and concealer and a brightener to make it seem like I had naturally perfect skin. I'd lost another two pounds, and one day when I caught sight of my image in the studio mirror, I didn't recognize myself.

Hollis emailed the details for Gigi's mother's memorial service the next week, and I signed up on the meal rotation website and ordered dinner to be delivered from Italianissimo. No matter how chaotic life got, there were certain obligations one never, ever tried to get out of, and paying one's respects to a friend who'd lost a parent was at the top of the list.

I was back on the lunch circuit, reconnected to the grapevine, and was thinking about throwing a dinner party and inviting Tatum, timing it after the TomorrowMakers gala and before the holiday season kicked into gear.

I floated the idea at lunch with Penelope Epstein and Emery Souza. Reaching out to Emery had required swallowing my pride, given our chronic low-grade feud, and I'd invited Penelope to act as a neutral third party. It seemed to be working—at least, until I brought up the dinner party.

"You'd have to keep it to three couples, four at the most, given your dining room," Emery said, breaking off bits of her scone but not eating them. She seemed to have lost her appetite after I took off my jacket, revealing my tight black Iro half-zip with see-through sleeves that showed off the definition in my arms.

I figured she was punishing me with that crack about the size of my apartment. "We've had twelve for dinner plenty of times. Though honestly, I'm thinking something intimate, maybe the Friday before Halloween."

"Isn't that the night Grace and Shayla are doing the progressive dinner?" Penelope said, adding a slow stream of Splenda to her tea.

"The what?" I said, realizing my error too late.

"You didn't know about it? I assumed you'd be hosting it with them," Emery said, barely able to conceal her glee. "You're coming, though, right?"

"Oh, yeah . . ." I said, "I totally forgot—maybe I'll move my dinner to the next week."

But my face was burning; I knew they knew I hadn't been invited. I took the lid off my coffee and blew on it, anything to create a distraction. "The coffee's always so hot here! It's a wonder they don't get sued."

"I think I'm doing dessert," Emery said, even though Penelope was shooting her looks. "I'll have Tina stay late so she can get the coffee going. Maybe I'll have her make a pavlova."

"So back to *your* dinner, Julia," Penelope said kindly, and I wondered why I'd never been better friends with her. "Were you thinking of any particular theme?"

I stuttered some response, and Penelope skillfully steered the conversation until Emery gave up and went back to sulking. After the proper amount of time had lapsed, we said goodbye and went our separate ways, and only when I was halfway home did I realize I'd left my jacket on the chair. Those mesh sleeves didn't exactly keep me warm.

It wasn't like I could ask Grace why she hadn't told me about the dinner.

So she was hosting a dinner party with her friend, who happened to be a former model and hung out with famous actors, and I wasn't invited. So what? It wasn't like she was required to invite me to every party she ever threw. All famous hostesses rotated their guest lists. Keeping the mix fresh was one of my own best tricks, and I always threw in a few surprise guests to liven things up.

But I'd never leave out my best friends.

I tried to ignore my hurt feelings and put all my energy into Lindsay's birthday party, which was now just two days away. Instinctively I knew that making a bigger deal of it—say, with a big Happy Birthday sign strung between the bikes or a treasure hunt around the gym or a slide show of the three of us set to her favorite song—was not the way to go; my best shot was to keep it understated but perfect, something I knew I could pull off. Like the vintage English sterling wine collar I'd given Garth for his fortieth birthday, the party needed to reflect my singular taste and style and remind my friends that I could never be replaced by someone like Emery Souza, no matter how many chairs she could fit around her dining room table.

Having Tatum there, making it clear I could summon her anytime I wanted, was a solid start. I spent the rest of the day gilding the lily and giving my credit card a workout.

I found myself in midtown Thursday after finishing the last of my errands for the party and decided to stop by James's office to surprise him. I was feeling better now that everything was in place, confident I'd nailed it, and I was thinking I'd treat myself and get hot chocolate with James at Maison du Chocolat.

His firm was located in a nondescript older building off Madison Avenue. I took the elevator to the sixth floor, admiring, as I always did, the old oak paneling with its scent of wood polish, the inlaid mother-of-pearl numerals. But when I reached his office, there was a placard on the door announcing that the suite was for lease. I looked up and down the hallway—maybe I was confused, had I gotten off on the wrong floor?—and then I reached for the placard and yanked it off.

Underneath was his company logo. I tried the doorknob, attempted to peer through the frosted glass. I could make out the contours of the built-in reception desk, but the Florence Knoll sofa and coffee table I'd chosen were gone, as was the large sign I'd had made for the wall behind the desk, a tasteful, spare version of the logo rendered in Prussian blue and gray.

I backed away from the door, feeling slightly nauseous. What the hell was happening?

I leaned against the wall and forced myself to think. The last time I'd been here had been—could it have been back in June? The week the children got out of school? We'd all gone out for burgers and shakes at Black Tap, and James told the kids he'd pay them five dollars for every book they read over the summer, a hefty increase from the quarter his own father had given him.

It might as well have happened in another century. The hall was empty and echoing, smelling faintly of old newspapers. James had given up his office—but why? And more significantly—why hadn't he told me?

I got out my phone and dialed, chewing on a nail while I waited for him to pick up.

"Hey," he answered, sounding out of breath.

"James? I'm standing outside your office. What used to be your office. What the hell is going on?"

There was a pause—and as you can only do with the people you know the best in the world, I was able to read an entire narrative into it. I sensed his guilt and fear and annoyance and regret, all before he spoke.

"Oh, Jules," he finally said. "I just didn't want to tell you while you were so busy with the new school year. I knew you'd worry, and I was afraid you'd blow it all out of proportion."

"Blow it—" I sputtered, my voice going shrill. "And how am I not supposed to worry? Tell me one thing, just one thing—do you still have a job? Do we still have an income?"

"Jesus, Julia, for Christ's fucking sake! Just stay right there—I'll come to you."

"But where are you?"

"I'm at—I'm down in the financial district. I was just walking out for lunch. Give me fifteen minutes tops."

He hung up, and I was left staring at my phone, practically hyperventilating. At this hour, there was no way he was getting here that fast—a cab would shoot up the FDR but then get mired on Forty-second Street. I thought about just going home, letting him show up and experience a fraction of the alarm I was feeling, but I needed to know what was going on.

I made my way down to the lobby and sat on a bench and waited. I watched the traffic go by, avoided eye contact with the guard behind his desk, resisted the urge to pace. It was close to half an hour before James burst through the doors, coattails flapping behind him, and threw his arms around me. I felt the stiff cotton of his shirt against my face, inhaled his scent of starch and aftershave and a faint note of sweat. He patted my back like I was a foundling kitten.

But I was in no mood to be coddled. I pulled away angrily. "What were you doing downtown, anyway? Paying off inspectors?"

"Christ," James muttered under his breath. "Can we go somewhere to talk?"

"Not until you tell me what's going on."

James raked his hand through his hair. He caught the guard's eye, nodded at him. "Hey, Monty, good to see you."

"Good to see you, Mr. Summers, been way too quiet around here without you."

"Yeah, yeah. Hey, take care, hear?" James took my elbow and propelled me out the door and onto the street.

"Did you have to do that in front of people we know?" he demanded once we were outside.

People we know—not something most people would call a security guard, especially since I'd never seen the guy before. But these were James's people: the anonymous toilers, the ones who kept the gears turning. I think he still felt like one of them himself.

"Can we at least go somewhere inside?" I asked. There was a Starbucks thirty feet away, and I headed toward it without waiting for James's response, but he hustled to get to the door in time to open it for me. I headed straight for the only empty table and sat, rigid and furious, while he got our drinks. I lifted the lid of mine and sniffed—he'd gotten my usual skim latte right, but that was only a minor point in his favor.

I took a small sip and set it down. "So?"

"Okay, look," James said nervously. "To start with, there's no reason to freak out, okay? You know this Mercer project has been a shit show for the last six months. It's been one fucking piece of bad luck after another, nothing we could have anticipated, believe me. The variances—I had Cora's *word* on them. Her and De Stasi, both. I mean shit, we let Cora take her whole goddamn crew to the Hamptons house for spring break, remember?"

I did indeed remember. We'd gone to Beaver Creek to ski, so

James let Cora and Josie and their two dogs use the house. James had even sent a case of wine—all to thank her for streamlining the process of granting the zoning variances required by the building plan.

"But I don't understand," I said. "You got the variances, so what's the problem?"

James looked down at his paper cup, which he had yet to drink from. "The *problem* is that DCAS is threatening to slap a stop work order on me because now they're saying the deed restriction should never have been lifted."

A cold tentacle of fear reached around my heart. I may pretend not to understand James's job when it suits me, but I got an A in Capital Markets and Investments and I knew the effect a stop work order could have on a project of this size: every day that James's crew was idle meant accruing holding costs, frustrating investors, and delaying the day tenants started paying rent.

"That's—okay, that's a problem," I conceded. "But they've got to understand—"

"There's something I didn't tell you," James said, his voice strangled. He looked up at me; his expression was that of a man about to walk the plank. "Finn pulled out."

I blinked, my mouth going dry. "When?"

"March." The skin at the corner of his right eye twitched. "When he found out the zoning didn't go through."

"How . . . how much was he in for?"

"Four point eight."

I felt faint. "Please don't tell me . . . James. James, tell me you didn't."

"I covered it. It was too late to—look, Jules. He got spooked. He's an idiot. He'll be kicking himself forever, but I had to act, you know? What was I going to do, let the whole thing go?"

Yes, I thought, *because this was our life you were playing with, and Mercer was just a building.* I recognized the name Finn; he was a frequent investor in James's projects, going back years. He'd come to dinner once with a few other investors and their wives.

"How?" was all I said.

"The, ah . . . I cashed in the Sankyo stock. And the, um, the insurance check from the Hamptons house. I'm so sorry, Jules. I should have told you."

I was speechless.

"This is temporary, Jules, you gotta know that, okay?" James said in a rush. "Marlowe says Special Investigations hasn't got a case. I mean, they can't legally *un*lift the restriction—especially since I had nothing to do with it. It happened before I ever submitted a bid on the place. But it's the activists. I mean they act like we're roasting babies in there—my guys can't even come to work without protesters trying to block the entrance. And they got to Cora and Larry and I don't even know who else."

"But construction hasn't stopped, right? They can't stop you working . . ."

"I mean, sure, for now," James said. "They're letting us go ahead with engineering and demo. Technically, they can't stop the rest unless they file."

My mind was racing in a dozen different directions. James had put up the money an investor pulled out; with all of the delays the project had faced, the initial development costs were undoubtedly going over. He couldn't afford the overhead so he got rid of the office . . .

"But where have you been working?" I asked. "Where's everyone else?"

James was shaking his head before I finished speaking. "We just set up some space at the site. And honestly, when you think about it, this is kind of a good wake-up call. What were we doing in almost two thousand square feet, when most of the staff work at home these days? And who are we trying to impress? I haven't sold a job out of the office in . . . I mean, I'm on-site, I'm at the Building Department. I'm meeting with the mucky-mucks in their offices. And before you ask me, Jules, I haven't laid anyone off, though if things don't turn around soon . . . but come on, I'd never leave my guys high and dry."

I was having trouble tracking. Unlike James, who was agitated, fidgeting, I could only handle one thought at a time. And the thought I was having was—

"Is this connected to the federal investigator? Truth this time."

"Oh, that—no, I mean yes, that was over a complaint someone filed. From a tenants' rights group. But it was dismissed, they were just sounding off, there wasn't any merit to it. Like ninety-nine percent of those bonehead complaints."

"You cooperated, though, right? With the investigation?"

"It didn't even get that far," James said dismissively. "Just a guy in a cheap suit with a bunch of questions he could have answered himself if he'd done his homework."

"So all these times . . . all these nights you haven't come home, where have you been? At the site?"

"Come on, Jules, you act like I'm never around. Haven't you noticed I've been home almost every night lately?"

"Yes, and I appreciate it, believe me. But what about when you're not? Where do you *sleep*?"

"I told you, we set up an office at the site. Temporary, obviously, but I've got all my stuff there. My files and shit, the couch. Look, let me take you out to lunch," James said, almost pleading. "We can go to Sparks. What do you say, I'll get the porterhouse and you can have the Cobb."

It was an old joke, from early in our dating days. Sparks had been a splurge for him at the time, and James had encouraged me to order their signature dish, a porterhouse as big as my face. I was on a perpetual diet at the time and had ordered the Cobb salad. But James, noticing that I'd chosen one of the least expensive items on the menu, blurted, *You're breaking up with me, aren't you?*

"I don't think so," I said. "I'm just going to head home."

"Aw, come on, don't be like that—"

"Where's the furniture?" I demanded. "The sign? What about the carpet I had put in that office? It was *custom,* James."

"It's—we saved some of it," he faltered. "What we could."

I pushed back my chair and stood. "So all this time, you decided that rather than tell me what was going on, you'd just keep it to yourself while you gambled with our lives. Our *children's* lives, James."

"I didn't—I wouldn't—" He got up too, his chair scraping the floor noisily.

"Just save it. Okay? I mean, why take me into your confidence now? After all, I'm only your wife."

With that inadequate exit line, I gathered my bags and left.

CHAPTER 28

James found me crying in the bathroom that night after I'd gotten the kids to bed.

"Hey, hey," he said as I tried to wipe off my ruined makeup. I pushed him away when he put his arms around me, but he wasn't having it; he just held me tighter until I gave up and cried on his shirt.

"I'm sorry," he mumbled. "For all of it."

"It's just . . . the stock?" I snuffled. As much money as James made, we'd been sloppy about funding our retirement, and that stock represented a big chunk of our savings. James liked to put our spare cash into aggressively paying down our mortgages. (I could thank my father-in-law for that instinct; Ed was one of those guys who equated debt with moral weakness.)

"We'll buy it back as soon as Mercer wraps up. Hell, we'll probably come out ahead."

I wasn't so sure about that . . . but what was done was done. "I'm sorry I was so mean earlier," I said. "It was just a shock, seeing that For Rent sign."

"You've got a right to be pissed. You put a lot of work into decorating that office."

We were falling all over ourselves apologizing, but I had the feeling we were avoiding the heart of the matter, the real reasons we'd ended up where we had. The truth was that James had never actually asked me to decorate his office; he'd simply tolerated it. If James had his way, he'd still be using the old desk that he got cheap at OfficeMax years ago because one of the legs was bent. And this whole business with Mercer—it wasn't like him to take such lop-sided risks. Sure, he thrived on adrenaline, but this was something else entirely.

"I think I'm going to cancel Lindsay's party," I said, turning back to the mirror and busying myself with a cotton ball.

"What? Why do you want to go and do something like that? You need a night out with the girls."

I smiled weakly at his reflection. "The thing is, James, I kind of went all out. Flowers, champagne, her gift . . . I spent a lot more than I should have."

He was already shaking his head. "Come on, Jules, we're not in the poorhouse yet. Besides, you're splitting it with Grace, so how bad can it be?"

That was a little fib I'd told James, along with lying to him about where we were having the party: I'd told him Matt was taking the kids to visit his mom so we were going to use their apartment. My lies were stacking up so fast, it was a wonder I could keep them straight.

"It's not just the money," I admitted. "Things have been kind of weird with them lately. Grace is acting . . . different."

"Girls are flaky—isn't that what you always tell Paige?" What I actually told Paige was something I'd heard at a talk Graylon put on last year given by a psychologist who specialized in adolescent fe-male relationships: she said that while "mean girl" behavior could and should be addressed and redirected, the instinct was develop-mentally appropriate and even necessary to forming a healthy self-concept. Or, in terms Paige could understand, it was fine to *feel like* excluding Maya Kim from her sleepover, but she had to invite her anyway because I made the rules.

"We're not girls," I pointed out. "Lindsay's turning forty-one."

"I thought you said Grace was the problem. Besides, it doesn't matter how old you are, some things don't change—even for guys."

I snorted. "I don't think getting arrested with Jack is the same thing."

"We didn't get *arrested,*" James corrected, chuckling at the mem-ory. When we were in Allentown for the holidays last year, one of

James's old friends had convinced him to do donuts on the top floor of a parking garage, which had resulted in a cop giving him a three-hundred-dollar ticket. "Guys are just better at working shit out, that's all."

He trundled off to bed, still laughing at the memory, while I took off the last of my mascara and found a few new lines around my eyes.

I didn't cancel, obviously—it would have required explaining things I didn't want getting out. There had been a time when I would have confided everything to Grace and Lindsay, not just what James had done but my fears and insecurities and regrets—but I no longer trusted them to keep it to themselves.

I took Tatum's afternoon class on Friday, and afterward she showed me the service door and gave me the code and confirmed that she'd bring Grace and Lindsay around 9:00 P.M. The last class ended at 6:45 P.M., so I'd have plenty of time.

When I got home, Benilda was getting ready to go get the kids, zipping up a puffy vest that made her look like a giant marshmallow.

"Flowers came," she said, jabbing a finger at the kitchen. "You ordered six? Is not a mistake?"

I'd forgotten to tell her they were being delivered. I hadn't even mentioned the party because she would have wanted to know whose birthday it was and why I wasn't having it here and I didn't feel like explaining—especially because Benilda had never mentioned Tatum's name since Tatum had moved out.

I went to check the flowers, six petite arrangements of white camellias, fuchsia anemones, and trailing pea vine in miniature tin pails from my favorite florist. My plan was to arrange them on the ledge under the mirror that ran along the side wall, flanking the cake in the center. Benilda followed me in and watched me carefully pull back the waxed florist's paper and inhale the cloying scent of the camellias.

"Pretty fancy," she observed. "Expensive, huh?"

I ignored that. "I'm taking them to a party. Did the delivery from Wine Emporium come?"

"Uh-huh. I thought it was mistake—second time this week they come."

"It's for the *party*," I repeated. I wouldn't miss Benilda tracking my drinking when she was gone, shaking her head at the sound of empty bottles clanking when she took the trash out. "Listen, when you come back could you go down to the storage unit and bring up my silver ice bucket? The plain one, not the one with the monogram."

"I have to leave at five."

"I know that, Benilda, but it'll take you all of ten minutes. I need to get in the shower."

"It's so messy in storage unit," she called after me as I headed for my room to get ready. "I don't know how I can find it."

James got home early, carrying a plastic-wrapped bouquet and even finding a vase to put it in. "For when you get home," he said, "and tomorrow morning you can give me all the gossip."

He was certainly trying to be a model husband since confessing about Mercer. I kissed him and squeezed his ass as a reward, and I was out the door by 7:30 P.M. in a lamb's-wool wrap and a black workout unitard that had cutouts at the hip bones and thighs. I was down to 121 pounds, the least I'd weighed since high school.

James insisted on carrying the champagne and ice and flowers and cake to the Uber and told me to have a nice time. When we arrived at Flame, I asked the driver to pull up to the service entrance and help me carry everything in and gave him a twenty for his trouble.

The service entrance opened onto a common hall with a door that led to the spin studio. Inside, everything was silent and still. I turned on the lights, thinking how surprised Lindsay would be when Tatum showed up instead of me. Imagining that moment—*You have to hand it to Julia*, I imagined her telling people Monday morning, *nobody throws a party the way she does*—more than made up for my trouble.

I'd never been in the studio alone before. The bikes waited patiently, like cattle at a gate. My footsteps echoed around the room; my reflection in the mirrored side wall made me jump.

I connected my laptop to the sound system and started the playlist I'd created for the party. TLC's "No Scrubs" came on, bringing back memories of a girls' weekend in Montauk a few years back. I could almost feel the salt spray on my legs as the three of us had walked the beach, collecting tiny bits of sea glass in our pockets. I couldn't wait to see the delight on my friends' faces when they walked in; I wanted that warm, comforting feeling back, of being loved, of belonging.

I lit the scented pillar candles at the front of the room and lined up the two dozen votives that I'd brought with me on the ledge along the side. I set the LED lights overhead to a confetti pattern and turned off the rest of the lights. As the tiny beams gently cascaded, it felt like being on the inside of a shaken snow globe.

While I arranged the flowers and the cake, the champagne bucket and the crystal glasses I'd brought from home—heavy Baroque-looking crystal flutes I'd found at the Hell's Kitchen flea market—I thought about the first time I'd come here, four months ago. I'd been twenty-six pounds heavier and plagued by a sort of generalized dissatisfaction, searching for something to inspire me. And I'd found it, for a while, but that brief moment of joy had shattered and now I felt tense all the time, primed for dangers that I couldn't see.

I was fixing the French wired ribbon on Lindsay's gift—it had gotten flattened on the way over—when I heard their voices. I took a last look around at the gorgeous cake piped with ganache rosettes, the candlelight reflected in the faceted crystal. Despite Grace's mocking, I'd tied a ribbon to the handlebars of the center bike in the front row, and set a glittery tiara on its seat: I was counting on Lindsay to think it was fun.

Lindsay and Grace walked in, dressed in workout clothes, laughing at something.

"Surprise!" I said, too brightly. Then, "I mean, I guess it wasn't a surprise . . . ?"

"I'm sorry about that," Grace said, dropping her gym bag on the floor. "Tatum texted to say she wasn't going to be able to pick us up after all, so at that point—I mean, it wasn't going to be a surprise anyway, so I figured we might as well wear our spin stuff so we didn't have to change until after."

"Oh wow, look at . . . all this!" Lindsay said, nearly tripping on Grace's bag. I caught a whiff of wine on her breath as she hugged me.

So much for my gift—cinnamon-colored leggings and a matching tank with intricate woven detailing from Carbon38 that I thought she could wear tonight. I'd even brought socks and an extra pair of spin shoes.

"Happy birthday," I said belatedly.

"I was still surprised," Lindsay said. "It's not every day I get to break into a building through the service door!"

"Oh, that was just, we need to come in that way because—"

"Is this from Lady M?" Grace was licking frosting off her finger; there was a gouge along the edge of the cake. "Oh my God, it's amazing!"

"We had a little bit of wine at my place," Lindsay confided as Grace nearly knocked over one of my Baccarat stems. "Drinking on an empty stomach, we're so bad. I'm *starving*."

"Is Tatum—is she on her way?" I asked, checking my phone to see if she'd texted me.

"Yeah, she was just running a little late—oh, look!" Grace had found the tiara. She set it on Lindsay's head, trying to fix it in place with the plastic side combs.

"Ow!" Lindsay yelped. "Ow, ow—" She slapped Grace's hand away, giggling, and the tiara clattered to the floor. One of the combs snapped off and the large fake ruby fell out and rolled away.

I grabbed the tiara and set it on the ledge. "Maybe we can, um, have some cake while we're waiting for Tatum."

I hoped they'd sober up before we got on the bikes. For the first time I wondered what would happen if one of us got hurt, especially since we weren't even supposed to be here. My cherished vision of the evening—the three of us cycling in a row, Tatum on the podium guiding us, Lindsay's favorite music playing, basking in the warmth of our friendship—was disintegrating. Tatum was supposed to be part of the surprise. I'd imagined the look on Lindsay's face when she came to the front door, not so different from when Paige got to meet Maddie Ziegler at a birthday party.

"I'll have cake," Grace said. "But where are we going to sit?"

Sitting wasn't part of the plan. I'd thought we'd spin first; I'd asked Tatum to do an easy half hour, nothing strenuous that would make us sweat. Then champagne and cake before heading to Elio's, where we'd have more wine and take the photos for Instagram that we couldn't take here. Sneaking into Flame would remain a secret between us, a private joke we'd share for years.

I cut three pieces of cake and placed them on dainty plates I'd brought from home. The dessert service had been my grandmother's, a fussy Royal Worcester pattern with big blowsy roses and gilt edges. I was disappointed that neither of them had even mentioned the flowers.

"We'll sit on the floor," I said with forced gaiety, plucking four of the votive candles from the ledge and setting them in the middle of the aisle between the bikes. "Just like a middle school party," I added, to show I was a good sport.

Lindsay and Grace exchanged a look. "I don't know about you, Linds," Grace said, "but if she suggests Spin the Bottle next, I'm going to have to pass."

I heard the back door again. "Be right back," I said, stung by her little joke. "That's got to be Tatum."

But Tatum wasn't alone. Holding her hand and walking unsteadily in five-inch platforms and black leather shorts was Brooke.

CHAPTER 29

"We're back together," Tatum crooned, her arm around Brooke's waist.

"Happy birthday." Brooke smirked. "It's like we have our own little birthday club. Remember celebrating mine, Julia? That was such a *special* evening."

"Don't be mean," Tatum said, playfully slapping Brooke's wrist.

"It's not my birthday," I said. "It's Lindsay's. Tatum was going to teach a private class."

"In *that*?" Brooke said, raising an eyebrow at Tatum's dress. It was tight, short, purple, and one-shouldered, and she'd paired it with red stilettos with satin laces that tied at the ankle.

"We *just* got back together," Tatum said, leaning in confidentially. "We're going downtown after this to celebrate."

I felt like screaming. The whole point of coming here was to offer Tatum to my friends, a rare prize to show my love for them. But Tatum was acting like this was the obligatory stop by a party when you're on your way to a better one, where you quickly drain a single glass of wine before heading for the exit.

"You were going to do a *class* for *Lindsay*," I said. "Remember?"

"Oops," Tatum said, putting a hand over her mouth.

"I don't think that's happening," Brooke said. "We'll have to do that another time, because we already started partying. I'd offer you some, but . . ."

Only now did I see that her eyes were dilated, Tatum's expression as dreamy and unfocused as it had been that night at Constellation. So all four of them were either drunk or high, too wasted to care about all the time and effort I'd put in. I heard a wet thump and turned around to see the cake upside down on the floor, its gold cardboard doily on top, Lindsay and Grace holding each other as they tried not to laugh.

"Happy birthday!" Tatum squealed, heading unsteadily for Lindsay in her high heels. She took Lindsay's hand and pulled her into a hug, then grabbed Grace's hand and they swayed with their arms around each other like they'd walked away from a car crash together.

Brooke got the champagne from the cooler of ice and started twisting off the cap. "It's like a fucking bridal shower in here," she said, nodding at the little flowers and the row of crystal flutes. "And what's with the music? Are you trying to put everyone to sleep?"

She handed me the champagne bottle and headed for my laptop. A second later Train's "Hey, Soul Sister" stopped abruptly, replaced after a few moments with some hip-hop ballad braced by a constant loop of *Fuck you, fuck you, fuck you,* turned up so loud I could feel it through the floor. Brooke threw back her head and shook out her hair, exposing the lace choker encircling her neck and the swell of her breasts in a black push-up bra, and then she started to dance, the bell sleeves of her see-through blouse swirling around her wrists as she moved.

"Come on, birthday girl, dance with me," she said, slinking over to Lindsay.

"I guess that means I get to dance with *you*," Tatum said with a giggle and grabbed Grace's hand.

All four of them started dancing in the aisle, moving to the pulsing beat. Tatum swung Grace dangerously close to the handlebars of one bike while Brooke backed Lindsay up to the seat of another and practically gave her a lap dance like that night at Constellation with Richard. There was so much aggressive sexual energy in the air you could cut it with a knife.

Grace and Lindsay loved it, though. They giggled and twerked, their hands in the air, their diamonds glittering. When Brooke grabbed Tatum and kissed her hard on the mouth, then slapped her on the ass, Grace and Lindsay cheered and Tatum danced teasingly up the aisle to the podium.

"Hey, be careful!" I called, visions of broken necks and hair caught in resistance knobs making me panic. "Let's stay off the bikes, okay? And we need to turn the music down. We're not supposed to be here, we can't—"

"Keep your shirt on, Grandma," Tatum said in a singsong voice. Then she turned the music up so loud it hurt my ears. I ran to the podium, awkwardly dodging around her, and turned the music all the way down.

"Nooo!" Lindsay wailed.

"Yeah, don't be a buzzkill, Julia," Brooke said icily, wiping out any remaining illusions that she'd forgiven me for giving her name to the police.

"A *buzzkill*?" I repeated incredulously. I spent five hundred dollars on flowers, another two hundred dollars on the ruined cake, and I didn't even want to see my bill from the liquor store—and all my so-called friends were acting like I was nothing more than a playground supervisor.

"At least don't turn it *all* the way down," Grace wheedled. "We're in a basement. Who's going to care?"

"Okay, but just for a few more minutes," I said tightly. "I think we should leave soon. We can go to Elio's, okay? I just don't think it's safe—"

"Where's that other bottle? Did you open it?" Tatum demanded, holding one of the champagne glasses upside down so that the last drops splattered onto the floor. She tottered toward the cooler, pausing to kick off her shoes. "Oh God, that's so much better."

I closed my eyes, wondering how I could have been stupid enough to bring glass into the studio, why I'd thought a cake was a good idea. I turned the music up just loud enough to prevent a mutiny. At this point all I wanted was to get them out so that I could clean up. Someone had stepped on the cake and tracked it all over the floor, and there was a puddle of champagne next to the cooler. The room reeked of it.

Tatum worked the cork out of the new bottle with a huge pop, and everyone shrieked and applauded. Brooke and Lindsay held the flutes while she poured, and then they all clinked glasses and drank, not even seeming to realize I hadn't joined them.

I took a trash bag from my tote and got down on my hands and knees, scraping up the ruined cake with my hands and dropping it into the bag. I used the pretty paper napkins I'd brought to scrub as much of the frosting off the floor as I could, but I needed some sort of cleaner to get the rest.

"Tatum," I said. "Tatum! I need to talk to you a minute."

She danced over to me, holding out her arms, but I grabbed her wrists and held them firmly. "Stop, just stop a minute."

"You really should have taken the Molly that night," she said in a disappointed tone. "None of the bad stuff would have happened if you did. Paige wouldn't have gone to the hospital and Brooke wouldn't be mad at you and—"

"Look, can you get me some spray cleaner?" I said.

She swayed a little. "I'm not sure where they keep it."

"*Fine*, never mind." I'd make do with the antiseptic spray under the podium. "Thanks a lot for ruining this whole night. Look, can you just take everyone to Elio's on Second and Eighty-fourth Street?"

"But Brooke wants to go to the Ruby Room," she pouted. "We got back *together*."

I dug my fingers into her wrists. "Just tell Grace and Lindsay to wait for me at Elio's and then you and Brooke can do whatever the hell you want, but we need to get out of here."

"Julia," she gasped, looking down at my hands. "You're hurting me."

I let go, staring at the red crescent marks my nails had left.

"Guys," Tatum called, turning away from me. "The party's over. Julia wants us out."

"Unless you want to deal with the cops when they show up for a noise complaint," I said, refusing to be cowed. "Grace, do you think you can manage to get Lindsay to Elio's, and I'll meet you there?"

"In *this*?" she asked, looking down at her leggings and tank top.

"Didn't you guys bring a change of clothes? Like we talked about?"

"You're fine," Brooke said, reaching behind Grace's head and pulling off the elastic holding her ponytail. She fluffed Grace's hair around her face. "Put on a little eyeliner and you're good."

"We'll figure it out," Lindsay said. "Come on, I want to *dance*."

Tatum was already heading toward the door. "I called an Uber, you guys, he's two minutes away!"

"An Uber?" Grace echoed. "It's only a few blocks!"

"I'm not walking in these shoes," Tatum said.

And with that my party was over, the sounds of their laughter echoing behind them as they left. I smelled something burning—somehow Lindsay's gift had gotten too close to one of the votives, and flames were licking at the wrapping paper. "Fuck!" I yelled—if the smoke reached the sprinklers I'd have an even bigger mess on my hands. I grabbed the closest thing at hand and sprinted to put out the fire, knocking things over in my rush.

Disaster averted, though now my lamb's-wool wrap lay ruined on the floor, singed and stinking among the shards of shattered crystal.

With the rest of them gone, it didn't take long to clean up. Everything went into the trash bags I'd brought, except for the two crystal flutes that had survived and the ice bucket that had been a wedding gift from my aunt and uncle, which I stuffed into my tote bag along with my laptop. I wavered before throwing away Lindsay's gift, but the flames had destroyed the corner of the box and the clothes stank. The whole studio still smelled faintly of smoke and champagne, even after I'd scrubbed the floor with towels and antiseptic spray, but I hoped the odor would be gone by morning. I took one last look around and turned off the lights.

I dragged the two trash bags into the narrow space between buildings and tossed them into the dumpster. I checked the service door to make sure it was locked, and then I walked down the street, waiting until I was a block away before checking my phone.

No messages. **Are you at Elio's?** I texted Grace and Lindsay, then tried to decide what to do. I was dirty and sweaty and shivering, and

I'd lost any desire to celebrate, but if I didn't show up I risked being labeled no fun.

No *fun*—it was the accusation I'd spent my entire life fearing the most. I'd fought my way into the limelight and kept fighting to hold on to it. I'd worked so hard to be proper enough for my mom, smart enough for my teachers, clever enough for my friends, cunning enough for my foes. The only person I'd never had to be anyone but myself around was James—and I'd rewarded him by ignoring what he wanted, and making him live *my* dream.

I'd finish this wretched evening, because I had never been a quitter and I wasn't about to start now, but then some things were going to change. I wasn't going to forget the way everyone had treated me tonight—and not just tonight, but over the summer and at Flame and after Paige was released from the hospital. I bought a bottle of water and some breath mints at the deli on the corner and used the bathroom to change clothes and did my best to touch up my face and fix my hair. No one had texted me back by the time I got to Elio's, but it didn't matter; they weren't there.

My only lucky break was that James and the kids were asleep when I got home, so I was able to wallow in self-pity all by myself. I left the ice bucket on the counter for Benilda and put the crystal flutes back in the cupboard, and then I took a shower, standing under the hot spray with my eyes closed for a long time.

I crawled into bed next to James, but I had trouble falling asleep. At a little after one in the morning my phone vibrated with a text on the bedside table.

Where were you, Grace had written. I scrolled through Instagram, and it didn't take long to find the four of them with their arms around each other in a bar I didn't recognize. Tatum had posted the photo at 12:38 A.M. and captioned it **Happy happy!!! Blowing out the candles with @sparklerparker #birthdaygirl #bestyears #best friends #birthdaysurprise #instacake #lovemygirls**

Grace had posted too, a selfie of her and Tatum in front of a dartboard, laughing. The caption: **Winning dart in the Triple Ring!** **@tatumfarris #winner #squadgoals #GameSetMatch**

I put down my phone; I couldn't stand to see any more. But a moment later I picked it up again and typed **I was at Elio's where we said we were going to meet**

I waited, but when she didn't text me back I rolled over, already regretting my text, my stupid idea for a party, the entire evening, ever meeting Tatum at all. I tossed and turned for a while, but I was almost asleep when Grace finally texted back.

No we said Ruby Room we waited there at least an hour

This time I turned my phone completely off and stuck it in the drawer of the nightstand.

CHAPTER 30

I woke up angry, remembering the cake lying smashed on the floor, the playlist I'd created with such care, the beautiful gift that was moldering in a dumpster. I could hear James and the kids in the kitchen making breakfast, but I lay in bed for a while, fuming. I'd been loyal to Lindsay from the start, putting up with her competitive side, laughing off her accusation that I'd gone after her husband. I'd hosted her for holiday dinners, cooked a week's worth of meals when she had her gallbladder out, spent a month creating a scrapbook for her for her fortieth birthday. And what did it get me? She'd left the party I'd thrown for her without even saying goodbye.

I forced myself out of bed, and wandered into the kitchen in my pajamas. Half-eaten waffles and abandoned glasses of milk littered the counter, and there was a long streak of something red on the floor. Henry was glassy-eyed in front of the television while Paige worked on a friendship bracelet, and James was putting on his jacket.

"It lives!" he said, coming over and sniffing my neck. "At least you don't smell like a skid row bum this time. How was the party?"

"Great," I lied, faking a yawn. "Everyone had fun. Are you headed to work?"

"Yeah, sorry about that but I have to catch up on a few things."

Given that our whole future now rested on this project, not to mention the fact that James had been on his best behavior, I couldn't really give him a hard time.

"Okay. Maybe I'll take the kids to a matinee or something. I think it's half off at the first show." I stood up on my toes to kiss him goodbye. "Maybe I'll even buy Junior mints at CVS and sneak them in. See? I bet you never thought I'd learn to live within my means."

I was teasing, but he had a haunted look in his eyes as he said goodbye.

James was true to his word and came home in time for dinner with a greasy paper sack full of wings and fries. After we ate, he challenged the kids to a game of Monopoly and I joined in, to their delight. James cheated, trying to steal the money from the middle of the board to make the kids laugh, and I sipped at a single glass of wine and tried to pretend that nothing had changed. *This is what matters,* I reminded myself, looking around the table, *family and our health and our marriage, all the stuff money can't buy.* I almost convinced myself.

James headed back to the office the next morning and I made a pot of coffee and told the kids to stay in their rooms until they'd decided what they wanted to be for Halloween and then I sat down at the kitchen table and finally turned my phone back on. I'd ignored it since Grace's late-night text over twenty-four hours before, the longest I'd gone without my phone since I lost it at La Guardia a few years ago.

It turned out Lindsay *had* texted to thank me, at a little after eight yesterday morning. **Thank you SO MUCH for a birthday to remember! I'm so sorry we left you with a mess I definitely shouldn't have started drinking so early** She'd added a row of hearts and the blushing smiley face emoji. After struggling to compose a response that didn't sound passive-aggressive, I finally gave up and didn't respond at all.

No word from Tatum. It took even longer to decide what to text her; finally I came up with **Thanks for ruining Friday night. Would have been nice to know you had no intention of doing what you promised. Feel like I might need to talk to the cops again after all.**

She texted back a few minutes later as I was reading the comments on Lindsay's birthday photos.

I made sure your "friends" had a good time not sure what else you were expecting and go ahead and call the cops if it makes you feel better tell them anything you want to about me I don't care

I stared at my phone, feeling almost punch-drunk from yet another hit. Tatum was calling my bluff; she must have done a little asking around and found out that she and Brooke weren't in any trouble. As I tried to absorb this new development, the phone rang in my hand, a local number I didn't recognize.

"Hello?"

"Julia? This is Linda Mendelsohn calling from the Tomorrow-Makers Foundation. We met briefly at last year's gala, but I'm sure you don't remember me."

"Of course I remember!" I said, forcing enthusiasm as I tried to place her. "Didn't you introduce the speakers?"

"Yes, it's one of my favorite duties as director of development."

Now I remembered; she'd worn a long shiny blue gown that looked like it belonged on a Texan mother of the bride. I pitied the staff at these events; they weren't paid enough to compete with all the couture on display.

"You must be busy, with the gala less than a month away!" I said, wondering uneasily if she was calling to twist my arm to increase this year's donation. It was a common practice when committee members were announced; the position came with certain obligations, among them ponying up eye-popping sums that you could then use to browbeat your friends into making big donations themselves.

"Oh, you know it." She had one of those pleasing, smooth voices that seem tailor-made for asking for money. "Listen, I don't want to take up too much of your time, but we're working on the press release announcing next year's committee so that it's ready to go the week after the gala, when excitement around TomorrowMakers is hopefully still high."

"Oh, that's a great idea," I said with effort, trying to inject some enthusiasm into my voice. "If the gala gets even half the coverage it did last time, you could probably sell out the event a year in advance."

Linda laughed. "Well, we received forty percent more applications for press credentials this year, so we have high hopes."

"And your social media presence keeps getting better and better." Look at me piling on the praise—apparently I was still willing to sell my soul for the right price. I was sure Linda could see right through me, but I didn't care as I imagined being photographed with Lindsay for *Page Six* and *Town & Country* and *Hampton Sheet*.

"Aw, thank you! I remember that you're good friends with Lindsay Parker, right? So you may already know she's agreed to chair next year's gala."

"Lindsay's fantastic. She's going to do such a great job."

"Well, she had very nice things to say about you too. In fact, she's put forth your name for a position on the committee."

"She has?" I said innocently, preparing to act surprised and delighted.

"Yes, she thinks you'd make a wonderful volunteer coordinator. I'm sure she'll be calling soon to discuss it, and I don't mean to steal her thunder, but I'm just trying to finalize our list."

"Oh. Wow." Volunteer coordinator . . . I tried to hide my shock. It was the worst position on the committee, requiring a ton of work and earning almost no recognition, the sort of job you took if you were desperate to break into an organization and didn't mind paying your dues. Which, given TomorrowMakers' rapid ascent on the charity circuit, meant plenty of women would be thrilled—but Lindsay had all but promised me assistant chair. How many times had we talked about the fun we'd have, the planning meetings we'd host, the favors we'd call in?

"I'm incredibly honored, obviously," I said, attempting to recover. "I'll look at my calendar this week and make sure I don't have conflicts with any of the key dates. Just out of curiosity, who else is serving on the committee?"

"Let's see . . . this is preliminary, of course, because everyone needs to look at their calendars. But there's Lindsay, and then Celeste Zapata for assistant chair, Mary Frances Whelan for promotions coordinator . . ." I stopped listening as she rattled off half a dozen more names. Celeste Zapata! I couldn't believe Lindsay had picked her—she hated Celeste almost as much as I did. But apparently things were different now; Celeste was probably a very different person when she wanted something from you. And since I'd heard Celeste was on the nominating committee for the American Folk Art Museum gala, it wouldn't surprise me if there was some quid pro quo going on.

I managed to end the conversation with a promise to get back to Linda. My answer would be no, of course—but first I wanted to find out if there was any way to quietly get my donation back. TomorrowMakers was a good cause, but my priorities seemed to have shifted.

Monday morning arrived too soon. I knew I'd see Lindsay at drop-off, and we'd have to have an awkward conversation about the gala committee. Grace and I appeared to be in a standoff, neither of us willing to apologize for what we'd said over text. And considering Tatum's part in ruining the evening and how we had left things, I was in no mood to go to Flame.

"What are you up to today?" James asked, coming into the kitchen and putting his arms around me from behind as I shook burnt crumbs out of the toaster over the sink.

"I might walk the reservoir, since the weather's nice," I said. "And I really need to figure out what we're going to do about a nanny. This is Benilda's last week."

"Oh shit, that's right." I could feel his breath on my neck, his hard chest against my back. "What would you think of trying it without a nanny for a while?"

"James," I cautioned, wriggling out of his grasp so I could turn and face him. "Don't even joke about it."

"Okay, okay. Sorry."

"Oh—and before I forget, we're going to a memorial service Thursday. It's at five at the Metropolitan Club, so can you make sure you're home by four at the latest? I'll have your suit ready."

Ordinarily this would set off a temper tantrum, especially since he'd never met Gigi's mother and hated the Metropolitan Club. I could see him gear up to protest and then stop himself. His restraint really was remarkable.

"Who died?"

"No one you know. I'll tell you that day—you'll only forget if I tell you now."

"Fair enough." He pushed a tangle of hair out of my eyes and kissed my nose. "I need to get going, but I'll see you tonight."

"Text me if you're going to be late."

"I will." He hesitated, then added, "I promise everything's going to be okay."

And those were the last words he spoke to me as a free man.

CHAPTER 31

I couldn't drum up the energy to do my makeup or figure out an outfit after James left, barely pulling on a sweater and jeans in time to walk the kids to school. As we joined the crowd outside the Graylon doors, I spotted Lindsay and Celeste talking near the stairs.

"You guys go find your friends," I told the kids. "I need to talk to Mrs. Parker."

Lindsay and Celeste fell silent as I approached. "Good morning, Julia," Celeste said, in an oddly formal tone.

"Good morning. And congratulations—I hear that you two will be running the TomorrowMakers gala together. I'm sure you'll both do a fantastic job."

"About that," Lindsay said uncomfortably. "I know you and I discussed how you could help out, but I'm not sure it's going to work."

"I already heard," I said. "Nice of you to recommend me for volunteer coordinator instead. I'm glad to know you have so much confidence in me."

"Look, can we talk about this in private? Maybe we can grab coffee and—"

"There's no need. Anything you need to say, you can say in front of Celeste, especially since she's going to be your assistant chair." I wasn't about to let her off the hook—the more people who heard me turn down her little volunteer coordinator consolation prize, the better.

The two of them shared a look. "It's actually not just the committee," Lindsay said. "There's something else."

"Go ahead," I said. "No time like the present."

"It's something that concerns me too," Celeste said. "I guess I'll just come out and say it—I'm afraid I can't allow Esme to come over to your apartment for playdates anymore."

"And that goes for Audrey too," Lindsay added, reddening.

"What—why?" I stammered. "Did something happen at school?"

"No," Lindsay said. "This is about what happened the other week at your apartment. Do I have to say it? With Paige?"

"I heard she could have *died*," Celeste said. "I know it was an accident, but just the fact that you keep that stuff around—"

"I can't believe you lied about it, Julia," Lindsay said. "I should have known when you told Grace it was a penicillin allergy—there's no way it would only just be showing up now."

"I don't know if you have a problem, or if it's James, but I genuinely hope you get help," Celeste said. "We've been friends for a long time, and you have my full support, you know that. But I have to put my children's safety first."

"Wait," I said. "I don't know what you heard, but—"

"My cousin has a problem with painkillers," Celeste said sympathetically. "It's everywhere these days. It's an epidemic."

"It wasn't painkillers! It was one stupid little tablet that didn't even belong to me. I'd forgotten I even kept it. And the only reason I had it to begin with was that I don't do drugs!" Nothing was coming out right. I'd raised my voice, and people were starting to stare.

"I don't want to get into the details," Lindsay said, holding up her hand. "They don't concern me or anyone else. Trust me, I'm not going to go around telling anyone. At least, not unless—I mean, you can't have other people's children over until you can really ensure it's safe."

"Don't worry," Celeste added. "Paige and Henry will still get invited to people's houses."

"It's not what you think! I was out with friends and one of them gave me Molly, it was in a little Altoids tin and I didn't know what it was at first, and it was loud and she ran off before I could give it back to her, and when I got home I just sort of dumped out my purse and the tin ended up in my bedside table." Even as the story tumbled out, I realized how improbable it sounded—just the sort of denial an addict might make, in fact.

How had Lindsay found out? It had to have been Tatum—she was the only person who knew, other than Brooke. And she'd called my bluff yesterday after we exchanged angry texts. Since I no longer had anything to hold over her, there was nothing stopping her from saying whatever she wanted.

Tatum told Lindsay and Lindsay told Celeste, and by the end of the week everyone would know. And despite what Celeste said, invitations for my children would dry up like the desert the minute the story got around.

Celeste put her hand on my arm. "Just promise to get help," she said gravely. "You can beat this, I know you can. We believe in you."

Half an hour later I was walking aimlessly through Central Park, having slunk away from drop-off before I had to face anyone else. I was watching a squirrel with its head in an abandoned Cheetos bag when my phone rang.

The caller ID showed an unknown number. If it were an ordinary day, I would have let it go to voicemail. But I answered before the second ring, spooked about what might be coming next.

"Julia." It was James, but his voice was off—hollow and hoarse.

"What's up?"

"I'm . . . I've been arrested, Julia. Stewart's on his way."

"Arrested?"

"They came to the work site."

"What in God's name for?"

"Look, it's a bunch of bullshit stuff about—I mean, it's the same stuff they're always fucking around with. Nothing that'll stick, I can tell you that right now."

But he didn't sound convincing—he sounded afraid.

And if James was afraid . . . I was terrified. "I don't understand. Where did they take you?"

Another pause before he finally said, "FBI building. Look, Jules, I don't know when I'm getting out of here—I just wanted you to know. But don't worry, okay?"

"Don't worry? Don't *worry*?" I was beginning to hyperventilate.

"I knew you were going to overreact," he said wearily.

"Let me talk to Stewart," I demanded. "I need to talk to Stewart."

"I just *said* he was on his *way*. And when he gets here, he's got a few other things to do—like keep me out of fucking prison, for one."

"Okay, then as soon as he takes care of . . ." *Out of prison*. Could we really be talking about this? "Just have him call me when he can, okay?"

"I will." There was a pause; I could hear him breathing. "Jules?"

"What?"

"Just . . . look. It's going to be okay."

But it wasn't. I could tell by his voice, the words he wasn't saying. So far today, I'd gotten a slap in the face from my best friend and shamed in front of everyone I knew. But all of that was nothing compared to the prospect of James going to prison.

"I'll come there. Should I come there?"

"No, no, don't do that. There's nothing you can do."

"Then . . . I love you, James."

"I know," he whispered, and then he hung up.

CHAPTER 32

James was wrong. The charges against him didn't go away, despite Stewart's efforts.

One thing quickly became clear: James had been withholding information not just from me but from his attorney too. Stewart called right before Benilda came home with the kids, but didn't have much to report yet. From the tone of his voice, I concluded this was the first he was hearing about the latest troubles with the project. I asked him if I should come to the federal building, and he gave me an emphatic no, promising to call me back as soon as he'd had a chance to talk to James.

I sent Benilda home, knowing she'd hear about what had happened from the other nannies soon enough. As I was heating up a frozen lasagna, Stewart called again. The reason for the arrest—James was accused of bribing city officials to expedite various permits and approvals—was only the tip of the iceberg. Stewart wouldn't tell me what else they had on my husband, but as I thought about what Garth Parker had reported to Lindsay way back in July, I realized that things may have been building for quite some time.

"When will you know more?" I demanded.

"Not tonight," he said. "Everyone's gone home for the night."

Not everyone, I thought—James was in a cell, probably surrounded by murderers. "But you'll be there first thing tomorrow morning, pounding on doors. Right?"

"Please let me do my job," Stewart said, in a pained voice. "Trust me, your husband is getting the best legal support money can buy."

"He'd better be," I muttered. "If I don't hear from you by ten tomorrow morning, I'm coming down there."

"There is absolutely no reason—"

"You're sure there's no way I can see James tonight?"

He actually laughed, not very nicely. I hung up before I said something I'd regret.

The arrest made the evening news. I watched it on my laptop with my earbuds in while the kids watched *The Lion King* for the thousandth time. There was a brief shot of James being escorted into the federal building, looking straight ahead as a reporter chased after him trying to shove a microphone in his face. The on-air reporter called him "one of New York's most successful real estate developers, with homes in the Hamptons and rural Pennsylvania in addition to a nine-million-dollar apartment in the city."

"Lies!" I shouted at my laptop, startling the kids, but it didn't seem right that they hadn't bothered to get even the most basic facts right—it was almost as if they were trying to make James look even worse. It was true that he'd paid off his parents' house, but we didn't own any property in Pennsylvania, and our apartment was worth five million, not nine.

Within minutes, my phone was blowing up. I deleted the texts as quickly as they came in until I gave up and turned the damn thing off for the second time in the span of a few days. I went to the kitchen to open a bottle of wine, but Henry followed me in.

"Where's Daddy?"

"Oh, honey." I knelt down and pulled Henry into a hug. "He has to work."

"But why are you so sad?"

I wiped my eyes on his shirt and tried to smile. "I'm not sad, I'm just hungry. Hey, I think that lasagna's about ready—how about me and you set the table?"

While Henry ran to get the placemats out of the buffet, I stared at the bottle of wine on the counter for a long moment, and then I put it back in the fridge, unopened.

Someone was going to need to keep their shit together around here until Daddy came home.

When Benilda arrived Tuesday morning, I told her I needed to speak to her privately and hurried her into my bedroom. "I'm not sure what you've heard," I began, while her face remained impassive, "but some federal agents are holding James for questioning. He didn't do the things they're accusing me of, but I'm afraid people will get the wrong idea and say, um, insensitive things to the kids. I'm planning to talk to them about it tonight, but I think it's best to keep them home today."

"All right, Mrs. Julia." Benilda looked like she was going to say more, but she changed her mind.

"I know it's a lot to ask, but do you think you can keep them entertained today so I can deal with this? I was thinking you could take them to Dave & Buster's or a movie or—or whatever you want. Here." I handed her $140, most of the money I had in my wallet. "Use this. I really appreciate it, Benilda, I know it's a lot to ask."

She looked at the money, then back up at me. "Mr. James is coming home?"

"Yes," I said forcefully. "He is definitely coming home. I'm just not sure when yet."

Once they were gone, I paced the apartment as the weak autumn sun slowly rose above the city. I used the automatic phone system to report the kids' absences, claiming dentist appointments, and when a call came from the school a few minutes later I didn't pick up.

I tried Stewart right after 9:00 A.M. but got his voicemail.

Finally I couldn't stand it anymore and read all the texts I'd ignored.

There were half a dozen, all from school moms expressing their shock and asking what they could do to help. I questioned their sincerity—I suspected most just wanted the details—and it made me realize that I had no friends in the city outside of Graylon. How had my world gotten so small? If the news made it beyond the New York metropolitan area, maybe I'd start hearing from old friends . . . except that I'd lost touch with most of them since having kids and moving to the Upper East Side.

At least no one was calling us names or saying James had gotten what he deserved—not yet, anyway.

Stewart returned my call as I was drinking my third cup of coffee. He told me James wasn't allowed to make any more calls—probably because he'd pissed off the cops who were holding him. "He's cooperating" was the way Stewart put it, "but he's not happy about it."

"Can you talk to him?" I pleaded, knowing all too well how James could be. "Convince him that it wouldn't hurt to try to be polite to these guys?"

Stewart cleared his throat. "He's, ah, pretty upset."

"Yes, I know that, but—"

"Look, I'll do my best, Julia. I'll know more after I've had a chance to see him."

"When will that be?"

"Ten-thirty or so—eleven at the latest."

"Is there any chance he'll be home today?"

"Doubtful, but—"

"Can *I* see him?"

"Julia, please understand, James was adamant that you not go down there, and I have to say I agree. He doesn't want you to see him in those circumstances and they very likely won't let you anyway."

"Fine," I said tightly, but only because I knew how ashamed James was. "But I want you to call me back the minute you have more information."

"I will."

"Promise," I said, sounding a lot like Paige.

"Try not to worry," Stewart said and hung up.

I gave the phone the finger. Then I went back to pacing.

I couldn't believe that neither Grace nor Lindsay had called or even texted. Yes, things were strained between us, but a few days ago we'd all been together in what was supposed to be a celebration of our friendship. Maybe Lindsay was embarrassed over her little stunt with the gala committee, or maybe she genuinely believed I'd turned into an addict—but what about Grace? Even if she believed I'd intentionally blown them off on Friday night and poisoned my daughter, this was an emergency. If the tables were turned, I'd be on her doorstep the minute I heard, ready to offer whatever she needed. I'd do it for either of them; they wouldn't have to ask.

And I was suddenly furious that they wouldn't do the same for me.

I called Grace, and it went to voicemail. I hung up and called again. No answer.

The third time, she picked up.

"Julia," she said wearily. "Shouldn't you be trying to get James out of jail instead of blowing up my phone?"

"I can't believe you," I said. "Do you have any idea how hard this is? How much I'm hurting over here?"

"*You're* hurting? What about your kids? Did you ever think about them when you were partying and leaving drugs lying around the house? Or James, did he think about their future when he was committing fraud?"

I was shocked by the coldness in her voice. "Grace, this is *me* you're talking to. You *know* me. You've watched me with my children since they were born. Have you ever seen me do drugs around them?"

"No, which is why I couldn't believe it at first when Tatum told me. And by the way, before you start blaming her, she only confided in me because she's worried about you. She wants you to get help. And so do I."

"If you're so worried about me, why didn't you call me? I've been right here ever since they picked James up yesterday, and I could really have used a friend."

"Sometimes a real friend has to give you what you need, not what you want. I'm trying to do what's best for you, Julia."

"What the hell is that supposed to mean?"

"I'm not going to argue with you."

"I'm not arguing! I'm just trying to understand how you could possibly think that ignoring me would make any of this easier."

"But coming over there and acting like everything is going to be fine would be worse. It would be enabling, and that would make me part of the problem. I'm not willing to do that to you."

"How exactly is giving a shit about me *enabling*?"

"I *do* care, I'm just choosing to detach to give you room to work on yourself. Have you considered going to a meeting? An AA meeting," she clarified helpfully. "I think they have one for drug addicts."

"I don't need a meeting because I'm not an addict. What I need is for my friends to have my back."

"I think I should end this conversation now," Grace said. "We're just going in circles. But I will offer you this—I am happy to watch the kids while you attend meetings. In my home, obviously. Just let me know when you're ready to get honest."

"Gee, I don't know how to thank you," I said—but she'd already hung up.

When I hadn't heard back from Stewart by 11:15 A.M., I called again.

"I was planning to call you" was the way he answered the phone, sounding annoyed.

"Well, we're talking now. When is my husband coming home?"

There was a slight pause. "There may be some things he hasn't told you."

These are not the words a wife wants to hear from her husband's attorney, needless to say. "Just tell me."

Reluctantly, he did. Mercer House's bankrupt former owner was now under investigation for fraud, and the city was arguing that James had been in on their plan to flip the property all along. Larry De Stasi was claiming that James had tried to bribe him and other council members. And the most vociferous of the community opposition leaders had accused James of breaking a pledge to set aside 20 percent of the units for low-income residents.

"That last one isn't a crime," Stewart said, "especially since nothing was put into writing, but it isn't going to help his case in the court of public opinion, obviously."

"If it isn't a crime, why are we even talking about it?"

"Julia, I am just trying to give you a complete picture." Now Stewart sounded offended. Such a delicate flower. "There was a time when none of this would have attracted much attention from the DOI or the feds, but they're cracking down on this sort of thing. The mayor especially doesn't want people accusing him of being soft on white-collar crime again. So unfortunately, they're going to push this as hard as they can."

"Okay." I took a breath, forcing myself to stay calm. "Can you please just tell me how bad this is? Give me the worst-case scenario."

"Julia . . ."

"*No.* Tell me."

There was a silence, and I pictured Stewart in some windowless room at the ugly brown-brick correctional center downtown, his heavily starched shirt and wool trousers—as casual as he ever got, even on weekends—a sharp contrast to the institutional surroundings.

"Well, it is possible that James could serve time," he finally said. "If they convict on all of it—bribery, extortion, conspiracy—he could be facing five, maybe eight years. But he'd never serve it all. They'll knock it down . . . and this isn't going to be Sing Sing, obviously. It'd be minimum security. And we can always take a plea agreement."

He could serve time. The words ricocheted around my brain like BBs shot into a barrel. "James can't go to prison."

"Julia. Listen. None of us wants that. I just wish—never mind. You and I both know how headstrong he is."

I'd endured Stewart Marlowe's patronizing attitude for years—but I was done. Not only was my husband's future on the line, but I wasn't the same woman I used to be. I was exhausted by trying to be a perfect wife, mother, volunteer, hostess. Maybe it was time to remember who I was before we ever moved uptown.

From now on, I would put everything I had into saving my family, and anyone who got in my way was going to have a fight on their hands.

"Let me rephrase that," I said. "James will *not* be going to prison until every avenue, every possibility, every opportunity has been exhausted. I don't care if I have to go down there and camp out on the steps, and by the way, don't ever again imply that it's in *James's best interest* for me to stay away. I don't care how many documents have to be reviewed, arguments have to be written, or dicks have to be sucked to save my husband. And if you don't feel the same way, then maybe you aren't the right lawyer for the job."

"Julia, please, slow down." Stewart sounded more alarmed than offended. "I don't know what I've done to give you the impression that I'm not one hundred percent committed. I was not aware that I was being, er, insensitive to your involvement and will do my best to avoid doing so in the future."

This is where we women usually apologize, right? Because we've been raised to be decorous at all times, to respect authority and convention, to bring dignity to any situation in which we might find ourselves, no matter how trying. We trust our husbands to engage the best counsel, and we defer to their judgment because it's their area of expertise, not ours.

Not today.

"Good," I said coldly. "Then I can count on a daily summary of your actions regarding my husband's case? Email will be fine."

Stewart cleared his throat. "That would, it would have to be approved by my client."

"Absolutely. So you'll ask him at the earliest opportunity after we hang up. And I have one more request. I'd like a detailed weekly report of hours billed, starting with everything you've done to date."

"Again, with my client's permission, and that is a question for the accounting department, but I'll see what I can do."

"Excellent."

I said a polite goodbye and hung up. And then I went to my bathroom, closed the door, and threw up. When I was finished, I washed my hands and picked up my phone. My eyes welled with tears as I dialed. She answered on the first ring.

"Mom?" I croaked.

CHAPTER 33

It took me a few tries to get it out, but at last I managed to communicate that James had been arrested.

After that, Mom did what Mom does. She offered terse condolences and a few Yankee gems like "It's best to keep busy to take your mind off it"—and then she started handling shit. She and my father would come as quickly as they could. She'd book a flight as soon as we hung up. She'd ask the neighbor's daughter to watch Bucky, their ancient yellow Lab, for a few days.

It didn't escape me that her initial reaction wasn't shock but resignation. Like she and Dad had known all along this day would come, that James would fuck up spectacularly and that they would have to pick up the pieces.

In the moment, all I felt was relief. As if I were a child again, my mother's brisk, efficient voice made it seem as though everything would be all right, after she put me through some unpleasant corrective measure to make sure that I learned from the experience.

But this wasn't a case of her picking me and Emily Craig up at Kendall Square after the boys who took us to the movies got drunk in the theater and got us all thrown out. Second only to seeing my daughter carried out of my home on a stretcher, James's arrest was the worst thing that had ever happened to me.

And then I immediately felt guilty because I was only humiliated—James was the one who was sitting in jail.

"Don't worry about rushing to get here," I told Mom. "In fact, you really don't need to come at all."

"Don't be ridiculous. We want to see the kids anyway—especially since we got to spend so much time with Lila and Margaret over the summer."

As always, I chafed at her reference to my perfect brother and his perfect little girls, but I let it pass. "Well, if you really don't mind."

We spent a few more minutes talking about logistics, though now I was anxious to get off the phone. When we finally hung up, I felt very slightly better. My husband was locked up, my friends couldn't seem to abandon me fast enough, but at least my mother was still on my side.

Mom called back as I was doing lunges in my living room and watching old *Hoarders* episodes to say she'd booked their flights and would arrive at 8:00 P.M. the next night. I moved on to planks and willed Stewart to call me, and when that didn't work I retrieved James's Doritos from the freezer, where he'd hidden them, and watched a documentary about women's prisons.

By the time Benilda returned with the kids in the middle of the afternoon, I'd eaten half the bag. All three of them looked thoroughly exhausted. I wiped my orange Dorito-dusted fingers on my sweatpants and told the kids I needed to speak with Benilda privately, and sent them to their rooms.

"My parents are coming tomorrow," I told Benilda. "I'm not sure how long they're staying. The thing is, it's going to be pretty crowded in the apartment so . . . I was thinking today might as well be your last day. I mean I'll pay you for the rest, obviously, but—"

"That's fine," Benilda said. "It's good to have your parents here until Mr. James comes home."

I wrote out a check, adding an extra week's pay, and she folded it without looking at it and tucked it in her purse.

"So, I guess I'll get the kids," I said awkwardly.

Henry was in Paige's room, pestering her to play Connect Four with him.

"Kids," I said, "something surprising is happening, but I don't want you to worry. Benilda is leaving."

"Leaving where?" Henry asked.

"Leaving us, not working for us anymore. She has a new job that is going to let her be closer to her family."

"You mean because her cousin died?" Paige asked.

"Yes. But we'll find a new nanny. Someone just as nice as Benilda. But right now, it's time to say goodbye."

"She's leaving *now*?" Paige said, jumping up off the floor. "For-ever?"

"I'm sure she'll come back and visit," I improvised. "And you can invite her to your birthday party."

"What about *my* birthday party?" Henry said. "Can I visit her?"

"Come on, buddy," I said, "we'll figure all that out, but right now we shouldn't keep her waiting."

In the foyer, Benilda knelt and held her arms out wide. The children walked into her hug, almost shyly.

"You have to take care of your family?" Henry said sadly, grabbing a bit of her hair and twisting it the way he had when he was much younger. "Couldn't they come live here? We have lots of room."

Benilda tsked and hugged them and kissed their cheeks. When I saw her brush tears from her eyes, I had to look away. I wondered if I should hug her too, but in the end we just nodded at each other, and she gave the children one last sad look and was gone.

Stewart Marlowe called soon after Benilda left, saying he had good news and bad news. He'd just gotten out of the arraignment, where James had been indicted on charges of fraud, conspiracy, and bribery, and his next court date was over two months away.

"Oh my God," I said, feeling like I'd been punched in the gut. "You mean he has to stay in jail for the next two months?"

"No—remember I said there was good news? His bail was set at a million dollars. He can come home as soon as it's posted."

"That's—that's amazing but—look, I can get the money, it's just going to take—I'm probably going to have to ask my parents and—"

"Julia, you don't pay the whole million," Stewart said, as though I was an idiot.

"I'm sorry! I've never bailed anyone out before!" I was almost yelling. "Can you just tell me what the fuck to do?"

Stewart sighed audibly before explaining that he could recommend a bond agent and that I'd only need to pony up 15 percent, which James had assured him we could cover from our money market.

"James gave me the name of your financial adviser," Stewart said. "Do you need to write it down?"

"Do you think I don't know my own financial adviser's name?" I shot back, having had just about enough of his patronizing attitude. "It's Jordan something."

"Jordan Vandersall," Stewart said. "I have his number as well. Shall I wait while you get a pen?"

By the time I had written down Jordan's and the bond agent's information, I'd calmed down a bit. "So what happens now? It's too late to get to the bank by five—if I get there first thing tomorrow, and they can wire it out by ten, how long does it take for the bond agent to process it? Do I have to go down there in person to sign something, or—"

"You're making this way too complicated, Julia," Stewart said. "Call the bond agent, do what he says, and James could be home tomorrow night."

"I want to talk to you both about something," I told the kids after they'd brushed their teeth. "And then we can read a book in my bed."

"In *your* bed?" Henry was amazed. "I get to pick the book!"

"Who cares?" Paige said.

We all climbed under my linen duvet and I tried to gather them into my arms. Paige resisted, giving me a suspicious look. "You never let us in your bed unless we're sick. What's wrong with you?"

"Nothing," I said. "I just wanted to tell you some very exciting news. Grammy and Grampy are coming to visit tomorrow, and Daddy will be home tomorrow night."

"Yay!" Henry said, doing a somersault and nearly falling off the bed.

"Why are they coming? We have school," Paige pointed out.

"Yes, but—it's sort of a special occasion. You know how I told you Daddy had to go on a trip? It was actually kind of a bad trip, and everyone is really happy he's coming home. Happy enough that Grammy and Grampy want to be here with us."

"Why was it a bad trip? Just tell us," Paige added, seeing right through me. "I can take it."

"Okay. Right. Well, there are some people—important people— who think Daddy made a pretty big mistake, and so they sent him to a . . . well . . . they're letting him come home while they decide if he has to go back there, which could take a couple months."

The kids watched me expectantly. *Do not fucking cry,* I told myself sternly.

"The thing is, you may hear some scary stuff at school. The other kids might even say that Daddy was in jail."

"Jail!" Henry squawked. "Oh *no!*"

"Is he?" Paige demanded.

"Um . . . kind of. I mean not a jail like on TV, more like a . . ." Actually, I had no idea. I'd tried googling holding cells at the federal building but hadn't found any images. "A place where they decide if people's mistakes are superbad or more like . . . accidents."

"Is Daddy going to have to go back to jail if they decide his mistake was bad enough?" Paige asked, her lip beginning to tremble. "Are they going to give him the death penalty?"

"Paige Marie Summers! Why on earth would you say a thing like that? Of course not!" I was bungling this badly. I wished my mother was already here. "Look, it's all going to be fine, I promise. Mostly what I wanted to tell you is that if kids say anything that upsets you, I want you to go straight to your teachers and ask them to call me right away. Do you understand?"

"If it's Carlos, I'll tell him to stop being mean," Henry said fiercely. "But if it's Sheridan, I'll tell Miss Chirichella. She needs to learn to keep her lips zipped!"

"Do I have to go to school tomorrow?" Paige asked, a single tear rolling down her cheek, breaking my heart. "Can't I just stay home until Grammy and Grampy get here?"

"Oh, honey—you can see them after school, okay? I just don't think it's good for you to be missing school."

"But what about Daddy? Why can't we go pick him up now?"

"Because people make a lot of really stupid rules sometimes," I said grimly. "Now how about one of you go get me a book."

"I know!" said Henry, crawling out of bed and hopping down. "Let's read *Captain Underpants and the Terrifying Return of Tippy Tinkletrousers*. It's about when George and Harold escape from jail!"

"Oh my God, Henry, you're so *stupid*!" Paige yelled as he ran out of the room, and then she started sobbing and threw herself into my lap.

CHAPTER 34

In the morning when we arrived at the school, I walked the gauntlet of all those accusing stares and hushed whispers with my head held high. Henry seemed to have forgotten all about last night's conversation and ran off to find his friends like every other day, but when Paige saw Esme Zapata pointing and whispering with Clara Otedola, she squeezed my hand tighter.

"I really don't think I should be in school today," she said.

Something delicate inside me threatened to break, and I knew that I would never be the same even if I managed to survive the plague of disasters that had befallen my family. It was all I could do to keep myself from marching over to Celeste Zapata and asking her what she thought she was doing gossiping about an innocent little girl in front of her children. I knew it wasn't that simple, but I no longer had any interest in turning the other cheek or reserving judgment or giving people the benefit of the doubt or seeing things through others' eyes. In fact, everyone in this town who was not related to me by blood or marriage had better watch their step, because I was past the point of caring about decorum or propriety or my reputation or my good name or any of the other invisible bonds that had kept us all in line for far too long.

I knelt down in front of Paige and took her hands.

"Remember last night when I told you that if any of the kids said something that upset you, you should tell your teacher?"

"Uh-huh."

"Well, I still want you to tell your teacher. But first I want you to look that kid in the eye and tell them that they had better shut their stupid ugly face or they'll regret it. Do you think you can do that?"

Paige's eyes went wide and her mouth fell open. Then, very slowly, she nodded. "Yes, Mommy, I can."

"Good. Because in the Summers family we don't take shit from anyone, do we?"

"Mom . . . you said *shit*."

I nodded. "Yes I did. This is one of those times when a bad word is the only word that will do. Okay?"

I held my hand up for a high five, and Paige grinned and smacked it hard before running off to line up with her class.

I blew her a kiss before walking away, nearly colliding with Celeste Zapata, who'd apparently been eavesdropping.

"I can't believe you'd tell your own child that physical violence is—"

"Fuck off, Celeste," I said, giving her the finger for good measure. I was on a roll.

I still had Brooke's number from the night we'd all gone out. I thought for a few moments before composing a text to her.

Hey Brooke there's something I'd like to discuss with you. Can we meet for coffee or a drink? My parents are visiting, so any time after Friday is good for me.

Almost immediately, she texted back.

I can meet after my class on Saturday how about 11 at Brewsters

When I went to pick the kids up, Emery Souza was the first to see me coming. She broke away from her friends and jogged over to intercept me.

"Oh my God, I heard about James, it's terrible!" she said.

"I'm not sure what you're talking about."

"Julia, it's *me* you're talking to. I just want to help. You knew

Anthony was in Institutional Asset Management at JPMorgan, right?"

"Uh-huh." How would I know that? I doubted I'd even recognize Anthony Souza.

"So I know all about this sort of thing, what James is going through. I mean, I *sympathize.*"

She was fishing for gossip she could trade on like a kid who makes friends by giving away Jolly Ranchers. The only surprising thing was that she was so transparent about it, but then again Emery had never been subtle.

"Really?" I said. "That's such a comfort, and so kind of you to share, Emery. I mean, I had no idea that Anthony had ever been arrested."

She took a step back, her face tightening. "I never said that. Only that I know it happens. I mean, it could happen to anyone."

"Sure," I said, winking. "I hear you. Frankly I'm surprised James has gotten away with it this long. I mean, it's one thing to skim off a company as large as JPMorgan, right? But James has had to basically cook his own books right under his accountant's nose, and that's no easy task, you know what I mean?"

"Hey, I didn't—"

"But it's okay. Our lawyer's mobbed up. If things don't go well in court, there are other alternatives." Another wink. "James won't mind cooling his heels on the inside for a while as long as the guy who dimed him out gets what's coming to him."

Emery's expression changed to confusion and disgust. I was breaking a cardinal rule by refusing to succumb to my humiliation; the only acceptable way back was groveling and starting at the bottom again, like when you land on a slide in Chutes and Ladders and end up all the way back at the kid with the broken dishes.

"I don't know why you think this is funny," she said, her face reddening. People were staring at us, but I was becoming used to it. In fact, it felt oddly freeing.

I spotted Grace standing with Annabel Marcus, both of them watching me. Annabel said something and laughed, and Grace leaned in to whisper.

Over there? That used to be my best friend, I wanted to say. It wasn't so long ago that she'd posted a photo of the two of us at a Central Park Conservancy luncheon with our arms around each other and the caption **Me and @2jule4school #bestfriendsforever.** For my birthday last year, she'd written me a poem that made me cry.

"You know what, Emery, you're right," I said dully, dropping all pretense. "It's not funny at all. My husband is in jail, and I'm actually pretty terrified right now. I barely slept last night. You want to know who I called when I found out? The only person I could trust not to tell everyone I know? My mom."

I'd never been so honest about something so damning before. I wondered if I was starting to truly lose my mind as I took a last look at the people I'd convinced myself actually cared about me before heading home.

CHAPTER 35

I told the kids they could wait up for my parents if they tidied their rooms. Before starting dinner, I made myself a cup of tea and pulled a chair close to the window. It was a typical rush hour on the Upper East Side, cars honking, pedestrians rushing, cops blowing their whistles. This was my city, my home, but I was starting to understand that I inhabited an island within an island. Down below, among the nannies pushing fifteen-hundred-dollar strollers and the well-dressed women getting out of cabs, were the maids and janitors and shop owners and messengers and waitresses, all the people who kept our rarefied little world turning. When they went home at night, they snapped at their spouses and yelled at their kids and struggled to pay the bills and saved a few dollars when they could. They ran up their credit cards and got foreclosed on and let their insurance lapse.

They had real problems. They didn't worry about getting invited to the right parties or appointed to the right committees, or whether their kids would get into the right private schools or whether some other mom would show up to the school fundraiser in the same eighteen-hundred-dollar dress, or if after paying thirty-five dollars for a spin class, they would get a bike in the front row.

And while I had no way of knowing, I imagined that when someone crossed them—when another driver took the parking space they'd been waiting for, or a neighbor played music loud when they had to be up for the graveyard shift, or a coach yelled at their kids at a soccer game—they did something about it. Turned their anger into action—and not just gossiping about them or leaving them off the invitation list for their next dinner party.

A pigeon flew by outside the window, dipping its wings before sailing in a big, lazy loop down toward the street and then disappearing from view. I hated pigeons, hated the mess they made, the way they fought each other over crumbs. But up here, nine floors above the ground, they flew wherever they wanted. They had complete freedom, and they didn't give a shit how anyone else felt about them.

I'd been so focused on the people I saw every day, so worried about impressing them, that I'd stopped asking myself what I really wanted. Now that I was losing everything anyway, maybe it was time to try to figure out the answer to that question.

Stewart Marlowe called while we were eating dinner to say that everything was in order for James to be released that night once the bond went through, but it would probably be late.

I tried to read a book to pass the time until my parents arrived, but I couldn't concentrate. Instead I helped Henry build a huge, shapeless Lego construction that he called an "attack monster" while Paige played on her iPad.

When my parents finally walked in the door, I burst into tears. The kids cheered and ran to hug their grandparents, and when she'd finally untangled herself, Mom patted my back like she was burping a baby, until I eventually stopped blubbering and wiped my eyes.

"Go freshen up," she said. "Then you can say hello to Dad."

"Mom, he's standing right here!"

"It's okay, sweetheart," Dad said. "Go ahead and fix your face. I'm not going anywhere."

I didn't have the energy to resist. I went to my room and splashed water on my face solely because my mom told me to, but I did feel better after. I let the kids stay up another ten minutes and then sent them to bed with a promise that Grampy would wake them the next morning.

For the next hour we chatted about the dog, the garden, what my brother was up to, the mayoral race. My parents argued about what color to paint the house (Dad wanted to keep it white with black trim, Mom wanted to go nuts and paint the shutters a deep pine green) and whether to tell their neighbors that they smelled marijuana coming from their teenage son's bedroom.

I knew they were trying to distract me, but I loved them for it. As midnight approached, I could tell that they were exhausted.

"Go to bed," I finally said. "I'll just nap on the couch until James comes home."

"I don't mind staying up," Dad said, rubbing his eyes.

"*Go.*"

I turned on HGTV and was watching people argue about whether to move or not when I remembered that Gigi's mom's memorial was the next day. I hoped my parents wouldn't mind watching the kids for a few hours so James and I could go. After a day stuck inside with my parents, he'd probably welcome the chance to get out. My last thought before dozing off was that it was a shame no one wore black veils anymore. It would have been a perfect time to go incognito.

I didn't hear James come in. When he sat down on the sofa and pulled me into his arms, it took me a second to realize I wasn't dreaming. I might have cried a little more.

He handed me the plastic bag from the jail with his wallet and watch and belt in it, and stripped down in the bedroom, leaving his clothes where they fell. He went into the shower and stayed there for a long time. I fell asleep before he came to bed.

CHAPTER 36

Everyone was up before me in the morning. When I came into the kitchen, the kids were sitting on my parents' laps, and James was dressed and shaved and making polite conversation. But it was like he'd left a part of himself behind in the holding cell. The man who'd come home was reserved, tentative, and he jumped when I tapped him on the shoulder to pour him more coffee.

After breakfast, Dad walked the kids to school and James watched the news. I reminded him about the memorial and he said he didn't mind going. Mom went through my cabinets and refrigerator and made a grocery list. She handed me her credit card, and I ordered it all over the phone. She had me call Sherry-Lehmann and order six bottles of her favorite Australian Sauvignon Blanc and another six of Pinot Gris for me, plus scotch for Dad. It was as though she was laying in supplies before a hurricane.

After everything arrived, she put together a casserole made with shredded turkey and onion soup mix that had been my childhood favorite. Since James and I would miss having dinner with them, her only chance to feed me was lunch.

"Eat more," she said. "You're too thin."

"Mom, I'm not. I'm healthy." But I ate a second helping anyway.

Mom decided to walk with me to pickup, and you should have seen the looks she gave anyone who dared to point or whisper. We stood alone at a distance from everyone else, but I made a point of waving at anyone who looked in our direction.

When Paige came out, I breathed a sigh of relief to see her walking with her friends like it was any other day.

"Any trouble?" I asked her after she hugged her grandmother.

"I can handle it," she said. "Can I go skiing with Braden for Christmas? It's not like I believe in Santa anymore."

"Absolutely not," I said. "And if you tell your brother about Santa you're grounded until next year."

Henry was one of the last kids to come out of the school. He was holding Miss Chirichella's hand and he looked like he'd been crying.

"Oh shit," I said. "Mom, do you mind walking the kids home while I talk to Henry's teacher?"

"Of course not, Julia," Mom said calmly, taking Paige's hand and steering her a few paces away. "Come on, Paige, you can tell me all about your day."

Henry broke away and ran the last few yards, throwing his arms around my legs.

"Henry's had a rough day," Miss Chirichella said. I was surprised by how kind her voice was.

"Oh, no. Was there more . . . fighting?"

"No, no, nothing like that. I'm very pleased with Henry's behavior since we talked about play rules in class. Unfortunately, some of the parents haven't been careful about what they discuss in front of their children, and there were some . . . things said."

I gently peeled Henry's arms off my legs. "Henry, lovey, Grammy's going to walk you home, and I'll catch up, okay?"

"Okay," he said doubtfully and trudged off as though he was going to his execution.

"Sorry, I just didn't want to talk about this in front of him," I said. "At least, not here. I did try to prepare them—I didn't go into details, but they know about their father's arrest. I assume that's what the other kids were teasing him about?"

"Well, yes." Miss Chirichella's cheeks turned slightly pink. "To be honest, I wasn't sure how to bring it up with you. If it matters, I was very impressed with Mr. Summers when we met."

"You were?"

"You look surprised. I thought he was a breath of fresh air. I probably talked to him for ten minutes at Curriculum Night and he didn't once tell me how to do my job. I mean, don't repeat that, please."

"What *did* you talk about?" I said, curious despite myself.

"Cars, actually. He's worried that Henry won't have any incentive to learn to drive. He asked me if I could talk about cars more in class. And trucks. And construction equipment."

"Oh, James . . ." I sighed.

"So . . . you're managing? I mean I know it's not my business—"

"Yes, I guess we are. My parents are here and—well, you know." I took a breath. "Can I ask you something?"

"Of course."

"Did you hear about what happened to Paige a few weeks ago? When she ended up in the hospital?"

"Mmm. I'm sorry to say it's been a popular topic."

"Then—why are you being so nice to me? Everyone else seems to be convinced I'm a terrible parent."

"Well, maybe you are. But I've been doing this a few years, and I've learned to try to tune out the gossip. Because anyone who will gossip to you?—they'll gossip about you." She smiled faintly. "I'd rather make up my own mind and take my chances."

Mom was making her famous spaghetti sauce, and she put the kids to work scrubbing vegetables and peeling carrots. We hadn't told them we were going to a memorial service, only that it was a grown-up party and they were staying home. When I came into the living room in my plain black dress, James offered his arm as though he'd come to take me to prom.

We didn't speak on the way to the Metropolitan Club. I walked in clutching James's arm with as much dignity as I could muster, greeting people with what I hoped was an unapproachably distant nod. I left James at the bar and made the obligatory circuit of the photo boards lining the main room, having to endure only a few uncomfortable encounters with people I knew and a brief conversation with Tatum in which we pretended that we were merely acquaintances. I only saw Gigi briefly in the receiving line, but she hugged me and whispered in my ear, "I can't believe you came."

"You're my friend," I said. "At least I hope you still are."

"You showed up," she said. "That took guts." She gave my hand a squeeze before moving on to the next person.

After we'd stayed what I judged to be an acceptable amount of time, I found James and we made our escape. We were in the grand entrance hall, mere yards from the exit, when someone called my name. I froze, feeling James flinch. Our eyes met, and there was something in his face that I'd rarely seen before: shame, or at least regret. It was like seeing a mustache on the Mona Lisa.

I braced myself for whatever new snub was coming, but striding toward us purposefully in ugly black orthopedic-looking pumps was Janet Erikson.

She opened her arms wide and folded me in a hug, and I smelled patchouli and yeast, hairspray and wool. She held on too long, finally releasing me and turning to James. She took both of his hands in hers.

"You remember Janet," I said.

"Yeah, yeah," he said vaguely.

Janet released him and turned back to me. "I'm so sorry, sweetie. What a week you've had."

I searched her face for signs of sarcasm, but there wasn't any. "Thank you. Were you friends with Mrs. Dickinson?"

"Oh, you know—we've been running around in the same circles for thirty years. Although honestly, I can't say I ever really knew her all that well. She wasn't one to bare her soul."

I couldn't believe she said it; Janet seemed constitutionally programmed to say exactly what she was thinking.

"And of course I know Gigi," she continued. "Now, *she* shows a little more promise. Drove Lydia nuts when she was growing up."

I tried to think of a response while Janet dug in her purse.

"You've got my number," she said, taking out a card case and a plastic Bic. "I want you to come over and forget your troubles for a night. Just me and you, Terry's completely consumed with a paper he's presenting next month. Are you free at all in the next few days?"

"That's—it's—I'll have to check," I stammered. "It's so kind of you."

Janet took out a card and scribbled something on it. When she handed it to me, I saw that she had written her address on a thick ecru honest-to-God calling card, the kind my grandmother used to keep in an ebony box on her desk, the engraving plates ordered from Dempsey & Carroll as soon as she was married, with nothing but her new name in English script.

As if I needed Janet to tell me where she lived.

"Any night's fine. Just let me know." She gave me another hug, a quick one, and then gently looped a stray bit of my hair over my ear, a gesture so tender that I teared up as she turned and headed back inside.

"What was that all about?" James asked, but I just shook my head.

CHAPTER 37

Henry came running when we came through the door, holding up a Playmobil figure clutching what looked like a spear with bloody entrails impaled on the end.

"Look what Grammy and Grampy brought me!"

"It's a campfire play set," my mother said proudly. "See the little wiener?"

"Everything okay, pumpkin?" my father asked.

"Everything's fine," I said. "It sure smells good in here."

"We haven't eaten yet! We didn't expect you back so soon."

"I got needlepoint!" Paige said, showing me a square of canvas with a row of uneven red stitches. "Grammy's teaching me!"

"I brought you a little something too." Mom beamed, handing me a bag from E. A. Davis, where she'd always taken me for school clothes. Inside was a Pepto-Bismol pink Deans of Scotland sweater.

"Thanks, Mom," I said, my eyes misting, though I'd never wear it. I knew it was her way of taking care of me.

"Who wants to help me make breadsticks?" Mom asked brightly.

"Me!" the kids chorused.

"You'll mess them up, Henry," Paige said sternly. "Mom, if he helps he'll wreck them."

"Not another word if you want to help," I said automatically.

James came out of the bedroom, already changed into jeans and an old flannel shirt and looking much more like himself. "I was wondering if I could talk to you."

"Oh—I was going to see if Dad wanted to go for a walk," I stammered. I knew we needed to talk, but I didn't want to do it with my parents in the other room. I was more than happy to wait until they left.

"No, you go ahead, sweetheart," Dad said. "I think I'll help the cooks."

"You can't cook, Grampy!" Henry chortled. "You're a bad, *bad* cook!"

James took my elbow and steered me into the bedroom and shut the door.

"We haven't really had a chance to talk since I got home," he said.

"Did my dad . . . say something to you? This morning, before I got up?"

"Nah, he's been cool." James jammed his hands in the pockets of his jeans. His suit and shirt were crumpled on the bed where he'd tossed them. "Especially because, I mean, shit. I'm supposed to take *care* of his daughter, you know? Not . . . this."

"James . . ." I put my arms around him, feeling the tension in his back. After a moment he relaxed and wrapped his arms around me. I rested my head on his chest, and we held each other.

"I don't know exactly what's happened," I said, "but I can understand you getting scared of losing the deal. Of . . . not being able to provide for us. If that's why you did what you did, then that's all I need to know."

He didn't say anything for a moment, and then he gently disentangled himself. "It's complicated, Jules," he mumbled, and then he left the room.

By unspoken agreement, my parents were only staying two nights, long enough to reassure themselves that I was all right but not so long that they'd have to intervene in what they considered our private business. If James was cleared, the whole episode would never be mentioned again, and if he wasn't, they'd be back with lawyers and money and whatever else it took to make sure that the kids and I would be fine. James, at that point, would probably not be a high priority.

But before they left the next night, Mom had planned an outing to cheer me up. We dropped the kids off at school together, and then she and I went to the spa at the Peninsula hotel while James took Dad to the *Intrepid* Museum for a below-the-decks tour of the decommissioned aircraft carrier.

After our massages and seaweed wraps, as we were soaking in the plunge pool, Mom told me she'd set up an account for me at Child-Minders. They were the babysitters you used when you were desperate—when your nanny called in sick, your kids got sent home from school, your husband forgot to tell you about a work event—but I figured these qualified as desperate times.

The account was linked to my mom's credit card. I protested just enough to be polite.

"Consider it an early birthday present," Mom said.

"My birthday isn't for ages . . ."

"Well, Christmas, then. The point is, it's an investment in your sanity. You have to be the strong one in the family now, Julia. Do what you need to do."

I gazed at my mother across the steam rising from the bubbling jets. Around her neck was the pendant Dad had made from her original engagement ring when he bought her a four-carat emerald-cut diamond for her fiftieth birthday. She rarely wore that ring, but she never went anywhere without the pendant.

The women in our family, we mate for life. I thought of my friends who barely tolerated their husbands; and of Janet, who'd found her sweet, awkward scientist. There were marriages made of love and others made of sharpened knives and many, many in between, and I had been lucky but I had also been complacent. I'd counted on James to take care of us but I hadn't noticed when he faltered, when my expectations forced him to bend in ways that ended up breaking him.

When we got home, Dad had picked up the kids and was playing Crazy Eights with them at the kitchen table. Henry had blue smudges around his mouth and he could barely keep his eyes open. My father looked exhausted. Only Paige seemed to have any energy left.

"Daddy left," she said, pulling a card from her hand and tossing it on the table.

"Where'd he go?"

I was hanging our coats in the hall closet, but when no one responded, I turned around, my hands on my hips. "Well?"

My parents exchanged a glance. Mom took Henry's cards out of his hands and laid them on the table.

"Go to your rooms, please, you two," Mom said. "Scoot. Grampy and I have a little surprise for you before we leave, but only if you're very good so we can talk to Mommy for a bit."

"Talk to Mommy about what?" I demanded, suddenly getting a very bad feeling. But my children knew a bribe when they heard one, and they disappeared down the hall.

"Sit down, sweetheart," Dad said.

"I don't want to sit." My voice was shrill. "Tell me what's going on."

"Now hear us out," Dad said. "James was the one who decided. We didn't tell him he had to leave, obviously. We would never do that."

"Oh my God," I gasped. "What did you do?"

"James and I had a talk," Dad said. "Man to man. You know we love—"

I shot him a look so full of vitriol that it actually stopped my father in his tracks.

"You know that we care very much for James," my mother amended.

"You don't. You don't! You never have."

My father reached up and took my hand, and I let him. He looked so tired. My father was a healthy and energetic seventy-one, but in this moment, he looked like an old man.

I was starting to shake. "Please," I whispered. "I know you've never liked him. But—but he's my husband, and I need him. I need him, Daddy."

Dad patted my hand. I'd scared him. But he'd scared me first.

"It's not as bad as all that. He's just decided to stay at his office for a while," my father said gently. "We were talking, you know, and the kids . . . James just thought that the less they're exposed to, um, the current state of affairs, the less they'll have to worry about—because they'll hear things. People gossip, it's human nature. But the mothers, you mothers stick together. You stick up for each other. See? You'll have your friends to support you, you'll take care of the kids, this whole thing will blow over. It's not forever, honey, just for now, until things get back to normal."

I glanced at my mother, but she wouldn't meet my eyes. She'd known all along. That line about the mothers sticking together—she didn't correct him, even though she knew that my so-called friends tore me apart when they smelled blood. It had been the same way twenty years ago, when she used to wait for me at lacrosse practice, gossiping with the other mothers by the Winsor fields.

Maybe she was the one who gave him the line, though. Maybe it was my father who'd needed convincing to betray his only daughter.

"Did you pay him?" I demanded.

My father reddened—I'd scored a direct hit. Neither of them would look at me.

But . . . as angry as I was at them, a part of me understood. They were protecting me, just as I'd protect my own kids. And it pained them to do it, I knew that. It wasn't until I became a mother myself that I understood that one of the greatest sacrifices parents make is to bear the burden of their children's contempt.

"It's okay," I said. Dad patted my head, clearing his throat.

"He didn't take it, sweetheart. The money. I thought you should know."

But I already knew. That was my James. Unlike my parents, I knew him through and through.

Mom and Dad were on the 6:30 A.M. shuttle, and they liked to get to the airport early. Once they were packed and their Uber called, they stood in the foyer with their suitcases, looking slightly guilty.

"We left something for you in our room," Mom said. "It's no big deal. Use it on the kids. Or, you know, do something for you. And for the love of God, use those babysitters, do you hear me?"

I sighed. "If you left cash in there, I'm just going to cut it up with scissors and mail you the pieces."

That actually made my father giggle. Which in turn made me tear up.

"I love you guys," I said, and I would have hugged them hard, if they were the hugging type.

CHAPTER 38

After they were gone, the apartment seemed unbearably empty. I'd tried calling James and sent him two texts, but he hadn't responded. I helped Paige with her needlepoint and let Henry show me the little plastic tents and campfire, but I kept thinking about James, alone in the empty building on which he'd gambled our future.

At a little after seven, I couldn't stand it anymore. I had to see him, make sure he was okay. The ChildMinders paperwork was lying on my desk, but I didn't have time to figure it out right now. And I couldn't think of a single friend who I was confident would help me.

But then I thought of Janet, who'd invited me to her home when no one else would even look at me.

I'd been so rude to her—but I was desperate. I called her before I could change my mind.

"Hey, sweetie!" she answered. I could hear conversation and laughter behind her. "I'm so glad you called! Can you come over? We've got people for dinner, you'll love them."

"I, uh—the thing is, I'm having kind of an emergency."

"What's wrong?" she said, her tone changing instantly. "Hang on, I'm going to step out of the room."

The background noise disappeared. "What's happening?"

"It's kind of a long story," I said. "I just need someone to watch my kids for a bit. I wouldn't ask if there was anyone else—"

"Julia. *Yes.* It's fine." She had that same take-charge tone as my mother. "We'd love to have them. Willa will be thrilled, since it's all adults here tonight, and there's more than enough food. Just come on over, you don't need to say another word."

Janet and her husband lived in the Mortimer Hart mansion on Park Avenue and Eighty-fifth Street, where Janet's grandmother had lived until she died. Rumor had it that Janet furnished the opulent rooms with IKEA furniture she and Terry brought with them from MIT, where he'd gotten his PhD.

"I don't want to," Henry whined as we got out of the cab. He was tired and cranky, and I'd changed him into his pajamas in case he fell asleep at Janet's. Paige had her needlepoint in a Ziploc bag; she stared up at the mansion in awe.

I'd barely had time to knock on the door when Janet opened it, wearing a flannel shirt over a faded pair of jeans and wool slippers embroidered with acorns. The house smelled amazing, and I could see people gathered around a long pine table in the dining room.

"You're here!" she exclaimed, crouching so she could look Henry and Paige in the eye. "Do you remember me? I'm Janet."

Henry shook her hand somberly. Paige glanced up at me, incredulous that I was going to let her call one of my friends by her first name.

Then it was my turn, and this time I didn't resist her hug. "I don't know how to thank you," I mumbled as I held on.

"Don't give it a thought. Do you have time to say a quick hello? Have a glass of wine?" She was already leading us toward the dining room, shepherding the kids with her hands on their shoulders. "Willa! Look who's here!"

Willa had grown into herself since I saw her last. Her braces were gone, and she'd cut her waist-length hair into a cute layered bob. "Hi!" she said. "Want to help me frost the cake?"

The kids eagerly followed her, and Janet took my hand and made introductions.

"You know Gina," Janet said. "And her husband, Mark."

I nodded, surprised. Gina's son had graduated the year after Paige started at Graylon, but I'd gotten to know her through the PTA. She was a gregarious southerner married to a surgeon, and one of the most popular moms at the school, someone I'd identified as competition the first time I laid eyes on her.

And yet here she was, looking perfectly at ease at Janet's IKEA table.

Janet continued around the table, introducing people. "That's Luis, he was our exchange student a few years ago, he's working in Brooklyn now. Sandy's one of Terry's colleagues, and we met Neil when he did some tree work for us. Oh, Terry, there you are, do you remember Julia?"

"Of course I do!" Terry set a steaming pot of chili on a trivet in the middle of the table. "Can I get you something to drink?"

"Honey, Julia's got to be somewhere."

After a chorus of goodbyes, Janet walked me to the door.

"I just want to thank you again," I said.

"You really don't need to thank me. Listen, why don't you let the kids stay over and pick them up in the morning? There's a playroom downstairs, Willa used to like to sleep in her tepee down there. I know she'd be happy to stay with them."

I hesitated. It didn't seem right to leave the kids with strangers, but the idea of having to come back to the party after going to see James was overwhelming. "Are you sure?"

"Absolutely. Don't rush over, either, we sleep in on Saturdays. Terry will get bagels, you can have breakfast with us!"

This time I might have hugged her first.

"Don't thank me again," Janet said, "or I'll have to fine you. A dollar in the swear jar. We've almost got enough for a Roomba."

I'd asked the Uber driver to wait for me. As he pulled up to the job site, he glanced at me in the rearview mirror. Scaffolding covered three sides of the building; pallets of lumber were stacked out front.

"You sure this is where you're going?" the driver asked.

A security guard was walking toward me as I got out.

"Can I help you, miss?"

"Hi, my husband is the developer of this building," I said. "He's working late and not picking up the phone and—"

"You mean James?" the man asked.

"You know him?"

"Oh, yeah. Mmm-hmm, that James. Come on, then, ma'am."

He walked slowly, pointing out every uneven patch of dirt, shining his light for me, keeping up a steady patter all the time. *James works all the time, but he's a good man, one of the best. You should be proud of him, all he ever talks about is his family.* I figured he and James had probably shared a beer or two.

It took two keys to unlock the entrance. The lobby was lit by too-bright bulbs in the temporary fixtures, the beautiful old mosaics and bronze fittings taped off with plastic. It looked so different from the only time I'd been here before, the day after James signed the deal.

James had lied—there was no office. There were no rooms at all, not yet; according to Carl, most of the upper floors were stripped down to the studs.

But through the lobby in the back of the building, a light shone under the sheets of plywood nailed together to make a box in the corner. A rough plywood door had been mounted on hinges, an open padlock hanging from the hasp.

"James?" I called.

I heard metal scraping the floor. The door swung open and there he was, still dressed in the clothes he'd worn this morning. His sleeves were rolled up, and his little makeshift room smelled like pizza.

"Oh, Julia," he said, sighing.

"You good, James?" the security guard asked.

"Yeah, all good, except I married a crazy woman, Carl. Nah, we're all set."

Carl chuckled obligingly. "You call me if she needs a car, hear?"

We waited until his footsteps echoed down the hall, and then James pulled me into his arms and kissed my forehead. Over his shoulder I saw that he'd rigged a desk out of a board and sawhorses, with a construction light clamped to a two-by-four. Against one wall was the beautiful Florence Knoll sofa from his office, draped with cheap-looking sheets and a blanket. There were papers all over the desk; half a sandwich sat next to his laptop, the lettuce wilted. The floor was bare concrete. Everything was covered with a layer of construction dust.

I pulled away from James. "I'm so sorry about Dad."

"Ahhh . . ." James jammed his hands in his pants pockets and looked at the ground. "No, he was fine. He was right. This is better. Look. I hated having the kids see me like that, okay? I hate having *you* see me like this."

I couldn't believe that James was defending my father, but I shouldn't have been surprised. All Dad would have had to do was express concern for my welfare to pitch James into a spiral of self-criticism. My family had long ago settled on the narrative that I had married beneath me, but James never quit trying to prove himself. The same man who would tell a ribald joke at an engagement party or wear a baseball cap to a Graylon parents' night could spend an hour getting ready for dinner with my parents, rehearsing topics to bring up with my dad and asking my opinion about what he should wear.

"Like what?" I asked. "Nothing has changed. There's no verdict, no proof, just—just a lot of talk. You're better than that—better than any of them."

James hung his head. "No, I'm not. Jules . . . you don't get it. I lied to you."

"Okay, fine, maybe you did," I said. "And there will be time to talk about that. But I don't believe you did anything I can't forgive you for."

Whatever James had done, he'd done it for me—to allow me to stay home with the kids, to hire help, to pay the outrageous school tuitions and mortgages on our apartment and summer home. He refused to accept a dime from my parents, even when that meant we spent our first year of marriage in a 550-square-foot one-bedroom apartment. Meanwhile, he somehow managed to send money home to his own parents. If you dug down under our opulent lifestyle and James's occasional expensive cigar, you'd find a man who cared little for the finer things, but never questioned that I deserved them.

"How can you say that? You don't even know what I did."

"It doesn't matter. You're *good,* James. You don't have to prove it to me. And I don't care what anyone else thinks—even my parents, especially my parents."

James shook his head and pulled me against him again. We stood, holding each other, not talking. I already knew I wasn't going to be able to convince him to come home, not yet. Most men wouldn't want their wives to see them living like this; my husband couldn't bear for me to see him idle. I felt the swell of that old, secret pride, the same feeling I'd had when he took me to his place the first time and showed me the bookcases he'd built himself.

"Are you going to be all right?" he finally asked.

"Of course I will. But the kids miss you," I said. "And since Benilda's gone, I'm going to have to go to Graylon twice a day, and they're going to eat me alive."

"Any of those bitches gives you a hard time, just blow them off. Who needs 'em? You've got lots of other friends."

Sweet James . . . he didn't have any idea. "Come sit with me a minute."

I led him to the couch and snuggled against his chest.

"Who's watching the kids?" he asked.

"They're at a sleepover," I murmured. "Did Dad really offer you money to leave?"

"Oh, it wasn't like that," James said. "He just asked if he could help tide us over."

"Ha. You don't have to defend him, you know."

"We kind of came to the same conclusion, actually. I need to do a little thinking. Your dad . . . well, he knows how things work. How this situation could play out. He just wants you to be prepared. Protected."

"Are you talking about jail?" I was tired of not talking about it. "I mean, prison. It would be prison, right?"

James took my hand in his, lacing our fingers together. He didn't answer for a moment. "Look, Jules . . . I've got some options here. I don't want to go into too much detail—not that you'd pay any attention anyway."

He smiled to show me he was teasing, but it was true. "I'm sorry I didn't know this was happening," I said. "That I didn't listen when you tried to tell me about it. It just . . . I know it's a terrible excuse, but those things happen all the time. The protests, the permit stuff, the zoning—I don't remember when it went from being just the usual to—to—"

"It's okay, I wasn't prepared for it either. Look, Mercer was a risk from the start. But the rezone was supposed to be a sure thing. Fucking council sat across the table from me and gave me their word. And I was too stupid to see Larry was setting me up so by the time he comes rolling in with all those other demands—and the debt service was killing me. All those delays—"

"Is that when you started . . ." I searched for a way to say it. Using our money. Giving away our family's financial security. Endangering everything he'd worked for.

James wiped his face with his hand. "I had to cut costs somewhere. I hired some nonunion guys—not for everything. But, you know, once I started—I mean, you can get some of these guys for fifteen bucks an hour."

That was perhaps the one thing he could have told me that truly shocked me. His dad had been a member of IBEW Local 375 since his eighteenth birthday, when his own father took him down to the hall and signed him up. When I met James, he told me that his fallback plan if he couldn't make it in Manhattan was to go back and join his father on the job. His commitment to the unions had never wavered, even as his projects got bigger and more lucrative.

"But—but that's not illegal."

"No, it's not."

"So . . . what exactly are you doing here?" I asked.

James glanced at the pile of paperwork. "Oh, you know, tying up loose ends . . . this is still my building, or at least it will be as long as this whole thing gets . . ."

There was that dark mood again. It was hard work, distracting him from it, but I had once been a Girl Scout, and I knew just what to do. As the motto goes, *I will try to serve God and my country, and to help people at all times.*

God and my country were going to have to take care of themselves tonight. But there was one person I was pretty sure I could help.

"Sit back and relax, sailor," I said, reaching for his belt. "And stop talking."

James was still sleeping when I left in the morning. I'd been lying almost on top of him all night, and he'd barely moved.

I took a last look at him as I stood in the plywood doorway. His face was serene.

"Goodbye, my love," I whispered, and then I walked through the empty lobby, my footsteps echoing all around me.

CHAPTER 39

I stopped at Dean & DeLuca for a crumb cake and a quart of fresh-squeezed orange juice, trying not to think of the balance in our bank account. When I got to Janet's, I could hear someone picking at a guitar. I knocked, and a moment later Willa opened the door, Paige in tow.

"Hi!" she said. "Did you have a nice night?"

I smiled. I may have even blushed. "I did, sweetheart. What did you girls do?"

"*Mom.*" Paige rolled her eyes. "It's none of your business."

"Oh, I see. Willa, is your mother in the kitchen?"

"I'll find her. Come on back."

We found Janet and Terry in a sunny den filled with houseplants, sharing *The New York Times*. They were sitting at opposite ends of the couch, their feet entwined. Henry was on the floor on his stomach, using a compass to make circles on a pad of graph paper.

"Mom!" Henry said, jumping up and nearly stepping on the compass. "We're going to Break Your Neck Bridge!"

"Henry, sweetie, we have to ask your mother, remember?" Janet said.

"*Can* we? Please?"

"It's actually Breakneck Ridge, if that helps," Terry said. "There's a nice little hiking trail there. Henry can handle it, no problem."

"Oh, you guys, you've done so much for them already! I can't impose—"

"Swear jar," Janet cut me off, grinning. "Dollar."

"Are you sure Willa won't mind? It looks like Paige hasn't given her a minute's peace." I had to admit it was tempting; I'd completed all the paperwork for ChildMinders and was planning to drop the kids off on my way to meet Brooke, but the notion still made me uneasy.

"Willa would *love* it. And then you can have the day to yourself, and come in for a glass of wine when you pick them up."

And so I was invited for drinks at the Mortimer Hart mansion for the second time in twenty-four hours. Not bad for the wife of a felon.

James texted me while I was walking to Brewster's, a pleasant half mile from Janet's.

What are u doing sexy

Well, that was good; those didn't seem like the words of a despairing man. **Missing my husband**, I typed back. **How about you?**

Missing u lots. Had a good call today. Things moving forward. Everything ok?

All good. Kids are fine. Are you eating?

Yes lol, he typed back. **Carl brought me tacos**

Glad you're surviving

I backspaced; it sounded too dire, begging the question of how long he could survive in that construction-site purgatory. I tried again.

Glad you're doing ok.

Love you xoxo

I dropped the phone in my purse as I reached Brewster's, a funky Yorkville coffee bar and vegan bakery. I spotted Brooke immediately at a little round table in back, reading a book with a threadbare cover, her hair piled on her head. She was wearing what looked like a 1950s girls' gym uniform, complete with bloomers, her trusty motorcycle boots, and oversize jade-green glasses, and she seemed oblivious to all the attention she was getting, though I was pretty sure it was an act.

My suspicion was confirmed when she said, "Hey, Julia," without looking up. "Just let me finish this paragraph."

I went to get a decaf, and when I got back, her hands were folded on the book and her eyes were closed, a tranquil little smile on her face. I checked the title: Doris Lessing's *The Golden Notebook.*

"Pretty ambitious reading," I said.

She opened her eyes, still smiling. "I'm not stupid, Julia."

"I never said you were. I never *thought* you were, believe it or not."

"So, what are we doing here? What did you want to talk to me about?"

"You know, I was half-expecting Tatum to show up with you."

Her eyes flickered; she dropped the smile. "Well, she didn't."

"Okay." Obviously we weren't going to waste any time on pleasantries. "I just thought there were some things you should know about her."

"Is that right," she said tonelessly, putting her feet up on a chair as though she was settling in for a movie.

I rolled out my little speech the way I'd planned, going through the months since I'd first met Tatum and describing all the red flags I'd missed. I described her cunning in targeting Graylon as a way to get her foot in the door with rich moms, how eager she'd been to meet my friends and worm her way into my circle. I told her about all the expensive things I'd bought for Tatum, the people I'd introduced her to. I was detailing all the ways I'd helped her move up through the ranks at Flame when Brooke covered a yawn and then interrupted me.

"You can stop."

"Fine," I said, irritated. "I'm only telling you because she's probably taking advantage of you, too, in ways you might not even know about yet."

Brooke snorted. "I know all this already. You're not telling me anything new."

"Oh, come on, Brooke," I said, finally losing my composure. "You need to wake up! The minute she's sure she's got her next move locked down, she'll dump you the same way she dumped me."

"You're a little late. I broke up with her last week. For real, this time."

I could feel the figurative wind leaving my sails. "Oh," I said. "What happened?"

"She butt-dialed me while she and that asshole were shopping—she was literally telling him she wanted Fred Leighton diamond earrings instead of pearls as a wedding present."

"Oh," I said again. That was pure Tatum; Brooke was telling the truth. "So . . . you told her you were done?"

"Not right away." Brooke sighed, dropping her own attempt at indifference. "First I asked her what the fuck she was thinking and when was she planning to tell me and then there was a lot of yelling and things got a little rough before I finally kicked her out. She swore she'd give me back all my mom's shit and of course she hasn't. Oh, and she blocked me on everything."

"That's—I'm sorry, Brooke," I said. "I mean, I'm really sorry. I got played by her too."

Brooke gave a bitter little laugh. "You don't even know."

"Know what?"

"What she's said about you. Who she said it to."

"Who—" I started, then changed my mind. "No, don't tell me. I don't want to know."

"You say that now," Brooke said grimly. "Wait until you're halfway through a bottle of Tanqueray Ten at three in the morning."

For the first time, I felt a faint stirring of sympathy for Brooke. "I guess I'll take that chance."

"Probably a good idea."

I let the momentousness of Tatum's latest betrayal sink in. How many times was I going to underestimate Tatum? When she and Brooke had gotten back together . . . the way they couldn't keep their hands off each other . . . I thought it was real. But Tatum was merely amusing herself.

Still, I couldn't help being curious. "Isn't it . . . awkward? At Flame?"

"I quit. I'm taking the LSAT next month, and I'm working on my law school applications. I took a bartender job so I can study during the day. Oh, and I'm apartment-sitting for a friend—no more taking money from my parents."

"Wow," I said. "You're really doing it."

"Unless I fuck it up. But yeah, I figure it's about time. And I'm a pretty good test taker. I actually got in everywhere I applied for undergrad—I only went to Rutgers to piss off my mom."

She flashed me a rare grin—it looked good on her.

"Well, I wish you luck," I said, meaning it. "At least one of us ought to land on our feet. Tatum—she's like a human wrecking ball, you know? I feel sorry for whoever she ends up with."

"I don't," Brooke said. "You can't tell me you didn't know what she was from the start, deep down. The signs are there if you're paying attention. We just didn't want to see it."

I thought about it; maybe Brooke was right. There were all those moments when Tatum's reactions were just a little off, when her expression would shift in a flash. But her lies were so convincing, especially when you wanted to believe her.

"Maybe," I conceded. "But even if that was true, there's the *scale* of it—I mean, at this point I'm convinced there's nothing she wouldn't do for money and power. Social power, anyway."

"You really think that's what she's after?" Brooke was watching me with those opaque ice-gray eyes.

"Well, what else does she want?"

"Safety," Brooke said without hesitation. "Security. Enough money that she'll never run out. She told me some things . . . not a lot, and I had to piece it together, but her childhood was basically a horror show. Her dad took off before she was born. She and her mom lived in some old-ass aunt's basement, and her mom was a doper, couldn't keep a job, brought home one man after another."

"So much for Tatum's story about her parents dying in a car accident."

"Most of them went after Tatum when they had a chance," she continued. "When she was in high school her mom hit some pedestrian when she was drunk and went to prison and by then the aunt was stuck in a chair drooling and pissing herself, and by the time the county got their shit together and put her in a home, Tatum was working two jobs and skipping school just to eat. She barely graduated and the bank took the house and she basically started turning tricks to get the money to come here."

I was speechless; I'd known Tatum had a difficult childhood, but not on the scale Brooke described. How did anyone even survive something like that?

But I guess that was the point.

"Did she ever even act?" I asked. "Was she really in a Broadway show?"

"Ha. Not that I know of, unless you count all the times she lies. She probably would have made a pretty good actor, come to think of it."

I felt myself tear up unexpectedly, but it wasn't out of pity or even sympathy for Tatum. "Do you ever think about . . . if you'd never met her? How much pain you could have avoided?"

"It's pointless to think like that," Brooke said. "Besides, even when it's over, and you've got the scars to prove it, you can't be sure you wouldn't do it again. And you're lying to yourself if you don't see that."

"I need to go," I said, pushing back my chair with more force than necessary. "Like I said, best of luck with everything, and . . . and . . ."

"Keep in touch?" Brooke suggested mockingly, picking up her book. "Sure, Julia, that's just what I'll do. And good luck to you too."

CHAPTER 40

I arrived at the Eriksons' mansion as the sun was setting, turning the windows gold. The afternoon had become chilly and I was wearing my favorite woolly coat. I'd picked up a pot of orange mums nestled in pinpoint ivy, and when Janet came to the door I felt almost shy.

"Those are gorgeous!" she said, taking the mums. "I hope I don't kill them. Terry wants to put in an herb garden, but the last time we tried that, the mint took over our entire backyard in Cambridge."

It was quiet in the house, the faint sounds of a television coming from the basement. "The kids are wiped out from the hike," she said. "I put a movie on for them."

The dining room had been cleaned, but pans and trays were stacked on the table.

"From the potluck," Janet said. "I think most of our dishes at this point came from other people."

She took me into the kitchen, which was enormous by city standards and cluttered in a homey way with shelves of cookbooks and a collection of ceramic pitchers and antique advertising signs sharing wall space with Willa's drawings. On the refrigerator were Willa's spelling finalist certificate and photos of the family going back to when Willa was swaddled on a much younger Terry's chest. Janet poured us each a glass of wine and moved a pile of papers off the kitchen table, and we sat down.

"Terry always leaves his papers out," she said. "He left for the airport a while ago, so at any moment I expect he'll call in a panic because he forgot some piece of paper that he made notes on and I'll have to find it in that mess. Hey, how does a German physicist drink beer?"

"Um . . ."

"In *ein stein*!"

I couldn't help laughing, not at the dumb joke, but at the sheer joy she took from it. "What's it like, being married to a genius?"

"What's it like being married to a builder?" Janet said, smiling. "Don't you think it depends on who specifically the genius and the builder are?"

"James is a good man," I blurted.

"Aw, sweetie . . . I believe you. I figure most of us are good and most of us are assholes, depending on the day. I'm not going to judge. I mean, I judge all the time, but I kind of go with my gut, you know?"

I thought of Gina and Mark, breaking bread with the Eriksons' arborist. I wanted to believe it could work, Janet's happy vision of people getting along, that all you needed was good intentions and a positive attitude to insulate yourself from the judgment of the outside world.

"I have to ask you something," I said. "Why were you always so nice to me? I didn't . . . treat you very well."

Janet shrugged. "Honestly? You weren't afraid to be yourself. The first time we met, when you were new in the city, you told us this wild story about trying to buy some stranger's purse and how you ended up trading her for it."

"I'd forgotten about that. I still have it." I had been sitting on the steps of the library eating a sandwich on my lunch break when a girl sat next to me, setting down a canvas tote painted with a brilliantly colored dragon, embroidered with beads and tiny mirrors. Along the bottom was stitched *If the sky could dream, it would dream of dragons.* "I traded the Burberry work bag my mom bought me when I got my job."

"Yes, exactly!" Janet's eyes sparkled with merriment. "And yeah, I was a little worried when that crew got you in their clutches, but I saw how you were with your kids—how you let Henry wear that wolf hat to school, how you always got down on the ground to kiss them goodbye. And James, whenever I saw him at school events, I could tell he was miserable, but he was there anyway. That says a lot."

"Still." I looked down. "I've been a bitch to a lot of people."

"So don't be a bitch anymore, if you can help it." Janet grinned. "Besides, I doubt people really noticed. You'd have to do something really spectacular to make an impression on some of those women."

"You make it sound so easy. To, you know, ignore what people think and just be yourself."

Janet picked up her glass. "Sometimes it's easy, and sometimes it's not," she admitted. "That's why there's wine."

We drank and we ate potato chips and we made fun of the mean girls like we were in seventh grade, and we talked about our kids and our families. Janet opened a second bottle and we checked on the kids—Henry was fast asleep and Willa was teaching Paige origami—and then Janet gave me a tour of the house, which was decorated with a mixture of priceless antiques and castoffs, threadbare Persian rugs and family photos in plastic frames. Gorgeous millwork and inlaid floors were obscured by baskets of laundry and stacks of books and papers and a dusty treadmill in a spare bedroom, making it clear that no housekeeper darkened those doors. Then we returned to the kitchen table and continued where we'd left off.

Janet was telling a rambling story about how she and her sisters had snuck out one moonlit night at their grandparents' summer house in the Berkshires when I interrupted her.

"My life is kind of fucked up right now," I said, slurring my words a little.

Janet set down her glass and regarded me thoughtfully. "That sounds interesting," she said. "Do you want to talk about it?"

It turned out that I did.

I slept in Janet's guest room that night, Henry curled up next to me under a quilt Janet's sister had made. Paige slept in Willa's room. I had a bit of a hangover in the morning, but when I came downstairs, I could smell coffee already brewing.

Janet was at the counter, unrolling a tube of Pillsbury cinnamon rolls. "Oh God, you caught me," she said. "Willa loves these. Nothing but chemicals."

"Janet . . ." I said.

She set down the tube and grabbed my hands. "If you're about to tell me that you were drunk last night, that you said some things you shouldn't have, don't worry. I like you even more now that I know you're as much of a mess as everyone else."

"I'm not sure I remember everything I told you," I admitted.

"You know what I think? You need a decent therapist."

"Maybe when things settle down—"

"That's the *worst* time to talk to a therapist," Janet said, returning to her task. "I mean, shit. Strike while the iron's hot and all that."

"Did I, um . . . did I happen to mention the part where James is living in a plywood box and pissing in an alley?"

"Yup. But my favorite part was when you told Celeste Zapata to fuck off. I've been wanting to do that for a long time."

"It's just—I don't know what I'll *do,* you know? If James ends up in prison. I mean, I could take the kids and go live with my parents, I guess—"

"Screw that," Janet said. "You'll figure it out. I mean, I know it's easy for me to say, when I won't ever be able to spend all my money even if I live to be two hundred years old, but when I met Terry we lived on his grad school stipend and what I made teaching ESL, because I couldn't touch my trust until I was twenty-five. And it wasn't the end of the world."

"But the schools . . . the kids. And I don't have any marketable skills."

"Now you're whining," Janet said. She'd gotten the container partway open and dough oozed grotesquely from the cardboard slits. "Here—make yourself useful and see if you can get these out while I find a pan."

CHAPTER 41

Tuesday morning, I was dropping the kids off at school when my phone rang. I was getting used to the chill that greeted me every time I showed up at Graylon, the way conversations shifted and my old friends pretended not to see me, but when I saw it was James, I was happy for the distraction.

"James?"

"I'm coming home."

All those papers I'd seen on his plywood desk? They weren't financial documents at all—they were email printouts and copies of receipts and invoices and the notes James had begun pulling together, and taken as a whole they made a very convincing case for a story that James had never told me.

It was the tale of a young man who wanted to be a part of a magnificent city, to be able to show his children the work he'd done someday and say, "Daddy built that." Who wanted his father—whose wallet still contained the union card he'd carried proudly for almost fifty years—to know that his son had made something of himself.

And it was the story of a successful man who never forgot where he came from, who took care of his employees and tried to treat people fairly. But also, of a man who fell in love with a girl from another world, one that required him to adapt and sacrifice. Who took a giant risk that, if it paid off, would give his wife everything she could ever want and his children all they would ever need.

James made mistakes. He trusted the wrong people and ignored warning signs, and he waded too far into too many gray areas. As financial pressures mounted, he tapped our own savings to service his debt. He got sloppy—he got desperate. He gave in to the strong-arm tactics of the city council and the community groups and started taking shortcuts to win their cooperation. It turned out that everyone had a price.

There was another villain in the story: the construction union, whose members he had employed for so many years, despite the fact that their labor cost as much as four times what could be had on the street. When James jobbed out a few contracts to nonunion crews, they showed their true colors. All those years of friendship evaporated. A man came to see him; it wasn't a friendly meeting, but what could James do? Then another man came to see him, bringing photos of our children walking into Graylon and me coming out of Flame.

The morning after I'd gone to visit him at the building site, James had made a decision that went against everything he'd once believed about loyalty and honor. The world had changed since he set out on his own; the politics of the building game had metastasized. The feds had known exactly what to ask James when they first picked him up. They made it clear that he was small potatoes, that if he'd help them nab their real quarry, they would lose interest in prosecuting him.

That might seem like an easy choice, if you're not James—if you didn't cut your thumb and mingle your blood with that of your childhood friends as a symbol of everlasting brotherhood; if your best friends weren't still guys from high school who painted houses and laid sewer lines for a living. If your mind didn't still echo with the rule you learned as a child: *Once a snitch, always a traitor.*

James had to get there in his own time—but get there he did.

While I was cleaning our apartment on Monday morning, James had been attending a meeting at Federal Plaza, giving the feds everything they wanted and a bonus too. He offered up enough on Cora

Rivera and Larry De Stasi that the investigators were able to connect it with what they already had in three separate unrelated complaints. With the pair indicted on charges of fraud, grand larceny, and falsifying business records, the city council was in for a shake-up. And it turned out the FBI had been closing in on a union racketeering case for months—but James gave them the final proof they needed.

This didn't happen all at once, obviously. It took a few months, but the charges against James were dropped within days of his meeting with the feds. James gave a *New York Times* reporter an exclusive, earning a top-of-fold headline in the business section: PROSECUTORS MOVE TO DISMISS CHARGES IN MERCER HOUSE DEVELOPMENT DEAL.

Overnight, we were freed from social Siberia. Guilt over the way my friends and acquaintances had treated me had little to do with it—no one could resist the allure of a scandal, and James made an appealing hero. Milly Prasad called to invite us to their place in Jackson Hole over the Martin Luther King holiday weekend. At the rescheduled meeting of the book club, Tatum kept looking at me nervously as she went on about the benefits of the Kegan Diet, and Grace drank too much and tearfully called me her best friend in a toast.

But I'm getting ahead of myself.

After James's public exoneration, he took a few days off. We didn't do much, dropping the kids at school together and then wandering the city the way we'd done when we first met. We held hands and bought lunch from street carts and came home in time to make love before school let out—and sometimes we did it again when the kids were asleep.

A week after the *Times* story ran, I called both kids in sick to school, and the four of us took a tour of Mercer House, breathing the good clean smell of sawdust and stepping over two-by-fours. Forty-two apartments would soon house families, 20 percent of which were set aside for low- and moderate-income residents. We all wore hard hats, and James ordered lunch for the crew and gave Carl a gift certificate to take his wife out for a nice dinner.

Afterward, we walked to the subway station that James had agreed to refurbish as an expression of good faith to the interim councilwoman. Henry was out of his mind, since riding the subway was his favorite thing in the world. But James seemed almost as excited.

"They brought this tile all the way from Ohio a hundred years ago," James told the kids, his voice a little husky as he ran his hand along the beautiful old mosaic. "Guys like your grandpa installed it by hand."

As I watched my husband proudly show our children how our city was built, I couldn't wait to get him alone. Turns out I have a thing for a bighearted man in a hard hat.

EPILOGUE

Almost nine months to the day after James was cleared, and one week before the first tenants will begin moving into Mercer House, Summers Properties is holding a reception for community leaders, city council members, and the press in the restored lobby of the building. Four hundred guests are coming, including a large contingent of our friends, for no other reason than that I'm the boss and I can invite anyone I want. (Okay, technically, James is the boss—but he's more than happy to cede this sort of thing to me since he doesn't have a lot of patience for projects that don't involve power tools.)

Benilda is home with the kids. Surprised? A few days after James was exonerated, I texted her and asked her to meet. I drove all the way to Queens and took her to lunch at the nicest place I could find on Yelp. I asked her why she'd really left us, and though it took her a while to admit it, she finally made it clear that while her cousin lay dying, all I seemed to care about was dieting and going to Flame and partying with a bunch of *magputas*.

Also, she was *really* unhappy about having to clean up after Tatum. *Worse than living with a pig,* she said.

I asked for her forgiveness—and then I asked her if she'd come back for a 30 percent raise. To sweeten the pot I told her we were selling the Hamptons house, that she'd have paid time off to be with her family while we took the kids on a summer vacation to a ranch in Montana. (James's idea, obviously.)

I've carefully curated tonight's guest list to ensure positive coverage from friendly media and limited access to our detractors, of which there are still a vocal few. Despite James being cleared and the very public manner in which the scandals involving the city council and the union played out, as well as a statement of support from the mayor calling the project "a sterling example of mixed-income housing," James still sometimes draws the ire of activists. I've decided they're like sand flies—you'll never escape them, but you can minimize the nuisance by covering your area of the beach with a big towel. In our case, that towel is my recent involvement in various programs working to ensure access to the city's treasures for disadvantaged and marginalized youth. It's amazing, the credibility one can build by giving one's time and money to Arts for All or City-Parks Play. (Deft use of social media certainly helps. I post a lot of pictures from community events these days. Hashtag GiveTillItHurts, anyone?)

For you cynics who think my philanthropic work is motivated only by the interests of James's company—you're wrong. There's also the satisfaction of telling those bitches who turned on me during our difficult time that they can just run the book fair or the skating party or the winter coat drive all by themselves. I took great pleasure in turning in my resignation as class mom. My replacement certainly has her hands full.

James and I are bulletproof these days. I'm sure that in time the goodwill generated by publicly sticking it to some of the most hated institutions in town will fade. But for now, I'm very much enjoying not having to give a shit what people are saying about me.

Among our guests tonight are many Graylon parents, including those who once told me they'd never let their children play in our home again. That little incident seems to have vanished from everyone's memory. Even Grace and Lindsay are coming, though I don't really see much of them anymore outside school.

Oh—and Tatum and her fiancé are attending.

Believe me, I'd rather they didn't. I avoid her whenever I can—I'm working out with a trainer at the gym in my building these days—but since she's on many of the same guest lists as I am, it's not always possible. They've been invited tonight because Augie Craft has a financial stake in James's new project. (Surprise! But I bet you saw that coming.) James has taken on a partner who handles the finance side of things, allowing him to focus on managing the projects on the ground. When she sent me the investor list, I had no choice but to invite them all. Besides, I can't afford to snub Tatum publicly. Her Instagram posts routinely get thousands of likes these days, and she has something like fifty thousand followers—yes, I admit I still check—and she's managed to get herself on the board of Arts for All, for whom she has planned a fundraiser at Flame with a ticket price of a thousand dollars per rider. It sold out in an hour.

Since her recent engagement, the future second Mrs. Augie Craft has been flashing her huge diamond—and her tiny baby bump—all over town. I may have scratched out a successful second act for myself, but I don't hold a candle to Tatum, who apparently has more lives—and more cunning—than an alley cat.

Just as I'm making a final inspection of the centerpieces, James finds me. He looks debonair in the vintage herringbone jacket I found for him so he can deliver his remarks in period-perfect style in front of the photographs from the building's grand opening in the twenties, which I've had blown up and hung on the walls.

James has cut himself shaving, and there is still a bit of toilet paper stuck to his chin, which I flick away before giving him a kiss. "That's for luck," I say. "But you won't need it. You'll be great."

James grabs my hand and presses it to his heart. He opens his mouth to say something, clears his throat, and shakes his head. "I couldn't have ever . . ." is as far as he gets before he has to clear his throat again.

"It's okay," I say. "Go do your job. Kiss some ass and stay on brand."

He rolls his eyes, but he's smiling as I shove him gently in the direction of Colbert Liu, who has taken over Cora Rivera's seat on the council. I'm heading to the entrance, where I will receive the guests who are starting to arrive, when a familiar face catches my eye.

But Tatum saw me first. She says a few words to Augie and heads my way.

It takes her about twenty seconds to cross the expanse of original tile that was found under layers of linoleum, and in that time I try to gauge what has changed since we last spoke. With the baby coming, she's cut down on her teaching. She seems more sure of herself. She works hard at sustaining the narrative of her romance with Augie Craft, in which she offered support to a friend at a time when his life was made a living hell by a wife who was slowly losing ground to her borderline personality disorder. Poor Nan—she toughed it out for a while, but the strain of seeing Tatum and Augie at the club proved too much for her, and these days she's living full-time in Phoenix at the home she got in the divorce.

Tatum's wearing flowing ivory silk trousers and a simple sleeve-less turtleneck that shows off her sculpted torso, her perfect breasts, and yes—the barely noticeable swell of her stomach. Her heels are so high and narrow that you could use them to stab your enemies to death. A luminous black sea pearl is suspended from a long, thin gold chain around her neck, and it's easy to imagine some strapping island swain diving deep into the sea to find it for her. Her real lover isn't nearly as appealing—thirty pounds overweight with small eyes and shorter than Tatum even when she's barefoot—but he's on the *Forbes* list, and that can do a lot for a man's appeal.

"Hello, Tatum," I say coolly when she arrives. "You're looking well."

"Aren't you kind?" she says. "What a lovely party. Thank you for inviting us."

"You're so welcome. James and I are so pleased that our friends could join us to celebrate. Mercer House is very close to both of our hearts."

We gaze at each other, having delivered our lines; our duty is done and we can safely ignore each other for the rest of the evening. But before she turns to go, Tatum leans in close enough that I can see the knots in her eyelash extensions and whispers something in my ear.

Then she walks away to join Augie, who's grinning like he can't believe his luck. Poor fool.

I spot the Ericksons, and Janet and I rush toward each other and hug—no air kisses for us. "What did she say to you?" Janet asks as she takes my hand and leads me toward the bar, leaving Terry to fend for himself in the husband parking lot, the group of bored men that always forms at these things.

"She told me my bra strap was showing," I tell Janet.

We share a laugh and a high five, we two who are perhaps the only women in the room remotely comfortable in our own skin.

But that wasn't what Tatum really said. Maybe I'll tell Janet the truth later, one of these mornings when we're walking around the reservoir together after school drop-off. Or maybe I'll keep it to myself. As Janet hands me a glass of cold, straw-colored Sauvignon Blanc, Tatum's words echo in my mind.

I always knew I'd win.

But that's the problem with narcissists: they lack self-awareness. Tatum believes that the diamond ring, the sumptuous townhouse, her minor celebrity will insulate her forever. But no one sheds the shackles of the past that easily.

"Ladies!" James calls, heading toward us with his arm slung around the shoulders of none other than Terry Erikson, who is grinning from ear to ear. "You gotta hear this one. I had no idea physicists had a sense of humor."

"Did you steal my joke?" Janet demands.

"God help us," I deadpan.

"A neutron walks into a bar and asks how much for a beer," Terry says. "And the bartender goes—For you, no charge."

And the four of us laugh like it's the funniest thing we've ever heard, as the beautiful people sparkle and shine all around us.

ACKNOWLEDGMENTS

While creating this story, we were aided by many talented people who gave generously of their time and wisdom. In particular we send out our thanks to David Yudelson, Esq., who educated us about real estate crime, and Rachael Herron, whose many years as a 911 dispatcher came in handy when we wrote our fictional emergencies.

Our agents, Barbara Poelle and Jenni Ferrari-Adler, shepherded us most ably through the writing and submission process and helped match us up with our editor, Shauna Summers, whose brainy guidance made the book better and whose grace made the project a pleasure.

To the team at Ballantine Books who attended to every detail—keeping us on schedule, ensuring the prose was as spotless as could be, cloaking it in a gorgeous cover, and knocking down doors to introduce it to the world—you have our deep gratitude: Lexi Batsides, Jennifer Garza, Ashleigh Heaton, Jennifer Hershey, Kim Hovey, Belina Huey, Emily Isayeff, Courtney Mocklow, Jennifer Rodriguez, Quinne Rogers, and Kara Welsh.

—SL

As Elton John sings in my favorite song of all time, *Mona Lisas and Mad Hatters,* "I thank the Lord for the people I have found." I surround myself and share my life with the best people on the planet; they are all unbelievably understanding and supportive, and make the lows bearable and the highs even more magical. I can't name everyone, but thank you all for your kindness, enthusiasm, loyalty and friendship.

A few people must be thanked specifically . . . First and foremost, Kristin Morse, the initial person I entrusted with the kernel of an idea that became this novel. She kept my confidence for nearly eight months, and always made me feel like this could all actually happen. Whether we were sitting at the same dinner table for hours, or texting from opposite sides of the planet, she has always, always, always had my back, and I feel immense gratitude for her and for E.G., her husband. Eleisa and Patrick Coster, Laura De Girolami and Marc Vander Elst, Elizabeth Robilotti and Rit Aggarwala—my children's godparents have consistently epitomized the meaning of friends who are family. I am thankful for my decades of friendship with them, and have complete adoration for the children they have produced. And Hannah Zaks and Matthew Shyman, who have gifted me in my middle years with an incredibly fun and easy friendship filled with so much love and so few boundaries . . . thank you both for everything, which is way more than anyone could ever imagine.

I have many other friends whom I have met in my crazy world who keep me sane; they celebrated early and helped me with details and ideas I couldn't come up with myself. My champions: Laurel Fine, Suzanne Dawson, Angelique Famulak, Caitlin Pannese, Lauren Katz, Noelle Penna, Jaime Neary, Elizabeth Villar, Lauren Epstein, Jean Kim, Kemp Steib, Bona Yang, Carolyn Sterling, Shailini Rao, Sophie Herzig, Eve Madison Rodsky, and Melinda Koulbalides. A general shout-out to the amazing women in the Collegiate '27 class for all the laughs and the overly generous pours, and to Collegiate itself for inviting my family into a truly extraordinary community. I still cannot believe how lucky we are to be there.

There are not enough words in the English language with which to thank my incredible agent, Jenni Ferrari-Adler. Quite literally, without her there would be no *That's What Frenemies Are For.* She explained everything and kept me relatively calm, a feat most would find impossible. Thank you for taking a major chance on me and this project. Your guidance, patience, commitment and knowledge have made it all possible.

As for my family: My parents have loved and supported me every single day of my life. My mother, Marcia Fox, published her own book and planted the kernel in my mind when I was a child that I would write one day. My father, Robert Rosenberg, with whom I'll be sympatico forever, was my favorite person to shock with my news, and his reaction still makes me giggle. I hope I've made you both proud. Thank you to my decidedly un-wicked stepmother, Pamela Rosenberg, who keeps my children entertained and full of pancakes, cookies, and cotton candy when I need to work. And Leland Gershell, my husband, who looks dashing in his blazer and tie but who can also climb a ladder to fix and install anything: Nineteen years later, my love, it still had to be you. Thank you for always being by my side; we have created a beautiful life together. And finally, Caroline and Alexander, who have been beyond patient and who are my everything. Caroline, the bravest person I know, and Alexander, the funniest—you both bring me so much joy: I cannot wait to see what wonderful things the future holds for you both.

—LG

ABOUT THE AUTHORS

SOPHIE LITTLEFIELD is the author of more than twenty bestselling adult and YA novels. She is the recipient of an Anthony Award and a *RT Book Reviews* Reviewers' Choice Award, and she has been shortlisted for the Edgar, Macavity, Barry, and Crimespree Awards. *The New York Times* has called her "a regular writing machine."

sophielittlefield.com
Facebook.com/Sophie.Littlefield.Author
Twitter: @swlittlefield
Instagram: @swlittlefield

LAUREN GERSHELL was born and raised on the Upper East Side of Manhattan, where she now lives with her family. She holds a B.A. and law degree from Columbia University. *That's What Frenemies Are For* is her first novel.

laurengershell.com
Facebook.com/laurengershellauthor
Twitter: @laurengershell
Instagram: @laurengershell